To dea

with thanks

Gulls Walk

2. 17. 11

Gulls Walk

Barbara Nugent

To order additional copies of this book, contact:
Xlibris Corporation
1-888-795-4274
www.Xlibris.com
Orders@Xlibris.com
48138

Dedication

This book is dedicated to a very dear friend,
Elizabeth Burman Patterson
Who taught me a new dimension in time.

ACKNOWLEDGEMENTS

With love and grateful thanks to my children, Gregory, Rachel, Giles and Rowena, and especially my husband Gerald, who has been chief-cook-and-bottle-washer while I muse. Their encouragement and belief in me has meant more than I can say.

CHAPTER ONE

Rowena Pentraegon looked up at the gloomy skies, shivering as she stood for a moment under the porch of the old manor house. June in Cornwall was supposed to be sunshine and warmth, but today was cold and dismal, and a heavy rain was still falling. Appropriate for the misery of her grandfather's funeral she thought bleakly.

The few family friends, who had come to the church to mourn the death of Morgan Pentraegon, murmured words of sympathy as they straggled past her to where Trevy, the housekeeper, had laid out a buffet lunch in the dining room. Rowena started to follow them, but she hesitated in the silence of the Great Hall, still trying to come to terms with her loss.

Overwhelmed by loneliness, she felt drained, both physically and emotionally, for she had slept little the last few nights as she tried to grapple with the bitter truth that she was the last of the Pentraegons. She had no other family. Her parents had died in an accident when she was a baby. And now, devastatingly and unexpectedly, so had Gramps.

How was she going to manage without him?

James Whitford, the family solicitor who had stood waiting for her, gently touched her arm.

"Miss Pentraegon, I wonder, may I have a few moments with you in private?" He cleared his throat, wishing he need not worry her now, but no time would be good for what he had to say.

She managed to drag a smile from somewhere.

"Of course, Mr. Whitford, perhaps the library?"

She led him into the long, oak-panelled room and invited him to use her grandfather's desk. As he placed his briefcase on the scarred leather surface, the old man began to speak of his concern and regret, but Rowena's mind was still too numb to register. She turned away to hide the tears and moved to the window.

After a few moments, somewhat uncomfortably, the lawyer went over to the glass display case near the fireplace, took the key and opened it. He peered down at the various pieces of memorabilia enclosed there, his old eyes searching out one of the ancient documents. Carefully, he began to read aloud.

Hereafter I do bequeathe my house, Gulls Walk, and mye lands to mye first borne Son, and to his Son after Him, on and on, In Perpetuity. Maye no Man or Woman, be they King, Queen or Commoner, yntrude upon the House of the Pentraegons.

The silent girl found her lips moving to the words; she had learned them with pride and delight as a small child when Gramps, with some amusement, had taught them to her. But James Whitford's expression was sombre as he returned to the desk. Perching his gold-rimmed spectacles more firmly in place, he drew a sheaf of papers from his briefcase. His voice was almost apologetic as he continued to speak.

"I have your grandfather's will here. I will read it in total later, but I wanted to prepare you."

With some emotion, he cleared his throat. Rowena's eyes softened as she remembered that he, too, had been saddened at the sudden death. Morgan Pentraegon, the fourteenth in line to inherit Gulls Walk, had been his lifelong friend, too.

Turning to face the old man, she attempted to swallow the lump that had persistently blocked her throat during the funeral service. The corners of her mouth lifted a little as she tried to show her sympathy.

He watched her with some concern, then his eyes returned to the papers spread in front of him. Removing his glasses, he polished them to give Rowena a breathing space. It hurt him to see her grieving so. He cleared his throat and continued.

"The unbroken law by which all Pentraegons have passed on Gulls Walk has been through the male line. Your grandfather intended to make no exception, and the implication of his will is clear. He states that after various bequests to the servants, all other properties and moneys are to be divided between his children, and there after, his children's children. But Gulls Walk shall revert to his son or grandson . . . and so on."

He paused, watching Rowena as she tried to concentrate.

"Though the will was made when his son was still a child, it remains valid. He had updated parts of it, the bequests and so forth; but after your father's death, he desperately wanted to leave the house to his great grandson, your son, thus keeping the line unbroken."

Rowena was startled. She looked up sharply. She hadn't even thought of marriage, and she was the last Pentraegon. There were no others, male or female. Did that mean she would not inherit the house, not be able to carry on living at Gulls Walk? Bewilderment gave way to an unexpected fear.

Before she could speak, the old man held up his hand. "It's all right, I know there is no son, grandson, or great grandson to inherit, so no longer is this a case of primogeniture: inheritance by the eldest male descendent. In any case, that rule was abolished by the Administration of Estates Act many years ago, and the law now says that . . ." he searched through his papers for the exact words: ". . . The disposition of such moneys and properties as are within an estate shall be divided proportionately between such offspring as are of that family. All descendants, or other known relatives of equal degree, shall take equally in such succession."

Rowena sat down abruptly on the window seat as she tried to digest the legal phrases. Did he mean that someone else could lay claim to Gulls Walk? She had never heard of any other relatives. Her grandfather had been an only child, as had been her father, and herself. For a moment, the possible loss of her home disoriented her.

Eyeing her with concern, the lawyer wished he need not continue, for now came the difficult part. But first, he tried to smooth the way.

"You are the only living direct descendant, my dear; therefore, you are sole heir. So of course I can see no obstruction to your inheriting Gulls Walk."

She sighed in relief. The moment had been overwhelming. The idea of having to give up Gulls Walk had not occurred to her until then. Apart from time away at college, she had known no other home. But she wondered why Mr. Whitford still looked so grave.

The lawyer worriedly removed his glasses again and tapped them against his teeth as he shifted uneasily in his chair. Perhaps he should not have lulled her into this false sense of security, but he knew how much she loved the old house. Unfortunately there were difficulties, which seemed to be insurmountable.

"Even though Gulls Walk is undoubtedly yours, I am afraid there is still a problem." Uncomfortably, he rustled his papers. "The estate will be subject to death duties."

"Death duties?" Rowena repeated questioningly.

He paused, hesitating in concern; then slowly he continued. He had no choice.

"Gulls Walk is a valuable property in the eyes of the state, and it will warrant a pretty stiff tax that will have to be paid; but I'm afraid your grandfather left very little actual cash."

Rowena felt bewildered again. She and Gramps had never needed much money. She could cope with that. In any case, she was quite capable of making her own living now she had graduated. But what sort of tax? The old man paused and cleared his throat as he watched her. The law could be a hard taskmaster in these circumstances.

"Morgan Pentraegon was living on a fixed annuity that was sufficient while he was alive. Unfortunately, it ceased when he died."

He paused again, fearing some sort of reaction, but Rowena didn't interrupt him. She knelt on the window seat and pushed open one of the lead-mullioned windows. With a sigh, he put down his papers and got to his feet and moved to stand beside her.

The rain had eased and was now little more than a fine summer drizzle. A pale sun was trying to peep through. The gardens of Gulls Walk looked so sparkling, fresh washed, beautiful; indeed, so peaceful in the crystal-clear light. He could smell the scents he always associated with Pentraegon Cove, the salt air from the Atlantic, the new mown hay, and the roses: always the roses.

James Whitford sighed as he turned back to his client. He wished he could leave the details of his bad news unsaid. Again he tried to soften the blow.

"Most of the land has been sold over the years, as you know. Luckily, the few acres remaining in the estate are yours, and all the contents of the house. Your grandfather deeded them directly to you when your father died, so you have something on which the government won't require death duties." He paused. "As for the rest . . . ."

His expression showed his concern.

"My dear, I'm so sorry; in order to pay these taxes you will probably have to sell quite a large part of your inheritance. The last few acres, even your beachfront property, may have to go if you are to keep Gulls Walk. And after the government has taken its share, it will mean there will be almost no money left to maintain the house. I know this is a bitter blow, but I feel responsible for finding the right solution; though, of course, I understand how much Gulls Walk means to you."

He looked down at the too-silent girl. Her face had taken on a drawn, waiting quality. She lifted a hand to her throat. Pride was apparent in every graceful line of her body. She turned to look at him; it was so difficult to concentrate. What was he trying to say?

"Please continue, Mr. Whitford, I'm not made of glass."

Her courage gave him the impetus he needed. "My dear, your grandfather would not wish you to be saddled with a burden too heavy for your young shoulders. And surely Gulls Walk is far too big for you, even if it is possible to meet all the tax obligations."

He took a deep breath. Now came the worst part.

"In order for you to have a reasonable income on which to live quite comfortably, maybe the most practical thing for you to do is to sell the manor house."

Rowena froze. Sell her home? This was far worse than she had imagined.

Her face was white and pinched; money had never mattered very much to her, but if it meant losing her home, she must pay closer attention.

"Sell Gulls Walk? You can't mean it?" Rowena's expression crumbled.

"I'm afraid so. I'm deeply sorry, my dear; but selling the house really is the most practical solution." James Whitford watched his client as she got to her feet; he hated to be the bearer of such bad news. He moved back to the desk and glanced again at the legal documents lying there, giving Rowena time to recover.

She took a step toward him, then wanting to hear no more, she turned away, hardly aware of the lawyer's continued concern. Understanding her withdrawal, he leafed again through the papers. If only there were something he could do to ease her pain, but he had to persist.

"I'm so sorry, but that is the most practical solution, my dear. Selling the manor house will solve any financial problems, even leave you with enough money to start that dress designing business you so often have talked about."

She felt overwhelmed. It was all far worse than she had imagined. For over four hundred years there had been Pentraegons at Gulls Walk, and her ancestors had lived in the valley long before the house was built. Now the family lawyer was telling her that she, the last of the Pentraegons, must sell. Bewildered, she tried to gather together her scattered thoughts.

"But there has to be another way, Mr. Whitford. Surely the taxes can't be so bad. My forefathers will turn in their graves if I do what you suggest." She began to pace the library. "No, I can't sell. There must be something else that I can do."

The old man sadly shook his head. Deeply concerned though he was for her, he knew the cold, hard facts better than did she. Her grandfather's death earlier in the week had been tragedy enough, since he had been Rowena's only living relative. But to compound her troubles, not only was Morgan

Pentraegon's income gone, he had left his granddaughter only a small legacy. And there were few valuables remaining in the house to sell, certainly not enough to settle the death duties and keep up the constant repairs Gulls Walk always needed, and take care of the remaining acres around it.

Yes, the house must go. She would at least then have some money to live on; and what use was such a large, rambling place to a single girl so far away from the bright city lights that young people seemed to crave? A nice apartment was much better. She would be well able to afford that. Sentiment was a fine thing, but one had to he practical.

The old man sighed. As he looked into Rowena's anguished face, the plea in her eyes wrenched at his heart. Having to endure alone the death of her grandfather was devastating enough. And now, added to that, the potential loss of her beloved Gulls Walk, the only home she had ever known, was tearing her apart.

This will not do, he thought as he carefully folded Morgan Pentraegon's will, trying to hide his own distress. He attempted to ease the moment.

"Now, my dear, though I'm afraid those death duties will be substantial, there is enough money for a little while. You don't have to make a decision today."

He grew silent, watching her reaction. The reading of wills was difficult at any time, but today he, too, felt a personal loss.

"I'm so sorry, Miss Rowena," he repeated; "I wish there were something I could say that might help."

Again he removed his spectacles to polish them, for his eyes had grown misty. He sighed, remembering his own youth. He had known Morgan Pentraegon's grandchild since she was a tiny baby and had watched her grow from a mischievous tomboy into slender, enchanting womanhood. Perhaps she was not strictly beautiful, but she had a quality he found hard to resist. It was difficult to look into those enormous eyes and have so little comfort to offer.

Standing there, in numb disbelief, Rowena seemed more like a frozen statue than her usual, vibrant self. Even her glorious mane of auburn hair had been subdued and drawn back, tied with a bow of conventional black. Beneath a faint summer tan, her face was pale, showing the fragile, almost porcelain-like translucency of sleepless nights. Shadows sculptured the contours, emphasising the deep circles under her eyes. It was as if the light had gone out of her.

What more could he say or do?

Abruptly, Rowena looked away. She could no longer bear to see the pity clouding his face.

Blinking back the tears, she returned to the window and gazed across the walled garden to the wide panorama of Cornish coast land, with the high cliffs of Trenallack Point cupping the cove in its giant hand. Shimmering in the watery sunlight breaking through the scudding clouds, the vast Atlantic beyond murmured its usual complaint at the storm now dieing away. It was a timeless scene. How could she endure the thought of leaving?

Yet she must try to hold back the awful feeling of disaster. It was threatening to destroy the remnants of poise she had tried so hard to maintain all through the ghastly funeral service, for she still had responsibilities. Taking a deep breath, she lifted her chin, striving for control. Making an attempt at a smile, she turned back to the waiting solicitor.

"Thank you, Mr. Whitford. You have been very kind. I know that my grandfather's death was a blow to you, too." Her throat felt swollen and dry. She swallowed, fighting to keep her voice firm. "I'll think of something." The small smile spread. "We Pentraegons have been down before." Brave word from the last of the line.

James Whitford allowed an answering twinkle to appear. "That's the spirit. Your grandfather was always so proud of you." But his eyes misted again as he stood up. He could see no hope for the retention of Gulls Walk. If only old Morgan Pentraegon had not so blindly and stubbornly refused to face the possibility of an early death. The sinking of most of his money into that annuity had been a mistake. He should have made better provision for his granddaughter.

The solicitor moved to the door. He hesitated, and then he decided to leave the details to later. Now was not the time. Enough was enough. He had, over the years, learned something of Pentraegon pride. He must, at least, allow his client that.

"I'll join the others, my dear. If you want me, I'll be in the dining room. Perhaps you might have some further questions."

Closing the door softly behind him, James Whitford stood for a few moments in the quiet of the Great Hall. Maybe later she would be more ready to accept his suggestions. He sighed. He felt chilled. He was getting old, too old to fight against the inevitable. Finally, he went to seek the comfort of a glass of sherry.

Rowena returned to the window, miserably thinking back over the last few hours.

The funeral service had been a nightmare, unreal. And she had found it difficult to concentrate when she and the various family friends returned to the house. She knew she should be with them now, politely listening to their condolences, but perhaps a few more minutes were excusable.

It was hard for her to believe that less than a week ago, just a few days after she graduated from art school and returned to the valley, her beloved Gramps, hale and hearty, had been cantering beside her. She was riding her dainty Firefly, and he, Goemor, his black stallion.

Then came the massive heart attack, sudden, totally unexpected. Morgan Pentraegon slumped in his saddle and slid sideways, one foot still held in the stirrup. His body lurched, hung heavy and lifeless as Goemor tried to counterbalance the uneven weight.

Rowena had managed to grasp the reins to halt the frightened animal as she sprang from her own horse, but she was too late to do more than release her grandfather's body. The strange, neighing cry from the stallion was something she was not likely to forget; it was as if Goemor knew and was mourning with her.

And now, according to the will, she must face the bitter fact that life as she had known it in her own small corner of Cornwall was over. Dear God, she was not ready for that.

Her mind shied away from the present and wandered back as she remembered how Gramps used to talk of the sons and grandsons who had inherited Gulls Walk. Little had he known that she was to be his only living descendant, that he was never to see his own great grandsons.

When he first married, he and his wife Felicity intended to have a large family. But when their only son Andrew was still only small, there had been the tragedy of a stillborn, second child. Weakened by the difficult birth, Felicity soon followed her baby. Desolate at both deaths, Morgan Pentraegon did not remarry.

Eventually, his son grew up and married, and Rowena was born. Nobody minded that the first child was a girl. There was plenty of time for more children, the family thought. But Morgan's tragedies were not over. Rowena's father, never over cautious, went sailing with his wife on a windy day. The boat was overturned and its passengers were drowned.

Rowena had been too young to understand, and her grandfather put away his own sorrow, determinedly taking on the care of the tiny child. From then on, the two were inseparable. Morgan Pentraegon was all that she needed, and Rowena was his whole life.

"It's your turn now;" her grandfather used to say as she was growing up; "you'll marry and produce lots and lots of great grandsons for me. They'll be Pentraegons, whatever your husband's name, and we'll have a new dynasty." They laughed at the future; she had taken no notice of his occasional frown of concern.

But now he was gone. Rowena shivered as icy fingers of loneliness closed tighter around her heart.

This wouldn't do. She tried to pull herself together, forcing her mind to concentrate on her grandfather's will, and the future. Even though there was little money, there must be some way to save Gulls Walk. But first, there was the present to take care of. She wrapped her arms around herself. Why was she so cold? Shock, she supposed. No wonder she felt insecure, defenceless, and yet so ridiculously naive. She had been living in a fool's paradise. She searched her mind for something, anything to ease the moment.

Then she remembered; Mr. Whitford had injected a brighter note. There was a little time. Grasping the thought, she turned away from the window and hurried out of the library to find him. She needed to verify that one grain of hope. The kindly lawyer had returned to the Great Hall and was waiting for her.

"Mr. Whitford, please, you said there is a little time before the . . ." she could hardly bring herself to form the question, "before the death duties have to be paid?"

He took her hand, glad that she seemed ready to talk. "Oh, quite a little time. Government agencies are not known for their speed. A few months at least. And there is no reason why you shouldn't carry on living here until then." The old man smiled kindly to ease her distress. "I can dispense enough money for general expenses, and wages, of course."

Rowena sighed with relief. "Thank you so much, Mr. Whitford. I'm sorry that I haven't been very bright. I still am not used to Gramps being gone." He patted her hand with understanding.

But after he and the other guests had left, she wandered around the house looking at it with new eyes, wondering if there could be any solution to her problems. She had inherited not only the manor house, but also the responsibility of carrying on what so many generations had left to her.

She could not, indeed, must not sell.

CHAPTER TWO

Desperately needing to be alone, she took herself early to bed, hoping to sleep. The last few days had exhausted her to a state of numbness. But all night she tossed and turned, her mind trying to find a practical solution.

Finally, while it was still dark, she dressed and crept out to the stables to saddle Firefly. Perhaps the night air, and the winds from the Atlantic, which always buffeted the high cliffs around the cove, would clear her befuddled mind.

Carefully, keeping to the edge of the broad lawn as much as possible to avoid disturbing the sleeping household, she wended her way to the bridge. There, she paused for a moment to listen to the beck gurgling cheerfully past the manor on its way to the ocean. The heady scent of early June roses, mingled with the sharp tang of salt air, were tantalising nostalgia of other summers; but sadly thrusting the unbidden memories away, she turned to climb the winding path to Trenallack Point.

When she reached the top, she dismounted and allowed the mare to graze. It was still too dark to see through the shadows and the residue of the fog that had rolled in from the sea during the night, so she threw herself down on the grass to wait for morning light. She willed the murmur of the waves to bring her at least some measure of peace.

As the pewter light of pre-dawn sharpened to silver, the veil of mist stirred and lifted. Beads of moisture quivered in the quiet air above the valley. Stretched out on the coarse turf of the headland, with her chin cupped in her hands, Rowena watched, waiting for the first glimmering rays of daylight, and the usual upsurge of pleasure she always felt when the distant house emerged from the shadows.

Today it was hard, even though she concentrated on the moment, determined to savour to the full the first, finely-etched outlines of Pentraegon Cove, and Gulls Walk nestling in its valley.

The dawn was still, turning yellow, as the sun's first rays defined the far cliffs. She lay motionless, not wanting anything to change, wishing that it could be like this for ever. Strange how there was no going back, that the carefree simplicity of yesterday's childhood could never be recaptured.

An oystercatcher appeared on the shore, its long beak probing the seaweed left by the tide. It hopped comically out of the way as a wave lapped too close. And farther out in the bay, she watched a cormorant dive into the cool depths of the water hoping to catch an unsuspecting fish. A bitter smile touched the girl's lips. The inevitability of nature, she supposed, was the only permanence in this world.

She stood up, brushing the bracken from her jeans as she moved closer to the cliff edge now that the light was brighter. Her feet dislodged loose shale, which rattled down the path, and a colony of startled gulls flew from the craggy ledges, up, over her head. They squawked their irritation, then lifted into smooth flight as they, too, wheeled toward the Atlantic in search of breakfast.

Tears stung her eyes. She wiped them away. Seagulls had been strutting on these Cornish cliffs long before her family had given their name to the cove beneath, and the Pentraegons' dynastic efforts seemed ephemeral by comparison despite the hundreds of years they had lived in, and finally owned, the valley. She shivered a little, waiting until her emotions were back under control, trying to isolate herself in the beauty of the scene.

Over the humped back of the storm-carved cliff bordering the far side of the cove, she watched the thin slivers of gold spread across the eastern horizon. They burnished the high fields beyond Home Farm and crept downward to the wide, terraced slopes of the house that nestled against a filmy tracery of bright-leafed trees, and the darker branches of cypresses.

Gradually, the sun's full splendour brought fire to the tall, mullioned windows of the ancient pile sitting proudly as sentinel of the valley. The brilliance gave startlingly life to the carved granite, and to the buttery creams of the old bricks. It brightened to silver the stone-faced parapet that edged each wing. Indeed, the house glowed, like some rare jewel, proud of its history and heritage: an aged great lady, dressed in all her finery, daring the world to see the decay.

This was Gulls Walk, Elizabethan manor, the Pentraegon's family seat, and Rowena's home. She loved it deeply, desperately, and was more determined than ever that somehow she would manage to keep it. She had been bequeathed a legacy of trust as well as a house, and it was the only family she had left.

The sun's warmth reached up the slope to where she stood, causing her bitterness to lift a little. She pushed back the mass of curls tumbling in disarray around her face, trying to hold onto the pleasure of the moment. There was little point in feeling sorry for herself. Maudlin sentimentality never helped.

But still her eyes lingered on Gulls Walk where generations of Pentraegons had lived and died, happily and sadly, yet always determined to remain. So would she. Grandfather hadn't expected to die. And now, as the only Pentraegon left, surely she, too, must find a way. How dare she, as Mr. Whitford had suggested, even consider breaking generations of trust?

She shivered again as she felt the morning breezes whisper around her with memories of long gone times; of the first pirate Pentraegon, the beginnings of Gulls Walk, and its history as her grandfather had told her years ago. She seemed to hear his laughter and the deep timber of his voice as he read from the little booklet written by one of their later ancestors. It had been her favourite bedtime story, and she knew it by heart.

She had brought a copy with her, and seating herself on one of the boulders, Rowena opened it and remembered.

A History of Gulls Walk, Pentraegon Cove, Cornwall

Gulls Walk was built at the end of the sixteenth century, and since then it has passed from father to son or grandson down through the years in an unbroken line, just as its founder had always wished. But its birth was at a time of great turmoil in English history.

In October of 1588, one of the great Spanish galleons from King Phillip's Armada fled from Drake's fire ships and struggled round Cape Wrath at the Northwest extremity of Scotland. It then turned south toward Spain and, endeavouring to avoid the autumn storms in the Atlantic, limped down the coast of Ireland. The captain tried to land on its southern shore, as did other foundering ships, but was greeted by savage peasants and fishermen who attempted to rob the living as well as the dead. Though they were in desperate straits, the weary crew put back to sea, hoping to sail to home. Unfortunately for them, the galleon was blown off course and was wrecked on the rugged Cornish coast.

Excerpts from the old pirate's diary tell something of his participation in the story.

I, Morgan Pentraegon, yn Christian spirit, despyte that some calle me Pyrate, and some, Anti-papist, my Landes being stripped from Mye Famyly during Mary's reign, rowed with Mye Men to a doomed Ship, kyndly rescuing those whom our Lord wished. Such goodes as We could We brought to a place of rest.

Later, the old reprobate wrote details of the grateful sea captain's relief at being rescued from a watery grave; but little of the crew, many of whom must have died from battle wounds and fever before they even reached the Cornish coast.

Seemingly, more were drowned—by nature, or by man is not known—and their number was never recorded. But prayers were said for the Spaniards' Catholic souls, and the wealth they had brought was removed before the galleon sank.

The captain, who was a handsome devil according to Morgan, acceded, though perhaps not too willing, to the local laws of salvage in return for his life, and he remained with the Pentraegons until his wounds healed.

But Morgan's enthusiasm waned towards the Spaniard whose roving eye had caught the attention of his daughter, an auburn headed beauty, as have been many Pentraegons since; every generation or so, such a daughter is born into the family and is usually called Rowena. Morgan's last comment on the subject was short.

Of such Treasures as I hath, He shalle share when He Return. But not tille then, that of Mye Beloved Rowena.

Whether the captain ever did return, we do not know, but when he left Cornwall he was given a bronze chain, a presumed replica of which rests to this day in the library at Gulls Walk.

The Virgin Queen should, of course, have had first claim on the spoils from the galleon, for all confiscated treasure, by royal decree, was hers. But somehow, the whereabouts and quantity were never divulged. And the cove was a long, long way from London.

Maybe it was a guilty conscience, but more likely, an elaborate toast to Her Majesty. Anyway, Morgan Pentraegon bought back his confiscated lands and built an exquisite house in the popular style of the time, an elaborate 'E' to commemorate loyalty and obedience. It proclaimed to all that his allegiance to Her Royal Personage should never be suspect.

There was something of humour in the gesture as he bequeathed bricks and mortar in lusty legacy of tithes and taxes never paid. Whatever the reason, Morgan kept his house. He embellished it as the years went by, enlarging and adding to the original three wings, bars of the renowned Elizabethan initial. He hinted at hiding the rest of the salvaged treasure, but none has ever been found.

Even the name he chose was part of his puckish sense of humour. Certainly, the sea gulls enjoy perching on the crenulations, which top the high walls. And after a storm in the Atlantic, they can still be seen strutting backward and forward enjoying their safety and comparative shelter.

But there were other, wingless gulls who enjoyed the protection of the secluded cove. Local pirates, and later, smugglers, referred to themselves by that name. Many were the times that human 'gulls' made the quiet walk from their long boats with contraband brought back from France; lace and silk for my Lady, and wines and brandy for my Lord. Yes. Gulls Walk is well named.

Of course, the family is respectable now. For centuries, the Pentraegons have been loyal and upright citizens, staunch supporters of the Crown.

And, Rowena knew, as their honesty increased, their fortunes waned, something about which she had not been concerned until now.

She sighed as she tucked away the book and remounted Firefly. That was yesterday's story. Today she had no Gramps to chuckle with her over those past events. She had to face her own bleak future.

She gritted her teeth as she urged the little mare forward and wended her way back to the house, to all the new problems awaiting her.

CHAPTER THREE

When Rowena entered the kitchen, Miles Gilbert, her neighbour who owned Home Farm, had arrived and already helped himself to morning coffee. He looked his usual cool, aloof, immaculate self, and she found herself feeling faintly irritated; she was only too conscious of the dishevelled mess she must look. The ribbon she used to tie back her hair had become loosened in the wind, and recalcitrant wisps were curling like small flames around her face. Her old sweater and jeans had picked up a liberal amount of grass stains and burrs and were rumpled and creased. She felt a stirring of resentment. He looked so much in control.

Miles scraped back his chair and got to his feet. He came over to Rowena and put his arm around her shoulder.

"And how is Precious this morning?"

It was an old joke. When they were both children, an ancient, rather witch-like spinster in the village had called everything precious; from the apples on the trees in her orchard, to the mushrooms she gathered in the nearby fields. One day, Miles and Rowena were persuaded to take her a basket of food from the manor house kitchen. In typical devilish mood, Miles hid a frog under the linen cover. When it jumped out, the old crone cackled in amusement, calling it precious. Only Rowena was frightened, and Miles laughed. With thoughtless, childish cruelty he seized upon the name; thereafter, Rowena became Precious in twisted reconstruction of the old fairy tale, *The Princess and the Frog*.

Rowena never forgot the careless malice of the taunting label, but she now accepted it like a worn shoe that still pinched a little.

She sighed, but she recognised that today Miles used the name affectionately from force of habit. Normally, she paid little or no attention to it, but her nerves were too tightly strung. She was no longer a child to be patronised. Somewhat abruptly, she answered his question.

"I'll survive, I expect." Sympathy was one thing, but she had no intention of encouraging pity. She was aware that she didn't sound welcoming, but she was newly poor, and Miles always seemed to have plenty of money. The world looked different and made one wary when it turned itself upside down. Feeling a little guilty, she tried again.

"It was nice of you to come." The words were stilted, but she managed a smile. She knew she should be more grateful for the way he had journeyed from London for the funeral. It must not have been easy to change his plans. And Miles was almost a Pentraegon, the nearest one to a relative that she had left. In past centuries, his family had been tenant farmers at Home Farm, eventually buying it. They had lived there nearly as long as Rowena's had lived at Gulls Walk.

The Gilberts were equally proud of their history. Miles' father used to claim that their family was as old as the Pentraegons, that they were descended from Sir Walter Raleigh's half-brother, Sir Humphrey Gilbert.

According to legend, Gilbert came to visit Cornwall with Wart—as the first Morgan Pentraegon had called Sir Walter in his diary. Both Morgan and Wart had attended Oriel College, Oxford, becoming great friends; hence, the intertwining of the Gilbert family with that of the Pentraegons.

All three men sailed together for their Queen in the latter half of the 1570's, variously on explorations, and the destruction of Spanish shipping. No wonder the first Morgan showed little conscience when a galleon from the Armada was wrecked off their Cornish coast.

Sometime during the last century, as the Pentraegon fortunes waned, the Gilbert family prospered. They expanded the farm, purchasing more and more land from the manor. Gradually their holdings developed into quite a thriving business, growing vegetables and flowers for the London market, and rearing pedigree cattle. They also became involved in local and national entrepreneurial activities, including fishing.

Now only Miles with a small staff lived at Home Farm. His father was dead, and his mother had retired with her arthritis to the warmth of the south of France. More often than not, though, Miles was away in London leaving a manager in charge, or he was travelling around Europe dealing with some new enterprise.

Sometimes he appeared unexpectedly, often having sailed on one of his fishing boats from Penzance rather that come by more conventional transport. If he had time and had not brought visitors, he used to drop in on Rowena's grandfather who seemed glad of his company during the lonely months when she had been away at college.

It was kind of him to come. Rowena swallowed her irritation. He was so nearly the brother she had never had, only six years older than her own twenty-three. And she needed a friend.

Aware of his kindness, she rested her head on his shoulder. For a moment, it felt good to be held close and comforted, and she forgot her unreasonable resentment. Then she pushed him away. Miles released her and pulled out a chair for her. He picked up his coffee cup and perched on the edge of the table.

"Your grandfather meant a great deal to me, too, you know, Rowena. I thought I might be able to help. You always did need a bit of looking after." He grinned gently, but Rowena avoided his eyes.

She swallowed the memories, and the lump in her throat. Did he have to treat her like a child? She never could hide much from Miles, but her wound was still too raw to accept pity.

She wanted to change the subject and looked toward the housekeeper who was stirring something on the stove.

"Good morning, Trevy. Your coffee smells delicious as usual." Rowena felt faint stirrings of hunger. She hadn't eaten much during the last few days. Mrs. Trevain bustled over to the table.

"Let me pour some for you, Miss Rowena. Now, Master Miles. You leave her be; she's been up that dratted cliff, I'll he bound." She felt the thin sweater and shook her head. "You'm likely to catch your death of cold lying on that damp grass." Like most of the locals of her generation, she had a strong distrust of night air, and each evening closed all the windows tightly before going to bed. Gramps and Rowena had often been amused by her foible, usually quietly opening the casements again in their own bedrooms. Rowena remembered their conspiratorial grins. Dear Gramps. The tears stung the back of her eyes.

She busied herself with her coffee as a dish of fluffy scrambled eggs was placed in front of her. She took a slice of toast and began to eat. It was a good excuse to keep looking down at her plate. Trevy touched Rowena's shoulder gently before hurrying off to organise the day's housework, mumbling something about dust and dirt not staying away, even for a funeral. Sniffing, she wiped the corner of her eye with her apron as she left.

Miles rested his long fingers on Rowena's arm as he shifted his position to a chair beside her. Rowena looked up at him and found herself examining him in a new light. He had always been there, and she had taken him for granted, she realised; but his expression was different now, wary almost.

He was pale as usual; too many board room conferences she supposed. Tall and thin, Miles had what Rowena used teasingly to call romantic, Celtic colouring: black, black hair, with dark brown eyes, deep as agate. Her own colouring she had always deplored as being somewhere between carrot and copper; and her eyes, which she considered to be too large for her face, had a hazelish tint, except when they turned a deeper green. That was when she was upset or angry.

She wondered why anger was welling inside her now. Perhaps it was her own fault, but Miles managed to make her feel awkward, juvenile almost.

Totally unaware of her own eloquent beauty, Rowena gazed into his narrowed eyes, wondering what to say to him, where to begin. In distraction, she removed her arm from his touch. She was too miserable, and he was reawakening the nerves she was trying to control. That morning, everything about her life was so damnably awful. Only Gramps would have understood how she felt.

She tried to swallow more of the food in front of her, but it stuck in her throat; her appetite was gone. Finally, she put down her fork. Oh, how she missed Morgan Pentraegon. Needing him so much was becoming almost unbearable. She gulped, trying to hold back the tears, trying to hide this feeling of being so desperately alone. She turned away. A wracking sob shook her body as she anguished, "How on earth am I going to manage Gulls Walk without Gramps?"

Miles' chair fell back, and she found herself dragged to her feet and pulled close into his arms. He began to stroke her hair as he spoke softly into its unruly mass.

"Come, Precious. It's all right. Gramps wouldn't want you to worry. Being alone in this house is too much for you any way. I'll take care of everything." He half chuckled. "Of course, you could always become Mrs. Gilbert and give me the worry of taking care of Gulls Walk." That also was a family joke. He used to say that if the only way he could live at Gulls Walk was by marrying Rowena, then he would just have to swallow his medicine.

He talked on, doing his best to soothe her. "Gramps used to tell me to look after you when you were little, remember? Old customs die hard, you know."

He tried to cajole a smile out of her. Again, she leaned against him. Perhaps any comfort was better than none. Then she felt his hands, with practised assurance, move over her body, finding the soft curves.

Startled, she wrenched away with a strange feeling of distaste. He would never have touched her so intimately if Gramps had been around. She had not been unaware of the odd look of circumspection that her grandfather had given Miles from time to time as she was growing up.

Rowena gulped. Take care of her, indeed! Damn it all, no! She could take care of herself, thank you. He was patronising her again. She tried to pull herself together. Then his words began to penetrate as his arms tried again to curl around her slight figure. Marry him? It sounded more as if he wanted to marry the house!

Angry, and yet aware of feelings of guilt, for surely he meant well, Rowena turned back. She tried to smile politely at him before carefully releasing his hands. "Thank you, I don't want you to feel obligated because of Gramps." Miles probably only intended to be comforting anyway. As far as marriage was concerned, she was startled how much she disliked the idea.

What was wrong with her? Marriage would be the perfect solution. Miles always seemed to have plenty of money. She could continue to live at Gulls Walk and life would go on as usual. For a moment she was tempted. The last few days had been almost too much for her, and she couldn't bear the thought of leaving her beloved Pentraegon Cove.

She moved to the window and looked at the mellow peace. The sun had risen fully now, and the rolling swell of the Atlantic sparkled in the bright June morning. Below her was the herb garden, which some long-forgotten ancestor had planted, with the ancient sundial shadowing the hour.

Beyond it, protected from the Atlantic winds by the high stone wall, her eyes registered the pallet of colours rioting in the flower borders edging the wide lawns. Holly hocks, brilliant purples and magentas, bent gracefully to the softer blues and pinks of the lupines. White Shasta daisies and great clouds of grey-blue lavender nudged gentian, phlox, and delicate columbines.

And behind, smothering the old walls that protected the garden from the sea winds, were morning glory entwined with honeysuckle and ivy. And roses, roses everywhere.

It was all so poignantly beautiful. Dear God! She couldn't lose Gulls Walk.

But suppose she had no other choice? She came down to earth. Perhaps she shouldn't be too hasty. Miles loved the house, of course. Maybe almost as much as she did, and she had no doubt that he was fond of her. But she had not told him about the death duties yet, and surely he wouldn't want to marry her at her reduced value, particularly if, in the end, she could not raise the taxes. Miles would hardly want to start married life with a millstone of debt around his neck, in spite of his love for Gulls Walk.

No. Marriage was definitely out! And certainly, she was too proud to ask for help from him since she was not willing to offer herself in return, or the house.

But her mind must be wandering after her sleepless night. The prosaic morning light made her doubt if he were really serious. She pulled herself together. Dear Miles; he meant well. For the first time in her twenty-three summers, she found herself being aware of a sense of maturity, of being older than her years. Her growing up was happening faster than she wanted. She lifted her chin, her emotions now well under control.

A determination began to crystallise, and with it, a tenacity she didn't know she possessed. She was not willing to allow defeat. The gardens, the land, the house, they were hers. She'd decide who would share them. She'd work her fingers to the bone to keep them. Though how, she had no idea as yet.

She turned to touch Miles' arm in gratitude. He meant only to be kind, she thought. But he had a strange, waiting expression his face. His eyes, never easy to read—not like hers, which expressed every feeling—were almost shuttered by their heavy lids. Rowena pulled back, not quite understanding her own hesitancy. She needed to, had to, say something.

"I really am grateful, Miles, you are very sweet. If no one asks me in twenty years time, I'll consider you." She tried to make a joke of it. After all, he could not really be expecting her to say yes.

"Well, the offer still stands if you decide to change your mind." He didn't smile this time, though his eyes still held sympathy, she thought. But she dismissed his words as only polite conventionality. She accepted that he felt a duty to her grandfather's memory.

She took a deep breath. It was time to tell him about her straightened circumstances.

He listened as Rowena repeated what Mr. Whitford had said. She had never had any secrets from Miles and saw no reason to begin now. A faint frown crossed his face. Then he again put an arm across her shoulder. Carefully, he said, "I'll lend you the money." Rowena pulled away sharply. She hadn't told him for that reason. She wasn't prepared to be beholden to anyone. Surely he knew enough about Pentraegon pride by now!

"No, Miles, thank you. This is my problem. I'll handle it somehow." She found herself avoiding his eyes. "Of course, if you have any bright ideas . . ." She managed to laugh; "maybe I'll win a lottery."

A wry grin touched his lips. "Perhaps Whitford's idea of selling Gulls Walk may be the best thing if you won't accept any help from me."

Now Rowena was hurt. She didn't expect that from him. He knew how much the house meant to her.

"Over my dead body!" She turned away, trying to control the anger that threatened to break through her hard-won self-control.

"Oh, I meant that you could sell it to me! It will still be in the family, so to speak." His voice was curiously colourless, and there was a moment's silence as he waited.

Rowena shook her head vehemently, not trusting herself to speak. The Gilberts already had so much of the Pentraegon land as well as the farm. Suddenly, she felt frightened. And yet, if anyone should buy Gulls Walk, why not Miles? But she managed some sort of strangled negative, then hurried toward the door to the garden. She needed to get away from him, from everyone.

"Well, at least give me first refusal if you do decide to sell," he called after her; "surely I would be better than strangers?"

Rowena murmured something or other. The conversation had become too difficult. There seemed to be a distance between them—of her own making, no doubt. She felt awkward, strangely threatened.

Yet she was grateful to him. After all, he had dropped everything and come down from London without her asking. Perhaps she had been rude.

Quickly, she looked back, with her hand on the latch. He deserved appreciation at least. There was no need for her to have been so abrupt.

But still she hesitated, and she watched Miles move to the hall door to leave. He didn't notice her turn, and she could have sworn she saw a smile touch his lips as he went out.

Rowena spent the greater part of the day wandering around Gulls Walk looking at everything with new eyes. She had not noticed how threadbare the curtains had become, the carpets, too. Perhaps It was foolish to try to squash the feelings of hopelessness. What possible future could there be? Yet she had to find some purpose.

She still had her share of the morning chores to do. Everything was well polished, Mrs. Trevain and the servants had seen to that.

But the vases, which held their usual profusion of flowers, needed to be freshened, for Grandfather had loved them too much for anyone to change the habits of a lifetime. In season, there always were plenty in the gardens, and Miles allowed her to pick any more that were needed from his fields. It suddenly occurred to her that perhaps these were usually paid for, and she wondered how she could bring up the subject to Miles.

She had never seriously thought about money before, since there had always seemed to he enough; consequently, it was a subject about which Gramps had never spoken. Sharply aware of the shortage of it now, she realised that she must take a cold, hard look at Gulls Walk household accounts in the future—if there were to be a future.

This wouldn't do. She must take a hold of herself. She had better talk to the solicitor tomorrow and find out just how long she could last. The small allowance, which Grandfather had given her as usual last month, suddenly seemed pitiful. It would last no time. And then what?

By late afternoon, Rowena was weary, and she threw herself down on the couch in her own little sitting room next to her bedroom in the west wing. First she rang Mr. Whitford to make an appointment for the following morning, and then she decided to call Meg.

Rowena and Megan Haversham had been at school together; and afterwards had gone to the same college where both had studied Art. Rowena had always been interested in fabrics and enjoyed creating strange, and occasionally to her surprise, rather elegant garments. So fascinated had she been that she stayed on an extra year, and her work had even caught the eyes of a couple of fashion houses.

Megan had often been her model, being tall and willowy, and both girls used to get a secret amusement out of listening to casual strangers asking from where Megan had bought whichever outfit she was wearing at the time. Indeed, once they had both finished art school, if it had not been for Rowena's longing to return to her beloved Gulls Walk, they might have started a boutique somewhere. But one could hardly do that in the local village; neither of them was that naive. So her friend now taught art at the day school both girls had attended.

The phone call to Megan at the flat she shared with a couple of other teachers caught her as she was walking through the door. After a tiring day organising some sort of art show for her pupils, she greeted the call with pleasure, ready to fill Rowena in, as she did from time to time, on her classes' latest escapades. Usually this caused them to chuckle together remembering their own less-than-perfect behaviour when they were teenagers.

"Thank goodness there is someone sane in this wretched, Old World." Megan chattered. "You'll never believe what the little monsters did today." Rowena listened half-heartedly, and Megan finally stopped, remembering the funeral. "But you don't want to hear my drivel. How is everything, Precious?" Miles' name had not been limited to the family. Today, his use of it had made Rowena particularly dislike it, though she knew that both he and Megan meant nothing by it any more.

"The name's Rowena," she snapped.

There was a moment's silence while Megan digested the flare of temper.

"What's the matter?" Her voice softened and become serious. "Was the funeral too dreadful? I'd've been there except for school . . . ."

Rowena choked, feeling the wretched tears returning. "Oh, it was awful! Can you come over?" Her words trailed away. She knew she had no right to bother Megan who lived some miles the other side of the village, and who had had a long day. But she did so need someone who would understand. "Please." she added.

She heard a few hasty mumbles in the background.

"I tell you what, Rowe," Rowena winced. The abbreviation suddenly sounded so childish. Good Lord! Had she aged so much in the last few days? "It's Friday, and I don't have any particular plans. Why don't I come for the weekend? Will that help?"

"Oh, Megan, will you? You're an angel of mercy." Rowena put down the phone, feeling a little better.

Exercise, that was what she needed now. After asking Mrs. Trevain to prepare a room for Megan, she hurried down to the paddock where an eager Goemor was literally champing at his bit. She decided that the quieter Firefly would have to wait for another day, particularly, she remembered guiltily, as she had not exercised the stallion since her grandfather's death. She saddled him quickly.

They climbed Trenallack Point and galloped over the headland, both of them revelling in the wind and the freedom away from the sadness of the house. If only they could ride on forever and forget the worries.

Gramps, dear Gramps. His death had left such an aching void. She had no idea how she was going to manage without him. Goemor responded to her need as they sped across the open country, but it was only a temporary escape. Too soon it would be time to return.

CHAPTER FOUR

Rowena had stayed out too long. She saw her guest's little car turn onto the gravel driveway leading down to the house; Megan must have dropped everything and left home almost immediately.

Cantering back, regretfully leaving the freedom of the wide-open headland where the evening sun had bathed her in its peace, Rowena was, nevertheless, glad that her guest had arrived. For all Megan's beauty, she was not given to flights of fancy and would put everything into some sort of proportion. At the very least, she would cheer up Rowena's sombre mood.

When she reached the stables, Megan, her face flushed, was leaning on the herb garden wall talking to Miles. Knowing how she herself enjoyed the breeze, Rowena supposed that Megan had driven with the windows down. She really was extraordinarily lovely, tall and graceful with long, silky blonde hair.

She should live closer, Rowena thought, and then both her good friends would always be near. But she frowned somewhat bitterly to herself as she hastily dismounted; any nearness to Gulls Walk was hardly likely to be of value to her for much longer unless she came up with an idea quickly.

She was unconscious of her grim expression as she turned to greet them, causing Megan's bright smile to fade. But she caught the glimpse of uncertainty that passed between the two standing there. Rowena pulled herself together. Some hostess I must look, she thought.

"You're a sight for sore eyes." She managed a grin. "I hope you didn't break any speed limits." That was usually a source of amusement to both of them. Rowena was the one with the tickets. Megan was staid and law-abiding, particularly now that she was a local pillar of the community. Teachers were expected to fall into that category in their part of the world. And she took her position seriously.

Her smile returned. "You needed me, so I came." Rowena realised that to Megan it was as simple as that.

She was a dear, uncomplicated soul, Rowena thought, wondering what she had done to deserve such good friends. Both had come when she needed them. She suddenly felt guilty, selfish, regretting her uncomfortable thoughts about Miles. She really did take a cold, hard look at herself that day. What right did she have to presume that the world should revolve around her problems?

Leaving Goemor in the competent hands of Jason, the stable boy, Rowena linked arms with both her friends and dragged them into the house.

When they seated themselves in the library, Miles, with a beer, the girls, with long, cool lemonade, they began to discuss the problem of Gulls Walk. Rowena listened as improbable, moneymaking schemes were banded back and forth. Opening the house to the public seemed a possibility.

"Too impractical, no parking space, no paved entrance road, no money to refurbish or repair," said Miles.

"How about a restaurant?" suggested Megan. Rowena shuddered at the thought, but the same problems applied.

"There must be something you can sell. There should be antiques worth a fortune." Megan's art studies had been almost totally of the modern school. French impressionists were the limit of her historical interest.

"I'm afraid that all the good stuff was sold years ago. Antiques we certainly have, but they're mostly nineteenth century, except for the sea chests, which have more sentimental value than anything else."

"What about the Queen's picture?"

"No!" Rowena sat up, her voice sharper than she intended. Never, never would she separate the portrait from the house. "No." she repeated more quietly. The subject was closed as far as she was concerned. Elizabeth's portrait had hung in the library since the house had been built. It belonged in Gulls Walk even more than she did.

Rowena was glad to leave the subject when they went into dinner. She had the beginnings of a headache. In spite of her long gallop over the cliffs, her sleepless nights were catching up with her.

An extra place had been laid for Miles. He was usually invited to dine at the manor house when ever he came home alone, even though that had been less often in recent months, for his business kept him so much in London or abroad. Gramps enjoyed those occasions since so seldom were there visitors to the valley. Once, during the Easter holidays, Rowena had seen quiet, dark suited, city men walking around the farm, but they had spent their time in long conferences, making no effort to enjoy the local scenery, or meet Gramps.

Rowena smiled gratefully at the housekeeper. It had been a long day for her, too, particularly after the funeral yesterday. Trevy normally went to her own room by this time in the evening, leaving dinner prepared in the oven. Gramps and Rowena usually served themselves, enjoying their times alone. Rowena's smile slipped a little at painful memories.

With her usual kindness, Mrs. Trevain was pleased that there were friends to dine with Rowena. Favourite dishes had been prepared: ice-cold vichyssoise, fresh garden salad, crisp roast lamb, and small new potatoes flavoured with the mint that always seemed to be threatening to take over the herb garden. The housekeeper had even shelled some early peas, tiny and sweet, and made a raspberry syllabub.

It was all deliciously tasty, but Rowena found she could eat almost nothing. She toyed with what was on her plate to please the old lady, thankful to see that Miles, and even Megan, made up for her own lack of appetite.

By mutual agreement, they talked of other things through dinner. Her guests obviously thought that Rowena needed cheering up. They discussed current events, the places Miles had visited, and even the success of a particular dress of Megan's that Rowena had made.

But her mind was unable to concentrate; she kept churning over her troubles, which were like a nagging toothache. Before the meal ended, her headache was almost blinding, and she begged to be excused. She retired to her bedroom leaving the other two chatting companionably over coffee. She was glad that they could enjoy each other's company and forgive her lack of manners.

It had been a long, long day.

On Saturday morning, before Megan was up, Rowena drove into town to the lawyer's office. She was determined to know as much of her financial situation as she could. Mr. Whitford was waiting for her.

She knew she was not looking her best. It had been another bad night, and the circles under her eyes were darker than ever. Gently, she was shown to a chair, and coffee was brought. She was glad of it. She seemed unable to get warm. Delayed shock, she supposed.

"I think that I might have some good news for you." The lawyer looked warily at Rowena. After her outburst when he had explained the will to her, he must have expected little enthusiasm.

"I have been talking to my land agent, and he seems to think that we could very easily sell the land between the house and the sea."

Rowena sat up, ready to bristle with arguments.

"Now, Miss Pentraegon, wait until I have finished. I understand that you want to keep all the property, but we have to be realistic. There is a tremendous demand for land, and a piece such as yours, private, having its own lovely beach, could fetch quite a large amount of money, possibly enough to pay most of the taxes on Gulls Walk." He sat back, waiting for Rowena to speak.

Vivid memories came to her of playing among the wild flowers and the coarse grasses of the dunes; of scrambling over the rocks to build sand castles on the beach; of casting off from the pier in Miles' boat to go fishing, and waving back to her grandfather on the terrace. All these burned through her brain, bringing with them an almost physical pain. To give up any of her beloved Gulls Walk seemed sacrilegious.

Yet she knew she had to be practical. She had no right to be so selfish. Perhaps others deserved to fall in love with Pentraegon land and its quiet cove, though it would hardly remain quiet for long if she sold it. But Rowena shuddered as she realized that she was not yet prepared to be so altruistic.

"Is there no other way?" Even to herself, her voice sounded frail and defenceless. The sleepless nights had exhausted her.

"I'm afraid there seems to be little else we can do." James Whitford rubbed his long chin. "But it will be some months before you will have to make that decision, of course. The law can work in your favour, you know. Probate will take time. But we must be prepared. Let me at least put the property on the market and see what sort of interest it will engender. Legal costs will come out of the total value of the estate, so you will incur no extra expense."

Rowena nodded her head in some sort of vague half-agreement. She got to her feet to leave, with no heart to ask for details. Even her questions about personal expenses seemed unimportant after this body blow, though it was a possible solution, and kindly meant at that. She moved to the door.

"Actually," The old man rose from his chair; "I do have some thing else that might be of interest." He opened a drawer and took out a letter. Rowena noticed that it was a heavy, vellum paper. A crest of some sort was embossed at the top.

"It will be only a temporary help, you understand." He looked at her over the top of his glasses. "It will solve nothing in the long run. But it might alleviate any immediate financial strain." He coughed gently. "Of course, if you have too much on your mind to consider anything at the moment, I will not bother you with this, though I thought that perhaps the money would come in handy." He folded the letter to put it back into its envelope.

"Wait. What money?"

Dear heavens! She must look a mess if he thought she was utterly incapable of making any decision. Where was the spunk on which she usually prided herself? Rowena pulled herself together. "I've become a little more realistic in the last few hours, Mr. Whitford."

She leaned forward. Yesterday's wandering around the house had shown her so many places that needed money. Whatever happened in the future, she could not bear to think of her beloved Gulls Walk falling into further decay. The main structure her grandfather had kept in reasonable repair and up to date, but there was so much else she had noticed that needed attention; the sort of things of which a man would not be aware.

But why was she even bothering? The land might not sell, and the inheritance duty might be far more than the sale of the land would realise, anyway.

Damn it! That was giving up! If the letter contained anything that could remotely engender money, she would listen. How quickly one can become mercenary, she thought.

The solicitor hesitated, then re-opened the folded sheet.

"Would you consider renting?" Rowena looked startled. He hurried on apologetically. "Just one wing, you understand. He need not infringe on your life style."

He? Who was he? Her mind flew back to the house. Certainly the east wing was hardly ever used, unless there were visitors, and that was rare. Though the house was small in comparison with the great stately homes, it did have more than a dozen bedrooms, four of which were at the east end of the house.

But that would mean she would have to share her home with a stranger. She was uncertain. Yet what did that matter? It looked as if she would have to share much more in the very near future. Perhaps such an arrangement might help prepare for that time. Rowena took a deep breath.

"It's a possibility." But she was not ready to be enthusiastic. It depended on who the tenant might be.

Clearing his throat, the old man opened the letter and gave Rowena the salient points.

"It seems that one of my legal connections in Spain has a client who is looking for a place to rent somewhere along this area of coastline. He is something of a horseman and will need a good animal to ride; I thought that Goemor's Arab pedigree would certainly satisfy him. Also, he has a yacht that will require moorings; the dock is in good repair I believe?" She nodded dumbly. "Most importantly, he is looking for privacy. The gentleman will bring at least a couple of members of his staff to take care of him. He will pay well for the right accommodation, a quite large amount, it seems."

Rowena whistled as she heard the sum. Mentally, she translated it into repairs to the woodwork; fresh varnish and a new coat of paint; even curtains; and oats for the horses. And she could buy sadly-needed new sheets and towels. Her spirits lifted, despite the worry of the future.

Her eyes brightened. "What do you think?" she asked. Surely Mr. Whitford would be unlikely to recommend anyone not suitable.

"Well, it would certainly help your present finances. But it is not for me to persuade you. You must make your own decision. Why don't you go home and think about it. I have a month to find a suitable place if you are not interested. I have been looking around, and I'm sure there are other places available.

"But one of the criteria is total peace and quiet, and that is hard to find. He just will not stay in a place where he is likely to have any outside interference or disturbance of any kind. About that, he is adamant."

Quickly, she made her decision. The desire for quietness appealed to her. Yes. She wanted this tenant. She, and Gulls Walk, needed the money. It seemed almost poetic justice that a Spaniard should share the house. In any case, she wouldn't have to see him much. She could stay with Megan if he proved too ghastly. She laughed, with a certain grim humour.

"I'll do it. I'll rent the east wing. Thank you so much, Mr. Whitford." Then a sudden thought struck her. "Will he pay in advance?" That part of the house needed even more doing to it than the rest, and a month was not very long.

"I'm sure that can be arranged." The solicitor's eyes twinkled as Rowena looked eagerly at him. She supposed anything was better than the morose mood with which she had entered his office. "I'll make a list of his requirements for you, and inform him of your decision. His agent will come in the next few days to check out the house and area, but since peace seems to be of first important, we should have no problems there."

He folded up the letter and, with some relief, waved aside her thanks. Content with his morning's work, he ushered Rowena out of the building. She climbed into her car as she said good bye, feeling as if there might be just the smallest glimmerings of hope. At least she wasn't going to starve for the next few months! She had dreaded having to ask for more money to augment what was left of her allowance.

And just having something to do, something she could get her teeth into, made her feel better. It meant she could put off any eventual decision. Dear Gulls Walk. In the last few years she had not been looked after as she deserved. Perhaps a small facelift might make up for the neglect. Rowena couldn't wait to get home to start.

CHAPTER FIVE

Rowena was greeted with rather less enthusiasm than she had expected when she told Miles and Megan about her prospective tenant.

"What on earth good will that do?" Almost angrily, Miles thrust the words at her. "It will mean a great deal of work. And to what end? I'll give you money until you sell the land if you are so short. Indeed, I'll buy the land. I've already told you that. We don't want strangers at Gulls Walk."

She bridled a little. Miles was rushing her. In any case, she hadn't decided whether she intended to sell. Oh, she knew his offer was kindly meant, even though he seemed so annoyed; but Rowena wanted to be beholden to no one. His concern for her was all very well, but he was missing the point.

"No. I don't need a handout, thank you, Miles. And I'm not going to cut a slice off Gulls Walk just yet. As to what good having a tenant will be, it will be good for Gulls Walk. Just look around you. This place hasn't been decorated in years. It's an opportunity to spruce up the old girl a bit. Oh, I know I may lose everything, but I can't bear to let her die." Rowena suspected that she was being rather melodramatic, but surely Miles cared almost as much as she did?

Even Megan, who usually was docile and followed in whatever direction others chose to lead her, was negative.

"You won't have the house to yourself. We won't be free to come to visit you whenever we . . . whenever you want us." She stopped speaking and looked to Miles for support. Rowena began to feel defensive.

"Oh, yes you will. I'm only renting the east wing. He will be bringing his own staff, so we won't see much of him. And if he becomes too much of a nuisance, I'll come to stay with you." She smiled as brightly as she could at Megan; they had been good friends for so long.

"Come on. Be glad for me, both of you. I know that when the entire legal hassle is over, I may end up without Gulls Walk, but at least I can try to keep my head above water for the time being."

Rowena sounded as if her beloved house was about to float out into the deep Atlantic, but even a drowning man will swim until the last wave swamps him. Wincing mentally at the uncomfortable picture her mind was painting, she turned away to look out of the window. The tears were smarting behind her eyes. She had come home so eagerly, ready at least to try to make a success of this new venture. Perhaps she had been fooling herself, but anything was better than the desperate moods she had endured over the last few days. She so needed to be doing something, anything that might stave off the day of judgement. Perhaps she was trying to hold on to her fool's paradise. But she'd had enough of mixed metaphors for one day.

Megan reached out a hand to touch her arm. "Of course, Rowe. You're right. I didn't mean to sound such a pessimist. It's just, well, why waste the time left. There is nothing you can do, and it's summer. School will be closing soon. We could have such a lovely time, bathing, fishing, and just lazing."

Inwardly Rowena smiled, though somewhat ironically. The last time that Megan had gone fishing, she had caught nothing but a very sunburned nose.

Rowena found herself feeling less than charitable and gave herself a mental shaking. Maybe it was not fair to expect either of them to understand. Truth to tell, she didn't understand completely herself. Was it just that she was trying to hang on to her history and to bricks and mortar? She remembered a quote from Cyrano De Bergerac: Something about 'Love worships at the shrine of past memories.'

Was that what she was doing? Shouldn't she, perhaps, move on, let Gulls Walk go to a new owner? It would surely sell for a good price. And once the taxes were paid, she would still have enough for a regular income on which she could live reasonably independently, or even start up a business designing clothes for a living.

And she supposed Miles would be that ideal owner. She sighed to herself as he pressured her further.

"A tenant will solve none of your problems, Rowena. What you need is a solution that will cover them all. Let me at least talk to Mr. Whitford about buying the house or the land. I always promised your grandfather that I would take care of you. I can't let you turn your home into a common boarding house. Gulls Walk and the farm have always had only Pentraegons and Gilberts here. We don't want anyone else."

Damn it all, thought Rowena grimly. That was not fair. One extremely well paying tenant wasn't exactly like taking in lodgers! Couldn't they see that she was trying so hard to be practical and realistic? She refused to accept what to Miles and Megan appeared to be obvious. She must not give in without at least an effort. Every instinct resisted the thought.

A grim determination began to surface. The burden, if burden it would be, was her inheritance. It was bound to her as tightly as if it were parent, child and lover all in one. She could not, indeed, had no right to reject that which four hundred years had nurtured. She was the last of the Pentraegons, and the responsibility was just as much her birthright as it had been Gramp's, or any of the long line of ancestors who had lived and loved in this, their own piece of Cornwall.

For the rest of the day, Rowena concentrated on that: a clarity of single-minded purpose that nothing Miles or Megan could say would shift. She did not even attempt to explain; in any case, she couldn't find the words: not ones that they would understand.

Leaving them to their own devices, Rowena searched the house making a mental list of all the things that would have to be done before her Spanish tenant arrived. It was such a long list that later, as she looked back, she wondered why she hadn't crumbled.

She had only a month to work a miracle.

On Sunday evening, Megan went back to her own home. To be fair to her, she did offer to come to help when the term was over—coincidentally, about the same time the Spaniard would be arriving. And she wished Rowena luck.

Before Miles returned to London the following morning, he renewed an agreement he had established with her grandfather over the last couple of years to rent some of Gulls Walk's remaining land for pasture. Rowena had not realised that the payment was in ample supplies of produce from the farm, including all the flowers she could pick. No wonder Gramps had not bothered her with housekeeping bills, particularly since there was little he had to purchase from the village. Indeed, over the last few years, he had maintained less and less contact with anyone outside his own property.

Apparently, Miles' rather dour farm manager Heron had seen to it that a basket of meat, dairy produce and vegetables was delivered each day. The deep freeze was kept stocked, and extra fodder was available for the horses when ever necessary. If Trevy ran out of something, a phone call had been all that was needed to have it included in the daily delivery.

Rowena felt relieved, yet sad, as Miles explained the details. Oh dear, how self-centredly ignorant she had been. Before this week, it had not occurred to her to inquire about housekeeping. And Gramps had never discussed their finances. He must have found it all rather demeaning to make such arrangements, for in the past he would not have taken payment for the use of the fields. Only the last few years away at art school, and summers filled with research, were an excuse for her own unawareness.

She agreed to the arrangements with as much grace as her pride would allow—she owed Miles that. Also, with some guilt, she was glad that she had something to barter, hoping that the pasture's value really was equal to the farm supplies. Up to that moment, she had no idea how she was going to feed her household out of the remains of her small allowance. Now, at least that worry was removed.

But Miles still tried one last time to persuade her. "Give up this tenant idea, Precious. I'm sure he'll only be a nuisance. The little money you make won't be worth it."

Her nickname was the last straw.

"Oh, Miles, for heaven sake, let me make my own decisions. I will, at least, be doing something to enhance the value of the house. And if it doesn't work, I'll let you know." she flared.

"All right, all right. But don't say I didn't warn you!" He paused, perhaps realising he had said enough. "Look, I can't help being concerned. Someone has to take care of you. I'll come down and check this Spaniard over when he arrives. I'm not going to let you be hassled by some stranger. And don't forget. You've promised to give me first refusal when . . . er . . . if, after all, you have to sell the house or the land."

Rowena must have allowed her fears to show, or anger, maybe both. Whichever, Miles seemed to realise his tactlessness. He tried to lighten her annoyance with a smile. "Now Precious, don't worry. If I buy, you can throw yourself in as a bonus. Then you can still live here." He kissed her, certainly with plenty of fondness, perhaps deliberately not noticing her withdrawal. One could never tell with Miles.

But once he and Megan had departed, Rowena dismissed them both from her mind. She had too many other things to worry about.

Monday found her in her oldest clothes, rummaging through the boxes and trunks in the attics. Generations of long-gone Pentraegons had stored much of their ill-gotten gains there, as well as all the flotsam and jetsam discarded over the years. She was determined to find anything that might help her in her refurbishing attempts before she purchased new items. As a child, she had played happily with snippets from the yards and yards of old silks and satins packed in camphor balls in some of the ancient chests; who knew how long they had been there? The edges of the bolts were stained and faded, but as she began to unravel them, the rich colours shone as vividly as ever.

Rowena blessed her skill with a needle; she was surely going to need it. But she couldn't help shedding a few tears when she dragged out the heavy bundles of cloth, remembering the good times.

She took as much as she could carry downstairs to the east wing and spread them in a riot of brightness over the somewhat sombre furniture in the various rooms. Mrs. Trevain and the other servants soon joined her, bringing down other bolts and helping her select what she needed for new curtains and covers.

For the couches and winged-back chairs in the drawing room, she decided on a deep blue brocade, through which was woven a small, gold fleur-de-lis. A glorious, golden-yellow silk was ideal for the curtains in there, and the rooms above. There was even enough of a paler gold for the canopy and drapes of the ancient four-poster bed in the east wing's master bedroom.

Just the scattering of the cloth enlivened the whole area. Rowena felt the familiar excitement grow within her as she handled the fabric. Truly, she was never happier than when she was creating. She pushed away any dismal thoughts, determined to make the whole house as beautiful as she could.

Even Jason, the stable boy, eagerly volunteered to help, and in no time Rowena had them all at work scraping walls and floors that needed re-painting and re-varnishing. Then began the cleaning and polishing of panelling that had not been touched in years; even re-hanging doors that had not closed properly, probably for centuries. All the time, Rowena cut and pinned as if her life depended on it!

Soon she was dancing backward and forward through the rooms in her eagerness to create as charming a decor as possible.

The agent for the Spaniard came and went. Rowena, with pins in her mouth, was too busy to see him; but Mrs. Trevain gave him a carefully orchestrated—and limited—tour, with which he seemed pleased and satisfied.

Even someone from the probate office came to make a first assessment of the house. Rowena deliberately avoided any contact with him, leaving others to guide him through the general havoc they were creating and point out the worst of the decay. The lower the evaluation, the lower the death duties, she hoped.

Eagerly, the household worked together, lightening and brightening the whole wing until it shone like a mint-new penny. A couple of the girls from the village, under Rowena's direction, sewed the cloth almost as fast as she could cut it; and toward the end of the second week, the tenant's rooms were practically ready. Those for any servants he might bring had been smartened, and furniture from other parts of the house moved in to make the wing as self-contained as could be managed.

There was even a butler's pantry, which would enable small meals to he prepared in the east wing without the need to trail all the way to the kitchen; though Rowena supposed the Spaniard would want to use the main dining room should he need to entertain. That bridge she would cross later. Luckily Gramps had not got rid of the long table with its seating for more than twenty. She suspected that no one had wanted to buy it; there certainly wasn't much demand for that size of dining arrangement nowadays.

True to his promise, Mr. Whitford delivered a cheque on an English bank from the Spanish lawyers to cover the rent for the first three months. It seemed quite enormous to Rowena, but she pounced on it eagerly, laughing over the long string of names on the document she had to sign. 'Rowena Felicity Pentraegon' seemed small stuff beside 'Roberto Igado Guilio Alberoni Olivares'.

But by now she was in her element, not concerned that the names represented an unknown quantity.

The results of the cleaning efforts were beginning to show in other parts of the house, too. The staff had worked with a will, and Gulls Walk was starting to lift her skirts and glow with all the gaiety of an elderly debutante. At last it was time to go shopping.

What girl does not enjoy spending money? Rowena bought fine percale sheets, and lovely thick towels. She even threw out the old breakfast china and bought pretty Devon pottery, persuading herself that the staff all should enjoy a little of the new wealth the cheque had brought. The kitchen was brightened with presents of pots and pans, and she invested in a new vacuum cleaner. For the first time, Rowena realised how antiquated and out-of-date was the equipment with which the servants had struggled so long. Dear Gramps had no idea. He had seen to the plumbing and wiring and had brought the bathrooms and kitchen up to date, but so much more was needed. Rowena was sure he had never realised. Thank heavens for the cheque! But, oh dear! It was dwindling fast.

And the days were passing much too quickly.

All the windows throughout the house were polished until they shone like diamonds in the summer sunshine. The somewhat battered silver, what was left of it, was cleaned and displayed. Grandmother's Spode dinner service for twenty-four, one of the few treasures still remaining in Gulls Walk, was taken from its dark cupboard and placed on the shelves above the sideboards on either side of the fireplace in the Great Hall. The sun streaming through the long windows, also newly curtained with a creamy green damask from the chests in the attic, caused the glowing warmth of the fine porcelain, with its splash of colour, to lift the somewhat sombre face of the high, panelled walls.

Rowena hoped that when flowers were placed in their various containers, the Great Hall would look even more inviting. She was determined that it would be an exquisite introduction to the beauty of the rest of the house. Unless the Spaniard used the doors onto the terrace, he would have to traverse the hall's length, or negotiate either of the broad staircases to the upper gallery each time he went in or out.

Even the library, her favourite room, got its share of attention. It was in the central wing and, therefore, not really part of the house she had allocated to the Spaniard. But it housed Elizabeth's portrait, and the first Morgan Pentraegon's papers. No doubt if any room deserved a face-lift, this one did. Anyway, it certainly needed new curtains. Rowena found a bolt of woven brocade; a blend of pale blues and green intermingled with a soft, sunshine yellow, to lighten the worn, leather-bound books, and the dark panelling.

She smiled up at Good Queen Bess when all was finished, and she was sure that Her Gracious Majesty looked pleased.

As she hurried through the house, in and out of the newly furbished rooms, she put away any qualms she still had. Surely her Spaniard would feel he was getting his money's worth and not notice the underlying signs of indigence.

It was nearing the end of the third week of preparation when the first blow fell.

Mr. Whitford came to see Rowena with a glum face. They took their coffee to the terrace to enjoy the beautiful morning. She was feeling particularly happy; judicial moving of furniture had covered all the worst parts of the carpet in the Great Hall. It was now much more respectable than she had imagined would be possible. The cheque had been generous, but there was no way it could stretch to new floor coverings; as it was, there would be barely enough left to pay for the day-to-day bills that she knew would inevitably crop up.

"I'm afraid I'm not bringing you very good news," the elderly lawyer apologised. Rowena kept a cheerful smile on her face. At least he had not said that he was bringing bad.

"Oh, cheer up, Mr. Whitford. What sort of news could spoil a lovely day like this?" Rowena refused to be pessimistic. Everything had been going so well.

"I have heard from the office of probate." Her heart gave a sudden lurch of apprehension. "It seems I am not going to be able to continue to dispense quite so much in the way of wages for the servants." He looked worriedly at Rowena. "I have to put a freeze on all but the very minimum of expenses. That means there will be only enough money to pay the usual bills; rates, electricity and so forth; and just a skeleton staff."

Rowena blanched. A skeleton staff? How few was that? Her tenant was due to arrive so soon. What if he expected to use her servants as well as his own? She couldn't pay any of the wages; she had spent far too much of the cheque already. And she could not turn him away; it would be impossible to give him back his money. Bemused, she dragged her mind back to listen as Mr. Whitford continued.

"I have managed to persuade them that the house requires at least three servants. This they have agreed to. Surely this will be enough. Your tenant will be bringing a husband and wife with him who will take care of all his needs, so you are not likely to have to do much for him."

Typical male! Rowena was sure the dear man had no idea how much work there was in a house this size and thought that they probably could just dust a little less often. Well, maybe he was right. She gulped. What choice did she have? Thank goodness they had almost finished such a thorough spring-cleaning.

"We'll manage. We'll have to. Don't worry, Mr. Whitford. Thank you for everything. I'm sure you did your best." What else could she say? She didn't dare let him know just how much of the cheque she had spent. What if the Spaniard demanded extras that she couldn't pay for? The solicitor might feel duty bound to tell her tenant that the house could not be satisfactory looked after, since there was so little money left. Rowena smiled as brightly as she could, causing the lawyer's own worried expression to lift a little.

"The wages for all the present staff will be paid to the end of the month, plus whatever severance pay is their due. I will handle that for you. After that, I'm afraid you'll have to manage . . . ."

"Now, you mustn't be so concerned." Rowena gave him the same sunny grin with which she had greeted him. She promised him that there would be no problems; he was to forget his worries and need not even think about her, or Gulls Walk, until probate was final. The rent money was ample to cover extra expenses, she assured him, crossing her fingers. She dared not tell him how little there was left! The less he knew, the less he need worry; then he could put no spoke in the path of her new venture. She mustn't have him communicate any of her fears to the Spaniard.

Poor Mr. Whitford's look of relief was almost comical. Rowena knew that he must have feared a tirade, but she was learning. And she must give him no reason to feel the need to keep checking on her. The less he came to Gulls Walk, the better, she decided.

As soon as he had gone, Rowena rushed to consult with Mrs. Trevain. She needed her support more than ever now!

"How will we manage, Trevy?" She looked around helplessly. The stables, the gardens, the endless corridors. "When we cut back on the servants at the end of the month is just when Don Olivares is due." Things such as probate and selling of land were the least of her worries now! Rowena had been pitching in with the rest of the staff and had scrubbed her share of tiles and floorboards, and she had no qualms about continuing to do the same, but there was so much that needed doing each day.

Mrs. Trevain folded her arms and stretched herself to all of her sixty-two inches. "We'm have to be practical. That's what. We'm done it a'fore. We'm do it again!"

In the face of such calm assurance, Rowena began to feel better. What would she do without her beloved Trevy?

It was decided that the housekeeper, with her kitchen maid, Jeannie, and Jason, the stable boy, would be the ones to stay on.

"Reduced wages if we have to!" The housekeeper had glared at the younger servants, giving them no chance to protest, though both were much too loyal to let that stop their eagerness to help. Rowena only hoped that cuts in pay would not be necessary.

The four of them toured the house, each carrying a bundle of dustsheets, and they closed up as many rooms as possible. Grandfather's old room, the various other guestrooms except those in the east wing, all received their share of covers. Then the doors were locked.

Rowena began to feel a little better. At least the house was fairly manageable now. She blessed Jason as he promised to shoulder as much of the extra work as he could. He assured her that he would look after the garden with its interminable lawn-mowing, the gravel drive-way, which had to be raked regularly, and also the thousand and one jobs that always needed doing in a house like this.

Dear Gulls Walk. She loved her. But Rowena was only just beginning to realise what a demanding lady she was, and how she'd always taken her wonderful staff so much for granted.

Over the next few days, everyone worked on the remaining spring-cleaning. The garden was weeded and tidied, the long driveway was raked meticulously. Even those servants who were leaving worked harder than Rowena felt she had the right to expect. But she promised them they would be re-hired if and when fortunes changed. Truth to tell, by now she was so tired that a depressed reaction was setting in. She was well aware that even if she could hold on to the house, there would be little likelihood of those better days ever returning.

At last it was the end of June, and all but her faithful three departed. In a couple of days, the tenant would arrive. Rowena looked at her broken fingernails, and her work-roughened hands. Some lady owner, she thought! Perhaps she need see very little of the Spaniard. Surely he would not expect her to play the Grande Dame.

Little did she realise how true that would turn out to be, or what twists of fate would change the lives of all the people who lived in Pentraegon Valley.

CHAPTER SIX

The day before the Spaniard was to arrive, everyone rose at the crack of dawn to put the final touches to the guest wing.

Beds were made up with the new linen. The larder and refrigerator in the butler's pantry in the east wing were well stocked with a generous supply of food as a welcoming gift. On a table in the drawing room, Rowena placed some ancient Spanish books that she had found in the library. The old leather bindings looked quite charming, and even if the contents turned out to be dull, at least she had tried.

Mrs. Trevain, who had been cooking every day when she could find a spare moment, filled the last shelves in the freezer with the pies and cakes and casseroles she was sure would be needed. She was determined that the guest should be well fed, and a glorious welcoming dinner had been planned. She paid no attention to Rowena's protestations that food was not in the contract, in spite of the size of the rent the tenant was paying.

At least it was a relief that no payment was required for most of the ingredients. There were plenty of fresh fruits and vegetables in the kitchen garden at this time of year; and the Home Farm, true to Miles' promise, kept them supplied with dairy produce and meats in return for the use of the pasture. She blessed him for insisting that the value of feeding his cattle so conveniently close to his own farm was a boon he had no desire to lose. Frankly, she thought he was being kind, but now she was even gladder that she had accepted. She certainly could not afford to go out and buy everything Mrs. Trevain needed for her cooking spree.

"Be prepared! That's my motto," the housekeeper said, with great determination, and Rowena had agreed weakly. She must have been light headed with the constant lack of sleep, for the idea of her dear, darling, roly-poly Trevy as a girl guide so tickled her sense of humour that she hadn't the heart to stop the sweet lady's culinary efforts.

The day passed in the final flurry that precedes the arrival of any guest, and by supper time all that was left to do was fill the vases with fresh flowers. This, Rowena would do in the morning.

Then Fate dealt her second blow. Climbing on a chair to put away the last bottles of freshly made preserves, Trevy slipped and fell.

Running into the kitchen when she heard her scream, Rowena found the poor soul lying in a twisted heap with her leg folded under her.

The bright red, sticky mess, which had splashed in all directions, looked for all the world like blood. To find that it was only strawberry jam was a tremendous relief, but the leg, obviously broken, was serious. The housekeeper was well into her sixties and should have been thinking about retirement, not working as hard as someone half her age. She moaned tearfully as the ambulance was called, worried as to how Rowena would manage, and she chastised herself for being so careless.

Reassuring her, she was bundled off to the hospital with Jeannie to keep her company, and Rowena followed behind in her little car. Trevy had been almost a mother to the whole household, and the unknown Spaniard took second place to her well being.

Hours later, when the leg was set and the old lady was comfortably sleeping, the doctor eased Rowena's mind. Luckily it was a clean break. Even though she wouldn't be completely back on her feet for some weeks to come, there was no reason why she shouldn't recover fully. Rowena returned home feeling considerably relieved. The predicament they were in without Trevy seemed of little importance—until the following day.

That night Rowena slept like a log. Whether it was from shock or just sheer exhaustion, or, perhaps, because her housekeeper's injury had put everything in better proportion, she didn't know. But when the alarm rang in the morning, she jumped out of bed with more energy than she had felt for days.

She pulled on her gardening clothes and hurried downstairs; there was still much to do, particularly with one less pair of hands. She first rang the hospital to reassure herself that all was well, and then she went into the garden to gather fresh foliage and great armfuls of flowers.

In spite of Trevy's absence, Rowena found herself feeling quite excited as she filled the many vases with the fragrant blossoms. Jeannie and Jason fetched and carried for her, and soon her beloved Gulls Walk was taking on the air of a summer garden party. Rowena even began to sing a little, pushing away her concern about coping without dear Trevy.

By early afternoon, Rowena had finished. She was filthy but content. Surely the Spaniard could not help but be impressed with all that had been done. The rooms glowed and sparkled like an enchanted fairyland. No longer could one see the worn areas or the threadbare carpets. The house looked truly beautiful, even, maybe, worth the exorbitant rent Mr. Whitford had obtained.

But keeping it looking like this was going to be a problem. Tomorrow she would have to see about another housekeeper. Somewhat grimly, Rowena wished Trevy could have seen how lovely everything was. It just wasn't fair, after all the work the old lady had done, that she could not be there.

Feeling oddly lonely as she wandered around, Rowena straightened cushions, and rearranged some of the glorious golden roses that had always been her grandmother's favourites.

Not for the first time, she wondered if she had bitten off more than she could chew.

She began to feel nervous. The practical tasks of decoration had been fun, in spite of the long hours and her constant exhaustion, and she had delighted in the gradual blooming of her adored Gulls Walk. But, Rowena supposed, once her guest arrived, she must make some show of being the Lady of the Manor. Scrubbing the floors was hardly what a tenant would expect of her.

Her feelings were mixed as she wondered if she were capable of seeing to all the things that the wealthy Spaniard would need. But it was too late now. If she had to scrub those interminable floors, for she couldn't expect Jeannie, or a new housekeeper, to do all the rough work, then she would just have to do it early in the morning. And tomorrow she would try to find a suitable replacement for Trevy. She rather grimly hoped that Mr. Whitford could come up with another salary. She certainly would not let him cut the old lady's pay. Later she'd call him, but not just now.

She needed a break. Poor Goemor and Firefly had been given little exercise over the last few days. The Spaniard was not due to arrive until around six, so Rowena decided to saddle the stallion for a good gallop over the headland in the hopes of blowing away some of her qualms. They were returning in full force now, to hang over her head like an oppressive cloud. There was nothing more that she could do to the house, anyway. Even dinner was prepared, and the gentle Firefly would be quite happy to meander around the paddock; she could have her exercise tomorrow.

The weather had been threatening a change over the last few hours. It looked like rain, so Rowena took down an old jacket that Jason had left hanging on a doornail in the stable, and dragged it over her dirty gardening clothes. She tucked her hair under her riding hat, and grimaced in some amusement at the sight she must make. She knew there probably were streaks of soil on her face, but there was plenty of time for a bath when she returned.

She mounted Goemor, and they trotted up Trenallack Point toward her favourite ride. The sparkling air, with its faint chill of rain to come, felt good on her face. The fresh, salt breeze, and the cry of the seagulls wheeling over her head quickly dispelled the cobwebs from her mind, and she succumbed to a desire to race with the wind, fly from her responsibility and, perhaps, feel carefree again. She urged Goemor to a gallop, determined for the moment to forget the problems tomorrow would bring, or worrisome words of the future such as staff shortages, death duties and probate officers.

After a few miles, she turned the horse, and they began to retrace their tracks. When they reached a part of the cliff that marked the limit of Pentraegon Cove, Rowena urged Goemor down the path they regularly used to reach the beach. The tide was out, and she intended to canter home along the water's edge.

Perhaps she was a little careless; certainly she was not concentrating on the stallion's steps, for he had carried her this way to the sea many times before. Whatever the reason, Rowena was caught off guard when a bird crackled its way out of the undergrowth. With beating wings, squawking its peevish annoyance, it flew in front of Goemor startling him and making him shy from the sudden noise. The path was narrow, and sensing danger, he twisted around, his feet scrambling for higher ground.

Before Rowena was able to tighten her grasp on the reins, she was thrown from the nervous stallion's back and suddenly found herself careening pell-mell down the steep slope. Unable to stop herself, she rolled over and over, jarring legs and arms, and scratching her face on the gorse bushes. Somehow her hat stayed on, and she remembered blessing its hard protection; otherwise, she might have been knocked unconscious.

At last, winded by the fall, Rowena collapsed in a heap onto a soft sand dune at the foot of the cliff. Thank goodness it was not an area of the hard, sharp-edged granite that angles out to sea along much of the coastline. Who knows what damage she might have done to herself, then? But her main emotion was chagrin at her stupidity. She had not been thrown since she was a small child.

Lying still for a few moments, mulling over her bruised pride, she reluctantly recognising that if she had been more cautious, none of this would have happened.

She eased onto an elbow to watch Goemor who, with typical equine unconcern, was cropping the grasses half way up the cliff. He seemed to have come to no harm and Rowena breathed a sigh of relief. She loved him dearly, feeling him to be the last living contact she had with Gramps. But more than that, she couldn't afford to lose him; her Spaniard would he none too happy if all he had to ride were Firefly!

Gradually Rowena became aware of a shout and the sound of running feet. She turned her head as the sun was blocked out by the large figure of a man bending over her.

"You damned fool, Child. What on earth possessed you to ride down that path? Stay still."

Rowena began to protest that she was neither a fool nor a child, and that she knew exactly what she was doing! But dark, glowering eyes stilled her tongue. She winced as none too gentle hands began to feel her arms and legs.

"Don't move. You deserve it if I am hurting you. That horse is far too big for you. And much too valuable for you to be taking such stupid chances coming down a narrow path like that."

The stranger gave a relieved grunt, as his probing fingers found no break. She could have told him that, but by now she was too incensed at his high-handed manner. She was more shaken up than she was prepared to admit, but she wasn't going to give any interfering male the satisfaction of 'I told you so.'

"I'm fine. Leave me alone." Rowena snapped as she tried to struggle to her feet.

"Stay where you are, Child. You're not getting up until I've checked you all over. If you must behave with such a lack of responsibility, you must take the consequences." Firm hands moved up her rib cage under Jason's coat, deftly kneading the soft flesh, searching for injuries.

Her irritation began to smoulder, the title of Child rankled. The fact that she had been careless and deserved his annoyance did not help either.

"Let me go. I'm only winded. Leave me alone!" She repeated angrily.

She knew she was being rude and should curb her wretched temper; after all, he was only trying to help. But Rowena wasn't used to the utter contempt in his voice. Hastily, she tried to push away his searching hands as they crept too high. She found herself blushing violently.

"I'm twenty-three, no child, thank you. And how I ride is certainly none of your business."

Rowena looked up as the hands stopped. Piercing, velvet-brown eyes with golden glints looked down at her. She found herself thinking of chestnuts glowing in the firelight on a cold winter's evening. Perhaps there was some slight concussion after all; why was her mind wandering so? For one long moment, curious fingers trailed across her small breasts and a vivid shaft of fire exploded where they touched. Rowena gasped and shrank away.

"Ah, yes. The jacket had me fooled." The corner of his mouth twitched. With no embarrassment, the stranger straightened her clothes, then pulled off her riding hat. His eyes widened as her dishevelled, auburn mane tumbled in the wind as if it were a living thing, sparkling bright.

But mortified at the memory of his fingers and at the mess she knew she must look, Rowena grabbed her hat and crammed it back on her head with little concern how it fitted.

His voice softened slightly, but he continued to bludgeon her with words.

"That still doesn't explain why you are riding that horse down such a steep path. Does his owner know you have him?" The golden glint hardened again. "By the smell of you, I presume that you work in the stables."

"Well, sometimes." He could take that any way he wanted as far as she was concerned. "I have to get back." She struggled to rise.

He towered over her, and again she was aware of that same piercing look, and of thick, dark hair catching glints of sunshine. Below it was the stern face of an arrogant man; a face with harsh planes and crags, too powerful to be called merely handsome; a memorable face, the face of a dangerous adversary.

Rowena, usually fairly impervious to the male species, felt a strange jagged fear tear at her gut. To her intense annoyance, a trembling shook her like the fronds of a willow caught in the breeze. She gritted her teeth, fighting for control.

"Thank you," she finally managed to mutter, as he lifted her to her feet. For a moment she was conscious of hard muscles, and her nostrils caught the sharp tang of after-shave lotion.

Bewildered to find that her legs seemed not to know how to carry her, she staggered, resting her head for a moment against the rough tweed of his jacket. His harsh anger seemed to subside, and he held her close until her head stopped spinning.

Acutely aware of her own heart fluttering like a captured bird, and of the steady beat of his under her hand, for one odd moment she felt strangely as if she were floating on a cloud; drifting, drifting, out of control. Then memories of his arrogance brought her back to earth. Sharply, she struggled out of his arms.

"Thanks." She kept her voice cool as she strove to keep her balance. But her natural good manners made her pause. Somewhat unwillingly, she held out her hand, which he accepted in a hard grip. It was the least she could do, she supposed, in spite of his rudeness, for she had been decidedly ill mannered, too.

He turned her fingers over, feeling the calluses she had acquired in the last few weeks.

"Someone works you hard," he muttered. He frowned, looking searchingly into her eyes. The anger surfaced again. "But you still shouldn't be riding that horse."

He released her, and Rowena turned away to hide the blush that she felt rising to her cheeks; part anger at his arrogance, and part, the heady chemical reaction to sheer male dominance. She was shaken by more than her tumble down the hillside.

She whistled to Goemor to cover her confusion. Docilely, he came to her call.

"Oh, no you don't!" The harshness had not gone. "I suppose you think that you can just climb aboard and ride him home."

He pushed Rowena away, preventing her from mounting. Taking the trailing reins, he examined the stallion just as meticulously as he had examined its rider, except that his large hands were much more gentle and patient.

"You will walk him back to his stable. Do you hear?" The irritation was still there. "He is much too valuable an animal to be abused. He seems to be all right. No thanks to you. But you mustn't take any risks. Let this be a lesson to you. You wouldn't last long if I had anything to do with your employment. You're damned lucky he didn't fall, too."

Men! Rowena thought as she opened her mouth to protest. He didn't care a hoot that she might be too sore to walk. But she said nothing as she felt the tears prickle behind her eyelids. She certainly would not give him the satisfaction of seeing her cry.

Burning with indignation, she turned away. It was devastating to feel that one was considered of such little importance. She still smarted from the injustice of his accusation. Typical male chauvinist! Damn him! He had jumped to all the wrong conclusions. Rowena's anger was winning. She lifted her chin high.

But she was definitely aware of the chemistry.

She also was aware of bruises as she started to trudge through the sand in the opposite direction from which she had intended to go. The stranger stood directly between her and the path down which she had tumbled and was blocking the way to her own cove. She supposed she could edge round him, but he looked so menacing that she certainly hadn't the guts to try.

She felt her skin burn in mortification at the memory of his words, and her uncomfortable temper still smouldered; particularly as she had no choice but to take the long way home.

As she led Goemor back along the beach, rubbing her sore rear end, she carried with her the memory of his angry frown and was suddenly startled to hear a sardonic laugh. He must still have been watching her.

"Consider your tender derriere in lieu of the spanking you so richly deserve!"

Damn and blast him! But Rowena resisted the urge to shout back a mouthful of abuse that a dirty little stable hand might be expected to use.

Blushing with painful chagrin, she straightened her back and stonily kept her silence. She persuaded herself that it was a good thing she was never likely to see him again. Casual tourists rarely reached this lonely stretch, keeping to the more accessible beaches.

It was growing late and she needed to hurry; she had been away far too long. Rowena groaned. But, of course, the stranger was right. She must not risk riding Goemor until she had given him a thorough check. Yet she was so sore. How the wretched man would have loved that! To make matters worse, it started to rain. That was all she needed to complete her misery.

It was well after five when she walked Goemor down the driveway. She was surprised to see her friend's car parked near the front door, but thankfully, no other.

Good, she thought; Megan'll be able to entertain the Spaniard if he should arrive before I'm ready. Rowena hurried to the stables. Jason was not there. He was probably in the house helping Jeannie, so she quickly began to rub down the stallion, not wanting to leave him unattended.

She carefully felt Goemor's legs and was relieved to find no swelling. Perhaps the walk had been the best thing for him; may be for her, too. She threw a blanket over his back and gave him an extra feed of oats. She could do no more for the moment.

As she walked round to the rear kitchen door, too dirty to use the front, she heard voices from the terrace.

"Good afternoon." It was Megan, polite and vague as usual.

"Ah, good afternoon to you. I believe you are expecting me."

Rowena froze in her tracks. That voice. Damn! It was the wretched stranger who had done such a good job of reducing her to a quivering idiot. Who was he? Could such a virile, arrogant Englishman be a valet? He hardly looked like one. But what else could he be? She had been told to expect the Spaniard's servants sometime that day. If he were the valet, then that would mean he had a wife. The lawyer had said there would be a married couple. Poor woman, Rowena thought; but an odd feeling of disappointment settled in the pit of her stomach. She shook it away angrily and listened for more.

Megan replied.

"Oh, yes. But aren't you a little early?" From anyone else that would have sounded rude. Not from Megan, whose beauty was certainly enough excuse.

"Is that inconvenient?" That same sardonic laughter again. "Shall I go away and come back later?"

"Oh, no. Of course not. It's just that . . ." Megan's voice trailed away and she looked around uncertainly. "Oh, forgive me. Do come into the house." She turned to cross the terrace toward the door that led into the library.

Rowena ducked back out of sight.

As she showed the way, Megan asked the stranger if he would like tea.

"That would be very welcome, thank you. I have just walked up from the dock where your admirable Mr. Whitford informed me that I might moor the yacht. I hope my informality is not a problem."

He sounded so polite and was obviously charmed by Megan. He hardly looked damp, not like Rowena who was soaked to the skin. Of course, he hadn't had to tramp for almost hours in the rain. She found her anger starting to boil again.If it were not for him, she would have been back ages ago. If Goemor had not thrown her, the boor would never have seen her in all her grime; then she would have been able to present the same cool, calm picture that Megan was making now.

If, if, if. Angrily, Rowena pushed back her hair; she intended to take quite a lot of pleasure in seeing his face when she told him who she was! She would soon put him in his place.

He continued to speak.

"Have my staff not arrived?"

Dear God! So he was no employee. She felt her whole body deflate as the wind was knocked out of her sails. He must be the Spaniard!

But where were the accent, and the jet-black hair that she had imagined was the prerogative of most Spaniards? And the name? It had been a jumble of letters to which she had not paid much attention, scrawled at the bottom of the same contract she had signed.

Yet it had certainly looked Spanish. The first and last names, Roberto Olivares, were all she could remember.

She was aghast. What on earth should she do? She could hardly appear and introduce herself. He would be disgusted. He was not likely to think that Gulls Walk was in very competent hands if she were its owner. His eyes had already condemned her for her apparently thoughtless disregard for a valuable stallion, obviously considering her an irresponsible child. She had seen how he had shown more concern for the horse than for her, and he certainly had not approved of the way she had ridden Goemor. Horse lovers are quick to judge the human race by their treatment of animals. She knew. She did the same. He would surely consider her quite incapable of fulfilling his requirements, particularly as the letter from his secretary had pointed out very forcefully that peace and quiet and a tranquil scene were most essential. Damn the man! Damn and blast!

Suddenly, in a state of shock, Rowena went back over his contempt of her as possible repercussions hit her. What if he decided not to stay? What would she do? Suppose he pulled out of the deal? A mirage of muddled thoughts ran pell-mell through her frightened mind. She had to do something, but what? He surely mustn't see her like this. Once was bad enough. She had to stall.

She scurried into the kitchen as Megan opened the baize-covered door from the Great Hall. Thankfully, Rowena saw that she was alone.

"Oh, hello, Rowena. Your guest has arrived. He's asking for his staff. He's in the library. He says he would like tea. Did I do the right thing?" Her nose wrinkled a little as she looked at Jason's jacket, which Rowena had forgotten to remove.

"Oh, Megan, you love. Yes, you did very much the right thing. Er, did you tell him who you are?" A sudden germ of an idea began to crystallise.

"No. Sorry. I suppose I forgot to introduce myself. I'm bad at that, aren't I?" She looked contrite.

Rowena watched her friend's face carefully. "Perhaps he thought you live here." Pleased surprise and a pink blush spread, but not before a faint gleam appeared in Megan's eyes.

"Do you think so?" Her voice was breathless.

"And why not?" Rowena laughed. Her friend's blush deepened. "Of course you look so gorgeous, as usual." She waited for Megan's reaction. The suede, emerald green skirt that Rowena had made, and a figure-hugging, crisp white shirt, with a dramatic scarf of swirling purples and magentas, were certainly exquisite foils for her pale, blonde beauty.

The idea grew stronger. Perhaps it would work, and solve other problems, too. Rowena was usually able to take the lead with Megan, and flattery was a tool she had used before. Momentarily, she felt rather ashamed of herself, but she was desperate; she cared too much about Gulls Walk to worry over ethics. Nothing must happen to make the tenant change his mind about staying. Visions of the enormous amount of money she had spent flashed through her mind.

Megan touched her hair and she smiled with pleasure as Rowena continued. "You certainly add a great deal to the decor of this place. I don't suppose you can stay a while? I need every bit of help I can get."

Rowena's mind was doing all sorts of acrobatics. If Megan could be a kind of hostess, then Rowena need not even see the wretched tenant. Megan could play the Lady-in-Charge. Jason would take care of the horses, and she could keep out of the way until the Spaniard was well settled in. Roberto Olivares might even forget the so-called stable girl. By that time he might be so in love with Gulls Walk that he'd just laugh if he happened to remember their meeting.

Perhaps he would not even recognise her! No one need mention her name, or say anything about where she was. After all, he was renting only one wing, and meeting his landlady was not a condition.

Yes, that would do. And the arrogant man would hardly be likely to ask about someone whom he assumed to be a servant, even if they did bump into each other. She would be free to do all the extra chores that Jeannie couldn't handle. And for a while they could manage without another housekeeper, or another salary. This could be a blessing in disguise. Rowena put on her best wheedling smile.

"Please, Megan dear. You did promise to help me."

She was laying it on a little too thickly, but she was well aware that Megan loved to stay at Gulls Walk. Would she accept a position? Some position! Rowena thought. At least hostess sounded better than housekeeper did. But in Megan's eyes, living in Gulls Walk under any circumstances carried some sort of status. "It will be such fun to have you here." Rowena's eyes never left Megan's face.

"Oh, you're kidding!" Rowena winced. Megan's conversation was not scintillating, but since she usually had the sense to keep her mouth shut, most people didn't get beyond her lovely face; a face much more in keeping with the fairy tale princess she seemed to imagine Rowena to be.

"Actually, I'm not." Rowena waited a moment for a refusal, but none came. "Well, how about it?" Megan's face showed her bewilderment. "I have too much to do. Mrs. Trevain being in hospital has thrown so much more work on my shoulders. I don't have the time to play Lady Bountiful." She knew that would appeal to Megan. "You will help me so much if you'll move in for a while and be the house . . . er, hostess." To say housekeeper suddenly stuck in Rowena's throat.

What was she letting herself in for? But surely even Megan could manage on the few occasions when she and the tenant might meet. Rowena realised her explanation sounded pretty thin. After all, as owner, if she chose to wander around in stable-smelling jackets, no tenant should care. But perhaps Megan's brain wasn't functioning very well, for she didn't question the reasons, or take much convincing.

Good so far, thought Rowena; she had no intention of telling Megan just what had happened on the cliff.

"Oh, do you think I could?" she said. Now Rowena felt really guilty. It sounded as if she were doing Megan the favour.

"Of course. Now get out there and be polite." That should be easy. "Say you don't know. Or that I'm not available, or something. It'll be the truth. Say you are in charge for the time being. Just ask him about his journey or what he does. Men love to talk. All he'll want to do is look at your pretty face, anyway." The innuendo was lost on Megan, thank goodness. "I'll send Jeannie in with the tea." Rowena finished.

With a dreamy expression on her face, Megan wandered back to the library. Rowena breathed a sigh of relief and went to find the rest of her staff.

Both Jeannie and Jason were less sanguine than Rowena over her plan, but agreed to back her up. They both were a little bewildered by the stress on the amount of housework to be done, and Rowena's desire to keep it a secret. She had never shown any signs of snobbery before; they couldn't see what Miss Pentraegon was bothered about now. Luckily, they were too well trained to argue.

Tea was served with no mishaps, and afterward, Jeannie escorted the tenant to his quarters. Soon arrived the Spaniard's staff, a middle-aged English couple. The man was driving their employer's sleek, silver Jaguar, and she, a heavily loaded station wagon. They were full of apologies for having lost their way, but were mainly concerned about avoiding the ire of their master. They helped Jeannie with the serving of the all-ready-prepared dinner to the Spaniard and Megan, after which, his apparent hostess returned to the kitchen, full of smiles.

"He is so sweet." She blushed prettily. "He has business in the area, he says. He spends most of his time in London, or on the continent. But he's down here mainly for peace and quiet. I suspect that there's some deep, dark tragedy, and he wants to be alone, like Greta Garbo. A woman perhaps. He has that brooding look." She giggled lightly at her own attempt at drama. "He intends to sail his yacht a lot. He also wants to do some research, history, I think." Her voice grew uncertain. Rowena hid a smile as she visualised Megan trying to understand esoteric terminology. "His name is Roberto, but he is usually called Rob, the English way. His mother is English and he went to school here. That's why he doesn't have a foreign accent."

Megan hadn't wasted much time! Rowena grinned wryly to herself, but her lips twisted as she imagined what sort of research dear Rob would be doing with Megan around.

A little ashamed, Rowena felt angry with herself. She wasn't being fair. Megan seemed never to understand the effect she had on the male of the species. And deep down there was another reason why Rowena felt angry. Hurriedly, she squashed that thought. Gulls Walk was the most important thing on her mind at the moment.

So far so good: she hoped!

But Megan wasn't finished.

"He thought I was you." She looked faintly pleased. "I didn't know what to say, so I just told him that you had gone away for a few weeks, that I was in charge. Was that all right?"

Damn! A few weeks? That blew her intentions of confessing who she was when the Spaniard had settled in. Why hadn't she primed Megan better? Now she mustn't appear too soon. Certainly she couldn't joke lightly about their meeting. How could she explain the lie, which Megan had told? This was hardly a good introduction to the peace and quiet he had demanded. He might be disgusted and leave. Damn and blast! What a ridiculous, stupid mess. Well, a servant in her own house she would just have to be.

Gulls Walk, I hope you appreciate all I'm doing for you, she thought to herself, as Megan smiled at her helpfully.

CHAPTER SEVEN

It was late when Rowena crawled into bed. She decided to sleep in Trevy's bed-sitter behind the kitchen, for she was unlikely to run the risk of seeing her tenant if she kept to the back quarters. Her own bedroom she gave to her guest, who was more than content with the arrangement.

Particularly was Megan entranced with the high four-poster bed in which Rowena had slept for the last few years. At that time, her grandfather had decided his almost-grown-up granddaughter should graduate from a small bedroom above the library, where she had always slept, to her own apartment in the west wing. Rowena had been delighted and loved the carved wainscoting, and the low moulded ceilings where embossed swirls of flowers and ivy decorated each corner. She had spruced up her haven by treating herself to the last of the sunshine yellow brocade. With new drapes for the windows, she had intended the room to be an even cosier retreat from any possibly intrusive tenant.

Now, she could not help feeling a faint touch of irritation at the ease with which Megan made herself at home there. But Rowena chastised herself. She needed Megan; the least she could do to show her appreciation was to make her guest comfortable.

A long, hot bath, with a generous dollop of Trevy's lavender crystals, had soothed her worries and most of her soreness. It had been a disastrous day in many ways, but there was hope that she could salvage something from the mess. At least Don Olivares had gone to bed happy, praising the beauty of his own wing: so he had told Megan. A small flame of warmth curled through Rowena as she settled to sleep. Tomorrow was another day.

The alarm woke her as the first glimmering light of dawn was creeping over the horizon. For a moment she lay, wondering where she was. Her sleep had been so deep, the result of exhaustion. Then she remembered.

It was very early. Even Jeannie was not up yet. Rowena climbed out of bed and wandered into the kitchen to make herself a cup of tea prior to starting the day's chores.

First, she intended to flip a duster through the ground floor before anyone else stirred. Then she could change any flowers that had wilted, and all would be fresh and sparkling when her tenant came down stairs. In spite of her anger of yesterday, she wanted him to see Gulls Walk only at its best. She had a duty to give him his money's worth, she reasoned to herself, refusing to listen to any other strange, unbidden thoughts.

She got out the tea things, put on the kettle and stood waiting for it to boil. Her short nightdress clung to her slight frame, only partially covering her bruises.

Her mind wandered over the events of the previous day. She remembered the amber flashes of anger in her tenant's eyes as he had looked at her in fury, and she cringed a little. Damn him. He had no right to judge her. He had no idea what she had gone through.

She repeated her thoughts out loud. "Hell and damnation!" It didn't help the situation, but at least it gave her a moment's satisfying relief.

"I think your mother should wash your mouth out with soap." Startled, she turned around. She had not heard the door open. Aghast, she simply froze to the spot.

"If you are making tea, I'll have a cup, please."

Don Olivares, freshly bathed and shaved, his crisp, dark brown hair still damp, lowered his large frame onto the edge of the kitchen table. He was dressed immaculately in riding clothes: cream, cotton shirt open at the strong column of his throat; beige, cavalry twill breeches; and gleaming boots of expensive leather.

Rowena's breath caught in her throat. Her mind spiralled like broken glass, chasing splintered images of the distant Miles with some vague idea of help, then shivered to opaque nothingness. Miles seemed like a slender shadow in comparison with this man. Roberto Olivares was taller, tanned, more virile, exuding an animal magnetism like an aura around him. His eyes, with that same remembered amber sparkle, swept slowly up and down her scantily clad figure.

"I hardly expected to find the stable girl in here, dressed like some eastern houri." The hard mouth curved.

Wildly, she tried to think of some sort of escape, but her pride would not accept ignominiously turning tail. Damn him to hell! Now he had really seen her at her worse. But she was a Pentraegon. No man was going to brow beat her without a fight.

"Surely the politeness of knocking is customary where you come from?" Her chin went up as she spat out the sharp barb. Blast him! Not for all the rent in the world would she take any more of his scorn.

The Spaniard's eyes narrowed. She was such a tiny thing to be so spunky. The sun peeping in through the window caught an answering light in the untamed beauty of her auburn hair. It warmed her skin, softening the shadows beneath her high cheekbones. She looked like a delicate wraith who, at any moment, might disappear on some ethereal rainbow. Roberto Olivares watched her, startled at his own flight of fancy. Her agitation caused the silken fabric she was wearing to stir, and he was aware of the high pointed curves of her young body.

He watched the colour suffuse her face. What the blazes was she doing in the kitchen dressed like that? Suppose he was the sort of stranger who . . . ? Biting the thought from his mind, he allowed his anger to show. He noticed the deep purple welts on her slender thighs. She could have killed herself. His voice was sharper than he intended.

"Put some clothes on, for heaven sake. I'll make the tea." He got to his feet and moved toward her. "I have business in town this morning; I can't waste time standing here if I'm to try that stallion you so nearly ruined yesterday. He is the one that I'm supposed to ride, I presume?"

Indignation jolted Rowena out of her stupor. "Of course he is, and he is fine. Give me five minute, and you can see for yourself." Her eyes challenged him before she ran from the room—completely unaware of how he had given her a chance to preserve her own dignity.

Ten minutes later found them both, with mugs of hot, strong tea in their hands, standing looking at Goemor who was peacefully champing at an apple that Rowena had brought for him.

"Hmm. He seems to have suffered no harm." A doubtful tone still lingered as Olivares put his mug down. He ran surprisingly gentle hands over Goemor's withers, then down each leg, checking for any sign of tenderness. With total unconcern, the stallion continued to munch his morning treat.

"Well. Aren't we going riding, Child? You'll have to show me the best places, and a better way to get to the beach." The sarcasm was pointed as he reached for a blanket and Grandfather's saddle. "A canter in the surf will be good for him."

Angrily, Rowena stalked across to Firefly's stall. Damn the man. She knew that. Indeed, she had had every intention of taking the stallion down to the beach when she found time that morning. She fumed in angry silence as they each prepared their own horse.

Seething at the unjustness of the situation, Rowena jerked the strap beneath Firefly's belly, causing her to whinny in surprise.

"Don't take it out on her." The tenant's voice held just a glint of amusement. Immediately Rowena felt contrite. Dear Firefly. For a moment she rested her head against the dainty mare's neck. Scalding tears forced their way through tightly closed lids. Memories came flooding back of her darling Gramps contentedly saddling his beloved Goemor on so many mornings such as this.

Taking a deep breath, she reached back to her anger to keep from breaking down. Damn him, damn the Spaniard, damn Roberto Olivares, or whatever his name was. Why should he be the one to take over the stallion? And worse, Goemor didn't even seem to mind.

"You look after your horse, and I'll look after mine!" It was childish, she knew. No wonder he repeatedly called her that. But she felt like a child that morning. Lost and lonely.

Flinging herself onto the back of Firefly, she cantered out of the stable, not waiting to see if Olivares were ready.

As the high, open heath of Trenallack Point came into view, with its craggy outcrops of wind-smoothed granite, the angry lines on Rowena's face softened. A stiff morning breeze blew her hair in long, vivid streamers behind her. While climbing the steep path, she had dragged on her hat, in too much of a hurry to get away from the sardonic eyes of the Spaniard to make any attempt to contain the unruly mane. Soon she heard the slower stride of Goemor behind her.

Reining in the eager Firefly, she waited for Olivares to reach her.

"Well, what do you think of it?" She knew she had dangerously stretched his anger and owed him an apology. The tinkling sound of a cash register rang in her head. But her pride kept the words back. "I think it is one of the most beautiful places in the world."

She dared him to disagree. She allowed her eyes to wander beyond the headland to the far curve of the cove where the curling spume of the breakers glimmered in the morning sun.

"I would not dream of contradicting you." This time, she heard the laughter in his voice and had the grace to feel ashamed. He was perfectly within his rights to want morning tea, and to ride Goemor. Why was she being such a bear? So what, if each time he had seen her she had looked like the rag end of a floor mop?

"Good!" A widening grin touched her flushed cheeks. She relaxed and her green eyes sparkled. "Give me a head start, and I'll race you." At least she would show him that she could ride.

She was off like the wind.

She slowed to a canter when she neared the end of the Point, intrigued that he had not passed her. She turned Firefly to watch his slower pace.

"You let me win." she accused, laughter in her eyes.

"My dear child, if and when I try to beat you, I assure you, you will have no chance." The Spaniard drew Goemor to a halt and jumped from the saddle. After trailing his hand carefully over the stallion's rump, he ran his fingers down the hind legs. "This animal is not mine, I have no intention of damaging valuable property that has been entrusted to me." He looked up at Rowena with narrowed eyes. "I thought you would have more concern than to try to persuade me to gallop him until we were sure that he was healthy."

Rowena sagged in her saddle. Damn. She should have thought of that. Now he must really be sure she was irresponsible. But her innate honesty over-rode her distress.

"You're right. I'm sorry." She dismounted, and caressed the stallion's velvet nose. "I didn't mean to forget you, Goemor, my love." The stallion nuzzled her hand, hoping for another apple.

"No harm done." The Spaniard's voice was strangely neutral as he watched the concern on Rowena's face. "I think he is fine. We don't need to worry any more." Startled at the softness of his tone, Rowena's eyes widened as she looked up at him. She had expected more chastisement. For a moment, she thought she saw the gleam of those chestnut fires.

Remounting, they wended their way down a gentle slope to the beach.

They jogged along, almost companionably for a while, each enjoying the salty tang of the breeze. The horses splashed skittishly, lifting their legs high in the cold water, and the flurry of the small waves occasionally made them dance and caper as if they were young foals again.

Rowena laughed aloud in momentary happiness. The broader spectrum of the vast panorama spread before them was putting things into proportion. It was going to be all right. Perhaps now was a good time to tell him who she was. Her attempts at concealment seemed silly, her fears ridiculous. He was not the sort of man to change his arrangements just because his landlady was a little scatty. Her fears were only of her own imagination, surely.

"Why is he called Goemor?"

She was startled out of her reverie by the question.

"Oh, My gr . . . er . . . his name was chosen because of an old legend." She nearly blurted out the truth with no preamble. "There was supposed to have been a great Cornish giant of that name who lived thousands of years ago here in Cornwall. We Cornish people like to keep our links with the past. Being such a big foal, it seemed the obvious name."

She remembered the night Goemor had been born, how they had nearly lost the mother. Rowena had been eight at the time, and Gramps had trusted her to help. Those had been special times. She felt the tears well behind her eyelids.

Suddenly she had to ride, to ride fast. Perhaps the wind would blow away the sadness. She had thought that she was over the worst. Touching her heels to Firefly, she urged the mare into a gallop.

This time Goemor passed her easily. The Spaniard glanced at the frowning face of the girl, wondering what had sparked the sudden change of pace. He grabbed her reins, and hauled both horses to a slower gait.

"Damn it, Child. Are you totally irresponsible?" The anger was back in his face. "I came here hoping for peace and quiet, not mercurial shenanigans from a silly stable girl. There are outcrops of rocks all along this coastline. Do you want to lame these animals?" Gone was the easy companionship of the last half-hour.

Rowena glared at him, retaliation on her lips. "I have been using these beaches for years. I know what I'm doing. I know every rock along here." But she had the grace to feel ashamed, for the Spaniard could not see what lay beneath the surface of the tumbling waves where they were riding. His anger was understandable, and she mumbled some sort of an apology.

Ruefully, she recognised that now was not the time for her intended admission. His disgust with her was all too obvious. She guided Firefly out of the water and cantered carefully along the beach. She vowed to herself that she would behave perfectly all the way home and then leave the stable and the horses to Jason. Maybe if Senor damned Olivares didn't see her for a while, he would calm down and forget.

As they rounded the headland, the stone dock came into view. Moored to it, moving gently on the tide, was a long, sleek yacht; its beautiful lines made for speed. It gleamed in the sunshine. Rowena caught her breath. Further in shore, looking almost squat in comparison, was one of Miles' sturdier fishing boats, and she could see its owner standing on the deck. She had forgotten that he had promised, like Megan, to come when the Spaniard arrived.

Suddenly she remembered. Dear God, she couldn't have him calling her name!

Keeping just a little ahead of Olivares, she cantered down to the landing area. She jumped from Firefly, looping the reins over a rail, hastily calling back to the Spaniard that she would he only a little while. Surely, he would hardly interrupt her conversation with Miles without an invitation.

As she hurried along the walkway, she heard Miles' shout as he stepped ashore.

"Hi, Precious, and how is my princess?" Startled, Rowena grinned her relief. Never had she been so happy with her nickname. A little surprised at the warmth of her welcoming smile, Miles threw an arm around her shoulder as he reached her.

"Hello, Miles, now just shut up and listened." Rowena grasped his shirt in agitation. "Look, I don't have time to explain, but he doesn't know who I am yet."

"Who doesn't? What are you talking about?"

She lowered her voice.

"The Spaniard. My tenant. Him!" She was aware of the slow tread of Senor Olivares as he walked towards them. "He thinks I'm the stable girl. And I want . . . I have to keep it that way."

Nobody had ever accused Miles of being slow in the uptake. His eyes became slits, their heavy lids almost closing as he watched the tall stranger moving nearer. For now, he would play along with Rowena's little game, what ever it was. It seemed that she might really need his help. That was all to the good. He drew her closer into his arms.

"I'll be mum as the grave." He grinned down at her, kissing her quickly. Raising his head, he allowed his smile to include the approaching stranger. His eyes widened a little, as he became aware of magnetism and power. The smile faded.

"Good morning." The Spaniard's greeting was curt and impersonal. He didn't pause but passed them both to climb aboard his yacht. Then he disappeared below to the cabin.

Rowena gave a disgusted sigh of annoyance and dragged herself away from Miles. She didn't need any more complications right now, certainly not any more pressure. Casual greetings were one thing, but Senor blasted Olivares would assume that she was a flighty girl with only her own interests at heart. She had certainly left him quickly enough, with no apology.

Damn. Why did he always have to see her in the worst of situations? And damn Miles. Did he have to make such a production of their meeting?

Hurrying him from the dock, out of earshot of her tenant on the boat, she tried to explain. She had no intention of going into all the details; they were too embarrassing. Apart from which, she didn't want him to exacerbate the Spaniard's anger. Miles was quite capable of taunting the man for not having realised who she was, for he hadn't wanted her to rent the east wing in the first place.

She had a sudden premonition that help might not be forthcoming if she told the true problem. She decided to keep to the same story she had told Megan. Heaven help her if she were not convincing.

She told Miles first of Trevy's accident, then of the load of extra work, and how much easier it would be for her if she didn't have to be a lady-like hostess with nothing to do but look pretty. Visions of Megan doing just that suddenly annoyed her, but there was nothing she could do now. She was the one who had arranged the situation; she would have to live with it.

Miles listened in silence until she had finished. That same hooded look she knew so well gave her no clue as to whether he believed her or not. She stumbled as she rushed on.

"I thought that I could keep out of his way; I asked Megan to he hostess. I really can't be bothered with all that sort of stuff. You know me. It was sheer bad luck that he saw me today, and he insisted that we ride. I just didn't tell him. And now I can't. Damn it, Miles. He'll think I'm a liar. I didn't say I wasn't me, but I didn't say I was, either." Her voice trailed away. She fiddled with Firefly's reins, not wanting to look at Miles as she waited.

Suddenly he grinned. "What a silly pickle." He reached to give her another hug. She endured it, still waiting. "If that's what you want, then that's what it will be. You're Precious for good now. Yes?" He chuckled. She looked up at him; his reaction was certainly not what she had expected. The laughter glowed deep in his eyes, and he looked inordinately pleased. "Yes, I shall rather enjoy that. I will be so loving that he will never hear the name 'Rowena' pass my lips!"

With mixed feelings, Rowena thanked him as she remounted Firefly, and she watched him make his way up toward the manor. It had gone better than she had expected. But why did she feel that she had jumped from the frying pan into the fire?

CHAPTER EIGHT

Rowena waited for Don Olivares to return from his yacht. She could hardly leave him to make his own way back to the stables, even though he had walked up to the house yesterday. The path was clear enough, but she was feeling apprehensive about her abrupt behaviour. She felt she had better try to make some sort of amends. She wriggled in her saddle uncomfortably.

Miles had departed with a cheery wave, his step light and quick. But she was somewhat apprehensive until she saw him by-pass the manor and go toward Home Farm. Apparently he wasn't too concerned about comparing notes with Megan. Just as well, for they probably both would think she was ridiculous.

If only she had gone straight up to the Spaniard when he first arrived; or at least, after a bath, having made herself respectable. The worst he could have done was to have left there and then. His disgust with her had been pretty obvious. He certainly seemed to be a man who had little or no tolerance; she had seen enough of his high handed manner to know that. She must have been in shock to be so boorishly defensive when they first met.

Yet being rude to a tenant surely was not such a ghastly crime. She hadn't known who he was, either; and she had thanked him for helping her and checking that there were no bones broken, grudging though those thanks had been. And she hadn't actually lied. Allowing someone to jump to the wrong conclusions was not the same thing, was it?

But apart from that, she was well aware that the results of her actions were hardly conducive to the peace and quiet he had so definitely specified; or to the assurance that Goemor was the excellently-cared-for horse that he had been led to believe. He might think that her whole behaviour was totally incomprehensible and wouldn't stay to find out why. No, she couldn't blame him if he left. And would Mr. Whitford be able to handle the embarrassment of the spent rent?

She winced. The very problem sounded absurd. Spent rent! It jangled around her head like a stuck needle on an old record.

Her worry increased as she pondered the repercussions.

She had constantly annoyed Olivares. And words like misrepresentation fell like stones in the swirling well of her discomfort.

She shuddered as her earlier fears returned even more forcibly. Though she had no idea what a court of law might do, it certainly would not take kindly to the money she had spent unnecessarily, particularly if her tenant demanded it back. They might even bring suit against her. And that was impossible to handle, for she had so little of the Spaniard's cheque left, and almost none of her allowance.

No. Stupid as she had been, she had no choice. Even if he had been able to accept that she had not been irresponsible with Goemor, Don Olivares would certainly not tolerate her rudeness of the morning, her odd behaviour as they had ridden through the surf, or her rushing off and leaving him for the arms of Miles.

Dear God. What a mess! The man would never understand. If only Gramps were still alive. But her sudden deep sense of loneliness without him was too hard to explain to her tenant. It was too personal; still hurt too much. She could not fall on the Spaniard's neck begging for pity; though maybe in a couple of days she might pluck up courage to apologise—that is, providing she could get him to listen.

Oh, Gulls Walk, what a problem you have become, she thought.

Don Olivares walked along the dock toward her, a frown on his face. "I'm surprised you're still here. You certainly don't take your job very seriously." With a look of sarcastic disgust, he glanced up the pathway to where Miles was disappearing in the distance. "You need not have waited. I am perfectly capable of finding my way to the house. I cannot for the life of me understand why Miss Pentraegon employs you. A little tramp, running after your boy friend more often than not, probably, and certainly away from your responsibilities."

Rowena's mouth fell open in angry astonishment. But before she could think of any retaliation, the Spaniard mounted Goemor. Giving her not even a backward glance, he cantered up the path to the manor and the stables beyond.

Whew! she thought angrily. That was certainly putting her in her place. Drat Miles and his greeting! Well, what was she going to do now? Apologies and explanations were out of the question.

Damn! She swallowed hard, feeling like a deflated punch bag.

She took her time reaching the stable, hoping that her tenant would be gone. Jason was rubbing down Goemor when she finally arrived.

"Mornin', Miss Rowena." No one else was in sight. "He were in a right rare temper, that there Spanish man. I see'd why ye b'ain't too eager." With a soft chuckle, he gave the stallion a final sweep with the currycomb, then led him out to the paddock. Rowena took Firefly to her stall and set to work; physical effort was what she needed to ease her troubles. To Hell with the man!

For the next few days she saw little of Olivares, and that, only at a distance. He rode in the early morning, then went into Penzance for the greater part of the day. His staff dealt with his meals and the care of the east wing.

Megan was the only one to have any contact. She made a point of reclining on the terrace in the sunshine, ready to greet him on his return from each ride.

Rowena told her nothing of her early morning debacle with the Don; and Miles, apparently, had not mentioned it to Megan, either. So her sweet smile had the same warm welcome she had given Roberto Olivares when he first arrived.

One morning, when Rowena had been weeding in the garden, hiding under an enormous sun hat, she heard his courteous, smiling reply to Megan's greeting.

"You are looking extremely charming, Miss Haversham." His face had lit up; such a change from the scowl that had seemed to be his permanent expression. Rowena angrily grabbed her basket of weeds and moved out of earshot. She hadn't wanted to hear any more. Why should she be so upset anyway? It was important that Megan and the Spaniard should be friends. Wasn't it?

Finding that there was less work for her to do than she had feared, Rowena got the bulk of her chores done in the early mornings. Then, when she heard the car leave with her tenant, she saddled Firefly and rode over Trenallack Point to try to rid herself of her misery.

One afternoon, Miles joined her on one of his own mounts. He called her Precious as usual and teased her in his newly acquired status of declared amorata. He professed to the world dramatic jealousy of the very saddle on which she sat. She longed to flare back at him, but the less serious he was, the less he might be likely to question her on her avoidance of Don Olivares. And the less likelihood there would be of him learning how little it would take to persuade the Spaniard to leave.

She wasn't sure if she trusted Miles. She felt that he was playing some game . . . and she didn't know all the rules. Come to think of it, she, too, was playing games.

When they returned to the stable, Olivares was just driving into the yard. Miles made a great show of kissing her as he left, calling, "'Bye, Precious." quite loudly enough for her tenant to hear.

Blushing furiously, she ran into the kitchen, cursing the day she had included Miles in her attempts at deception.

Toward the end of the week, the weather broke with a vengeance. Since she could not go riding, when she had finished her chores, she took a long, leisurely bath. She washed her hair, leaving it loose. Afterward, she wrapped herself in a kimono, a delicate silk, patterned with swirls of vivid colour. She intended to dress when her hair dried.

Restless, missing her usual exercise, Rowena wandered into the library. She had spent very little time there since she had hung the new drapes, and she curled up in her grandfather's deep chair to enjoy the refurbished decor. She was cosy and comfortable, and soon the hairbrush slid from her lap as her eyes closed in sleep.

A particularly loud clap of thunder woke her with a start. By now it was late afternoon, and heavy clouds darkened the sky. She sat up, conscious of a chill in the air. She decided to draw the curtains and light the fire that was always ready in the hearth. Why shouldn't she spoil herself a little? Megan had gone home to fetch fresh clothes and wouldn't be back until the morning. And Miles had taken himself off to London again.

Settling back in her chair, she watched the fire light flicker, softening the dark panelling and quickly warming the room. She began to brush her hair into soft shining waves. For the first times in weeks she relaxed, enjoying the peace. "Well, Good Queen Bess. How do you like your refurbished surroundings?" She smiled up at the portrait.

Her Majesty haughtily kept her silence.

The painting, now darkened by the centuries, had been hung near the fireplace soon after the first Morgan Pentaegon finished the house. How good a likeness it was, no one had been able to say. The red wig and white, mask-like face were common to the few remaining portraits of her during her last years. In her hands, painted by some later artist, was a likeness of the house as it must have been in the beginning. Rowena never tired of looking at it, weaving stories of the past. She got to her feet and moved to trace her fingers over the lettering beneath.

EI QUAM SALUTAMUS CUM OBSEQUIO ET HUMILI TRIBUTO TENEMUS IN MEMORIA ILLIUS DIEI ET EIUS REGALIS OMNIPOTENTIAE

Much of it was barely visible now, but Rowena knew the words by heart, and the rhyming translation that an ancestor had contrived:

OF SHE WHOM HONOR WE DO PAY WITH OBEISANCE AND HUMBLE PENCE WE KEEP IN MEMORY OF THAT DAY AND OF HER ROYAL OMNIPOTENCE.

She always had a feeling that old Morgan had been less than reverent when he had those words inscribed. Idly, as she had many times before, she wondered if he ever had paid his humble pence. Probably not, since it was Spanish tribute, and salvage at that. No doubt he felt he had earned it. If the Spanish galleon had not been wrecked on their coast, it would probably have gone to a watery grave, anyway. She wished there had been some of its treasure left after all these years.

Rowena reached for a book and settled back in her chair. Still a little drowsy, she curled into a corner, almost lost in its depth.

Suddenly, she was startled to hear the clatter of the front door and the sound of voices. She heard Jeannie exclaim over the fury of the rain.

"You come on in, Sir. Out of that there wet. It be good for the land, but b'ain't good for the likes of we!" Rowena chuckled to herself at the motherly tones. Jeannie was all of nineteen if she was a day.

"Your people, they be gone shoppin', so why don't 'ee come into the library, Sir? There be a fire laid in the hearth. It won't take but a moment for me to light un. 'Ee set there a while and I'll get 'ee a nice, hot cup o'tea."

Rowena tensed in her seat as she heard the door open. She was well and truly caught now!

Jeannie came bustling in, Don Olivares behind her; his wet jacket was hooked over a finger and he was laughing at her fuss.

"Ye'll be foine 'ere, Sir. Oh, pardon me, Miss Pentraegon, I dun'know you be here. Oh, oh Lordie! What dun I say?"

With horror, she covered her mouth, gazing aghast at the frozen tableau: at the tall menacing figure of the Spaniard, the laughter gone; and at the white face of her mistress.

"Oh, Ma'am, I be so sorry. I didn't mean to let on."

"That's all right, Jeannie. You may go. Perhaps tea would be nice, don't you think?" Rowena rose to her feet. There was not much she could do now.

She felt as if her world were crashing about her ears. Proudly, she held up her head. She would at least go down with dignity.

"So, Miss Pentraegon? What game are you playing? Why the pretense? I think that some explanation is in order." The Spaniard's words were clipped and cold. His eyes glittered with anger. He dropped his jacket on a chair.

"Yes, You deserve that." Rowena hesitated, not knowing where to begin. She searched his face for understanding. Beneath his lowered brows, shafts of amber gold caught the reflection of the firelight in a grim gleam of speculation. A smile without humour touched his lips.

"It seems, Stable-girl, I have been labouring under a misapprehension." His voice was softer than she had ever heard it. But there was no softening of his manner.

"I'm sorry. The whole thing was a ghastly mistake. I was so embarrassed when I fell off Goemor. I didn't mean to avoid telling you who I was, but you were so rude. And you jumped to conclusions." For a moment, her anger flared, but oh dear, she was making it worse.

Still he waited.

"You called me a child. It rankled."

Suddenly it was too much. The whole miserable day came flooding back. She had been so hopeful that her efforts could help Gulls Walk; instead, her stupid behaviour had ruined everything.

He moved toward her. Startled, she drew back, holding her hand in front of her as if to ward him off.

"Please don't be angry. Look. You needn't stay here at Gulls Walk any longer if you don't want." A harsh sob shook her slight frame and her eyes welled with tears. All the tension of the last weeks crumbled into a ghastly weariness. She could take no more. Still he moved forward.

"Not stay?" The Spaniard's face was grim. "I would have thought that my staying was in your best interests; after all, I am certainly paying good money for the privilege. Or is there some ulterior motive that I don't know about? That you want me to leave?"

This concealment of whom she was seemed to verify that there were secrets in Pentraegon Cove. Were they the ones he had been sent to uncover? She was either totally naive, or a damn good actress.

Rowena shook her head, bewildered by his sudden sharp reaction.

Olivares continued. "Did Whitford have to persuade you to take me as a tenant? Perhaps you thought that I would be some quiet ancient whom you need seldom meet. And now you've discovered I'm not, you and that boyfriend of yours have decided you want me out. Obviously, you personally had no intention of making me welcome. For some reason, I'm in the way." Again that gleam of speculation.

The desk behind Rowena stopped her backward progress. He stood in front of her, so close that she was aware of the faint, heady mingling of scents; the harsh, masculine odour of outdoors; of rain and damp clothing; of the subtle after-shave he wore; and the smell of enormous anger. She could feel it: a living entity.

"Just why do you want me to leave?" His contempt stung like a whip. "Don't think tears will cover up your deception and rudeness. You have behaved like a spoiled brat each time I have come in contact with you. Since you seem to have such a dislike of my presence, quite evidenced by your having made a fool out of me, you obviously think that you can make me walk away." He laughed harshly. "You certainly can't expect me to succumb to such childish methods."

He paused. After the lease was signed, had she somehow discovered who he was? There seemed to be a sudden flash of understanding. Grimly, he continued.

"Are you hoping that I will leave?" He paused. "That if I break the lease, I will have to forget the money I have already paid out to you?"

Startled, Rowena stared up at him. Not for one moment had such a thought occurred to her. Indeed, just the opposite; for under such circumstances, she knew she would have to return the rent somehow.

The verbal battering continued.

"You're so typically adolescent. You think that you can lie and make excuses to hide your own bad behaviour!" His eyes blazed.

Dear God. This was worse than she had imagined. Had she been lying? Bitterly she realised that the accusation was true, in essence if not in fact. Numbly she waited in terror, not knowing what to do or to say.

He watched her as her eyes widened, accepting his knowledge, until he felt as if he were drowning in great pools of liquid jade, dark as a woodland pool. Damn her. Why did she have to look so beautiful?

"Oh, no, my girl. You made a bargain. You promised me peace and quiet, with full use of the amenities. And I am paying you well for it. I'll take all that Gulls Walk has to offer. But on my terms now. What the hell you think you are doing wandering around half clad, looking like some eastern houri . . ." The searing contempt in his eyes as he glanced at her thin attire was devastating.

Rowena shrank away, almost stumbling in her effort to avoid his anger.

Sharply, he reached out to steady her, feeling the icy cold of her body through the sheer silk. He tightened his fingers, making her flinch. Her bones were thin, fragile, as childlike as the rest of her appeared to be. Vulnerable.

She had no right to look so innocent.

Suddenly, his own rage boiled up past his normal self-control. His fingers slid down her arm, twisting it behind her back, holding her easily in one hand.

She had no resistance, was too distraught to understand, seeming almost lifeless, like a straw in the wind, with no will of its own. He drew her nearer until the full length of her body was pressed close to his.

Still she did not struggle, mesmerised as a small animal caught in the hypnotic gaze of a larger creature of prey. She became aware of every hard muscle of his strong frame; of an iron will, contemptuous, with the power to destroy.

Her small breasts, with only the sheerest of material between her and the harsher cotton of his shirt, were crushed, hurting, made aware of his heavy heartbeat. It was tumultuous, like a sledgehammer; thudding against her body with insistent torture.

His eyes narrowed to cold, calculating slits; his lips dragged into a thin, angry line. Suddenly, his face swooped down, blocking out the firelight. His mouth opened to plunder hers with harsh, withering power, a bleak kiss of punishment.

In an agony of emotion she came to life. Great, swirling storms dragged her back from the unutterable exhaustion that had numbed her, and she began to struggle.

His grip tightened, his free hand unwittingly dragging the thin material of her robe, uncovering the sweet curves.

Suddenly he was still. "Sweet Mother of Christ!" He breathed harshly. Appalled at his own actions, he pulled her kimono back in place and pushed her from him, making her stagger. "Damn you!" The words were bitter. What the hell was happening to him?

With shuddering effort she strove for control. Her mouth felt raped, swollen by the force of his violent anger.

"How dare you?" She reached her trembling arms around herself in protection. "Get out, get out, do you hear?" The last vestige of her strength was torn to ragged shreds.

"With pleasure, my dear Miss Rowena Pentraegon." He picked up his jacket and moved to the door. "Let that be a lesson to you. Not all men are playthings to be twisted at whim around your little finger. Whatever you expected to get out of me with that outfit, forget it. Save it for your boy friend!" His searing contempt burned down her body like a scourge.

As he left, Rowena sank to the floor.

Slowly she realised what his words had meant. He thought that her behaviour since he had arrived had been a deliberate attempt to hide something, a ploy to make him break his own contract, and so be unable to demand back his rent if he decided to leave. He thought that she was trying to get rid of him.

But why should he have been so quick to jump to that conclusion? It was almost as if he had expected it.

Yet through the shock crept a small flame of curiosity. Why the anger? Had someone given him such distrust of people; a disbelief in honesty, or lack of it?

She buried deep her shattered reaction to his kiss.

CHAPTER NINE

For a while, she sat in front of the fire, trying to restore her equilibrium. When Jeannie came in with the tea, full of distraught apologies, Rowena managed to soothe her, even to find a smile.

"No harm done." What a travesty of the truth that was. "He had to know sometime."

She took her tea and drank it thirstily. It was supposed to be one of the best things for shock. Grimly, she drank a second cup. At least she didn't have the worry of returning the Spaniard's money. That was some consolation. Well, maybe she could just disappear until the rental period was over, then she needn't see the wretched man. But that was months ahead, providing he stayed for the length of his contract. And she had better make sure that he did!

And damn it all, why should she leave? No. She must endure her tenant since the total rent was such a substantial amount.

Another thought struck her. Was it enough to prove that Gulls Walk could be a paying concern? Surely, on the strength of that, she could persuade a bank to give her a loan to pay off whatever the death duties might be. Perhaps that was wishful thinking, but for the first time in weeks, she began to see the light at the end of the tunnel. Pentraegons were fighters!

She took herself back to Trevy's room, telling Jeannie not to bother about supper. She wasn't hungry, and she had too much thinking to do. It hardly seemed worth dressing, late as it was; though if she went to bed early, she knew she would not sleep. She sat herself at the dressing table and brushed out her tangled hair. A new image: that's what she needed. No more will he see the brat he imagined her to be, she thought grimly.

And she intended to explain the whole thing from beginning to end, calmly, coolly and collectedly. It was just a silly storm in a teacup, anyway, wasn't it? But she shuddered, remembering just how passionately angry Don

Olivares had been—and she tried to bury her memory of the result of that passion.

A tentative knock on the door brought her out of her reverie.

"It's a note from that there Spaniard." Jeannie's eyes were as big as saucers, full of concern for her mistress.

"Thank you, Jeannie." She opened the note with more than a little trepidation. It was one thing to persuade herself that the situation could easily be cleared up, quite another to actually face it.

> *Miss Pentraegon,*
> *Dinner will be served in my suite at eight-thirty.*
> *I shall appreciate your presence.*
>
> *Olivares.*

Now what did he want? It was almost too much. Was there more she must endure? Bitterly, she wondered if the ghastly evening would ever end. She considered refusing the invitation, but after having had a dose of his temper, she knew he was quite capable of coming into her room and dragging her to the east wing. Shades of Victorian melodrama, she thought, a grim smile touching her lips. And dinner: she wouldn't be able to eat a thing.

Yet here was the opportunity she was waiting for. She'd just been persuading herself that all she needed was a new image, so she'd let him see that she was made of sterner stuff and show him Pentraegon pride. Four hundred years ago a Spaniard had been sent away because of a Rowena. Of course, she didn't want to send this one away, but she'd certainly show him that another Rowena could be mistress in her own house.

And she would point out to him just how rude he had been. After all, none of the misunderstanding would have occurred if he had not been so high-handed. How dare he treat her like a piece of tawdry baggage?

She felt quite hopeful as she lifted her chin, though the colour rose to her cheeks as she remembered the library.

But that ghastly amalgam of emotions was finally dissipating, and now she was beginning to realise that though the Spaniard did have a considerable right to be angry, there was nothing to stop her putting the whole situation in perspective. She had tried apologising, though he hadn't listened; but that didn't mean she shouldn't try again. And damn it all, he needed to apologise, too.

But why had he been so angry? Yes, she had acted stupidly—his calling her a brat was probably pretty accurate; but that surely didn't warrant the tearing rage. There must be something more. Was there another reason?

She dressed with care, feeling that she needed every bit of feminine armour for protection. His plunder of her mouth and body had so shattered her equilibrium that she had an intense desire to hide in a nun's habit. But he was not going to make a weak, frail thing of her again. No. This time she was going to keep her cool!

She chose a high-collared, white silk shirt, and tailored, black velvet pants. Sophisticated, no-nonsense, she thought; but she was unaware of how her vivid auburn hair flamed in contrast to the almost puritanical garb. She added her grandmother's long strand of pearls, glowing and creamy; then the merest touch of eye shadow, and lip-gloss the colour of newly opened poppies. Now she felt ready to brave anything. Well, almost anything.

Jeannie's words of supposed comfort followed her as she walked down the Great Hall. "We'm here, Ma'am. If ye need us." Quite what she and Jason expected, Rowena didn't want to know. Involuntarily, she shivered, not only because of the evening's chill after the storm. But a touch of wry amusement lifted the corners of her lips as she prepared for battle. The glint in her eyes boded no good for Senor damned Olivares!

Bartlett, the Spaniard's manservant, opened the door when she knocked. With a kindly smile he invited her in. She felt strange as she entered the wing that temporarily was no longer hers.

The drawing room was empty, and she looked around curiously. Books and magazines were strewn on side tables, and one or two paintings and ornaments had been added. The fire was burning brightly, its warm glow softening the corners, hiding any worn areas. In the flickering light, the golden yellow brocade of the curtains against the mellow patina of the oak panelling added a rich beauty, which even she had not foreseen. Truly it had become a lovely, gracious room, with the tang of lemon polish and beeswax mingling with the sweet scent of her grandmother's roses. She sighed with pleasure, the purpose of her visit forgotten. Almost overwhelmed, she felt her love for Gulls Walk swell within her. Her eyes misted with tenderness.

When she heard a tread behind her, she half turned, her delight clearly visible. For the moment, she put aside the horror of the afternoon.

"I had forgotten what firelight would do; you have made it all look so beautiful." She had no quarrel with Bartlett, and she turned fully, with a smile of appreciation on her lips, only to realise that the servant had gone, and it was Olivares who stood by the door.

She felt herself blush, remembering the anger and disgust she had last seen on his face. She drew herself up, trying to maintain her poise. His eyes were still as he watched her.

"Oh. It's you." Her voice was flat. No longer did it hold the lilt of happiness he had heard when he first walked in.

Her hair, burnished by the flickering flames, glowed around her face as if she were some glorious Botticelli Madonna. Once again she had startled him into flights of fancy. Perhaps he had been unnecessarily harsh. He certainly had been unforgivably rude. Why the hell did she make him so angry? She looked such an innocent.

Yet she had lied to him. As owner of Gulls Walk she must know what was going on in the valley. And whatever it was, he intended to find out. When he requested Whitford to find accommodation for him in the area, he had been astonished that the best available place was part of the very house he had been asked to watch, a stroke of luck he did not intend to lose. Of course, she probably expected some ancient who only wanted to watch the birds. Yes, a little arrogant indignation might fluster her enough to cause her to drop her guard. He chose his words carefully.

"Good evening, Miss Pentraegon, I'm glad you approve." He made no attempt to keep the touch of sarcasm from his voice, well aware that her compliment had not been intended for him. He cleared his throat. "Thank you for accepting my rather abrupt invitation. I think we have some unfinished business."

His words were cold, and he saw a flash of fear in Rowena's eyes.

Yes, there was definitely more to the quiet and peaceful surroundings of Pentraegon land, but perhaps continued antagonism might not help him find the answers he was seeking. He softened his tone.

"I owe you an apology. My behaviour was unforgivable."

Rowena looked at him uncertainly, not sure how she should respond. His reference to unfinished business had brought back all her fears of a broken lease. But the last words quite drove from her mind her intention to show him Pentraegon pride, that she was mistress in her own house; instead, she wanted to blast him with disgust and fury at his earlier actions. He warranted that.

But he spoke again before she could rely.

"Will you sit down?" He made no attempt to touch her as he indicated one of the winged-back chairs. "Perhaps we should begin all over again."

His eyes were still cold, but a faint smile touched his mouth. She found herself watching its curve: that same mouth that had burned her with its cruel kiss. The blush of embarrassment deepened as she dragged her gaze away. She tried to fan the embers of anger, which had flamed so strongly just moments ago, but the softer, almost sensuous shape of his lips differed so from their usual hard, thin line. She bent her head to the blazing logs. Anything was safer than looking into that lean, powerful face.

Olivares came to stand on the other side of the fireplace. "I can't remember having been so angry in a long time. I can only offer that as an excuse for my behaviour. If you had been a man I would have . . ."

The smile disappeared. Rowena flinched, but the remorseless voice continued. "Why did you lie to me?" There was silence. Wretchedly, she realised he doubted everything she had said. She shifted in her seat, not knowing how to begin. The fear was back again, darkening her eyes, and the misty sheen of sudden tears reflected the glow from the fire.

The Spaniard hesitated. Hell! She was such a slip of a girl. Softening his voice somewhat, he spoke again.

"Your actions, from the first moment, have been those of a very prickly porcupine; as if you couldn't bear the thought of anyone criticising you or your treatment of Goemor. You behaved like a spoiled child who has never been curbed." He intended to sound faintly amused, but he felt his temper, which he had meant to keep so carefully under control, flare again.

"Damn it all, girl. You could have been killed. Your riding was dangerous, reckless. Apparently you assume that because you own this place, you are a law unto yourself."

The amber sparks in his eyes pierced her like sharp barbs, and she flinched again as she looked up.

Was that how others saw her? Had she been so full of her own woes that she had not thought of anyone else? Shameful memories of her manipulation of Megan caused the blood to rise again to her cheeks. But before she could protest, he continued, this time more calmly.

"But perhaps I should not have judged you so harshly. After all, Goemor is your horse. I suppose you have the right to do what you choose with your own property."

Aware of the scorn, Rowena flinched, though surely his accusations were unfair. Suddenly it mattered to her that he change his opinion. The incident in the library was startlingly vivid in her mind; his contemptuous disregard for her, the total lack of respect, and the devastating awareness that she was nothing but an ugly thorn in his side. His words were like a cold wind. Harshly, she dragged air into her lungs. Then her own anger erupted into equally sharp accusations as her temper flared, too.

"You have no right to be so judgemental. You know nothing about that path, or the coastline, or about the circumstances as to why I was riding Goemor there, or why I fell."

Her eyes widened in indignation, their intensity causing them to glow darkly. She lifted her chin as she made her passionate defence.

"I absolutely refuse to let you criticise me when you don't know anything about Gulls Walk, about what I have just gone through. My grandfather . . ." No, she didn't want his pity; she changed directions. "That was the first time I have fallen off Goemor in all the years I have ridden him!"

Rowena gulped. Her own anger helped. There would be no tears this evening. "And what's more, the path is one we have used hundreds of times. It was a bird that suddenly startled Goemor." Here was her chance to make him realise that she was not irresponsible or a brat. That particularly had rankled.

In her eagerness, she leaned forward, her eloquent green eyes enormous above the delicate curves and hollows.

Olivares watched her beauty glow. His anger melted.

"I stand corrected." Perhaps he had been hasty. Her explanation was reasonable. But she could so easily have been killed. He remembered the overwhelming fear he had felt as he had seen the thin body crumble. Olivares had seen so much of the ugliness of the world, but it never inured him to the hurt of the innocent—if she really were innocent. Mentally, he shrugged his shoulders.

"I obviously have accused you unfairly, I'm sorry." He owed her that. But he continued to probe. "Though that still doesn't explain why you lied to me, letting me believe that you were a servant. I suppose you made Miss Haversham lie, too."

The golden glint was back in his eyes. The familiar lines narrowing his mouth returned. She had not tempered his judgement yet.

That was not fair, she had only wanted Megan to prevaricate a little. But she could hardly tell Olivares that. As for the rest. That was even less easy to explain. Such a jumble of agonising fears. She couldn't share all her misery of the last few weeks, talk about her loneliness without Gramps. The wounds were still too raw. So her words, when they came, sounded stilted, and not enough. But she couldn't help it.

"Not intentionally. It wasn't really a lie. I do work in the stables, sometimes. I just couldn't tell you the truth." She didn't realise how her face had closed, how in her deep introspection, she had shut out his overtures.

"And why not?" The sharp words were relentless. He felt that she was covering up something.

She moved uncomfortably in her chair. But the Spaniard had no intention of making it easier.

"You were so furious," she replied in a small voice. It would have to do. What did it matter anyway. As long as he didn't leave, she wouldn't have to return the money. And what more could she say? That she was desperately frightened of failing; of the death duties; of losing Gulls Walk?

Perhaps an alternative would do.

"I had been getting ready for you, and I didn't know who you were at first. I was dirty, I hardly looked like—like the Lady of the Manor; and the next time you saw me, it was the same."

Whatever he had expected, it had not been that. So vanity had been the root of it all. Suddenly his lips began to twitch. Then a low chuckle, warm and enveloping, reached out to touch her.

"And for that, I damned near . . ." He moved toward her, swallowing the ugly word, and reached for her hand. "I'm sorry. It was appalling behaviour. I promise not to be such a bear again." His smile broadened, and the golden lights, no longer cruel barbs, softened.

Gently he pulled her to her feet. "Come. Let's forget all about it and have dinner. I'm sure that Mr. and Mrs. Bartlett have laid on something special. They, too, are enjoying the peace and quiet of Gulls Walk." His chuckle broke into laughter as he led her to her seat at the table. Perhaps she really was as innocent as she sounded.

Roberto Olivares put himself out to be charming. As they ate, he talked of this and that, of trade between their two countries; of how the beauty of Devon and Cornwall had always attracted him, so like the northern coast of his own country. That was the reason for his choice of Gulls Walk for a temporary residence, for it had seemed a good idea to combine business, (something to do with wines) and pleasure. And he needed a rest.

He asked her about her own life.

"And what are you intending to do with yourself? Marry your boyfriend?" His inquiry was casual as he stirred his coffee. Then his eyes narrowed at her startled reaction to his words. Rowena, unable to control the flood of colour that suffused her cheeks, remembered the violence of her rejection of the idea when Miles had suggested the same thing.

"Oh. Never! I'll live here, at Gulls Walk, for the rest of my life. And I will never marry Miles."

Suddenly it mattered very much for the Spaniard to understand that. She pushed away from the table and went to the fireplace. For a little while, she had been able to forget her troubles. And now they all come flooding back. The present was only transitory. Though whom was she kidding? A temporary tenant was doing nothing more than postponing the day of reckoning.

But she wanted no more of the casual conversation of the evening. As soon as she politely could, she excused herself, hardly aware of the speculative expression on the Spaniard's face. But when Rowena lay in bed that night, trying to sleep, she felt more miserable than ever. She had surmounted one hurdle, Roberto Olivares intended to stay. But what of the bigger hurdle? What would happen when the probate people made their decision? Or when her tenant left? Would any bank really feel she was capable of paying back a loan?

After having wished Rowena goodnight, her host returned to stand in front of the last embers in the dying fire. He kicked the logs into a blaze, and gazed into the flames.

What had frightened her away, he wondered? Why had she been so adamant about not marrying Miles? And what was the reason for the fear he had seen lurking in her eyes? Something was worrying her, something much more serious than feminine concern to appear an appropriate landlady.

And this Miles. He seemed to be quite pleased with his role as Rowena's boyfriend; indeed, possessively so with his lavish endearments. And she had accepted them, too. Precious indeed!

So why was she so vehement about not marrying her neighbour? Why had she shut up like a clam when he tried to probe? Why did she leave so quickly? She was afraid of something, and what it was, he intended to find out. His anger returned, surprising him. Maybe the incidents were nothing more than storms in a teacup, to which he should not have reacted so violently, particularly as he had much more important problems needing his attention. But Miles Gilbert remained at the forefront of his mind. There was something decidedly curious about him, and the apparent control he thought he had over Miss Rowena Pentraegon.

CHAPTER TEN

The next morning Rowena pondered whether she, too, should go riding, bring to normalcy a relationship of polite hostess and guest. Was that what her tenant expected?

But she decided she wasn't prepared for that yet. Even though the Spaniard had seemed willing to forgive and forget her behaviour, the memory of the devastation she had felt when he had kissed her was still too vivid in her mind. Dear heavens, she had been kissed before. Her college social life had not been exactly dull. But never like last night. Her fingers traced the curve of her mouth as she re-lived the moment; then she found her body shivering with unbidden thoughts.

No. She pulled herself together. She would wait until Megan returned. They could face him together. Perhaps, with Megan's chatter, Rowena could sink into the background and show that she was prepared to be polite but fully intended to maintain a distance.

And yet she was ducking the issue. At dinner, the Spaniard had apologised for his actions, and he, too, had been polite. Even though she had tried to unbend, she had not been as successful. She remembered her smouldering anger, her inability to talk about Gramps, which might have sounded as if she were asking for pity; then her rather abrupt departure. She tried to shrug away the feeling of guilt.

But daylight was putting the events into better perspective, for she had to be fair and admit Roberto Olivares had every right to be annoyed and offended by her deception. Thank goodness that his reactions, when he discovered who she was, extreme though they had been, had not included lease breaking.

Yet somehow, the money didn't seem quite so important this morning.

Oh, Damn it all! Why couldn't she just forget the whole thing and start again? He had seemed willing. She, too, must at least try.

Megan came back early, before Olivares returned from his ride. She was surprised to find Rowena seated on the terrace, sipping a cup of coffee. Standing just inside the windows of the library, a faint frown touched her face; then her usual smile appeared as she stepped forward.

"Hi, Rowe, I thought that you were still in hiding. Won't Rob see you when he returns? He will hardly expect to find the stable girl sitting out here with me, will he?" She laughed in her usual vague way.

"Oh, he discovered who I am yesterday. Jeannie let the cat out of the bag." There was no need for more explanation, Rowena decided. She dismissed the subject with an airy wave of her hand.

"Isn't it a lovely day after the storm. It's a good thing you didn't try to come back last night. The roads must have been flooded." She rose from her chair. "Let me get you a cup of coffee. Perhaps some breakfast?"

"Oh, thank you, no breakfast. But coffee would be lovely." Megan looked curiously after Rowena's departing figure. The frown settled back on her face and her eyes narrowed as she watched for the horse and its rider to return.

"Good morning, Miss Pentraegon, Megan." The Spaniard reined Goemor to a standstill at the foot of the terrace as Rowena returned with a fresh brew. A faint smile lifted the corner of his mouth. "I'm glad the storms are over." He looked at Rowena.

Ouch! she thought.

"Yes, it's a delightful day." Megan chimed in with a beaming smile of welcome. "And what have you been doing with yourself while I have been away?"

Rowena was rather startled at what she could only consider to be archness on Megan's part. She sat back in some amusement to wait for more.

"Oh, ironing out a few problems; nothing of any particular importance." The smile had developed into a decided twinkle. "I'm delighted to see you back. The two of you make quite a picture of contrasts."

With an airy wave of his hand he was gone. Now what on earth did he mean? thought Rowena, somewhat crossly. He certainly ducked out with the last word.

Megan sat silent, drinking her coffee. Suddenly, she got to her feet.

"Will you mind too, too much if I go into Penzance for the day, Rowena? I really must do some shopping. School finished and I rushed over immediately. I just haven't had time . . . ." Her voice trailed away.

"Of course I don't mind. I certainly don't want you to feel that you are tied here." A touch cynically, Rowena found herself quite prepared to endure the absence of her friend. "Why don't you ask Roberto to drive you? It'll save your petrol."

Megan flushed a little.

"Oh. Don't you think that would be presumptuous?" But a small gleam appeared in her eyes.

"Not at all. I'm sure he will he quite happy to feast on your charms." That was unkind, Rowena chastised herself; she hoped that Megan didn't notice the irony. But Olivares' red-blooded maleness could thrive on someone else, thank you.

Jumping to her feet, Megan hurried into the house to change. Rowena remained where she was and poured herself another cup of coffee. Half an hour later, she heard lilting chatter and laughter, and a slow, deeper drawl as her two guests left the house. The soft purr of the silver Jag faded into the distance leaving Gulls Walk bathed in peaceful silence.

But there was still work to be done. Though somewhat loath to leave her comfortable chair, Rowena cleared the table and carried the tray back to the kitchen where Jeannie was washing up the breakfast things.

"Don't bother about lunch for Miss Megan, or for me. She has gone to town with Don Olivares, and won't be back till evening. I'll just make myself a salad, thank you." She smiled at the concern on the girl's face. "Don't worry, Jeannie. It's all right. He didn't eat me. And dinner was quite good, too. Delicious in fact."

Taking cleaning material, Rowena went into the library to tidy up. She re-laid the fire and dusted, eventually coming to pause by the desk where the Spaniard had taught her a new dimension to an age-old art. She wondered if the first Morgan Pentraegon's daughter had felt the same emotion that had rocked her to her very core. Had that sea captain forced his attentions, too?

She moved to the glass cabinet under Queen Elizabeth's portrait. Taking the key from its ledge, carefully she lifted out the old diary, gently turning the crinkled pages. She began to read with a deeper understanding of how that first Rowena must have felt. Had she found her Spaniard overwhelming, too? Yet eventually fallen in love?

Suddenly, devastatingly, with startling clarity, the enormity of what she was thinking hit her. Was that likely to happen to her? Dear God, no! A thousand times no! She actively disliked Don Roberto Olivares, with his ruthless disregard, his condemnation of her, his criticism, his unwillingness to give her even a chance to explain—until last night when she finally had made him listen to her bumbling attempts. But even then, he was tolerant rather than understanding. Yes. She definitely was not going to fall for him!

Thrusting the thought aside, she began to turn the pages until she found the section on the building of Gulls Walk. She was determined to put her tenant out of her mind. The penmanship and the archaic English had been difficult to understand when she was a child, but her grandfather had taught her well.

There were lists of building materials, objects purchased, wages paid. As she was growing up, learning more and more of her family's history, she had been awed over how much an Elizabethan penny would buy.

But she had paid little attention to the step-by-step picture of the growth of Gulls Walk. Now, every stone and timber had a more personal meaning. She reread the pages, visualising the number of men employed in the construction, and the great joy Morgan Pentraegon must have felt as he saw his new home take shape.

Some of the prices seemed strange in relation to modern methods. It cost more to have a mounting block placed than to lay the bricks for a hearth. And to build a wall of stone cost less than the pruning of the mulberry tree, supposedly the same one that still stood, though gnarled and ancient, in the corner of the herb garden. These odd inequities had always intrigued her. Even the cost of placing the sundial seemed exorbitant at seven shillings, when one considered that wages were counted in pennies.

But earlier ancestors had noticed these anomalies and searched in those places for old Morgan's treasure, yet none had been found. Ruefully, she wished she could discover its whereabouts. If it existed at all, dear Gulls Walk could certainly do with it!

She read on, noting other expenses.

Whatever the going rate, Morgan Pentraegon had certainly not scrimped. Dresses and over-garments, even shoes and slippers, in quantities not normal in that era, were paid for unbegrudgingly, often with light comments at the side. *Thys doth pretty my buxom wife welle.* was annotated beside a particularly expensive gown. Rowena chuckled. As a designer she could appreciate the pleasure Mistress Pentraegon must have felt.

Her mind drifted back to the clothes she had made for Megan. Had she changed into one of those outfits before she went out? Oh well. She was, no doubt, enjoying her afternoon with Don Olivares.

Rowena sighed as she put away Morgan Pentraegon's diary.

There was plenty of work to do; she hadn't even changed the flowers this morning. But she lingered for a few more moments. In its special box lay the replica of the bronze chain, which, supposedly, had been given to the Spanish sea captain before he left Morgan Pentraegon's home. Carefully, she took it out and allowed her fingers to wander over its uneven surface. Originally, there must have been words embossed on one side, though most of them had worn away over the years, or had broken off. On the other face was a rather crude version of what probably was the original galleon.

Indeed, she wondered why the chain had been kept at all. Her Grandfather had it valued once, but its worth was only historical, and that mainly because it was mentioned two or three times in the diary. But old Morgan had specifically stated that it must be kept carefully and had bequeathed it to his son. Yet he had never given a reason.

And so it had become almost a family joke, particularly in later years when Pentraegon fortunes were on the wane.

"We'll just have to sell the family jewel," was her grandfather's usual caustic comment, and he laughingly teased her about the chain if her pocket money ran out.

She smiled to herself as she put it back in its box. They had been good times, just Gramps and her.

But there was work to do. She locked the glass case and put away the key.

By early evening, the house was spic and span again. Rowena had taken a basket of her grandmother's beautiful yellow roses to Bartlett, partly in thanks for dinner, and partly as a peace offering for her tenant. Not that he would be likely to notice. She had exercised Firefly and herself with a quick canter over the headland. Finally, it was time to wash away the grime of the day.

She went up to her bedroom, which was now Megan's, and searched through her wardrobe for something to wear. Most of her clothes had been pushed to one side to make room for her guest. Feeling a little irritated, Rowena suddenly realised that there was no reason why she shouldn't move back upstairs.

Quickly calling to Jeannie to bring the keys, she began to pile her own things on to the bed. Grandfather's room was all clean and tidy. His clothes had been removed, and most of his personal belongings had been packed away. She had no qualms about sleeping there. Indeed, it might be comforting. And it had the same lovely view across the valley to the sea beyond as had her own bedroom.

When Jeannie came running up the stairs, Rowena unlocked the door. They pulled off the dust covers; then, between them, carried in and put away most of her clothes and made up the bed.

When all was done, she collapsed on the seat by the window. It was so good to feel the warm, afternoon sunlight, and to see the tranquil calm of her beloved cove.

She was tired; she hadn't slept well last night. Somehow, the effort to shower and dress seemed too much, so she opened the casements, then snuggled against the pillows, the soft rays bathing her in peace. Gradually, she fell asleep.

"Rowena, Rowena. Where are you?"

She had been riding in her dream over golden waves to a face in which amber lights glistened. She was happy, she didn't know why. She felt cocooned in warmth. Sweet breezes caressed her face.

Suddenly, a voice startled her.

"Oh, you're here, wake up, do. I've had such a lovely day. You won't believe what we've been doing, Rowe."

Drowsily, still trying to hang on to her dream, Rowena opened her eyes.

Megan's face smiled down at her, cheeks bright with colour.

Go away, were Rowena's first thoughts, but politeness dictated otherwise. "Hello, Megan. I'm glad you've been enjoying yourself." She was remembering how tired she had been after all the housework, but she hoped that Megan would miss the touch of sarcasm. Rowena pulled herself together. Megan was her dear friend who had so willingly come to help her. She had no right to begrudge her just one day in Penzance.

"And what lovely things have you been doing?" She sat up and smiled at Megan.

"We've been planning." Dancing eyes sparkled with excitement. "We're going to have a party."

"We are?" Startled, Rowena jumped to her feet. "Who's we?"

"Why, Rob. And a lot of his friends. We're going to have it here. Isn't it fun?"

"His friends? Here?" She felt she sounded half-witted. "Why? When?" She grasped Megan by the arm. "What on earth have you two been up to?"

Looking hurt, wincing a little, Megan pulled away. "You needn't grab me so hard. I've done it for you."

"For me? What have you done for me?" The soft haziness of her dream was gone now.

"Well. I wanted you two to be friends. How better to make it up than to have a party?" Smiling with satisfaction, Megan danced around the room; she was wearing the same green suede skirt again, and it swirled like waves around her slim figure.

Rowena gasped; the thoughtless girl. What on earth had she let them in for? Did she never think? The almost empty bankbook swam before her eyes.

"Oh, it's all right. You don't have to worry about the money; I'm not a complete fool. Look at this lovely cheque. And he says we can ask whom ever we like, too. Won't it be wonderful?"

"Damn it, Megan. You can't do this to me. The last thing I want is a party. And who said I want to make it up? I don't even like the man. Why do you think that I kept out of his way?"

Stopping suddenly, Rowena realised that she might be admitting more than she had intended. "I mean, he is a tenant. One doesn't make friends with one's tenant."

"And why not? He's gorgeous. How can you not like him?"

Rowena was not about to argue. She was treading on thin ice. Slowly, she reached her hand for the cheque.

"Whow! What does he want? A ball?" The amount was staggering.

"Yes. That's exactly what he does want. A fancy dress ball."

"You mean, *you* want a fancy dress ball!"

"Well, I did egg him on a bit, I admit." Giggling, Megan turned around. With an airy wave of her hand, she danced out of the bedroom. Then she turned back to say, "You'd better get changed. He's coming to dinner in an hour. 'Bye."

Rowena collapsed, her mind, a whirl. What had happened to her life over the past couple of weeks? An hour! She'd better rush if she were to have anything on the table. Mentally, she blessed Trevy. The deep freeze would have to do its stuff.

She hurried through her shower and scampered downstairs in her dressing gown to rummage through the shelves. Soup and salad, a casserole, and fresh strawberries. That would have to do. Back up stairs she ran to dress; there was just time while dear, faithful Jeannie laid places at the end of the long table in the dining room. Thank goodness she had redone the flowers there that afternoon.

Five minutes to the hour she crossed the gallery, hoping that the high flush on her cheeks would subside. She was damned if she wanted her tenant to think that she had made any special effort for him!

She had just reached the top of the stair when she heard her name called.

With the calm assurance of some magnificent golden lion, wearing a cream polo neck, and dark brown trousers, Roberto Olivares walked toward her from his own wing at the far end of the gallery.

"Good evening, Miss Pentraegon. I hope that not only Megan is inviting me to dinner." The amber twinkle reminded her again of roasting chestnuts and warm winter fires.

Confused by the churning feelings his smile aroused, she murmured a conventional, "Of course not."

"I'm glad." He paused. "Yes, I can see how my calling you a child must have rankled." The laughter deepened in his eyes. "No one in his or her right mind would make that mistake seeing you now." His gaze wandered up and down her body. "Not exactly a grubby little girl's riding gear!"

Indignantly, Rowena lifted her chin. She was prepared to meet this arrogant Spaniard half way, but she was damned if she was going to let him be so personal.

"I think, perhaps, that dinner must he ready." She was proud of the icy chill she managed to put into her voice. She started to descend the stairs, glad that he could not see the hot blush, which she knew must be spreading.

But secretly she was aware of quivers of pleasure dancing up and down her spine as his eyes followed her. The dress of deep midnight blue was achieving the effect she had intended! It was sleeveless, of soft jersey. Its draping, deceptively simple, touched only gently her slender body, suggesting rather than emphasising. But the back dropped in a deep U, belying the almost puritanical high neckline at the front.

Yes, it was one of her most successful designs. She had not had the courage to wear it before, but she was determined to eradicate the little-brat image and show some level of maturity. She had brushed her hair until it shone, and fastened it on the crown of her head, twisting and pinning most of the curls out of the way. Only a few wispy tendrils against her cheeks and at the nape softened the severe lines. To add the final touch, her grandmother's pearls glowed in the evening light. She hoped she looked every inch the mature Lady of the Manor. Certainly, she was enjoying the feeling of sophistication.

But she had taken only a few steps when she felt her arm held; she was sharply spun around.

"That's enough, Miss Rowena Pentraegon." The warmth had gone from his eyes. "I'm tired of this game you seem to take such a delight in playing. I am paying some pretty hefty bills here, and I'm entitled to a little more common courtesy than you seem willing to show."

Splinters of ice had taken the place of the amber twinkles.

"Look, I know that I upset you, for which I have apologised, and I'm very much aware of this wretched chip you carry on your shoulder. I'm sorry if I have contributed to it. But I'm damned if I'm going to put up with any more childishness."

Stunned, Rowena looked up at him, her eyes wide and fearful. She had angered him again.

"Oh, God!" he muttered. "Don't look at me like that." He lifted a hand to caress her cheek. She trembled at his touch. He remembered his own mental description of her the night before, a Botticelli Madonna.

"Come here." Roughly, he pulled her into his arms. What was he going to do with her? Damn. She was so soft and warm, with curves . . . . His arms tightened.

Rowena's control crumbled. She could do nothing right. Her stupid emotions had taken control again. Why did she react so?

"I didn't mean to make you cross," she gulped; "I just wanted to show you . . ." Oh, what, was the use. She couldn't tell him how miserable she had been. "I just . . . I'm not a child." Dear heavens. If anything sounded childish, that did. Why did she always say the wrong thing? "I'm sorry."

She felt her chin lifted. The amber glints were back.

"I know." His taut lips widened into a gentler smile. "But don't play games, Rowena. I haven't the time. Other people have troubles, too, you know. Try being yourself for once."

He lowered his face. She felt his breath on her cheek as his lips traced the merest whisper of a kiss against the corner of her mouth.

Jeannie was ready to serve dinner when they walked in. She had changed into a black dress and had found a pretty cap and apron to complete her outfit.

Bless her, thought Rowena, then wondered if Rob would consider all their efforts just more of the games he disliked. Thank goodness Megan was there to keep the conversation going while she attempted to swallowed the Spaniard's comments, and tried to blank out of her mind the feel of his mouth.

"This house is really quite beautiful. It's a pleasure to share part of it." Rowena was suddenly aware that the comment was addressed to her.

"Yes. My family has lived here for four hundred years." Her face opened a little. A small smile lifted the corners of her mouth. "I love the old lady."

That seemed to encompass so much. Olivares watched the warm glow brighten her cheeks.

"Tell me about her." He asked softly.

Startled, she looked up. There were no signs of his earlier anger, just warm interest.

Why not? she thought. Maybe he was offering her a new start. Suddenly she wanted him to know, to understand. Perhaps then he would realise just how difficult the last weeks had been. Her behaviour was not just the silly schoolgirl pique that he seemed to think.

She took a deep breath.

"The first Morgan Pentraegon built this house at the turn of the sixteenth century. It has been handed down from father to son or grandson until the last Morgan Pentraegon, my grandfather. He died just a few weeks ago."

She hesitated. "I am the last Pentraegon. My parents were drowned when I was a baby. The house is my responsibility now."

She hesitated again, then sat up straighter. She would tell it all. Or nearly all.

"But unfortunately, my grandfather left very little money. Of course, I don't want to sell Gulls Walk. I thought that I might have some chance of keeping it if I could make some money, take in a lodger."

She let out a sigh. There. Now perhaps he would understand. Except for the looming problem of death duties, she had explained her circumstances; she didn't need to go into further details. The soft rose of a blush touched her cheeks. "I'm new at this. And I haven't made a very good job of it, have I?"

As she looked at the Spaniard, a small grin curved her lips. A feeling of immense relief flooded through her. For the first time in weeks her impish sense of humour came to the surface. "How does it feel to be a drowning girl's last straw?"

Perhaps he would understand and forgive her now. Life didn't seem so bad after all.

For a moment, which seemed an eternity, the world was empty except for two deep-set brown eyes. A curious change came over her tenant's face. His expression softened, was now full of warmth. And something else. She thought it was almost a relaxing of tension. She supposed that it was just because she had told him the truth. And yet something was strange.

But her puzzlement passed. The Spaniard reached a hand across the table.

"I didn't know how recent has been your grandfather's death. Whitford should have told me. I'm so sorry."

"Oh, no. Don't be. I didn't want you to know. You might not have come if you had." Her eyes widened. That would have been awful. She felt the hot colour flood her cheeks again.

A faint twinkle softened the amber glints. "And we couldn't have had that, could we?"

"Oh, come on, you two. What's past is past. And we've got a party to plan." Megan's voice held a note of irritation. "Rowena, dear. You know you don't like to talk about losing the house. I wanted Rob's and my surprise to make you happy." Uncertainly she looked from one to the other.

"Perhaps Miss Pentraegon does not want a party." Rob's words were gentle.

"Oh no! I mean, yes. Let's have a party." Suddenly the idea seemed exciting. "Gulls Walk would love a party. The old dear has been sad too long. Yes. Let's make her dance once more. There were wonderful parties when my grandmother was alive; Gramps used to tell me about them."

A small cloud touched her brow, but determinedly, she brushed it away. Yes. A party would be such a grand finale for her beloved Gulls Walk.

CHAPTER ELEVEN

From that moment, the evening became full of laughter. Rowena determined to put behind her all her fears and worries, for Megan was right; there was nothing more she could do to solve her money problems. She remembered a rather appropriate motto which hung over Gramp's desk. 'Yesterday is dead, forget it; tomorrow does not exist, don't worry; today is here, use it.' And she refused to listen to thoughts of 'Eat, drink and be merry, for tomorrow we die.'

"What sort of fancy dress shall we have?" Megan turned to Rob. "Give us some idea what your friends would like."

"Oh, I don't know. Perhaps Miss Pentraegon might care to make a suggestion. After all, it is her house."

"Yes, Rowe; you love designing costumes. What do you think?"

"Really, Megan, I haven't thought about it. You were the one who started all this; but perhaps something in keeping with Cornwall." She pondered for a moment. "Something that would look right in this house; it mustn't be anything too bizarre. Oh, how about an Elizabethan Ball? The first Morgan Pentraegon had one soon after the house was finished. There are notes in his diary."

"Marvellous. That would be just wonderful," enthused Megan,

"Yes, it will be nice to see Gulls Walk in all her finery, with old-world lords and ladies. Sounds a good idea to me," agreed Olivares.

Rowena's eyes began to sparkle. A vision of her tenant in the rich velvets of an Elizabethan courtier brought a rosy glow to her cheeks.

"But I have one condition," the Spaniard continued.

"Oh, yes, anything, Rob." Megan leaned forward, determined not to be left out.

"That Miss Pentraegon also calls me Rob. I am decidedly tired of all this formality." Amber twinkles, chestnuts, firelight on a winter's evening. Rowena's blush heightened.

"Oh, if you wish. And I am Rowena."

"Rowena Felicity Pentraegon. I thank you. I thought it was a pretty name when I read my lease." He was silent for a moment. "And now you can work out the details. I shall be a swash-buckling Spanish sea captain come to see what I can steal."

Rowena gasped, her face suddenly paling.

Rob Olivares' eyes narrowed. What caused that, he wondered? Was it the word steal? Why should she fear that word? He had thought their problems were behind them, particularly since her shortage of cash was being alleviated by the substantial rent he was paying. And he had ironed out their misunderstandings. It had been a relief to find he'd misjudged her.

But now, once more, the doubts surfaced. Again he was conscious of undercurrents. He pushed back his chair, feeling a bitter sense of disappointment. Perhaps it was time he left.

With polite words of thanks, he rose from the dining table. It was late. Tomorrow was another day. "I have had a most entertaining evening; you both have been charming hostesses." But his thoughts were grim as he climbed the stairs. His implied intention to steal had only meant hearts. There was more to the entrancing Miss Pentraegon, and he intended to find out what it was.

Are well, one good thing was coming out of the new arrangements; the ball would be excellent coverage for his men. He could bring some of them in to help in his search, particularly as he wanted no one to know just why he was here at Gulls Walk. But he hated the thought of Rowena's possible complicity, and that his instinct had been wrong. He remembered his flights of fancy: a delicate wraith, a Botticelli Madonna.

The following morning, rather shyly, Rowena waited in the stable for Rob to come. She arrived early and had already saddled Firefly. Pottering around, she was trying to find jobs to do. Her mind wandered back over the previous evening, which mostly had been fun. The only disconcerting moment was when Rob had mentioned his choice of costume. Much of the day she had been so immersed in Gulls Walk's history that his suggestion had shocked her as if it were déjà vu. She had the overwhelming feeling that events, in some convoluted way, were repeating themselves.

"Good morning." The Spaniard's deep voice startled her; she hadn't heard him enter the stable. "I hoped you would ride with me today. Thank you again for last night's dinner." He smiled down at Rowena. In the sleepless hours of the night he had decided that he would withhold judgement. "I must remember to thank your servants. They produced a wonderful meal at short notice."

"Yes." Rowena hesitated. She had, so far, managed to hide her staff problems. "Well, actually, I have to admit we raided the freezer. Trevy, our housekeeper, prepared lots of food before you came. Unfortunately, she broke her leg, and since she is still on crutches, she has not come back to work yet. I just thank my lucky stars that she had made so much. Neither Jeannie nor I can cook as well as that."

She laughed a little nervously.

"Jeannie and you? Is there nobody else who cooks?"

"No, there's nobody else, period. Unless you count Jason." She might as well let him know the truth. "You wouldn't have stayed long if we had to cook for you!" She chuckled again, glad that she had made a clean breast of it. She prepared to mount. It was such a lovely morning and last night's talk of parties and guests had been fun.

"Wait a minute. You mean there is no one else to help in the house?"

"No, nor in the garden either. But we manage." She wished he would stop the questions. Gramps had never worried about such things.

"Rowena!" He reached for Firefly's reins. "Don't think you can brush me off. I want to know. Are you telling me that you, Jeannie and Jason between you are running this house? I don't suppose Megan is being much help."

"Oh, we manage. Actually, it has been fun. We love Gulls Walk, all of us. We've been happy doing it. As for Megan, well, she is a guest." Confession is good for the soul, they say. Rowena pushed on with the truth. "And I asked her to stay when I found out who you are. Remember that I looked such a mess, and I needed a Lady of the Manor. I did rather take advantage of her."

It seemed hardly fair to tell the Spaniard that Megan had been the one to come up with the tale about the owner of the house being away for some weeks, thus giving her no opportunity the next day to confess.

"So you see, it wouldn't be right to expect her to work." Her voice trailed away. Rob was looking like a thundercloud.

"Damn it all, girl; this house is enormous. How on earth can we think of a ball? The work will be horrendous. We must cancel the idea."

"Oh, no, don't do that. Gulls Walk needs it. She was dying by inches before we gave her a spring-cleaning for your arrival. Just to see her in all her finery one more time will be so wonderful. And," she paused, her voice dropped. "and I need it, too."

It was true; she did need it. She had been so sad when her grandfather died. She missed him so much. And the prospect of fun, though only transitory, had lifted her spirits. Yes, she truly needed the ball.

"Please, Rob."

Uncertainly, he paused. Since she so obviously was running the house on a shoestring, she could hardly be involved in the mysterious goings on along the local Cornish coast. Yet all his information had pointed to Pentraegon Cove. He shook his head to dispel the thought.

"I could get some help from the village." Rowena's voice was tentative. The cheque she had been given the previous evening was more than generous, as had been the rent for the east wing, but she couldn't keep on spending the Spaniard's money.

"All right, Rowena." Quickly, he made up his mind. "But make sure that you do. Also, you can't appear as hostess at your own ball with finger nails like these." He reached for her hands. "See that someone else does the hard work. No more scrubbing!" He grinned down at her. The amber lights were back.

"I'll wear gloves." She laughed. Suddenly the day seemed brighter. It was going to be a wonderful, wonderful ball. She determined to think of nothing beyond that. Her own eyes sparkled as she reached for Firefly's reins. "Come on, I'll race you, I'll show you who's boss around here."

Rowena reached the headland before Rob, who was still securing Goemor's saddle when she had cantered out of the stable yard. She paused at the top, enjoying the wind in her face. Wisps of clouds rimmed with gold were straggling away to the east where the morning sun was beginning its climb. To the west, the sky was silver, and the ocean, a vast expanse of indigo and lace, was calm and peaceful in the early light. She could hear the cry of the gulls as they wheeled out to sea for their breakfast, and the soft soothing sound of the surf as it broke on the beach.

Her heart sang as she touched her heels to Firefly's willing flanks. For a few glorious moments, she felt the magic of freedom, as if she, too, could fly as high as the clouds.

The thunder of Goemor's hooves brought her back to the present. Determined not to be beaten, she urged the mare into a gallop. Soon the wind was ripping at her hair, forcing the curls to fly rampant behind her. But the stallion was faster, easily passing her. He was contentedly champing at the grass, with his rider standing beside him, when Rowena reached the end of the headland.

"I told you that if I wanted to beat you, you would have no chance." With a broad grin, Rob reached up his arms to help her from her saddle.

"It's not fair! You had the much faster horse. If I had been on Goemor I would have beaten you." She laughed down at him as she dragged off her hat.

"Probably, but I don't intend to give you a chance. I'm sufficient of a male chauvinist to want my women subservient." That'll be the day, he thought, wryly.

As he lifted her from the back of Firefly, she placed her hands on his shoulders. He pulled her close so that she felt every hard muscle as he lowered her to the ground. His eyes darkened. "Though you are like mercurial quicksilver." he whispered, in a voice grown husky.

Startled, Rowena gazed up at him, her laughter dying in a throat suddenly dry. A strange jangle of nerve endings tingled through her body. All thoughts disintegrated into a kaleidoscope of brilliant colours as he brought his face closer. Her eyelids fluttered, then closed, waiting.

Rob groaned. He buried his face in the soft, sweet fragrance of her hair. It smelled of summer rain and an elusive perfume reminding him of flower gardens and country hedgerows. His lips trailed a line across her cheek to the corner of her mouth.

"My prickly porcupine," he murmured with a gruff chuckle. "I must be a masochist. You've stabbed me so many times with those sharp barbs of yours; it's a wonder I come back for more."

Rowena felt the tension ease out of him. He lifted his head and amber lights twinkled down at her. She gazed up at him, her own eyes wide, startled.

The temptation was strong. It would be so good, he thought. Gently, he pushed her away. He was here on business. He mustn't forget that. Far from pleasant business. Yet surely she wasn't part of it.

Quickly, he made up his mind. He kissed her on the tip of her nose, then let her go.

"Come on," he said. "I feel like a holiday." He whistled to Goemor who had wandered away, bored with the strange actions of humans. "Let's return the horses to the stable. We'll steal away before Megan wakes." He glanced at his watch. "I normally wouldn't get back for another hour, so she won't be on the terrace yet. A mischievous glint of laughter lit up his face. "We'll go sailing!"

Rowena tried to bring herself back to earth.

He cupped his hands and bent to give her a leg up onto Firefly. She took a few seconds to drag together her wayward thoughts. The kiss had only been a playful diversion, she realised. She shivered in spite of the warmth of the sun. Wheeling her horse, she cantered back toward Gulls Walk. Rob watched her for a moment as a sombre expression returned to his face, and then he followed her.

He caught up with her at the crest of the path leading down to the stables. He moved to one side to let her go first. "Hurry up, slow coach, the weather is too good to waste, and my yacht awaits." He grinned at her, determined to bury the nagging worry for a few hours.

By now, Rowena was well in control. "No, we really shouldn't, I haven't done any of the chores; though it's a lovely idea." She hoped she sounded quite calm. "In any case, I've masses to do." Her equilibrium had received too much of a jolt for one morning. Yet what joy it would be not to have to think about practicalities. She hadn't been sailing in ages.

"The devil take the house and the chores; we'll sort those out later. And don't forget you promised me you'd get those servants back. I'll pay their salaries. I'm your tenant, remember, and I won't take no for an answer."

To hell with the mystery of Pentraegon Cove, he thought. Whoever were involved, it was a beautiful morning.

Jason was working in the stable when they returned and added his persuasion to Rowena when the Spaniard told him of their proposed outing.

"O' course ye mun go, Miss Rowena, it be toime 'ee had un 'oliday. Oi'l tell Bartlett where ee be, Sir. Now, don't ee worry. Me un Jeannie'll see to everything. Oi'l see to the 'orses, and Oi'l tell Miss Megan that 'ee be gone for the day. It b'ain't none of 'er business anyhow." He set his chin stubbornly. He wasn't fond of Miss Rowena's friend, and he was quite capable of being dumb.

No wonder Cornish men made such good smugglers, thought Rob.

Somewhat helplessly, Rowena gave in. Perhaps Megan would not be too annoyed that she had been left out of the invitation. Hoping she wouldn't look out of one of the windows, they ran down the path to the dock,

"You see. I told you the house could manage without you for one day," laughed her tenant. "And tomorrow, when you call all the servants back, you can worry about nothing but the list of guests and your costume for our ball."

Rob left Rowena in the main cabin while he went to change his clothes. She looked around entranced. Mellow mahogany; shining brass; crisp, navy curtains and seat covers; shelves stacked with books; even some exquisite water colours; all obvious signs of wealth. Everything was neat and spotlessly clean but had an air of comfortable relaxation that suggested regular use.

She wandered around as she waited and noticed a collection of photos on one wall. There was one of a younger Olivares standing proudly by a blue marlin suspended from a fisherman's scale. Next to it was a picture of a woman with a small child; both were laughing and under was written, "All my love, Margarita."

Rowena suddenly felt cold. She had never asked. It hadn't occurred to her. She had just assumed that Rob was single because he had come alone to Gulls Walk.

She heard the cabin door open behind her.

"I see you've found my rogues' gallery." Rob chuckled. "That was one hell of an exciting day." It had been his first big fish. Suddenly he seemed younger, and she could imagine the boy he had been.

"But that was almost a dozen years ago." He grimaced ruefully before moving on to the photo that had held her attention. "I hope you will like my sister."

Rowena found she had been holding her breath. "I wondered." Her voice was husky. She crushed the extraordinary jolt of pleasure and cleared her throat.

"I think we will invite her and her husband to the ball, if they can get away." He rested his hands on the nape of Rowena's neck. There was a pause. As if he had sensed her unspoken thoughts, his voice deepened. "I'm not married, Rowena."

Then he was all laughter again.

"If I don't get this boat out to sea soon, we'll have Megan down here looking for me."

"My, you are big headed!" Rowena managed to match his laughter.

"No, just aware of the avaricious look some women wear like a calculator!"

Startled, Rowena tried to digest the concept. She would not have thought that of Megan.

They climbed on deck and Rob started the engine, gently steering the boat away from the dock. He had changed into an ancient tee shirt and paint-spattered jeans. The wind ruffled his hair and he looked as free as any Cornish pirate did, Rowena couldn't help thinking—or any Spanish sea captain!

She removed her riding boots, rolled up the legs of her own jeans, and happily pattered to the prow of the boat to help navigate past the rocks that protected the entrance to the harbour. The day was suddenly glorious.

Between them, they unfurled the sails and soon were tacking into the morning breeze. They sailed west until they neared the first of the hundred and fifty or so islets that comprise the Scilly Isles. Many of them are just lumps of granite, home only to the immense variety of sea birds that nest there. Most of the rocks are uninhabited and bare, but some have been terraced by the Atlantic storms, and coarse grasses and a multitude of wild flowers have taken root.

In the lea of such a one, they dropped anchor and hauled in the sails. A narrow strip of sand sparkled in the sunlight. Rowena remembered this island from a visit she and Miles had made there many years ago, and she had pointed it out to Rob when they were yet some miles away. It had two curious humps, rather like a bactrian camel, and a marvellous cave she had often wanted to explore again.

"Do let's go ashore," she pleaded, her eyes bright with excitement.

"Good Lord, girl. I brought you for a rest, not to go clambering all over God's half acre!"

"Typical lazy male," she snorted.

She subsided. After all, the sun really was incredibly warm. It would be nice to just soak it up in the calm of the quiet cove. She lay back on the soft pillows Rob had brought from the cabin.

"Now, don't get too settled, Miss Porcupine. Shall we use one of your barbs to spear our lunch?" Dropping a bronzed arm easily over Rowena's waist, her host grinned down at her. "We had no breakfast, remember?"

Rowena grinned back. "So you want me to work, do you? If you need me to fish, I'll dive overboard and swim away like a mermaid. You told me to be lazy; I shall expect caviar and champagne, no less." Oh, it was fun to joke and tease.

"What my lady wants, my lady shall have. Coming up, a bottle of the best bubbly and all the fish eggs your little heart desires." With a flourishing bow, he disappeared below deck.

Rowena giggled. Being at sea was quite wonderful, for all one's cares seem to drift away on the breeze.

In a moment, Rob was back. "I knew my sister kept a variety of swimwear on board." He held up a brightly coloured beach bag. "See if any of these will fit you. Try them on in my cabin. At least they will be better than those thick jeans."

Gingerly, Rowena looked inside. More conservative costumes were mixed up in a hodgepodge of scraps. Pleased, she hurried down to the cabin and spilled the contents onto the bunk. The swimsuits turned out to be too big, so she picked out the bright yellow triangles of a bikini. The colour was marvellous against her faint tan, but she blushed at the diminutive areas it covered. Oh, well, she thought, if his sister can wear it, then so can I!

Picking up a large, fluffy towel, which Rob had put out for her, she returned to the deck.

He, too, had discarded his jeans and shirt and was wearing brief, black trunks against which his dark tan gleamed. As she stepped out into the hot sunshine, his back was towards her, and she could see the rippling muscles across his broad shoulders.

"Good timing. I've just opened the champagne." He turned to watch her walk towards him. "Good fit, too!" He chuckled. "You do more for that than my sister does, though don't tell her I said so." But his eyes darkened. "I think I need this drink." Rowena felt the faint colour rise to her cheeks as he held out a second glass to her.

"Thank you." She reached for it and buried her nose in its contents. Not surprisingly, she sneezed. The laughter returned to his eyes and he took the glass from her as she collapsed on the soft cushions.

"I didn't really believe you!" she exclaimed. "This is wonderful." In amazement, she looked at the silver dishes winking in the sunshine. Cheeses, biscuits, ham; and one even contained a pot of caviar with slices of lemon and the thinnest wafers of brown bread beside it. It all looked quite delicious. She found she was so hungry she would have settled for hard tack, but this was ambrosia for the gods.

When they had finished the last of the champagne and scraped the pot of caviar clean, Rowena lay back replete. Feeling so comfortably full and delightfully tipsy, all she wanted to do was laze away the afternoon.

"This is bliss," she murmured, snuggling into the pillow; "wake me when it's time to leave."

"I thought you wanted to go exploring?"

"Later, much later." She closed her eyes. The utter peace of the afternoon, and the gentle rocking of the boat, soothed her to sleep.

The Spaniard watched her until he, too, relaxed. In repose, her face held only the sweet innocence of youth. There were still dark circles under her eyes, but the tension was gone. All his gut feelings refused to believe that she could have any involvement in international crime. He settled on a cushion beside her, his arms behind his head. He had a great deal of thinking to do, for he had found out nothing in the last week. There had been no visitors, other than Megan and Miles; there had been no boats in the cove at night—he and Bartlett had taken it in turns to watch. Indeed, there had been nothing suspicious. Perhaps the police were wrong after all.

But the evidence had pointed to Pentraegon Cove.

In a truck laden with contraband wine and spirits, which by chance had been stopped in a routine check, they had found an old bill of sale for flowers from the Pentraegon Cove Company. The driver had got away, and the truck owner was untraceable because engine markings had been erased and the number plates were false. Even the few fingerprints were unknown. The grubby sheet of paper had been caught under the padding of the driver's seat and long forgotten.

In itself, it proved nothing. Many trucks contracted to carry goods to the London markets.

But later, in a police raid on a night club, the remnants of a recently cut daffodil had been found in some empty wine cases from his own vineyards; cases that had an entirely different destination marked on their sides. And the season was far too early for the flower to have come from anywhere other than this south-western corner of England.

Working on those shreds of information, those in charge of the investigation had called Interpol and, eventually, Spain. He had become involved because of the theft of his own wines. No one would suspect him. After all, he was just one of many businessmen who enjoyed combining work with pleasure. And where he chose to stay was no concern of others. If those cases had contained only wine, he would not have volunteered to help. Pilferage from the docks was not unknown, and he could well afford to lose a few bottles; insurance would pay, anyway. But a few of the contraband bottles had contained something much more evil.

Rob sat up, thrusting his hands through his hair. He had no right to take the day off. Too many people were relying on him.

His restlessness must have disturbed Rowena. She opened her eyes and blinked at the sky.

"Good afternoon, Sleepyhead." He raised a grin.

"Oh, did I sleep long? I'm sorry." Her skin looked soft and faintly pink from the hot sun. She sat up in confusion.

"Not really. In any case, you probably needed the rest, and I'm not going anywhere." He reached a hand to touch her face. The rough calluses of his palm, hardened by leather reins, sent frissons of feeling through her. It seemed the most natural thing in the world when he bent his head to kiss her. At first, he was gentle, his lips moving lightly, tasting her sweetness.

Her own mouth trembled under his, having no will of its own. Then, with a sigh, he drew her close. Easing her back against the pillows, he bent over her, deepening the kiss until Rowena felt as if she were floating high into the blue haze above them. She lifted her arms and curled them round his shoulders and buried her fingers in his hair. He reached up to her wrists, almost as if he would pull her hands away, then trailed his own over the silken skin, down past her shoulders to her slender waist.

His fingers spread as he caressed her, and she felt molten shafts of fire flare through her breasts as his thumbs grazed the taut nipples under their tiny triangles of cotton.

Unable to resist, she arched her body into his hands, her desires splintering and exploding in a maelstrom of emotions.

But now was not the time. Rob groaned.

"No, my little porcupine. We must be touched by the sun." He pulled away. "Your grandfather would not be pleased." He dragged a crooked grin in place, but his eyes were grave, almost black. That was not the reason, but it would have to do. He had to remember why he was in Cornwall. He was too deeply involved with criminal investigations that still pointed to Gulls Walk. Yet surely she could not be part of them. Oh, it would be too easy to forget.

CHAPTER TWELVE

Chilled by his sudden withdrawal, Rowena clambered to her feet. She had thought of nothing in those last few moments. Most certainly not of her grandfather, nor of her responsibilities. Gulls Walk had been far from her mind. Now, with a faint shiver, she mentally clawed at her equilibrium. Maybe Rob had only been passing the time, responding to the mood and the moment, and to what was available; she had certainly offered no resistance.

She tried to pull herself together and turned toward the shallow beach and the cliffs behind.

"You're right." She managed to laugh. "Let's go exploring." But she didn't look at him. Her face would give away too much. "There's a wonderful cave. I'll get my clothes on." She was uncomfortably aware of her scantily clad figure. Changing would give her an excuse to escape. Roberto Olivares was no different from any other red-blooded male, she decided, but he still thought of her as a child. She felt sad; bitterly sad.

"Good idea. I'll clear these things and get the dingy ready while you change." Suddenly, they were being polite strangers. She should have offered to help, but she needed to be alone, if only for a few minutes. She hurried down to the cabin and closed the door. For a few glorious moments, she had believed Rob was different from that first Spaniard who had stolen the heart of that long-ago Rowena; he who had proved to be less than worthy of the poor girl's love since he had never returned.

Men! she thought angrily. Were they all just philanderers at heart? She had better pull herself together. She changed into her shirt and jeans and returned to the deck.

Rob, too, had dressed and had lowered the inflatable dinghy into the water. He held out his hand to help her, but she avoided it, preferring to climb down by herself. The less she touched him, the better she would be able to keep her emotions under control. The Spaniard looked hard at her but said nothing.

It was only a hundred yards or so to the shore, and soon they were beaching the dingy high above the waterline. The hot sand had been scoured by the storm that had raged a couple of days before. Even the grass and the spiky cacti, and the tiny wild flowers clinging to the cliff, seemed washed clean. The fresh breezes sang around the granite mass, mingling the salty tang of the sea with the scent of the warm earth.

Determined to shake off her depression, Rowena tried to fill her mind with the beauty of her surroundings and climbed up the rocks at the north end of the island above the sheltered beach. The winds grew stronger as she rounded the headland. Glad that she had changed, she shivered a little as the Spaniard caught up with her.

"Go slower, little porcupine." There was laughter in his voice. "I like your legs as they are, not broken." He moved past her. "Let me lead the way, don't forget my chauvinistic tendencies."

Rowena chuckled, she couldn't help herself. Her sadness lifted. Maybe it was good to be alive.

Hand in hand, they scrambled down to a large, flat rock that tilted away from the face of the cliff, hiding the opening behind from the sea. It formed a natural barrier against which the waves tumbled and churned, only reaching to the pebbled beach beyond at high tide. At some time, the rock must have broken away from the main mass of the cliff, leaving a deep crevice. Over the aeons, a cave had been hollowed out; the cave that she and Miles had found all those years ago.

Rob had brought a flashlight with him, and as they entered, he switched on the powerful beam. The floor of the cave sloped upward, above sea level. The loose shale and seaweed gave way to hard granite polished by countless centuries of tides. He shone the light over their heads, and as he swung the torch, it shadowed a jagged line at the rear of the cave. Seemingly, there was a fissure where the granite face had split.

"Oh, we didn't see that when Miles and I came." Rowena eagerly clambered over rocky debris. Carefully, keeping one hand on the cold wall, she turned the corner. Rob caught her and held her back when she would have gone farther.

As the light penetrated the space beyond, she gave a startled cry. An even larger cave than the one through which they had come opened up before them; it widened and sloped down to dark, still waters. Obviously, the sea had forced its way through a channel under the island and found its own level.

A metal structure framed the uneven walls. Piled high on it were crates and boxes. Every ledge, shelf and flat surface had been used. There must have been hundreds of containers, each of which was stamped with various markings; numbers and names of quantities and contents, logos of manufacturers, and details of shipping firms. All were jumbled together in casual disorder.

"What on earth? It looks like a modern Aladdin's cave!" Rowena exclaimed. Rob shone his torch closer.

"I hardly think that Aladdin had much to do with this." He rummaged among the boxes. "Stolen goods, more likely." He searched for a while. "I wonder?" But just what it was he wondered, he didn't say.

One particular case caught his attention. The lid had been loosened and pushed to one side. Carefully keeping himself between Rowena and the case, he reached in. She heard the rustle of some sort of packing material; next, the faint clink of glass; then silence. Putting the lid back, Rob turned to Rowena and hurried her out of the cave. His own face was grim. Long suppressed, bitter anger welled to the surface of his mind.

But her totally startled expression was balm to his spirit. His gut feeling had been right. He heaved a deep sigh of relief. She knew nothing. And he had found what he was looking for, though he would dearly have loved to spend more time examining the contents of those bottles—those that seemed not to hold liquid. Thank God, Rowena was obviously ignorant of whoever had stored the contraband, and what it contained.

Now, the less she knew the better.

To find the cache had been marvellous luck; but to be certain at last that she was not part of it meant even more to him. He felt as if a great load had been lifted from his shoulders. As she stood there, her lovely eyes wide in bewilderment, he longed to pull her into his arms. But now was not the time.

"Come on. We've got to get out of here. Who knows when the people who stored this stuff will be back."

"But what have you found? What's in those cases?" She hadn't been able to translate the various words that she could see on the wooden surfaces.

"Later. I'll explain later. We have been moored in this cove for hours. God knows who may have seen us. Let's hope they do their smuggling at night."

As he hurried Rowena out to the main cave, he looked back. There were no other footprints but their own, so the tides, which would rise later that evening, evidently reached to the edge of the sand and washed away any marks left. The rear of the cave was above the high tide level, and little light penetrated there. Had he not brought the torch, they would not have noticed the crack in the wall. A casual visitor would never guess what was hidden behind it. No wonder who ever had placed the contraband there had not bothered with a guard. It was the perfect hiding place.

Once over the promontory, Rob searched the horizon. They were too far from any of the inhabited islands, and though there were scattered boats in the distance, none were near; and none showed any signs of coming in their direction.

They launched the dingy and climbed aboard the yacht. "No time for sails; in any case, they are too visible." He started the engine.

"But what if someone does see us? Surely, they won't do anything. If smugglers hid the stuff, they are the guilty ones, not us." Like most Cornish people, Rowena had been brought up on tales of smugglers, and as often as not, they were just locals trying to make a few extra pounds. It was a sport, almost, though the quantity of goods in the cave was definitely excessive, she realised.

"You're probably right, but I have no intention of finding out." He grinned at her to lighten the look of concern on her face.

He steered a more northerly course, away from the distant boats. No point in tempting fate. Only when the island had slipped well behind them over the horizon did they unfurl the sails and set a course for Pentraegon Cove.

Rowena remained silent, not wanting to disturb the preoccupation of the Spaniard. But once he was able to relax, she could contain her curiosity no longer.

"What was in those boxes, Rob? You recognised something, didn't you? And you didn't seem surprised." He had looked grimly pleased, in fact, when he had read a particular label.

"Yes, I did recognise one of the names. It was Spanish."

"From your country? Then why didn't we bring that crate back? Do you know to whom it belongs?"

Rob hesitated. Though he was now sure that she had no idea of what was going on in the area, he had no intention of worrying her. His instincts told him that she was totally trustworthy, but that small, cold voice of caution held him back. There must be others in Pentraegan Cove who knew about the cache.

And why did Rowena have that strange reaction to Miles Gilbert's name the night she and Rob had dined together? She had been almost frightened as she vehemently denied his suggestion that she intended to become Mrs. Gilbert. Why the fear? What had she been hiding?

And Miles Gilbert knew about the island.

Yet part of the truth could not hurt.

"It was wine. Quite a lot of such cases have been stolen from the docks in Spain, including some of mine. I recognised several of the vintners' labels." He paused. He had told her enough. "But we mustn't tamper with anything in the cave that might alert the thieves. It's better left to the police." He thought for a moment. "Look, when we get back, I'll call the right authorities and they'll take care of it. I won't mention your name because there may be local people involved. After all, Cornish men have been renowned smugglers down through the centuries, and I don't expect they take kindly to those who report them."

Rowena searched his face. Rob was not telling her everything. He had been startled when he had seen the huge stack of crates and boxes, but his lack of surprise when he read the names on the logos suggested that he knew what he would find.

How could he have known?

But it was a problem for others, not her. She had enough on her plate with her own, so perhaps the less she knew the better. Still, she couldn't help being curious.

It was evening when they moored the yacht. The long summer twilight was casting its shadows as they clambered ashore. Taking her hand in his, Rob walked with her to the kitchen door.

"Now we have to face Megan." He smiled conspiratorially at Rowena. "I hope she will understand that I owed a little politeness to my hostess." His face crinkled in laughter. Then he became serious. "Remember. Not a word about what we have found. To anyone; the servants; or Megan. I'll make sure she doesn't pester you with questions," he paused; "and don't tell Miles, either." He reached for the latch, avoiding her eyes. He hoped to God that she obeyed him, but her enigmatic boy friend had returned to London, so there was little likelihood of that for the time being.

"Oh, evenin', Miss Rowena, and Sir; I do hope 'ee had a good time. It be such a lovely day."

"Thank you, Jeannie; yes, it certainly was lovely. See, I even got burned." She held out her arms. It was true; she was already feeling the faint tingling of discomfort. That would teach her not to sleep in the hot sun. Memories of those few precious moments on the deck of the yacht when she had wakened came surging back. She swallowed, turning to the window to look out, pride coming to her rescue. She must not make too much of what to her tenant was probably just an amorous moment. The view of the distant ocean, aloofly peaceful and unconcerned, unaware of the lives it touched, calmed her.

"Thank you, Rob. I enjoyed myself. But I expect you want to get back to your rooms to change." She moved to the kitchen sink, ostensibly to wash her hands.

Aware of his dismissal, a small frown touched the Spaniard's forehead.

"Yes; I need to take a shower." But he couldn't resist the dig. "A cold one, I presume." He had not liked the way she had closed up so quickly.

As he left the kitchen, Rowena heard Megan call to him. "So you're back. Where have you been?" There followed the deeper murmur of the Spaniard's voice.

"Good evening, Megan. We decided to play hooky and went sailing."

"You might have let me know you were going. I hope you enjoyed yourselves." She sounded rather petulant.

Rowena moved nearer to the door, shamelessly eavesdropping. She wondered if he would be discomforted by Megan's quizzing. His answer was quite clear enough for her to hear; probably deliberately so.

"Oh, yes, we had a delightful time. I thought Rowena needed a break; I treated you to lunch yesterday, so today was her turn. I thought it was only fair that she should have a holiday, too." Did she detect a touch of condescension, or was that for Megan's benefit? "I'm afraid the poor girl has a touch of sunburn, so I expect she will take herself off to bed." He started up the stairs giving Megan no opportunity for further questions. "Good night, my dear. I'll see you tomorrow."

When Megan entered the kitchen, Rowena was searching through the cabinets for calamine lotion. The 'poor girl' had not done much for her ego. But at least Rob had saved her from having to make excuses. The last thing she needed was to talk about the day. Though Megan could be vague over many things, she always wanted to know what Rowena had been doing; and this particular day's events were not for broadcasting. Not only their discovery of the contents of the cave, either!

"Hello, Rowe. You might have let me know you were going out with Rob. Nobody here seemed to know where you were." There was no malice in her words now, just gentle chastisement.

"Oh, sorry. It was a spur of the moment thing, and you were fast asleep." Rowena changed the subject quickly. "Next time I go shopping, I must buy some more calamine; this bottle is almost empty."

Pleading tiredness and too much sun to want a meal, Rowena quickly said her good nights and hurried up the stairs to her room.

Megan stood at the kitchen door watching her leave.

CHAPTER THIRTEEN

Rowena certainly had a good excuse for not going riding the following morning. Truth to tell, she was sufficiently sunburned to find riding clothes too uncomfortable to wear, and yesterday's chores needed doing.

She made arrangements with her old servants, who were all delighted to return to help with the ball preparations, and she managed to avoid any contact with Rob, who took himself off to Penzance for the day.

But that evening, Megan insisted the three of them sit down to plan for the ball. No mention was made of yesterday's outing, even when the Spaniard came to join them.

"I have a list of friends whom I think might like to come, Rowena." Rob handed her a sheet with about thirty names and addresses written on it. "We'll have caterers prepare the food, and I will see about the drinks."

He watched her face as she scanned the names. None of them was local, so the list would make excellent cover for the three men he had invited from Scotland Yard. Those names he had slipped in after a long telephone call late last night. They were to be 'holidaying' in the area toward the end of the month, and what more natural than that they should be included.

But in spite of his belief in Rowena's innocence, that cold hard voice of mistrust still would not let him discount Gulls Walk, certainly not Pentraegon Cove.

Having spent most of the day setting up his plans, Rob should have been pleased, particularly as the island cache of goods bore out the certainty that Interpol's hunch in the early spring had been right, though their own men had turned up no more information until now. Nor had spot-checking of London nightclubs and of trucks from Cornwall revealed anything.

The whole operation seemed to have died down.

Still, an eye was to be kept on the island, and any activity monitored. Of course, if any attempts were made by the smugglers to empty the cave, the police would have to step in. Though it would be easy for the authorities to remove the contraband, tracing the organisers behind the smuggling was even more important.

The arrangements had gone well; for this much, he was pleased. Interpol and Scotland Yard, too, had been pleased.

Yet Rob found it hard to smile cheerfully at the two girls as they looked up from the list, ready for more ideas. He eased forward in his chair, dragging his mind back to the present. "I have staff who will come to help with whatever needs to be done in the shifting of furniture, and the setting up of extra tables and chairs, and Bartlett is quite a dab hand at lighting. I have no intention of leaving everything to you." That should enable his men to roam freely.

Oh, the house can hold more than these." Megan held out the paper with its list of names. Hers had been the original idea, so Rowena was glad to let her enthuse over the prospect of a glamorous evening at Gulls Walk. She was still feeling guilty that Megan had not been included yesterday. There might have been less heartache if her friend had come, or secrets to hide. Inwardly, she sighed.

"Certainly this number should be no problem." Rowena tried to match Megan's eagerness, glad to have common ground, but the Spaniard had seen the shadow cross her face. What was bothering her now? Perhaps he could cheer her up.

"And you two can make up your own list. The more, the merrier." he said. But merry was not exactly how he was feeling. "You must have many local friends. And ask Miles, too." By all means, the enigmatic Miles must be there.

Pulling herself together, Rowena gave her attention to the new list that Megan was making, conscious of Rob's quizzical expression.

"Of course we will ask Miles. He will love the idea." At least, she thought he would; though she remembered his anger when she had first talked about taking a tenant. He hadn't been thrilled with the idea of a stranger on the premises. But this was different, and he would be happy to see Gulls Walk in a festive mood—as would she. Indeed, they all would be happy. She smiled brightly at the Spaniard.

"Oh, this is fun!" chattered Megan. "Let's ask the Peterson twins, and the Egans. Then there are David and Alison Maynard."

"And there are the Stedmans." Rowena included names of others who had been her grandfather's friends, ones whom she knew would love to see

Gulls Walk again, particularly in party spirit. They would all be glad to see the old lady dance once more.

"And we mustn't forget Mr. Whitford." Rob chimed in.

In one startled moment, all Rowena's fears came tumbling back. She had almost forgotten about death duties and her desperate need for money. She had been fooling herself, for she really was only marking time with a short-term tenant. She lowered her face.

"Of course." She answered in a colourless voice.

There it was again. This shutting out of the world. What have I said this time? thought Rob.

The list was completed, the date settled, and the next few days saw the dispatching of invitations and constant comings and goings of various of the Spaniard's people as plans were made. Since Miles was away, his invitation was left to wait for him at the farm; it hardly seemed worth while to post it as he might be home any time.

The old staff returned to help in the preparations and to relieve Rowena from most of her chores, and a couple of Rob's men became almost permanent fixtures as they cleaned windows and polished floors throughout the house, wherever visitors might wander. Rob swallowed his guilt over the secret, though meticulous, search he instructed them to make, for it had to be done. But not even the bottle of Spanish sherry in the library's decidedly sparse liquor cabinet could be considered anywhere near the quality of the wines in the cases on the island. He could feel only relief when his men reported back empty handed.

Now, if he could search the farm, perhaps he would find some answers there; but the best his men could do was keep an eye on the place, for either Heron or one of his workers was always about.

In the midst of all the hustle and bustle, Miles Gilbert returned.

"What the hell is going on?" He looked immensely angry as he accosted Rowena in the hallway late one afternoon, only a few days before the ball.

"Oh, Miles. How nice to see you back." She smiled uncertainly at him. "Didn't you get your invitation?"

"Yes, I did, but why a ball? I thought you were broke."

"I am. Nothing's changed. But Rob wants to throw a party."

"Rob? You mean the Spaniard?" His introduction to Roberto Olivares had been cursory, and they had seldom met after the first occasion on the dock. Apart from deliberately displaying affection to Rowena whenever the Spaniard was near—for no one was going to step on Miles Gilbert's preserves—he had ignored the man.

He wondered just what had been going on while he had been away. Rowena had shown little liking for her tenant before Miles had left.

"Yes, Don Olivares, of course. He's paying for it. And he told us to ask our friends. You are coming, aren't you?"

Aware that his anger was bewildering Rowena, he summoned up a smile. "Oh, that's a relief. I thought you might be trying to foot the bill yourself, and I was concerned." He hoped he sounded convincing enough. He put an arm around her shoulder and hugged her close so that she couldn't see his eyes. "Of course I'm coming. Wild horses won't keep me away." He managed to laugh, though the last thing he wanted was for the Spaniard to show such an interest in Gulls Walk; especially now.

A faint frown appeared on Rowena's face. Why was Miles so inordinately angry? But she tried to put away any worry as he kissed her forehead, attempting to smooth the lines away.

"Well, I can't be happier for you, Precious. I had been visualising you moping away, making every penny stretch as far as two. I thought you must have gone off your rocker! You can understand how that frightened me."

Suddenly, a new thought occurred to him. Seeing Gulls Walk in splendour surely would be even more likely to make Rowena want to hold on. And that could only be to his advantage. He needn't worry about the Spaniard, who was only temporary. After Olivares was gone, she would have to come to Miles for help. He would lend her the money. She would have no way to pay him back, so then, with a little gentle squeezing, he would marry her, which would be cheaper than buying the whole place. Ownership of the manor house was so near he could almost taste it.

Yes, the ball was turning out to be a good idea after all.

Much more cheerfully, Miles continued, "What's the party in aid of? I thought that you and the Spaniard were barely on speaking terms."

"Oh, that's all over. He isn't so bad really." Understatement of the year, she thought. "He has business people he needs to entertain, so he thought he would hold the party here, and he is paying me extra. I didn't tell him about the death duties, though. I don't want him to know just how bad things really are; you won't tell him anything, will you, Miles?"

She looked up at him in sudden fear. Whatever casual feelings the Spaniard had for her, she didn't want pity to be added to the list, for he would not be pleased if he had to leave before his lease was up, which could happen if the probate people came too soon, possibly demanding she sell the manor to pay the death duties.

That could also mean he might demand a return of part of the rent. Something about a sinking ship. Perhaps she was not being fair. After all, he was being kind: hardly a rat. But the metaphor seemed particularly apt.

Her concern could not have delighted Miles more. "Of course, I won't tell! It's none of his business anyway." He had not been unaware of the dark attraction of the man, and the less Rowena wanted to pour her troubles into Olivares' undoubtedly sympathetic ear, the better for Miles. "A party will be wonderful, I'm sure. We'll dance until dawn, my precious."

His anger had gone. Indeed, he now looked remarkably pleased. Rowena cringed a little at his pet name, but she understood and appreciated his concern for her financial woes.

"By the way," Miles continued; "I don't suppose you have a couple of extra invitations, do you? Heron has arranged for some potential cattle buyers to visit this weekend; he didn't want to put them off and risk losing a sale. They're older men who probably won't want to stay up late. I haven't met them, but I expect I should do my social duty. I can hardly leave them to their own devices."

"Of course you may bring them. They will be welcome." Rowena managed to smile at her neighbour. But the list was growing extremely long; she hoped Rob would not mind.

"Thank you, my sweet. I've missed you, you know, Precious; but I'm staying here until after the ball, so if there is anything I can do to help, let me know." He gave her another hug and kissed her, too busy with his own thoughts to notice the wry expression on Rowena's face—or the Spaniard who had just come from his wing and was standing in the shadows.

With a cheerful wave, Miles returned to Home Farm

Rowena had seen little of Rob since their sail to the island. There had been no more morning rides, for he had been busy with various trips to London. Today he had come back early having returned on his yacht from Penzance to where he had gone that morning. It was almost as quick to sail there as to drive through the winding country lanes, for Gulls Walk was off the beaten track; and it gave him an opportunity for the fresh air he missed by not riding each morning. He entered through the terrace door, so Rowena had not seen him return.

She turned from saying good bye to Miles with a small smile on her face, relieved that he had gone, and that he hadn't asked any more awkward questions. She shrugged away the fears he had reawakened, hoping he would keep his promise to remain silent about the death duties.

She lifted her chin; there was too much to do and she was determined to get as much pleasure as she could out of the next few days. Eat, drink and be merry! It was almost laughable. She managed a chuckle.

She nearly careened into the Spaniard as she crossed the Great Hall. Startled, she blushed as tingling warmth flooded her body. Whatever her fears and worries, she could not keep the glow of pleasure and the brightness out of her eyes.

"Oh, Rob; I didn't know you were back."

"Evidently." His own dark eyes were hooded. What the hell was going on? He had been so positive about her reaction of fear when he had asked if she were going to marry Miles Gilbert. And now, just in time to catch her neighbour's departure, Rob had watched her being kissed by him, and being called Precious. Why had she been so adamant that she would never marry the man? Had she changed her mind since then? She certainly looked happy enough. Yet he was so sure that he had seen not only fear, but also considerable distaste in her eyes that night at dinner. And also, he could have sworn that she had not been averse to his own approaches. He remembered the interlude on the yacht.

He was tired. The long days in London, and sessions with the local police, had brought little results; and research into Gilbert's out-of-town entrepreneurial activities had not uncovered the long-established wealth that his lifestyle seemed to suggest. But the bank's balance sheets showed regular, remarkably large influxes of money from his Pentraegon Cove company.

Oh, Rowena, the Spaniard thought, I truly believed that you had no part in this. He dragged his eyes back to the face looking up at him.

"I'm afraid we have two more guests." Rowena began, uncertainly. She had a feeling that now was not a good time. For some reason, Rob looked far from pleased. "I do hope that is all right?"

"Whatever you and Megan decide is fine." Abruptly, he walked away. He was in no mood for trivial details.

Bewildered, she watched him go. Her tiny bubble of attempted happiness hadn't lasted long.

The last few days before the ball were a whirl of activity. All the replies to the invitations had arrived, most of them with eager acceptance, and Rowena answered many inquiries as to choice of costume. Her reply was usually the same. "Just imagine you are coming to a party given by the first Morgan

Pentraegon. You can dress up as anyone from that period; a country peasant to a courtier of Queen Elizabeth."

Refusing to be daunted by her tenant's preoccupation, Rowena was too busy to worry, even about the smugglers. She had not been able to catch Rob alone so heard nothing of any police investigations, and there had been no reports of contraband discoveries in the local paper. He and Bartlett appeared from time to time to chivvy the various workers, and each time he gave her a quick glance, but he made no attempt to broach the subject. She supposed the police were taking care of it, and it was none of her business, anyway.

By now her mind was full of a thousand details. She poured over Morgan's diary with the caterer, and they found dishes that could be copied. The clever man was even going to try his hand at a boar's head surrounded by stuffed partridges. Of course, he was going to use a local pig and Cornish hens, but he was sure he could manage to create life-like tusks.

Rowena had rummaged through the remaining silks and satins in the old sea chests to see what she could find for their costumes. Megan was to be a saucy serving wench. A foamy, off the shoulder white blouse, with a black velvet waistcoat, was the top. The voluminous skirt, Rowena made out of some vividly striped taffeta that Megan chose, though it could have been designed for the Moulin Rouge rather than an Elizabethan kitchen. It certainly reminded her of costumes that Toulouse-Lautrec had drawn. But Megan was delighted with it; and to wear under, masses of petticoats were easily concocted.

Her own costume took a little longer. She made a tight-fitting bodice out of rich, embroidered, deep emerald-green brocade. Into it she set great puffed sleeves, which she slashed to show fine diamonds of cream satin. She contrived cuffs and ruffles from pieces of delicate Brussels lace that had originally belonged to her grandmother. She even managed to create a farthingale out of yards and yards of curtain cord wrapped around a wire frame. It held the skirt, made from the same brocade, away from her hips and emphasised her tiny waist. At the front, the material was divided to show a cream underskirt made from the same silk as the diamond shapes in the sleeves.

Rowena was pleased with the effort but decided it needed more sparkle. Rummaging through old costume jewellery, she found ropes of seed pearls and spent quite a few hours stitching them all over the sleeves and skirt until the whole costume glistened. When it was finished, she eagerly tried it on.

Perhaps it needed one more touch. She fastened a single, pearl drop earring to a fragile lace handkerchief and pinned the concoction to her hair to make a headdress.

Stepping back to look at herself in the long mirror, she couldn't help but be pleased. The vivid green enhanced her own colouring, and made her eyes darker, almost mysterious. The soft swell of her breasts against the froth of the delicate ruffles, and the slenderness of her waist, emphasised by the farthingale, suggested enough delights to enchant any man. A far cry from jeans and shabby shirts.

She found herself wondering what her ancestor had worn at that first ball, and if she had scorned the advances of any young men who tried to pay her court since her sea captain had gone. Had she stood in lonely isolation?

Rowena shivered. But enough of that; there was no time to daydream. Carefully, she hung her costume in the wardrobe, pleased with her efforts. No one, not even Megan, was to see it before the night of the ball.

Friday came. The Spaniard had spent the last two days in London. It was late when he returned, and he felt particularly tired as he entered the house. All police and Interpol inquiries about new smuggling organisations had reached a blank wall. And no one had attempted to land on the island where near by an old fishing trawler was being used as an observation point. He poured himself a drink and wandered into the Great Hall to see how everything was progressing.

Rowena stood looking at the mess left by the gardening people. Trees and bushes were banked in their pots at the base of the two staircases, and the dais between, where the small orchestra was to be. Both areas looked lovely, but in the morning she must see that the debris was removed and the floor buffed over again. Some of the workmen had been clumsy, not very good at their job. She hoped they would be more careful tomorrow.

"And how is my hostess?" Rob put away his worries and smiled down at Rowena. She had smudges of soil on her face. "I thought I told you not to do anything."

"Typical male!" she grinned back. It was so wonderful to see his smile. She felt a blush suffuse her cheeks. Turning away she waved her hand at the shrubbery. "I suppose you think this got organised by a wave of my magic wand."

He laughed. It was all he could do not to take her in his arms. "I might have known that you couldn't keep your nose out of everything." Gently he rubbed away a particularly grubby spot from its tip. "And I do know something of your magic."

His grin became lopsided as he took a handkerchief from his pocket. Taking her chin in his hand, he began to work on the rest of the smudges.

When he had finished, he dropped a light kiss on her forehead. Her mouth looked oh, so tempting.

"Well, tell me about it all. Are we nearly ready?" His eyes skimmed over the woodland effect that had been achieved. It looked like a paradise. A Garden of Eden, he thought, but was there a serpent?

"Almost. Only the vases of flowers have to be done, and those we will do in the morning. We've had such fun."

She was silent for a moment. "I've been looking in the papers. There's been no report. What's happening about the smugglers? It's all a bit scary."

"Oh, don't worry your pretty head. It's being taken care of. We've a party to go to, remember?"

He dropped an arm across her shoulder and turned to look around. That way, she couldn't see his face. His eyes had grown sombre. This waiting was beginning to get to him. There had been no unusual activity along the coast or at Home Farm. His men had turned up nothing. And night after night, the island was watched. Yet he felt a constant undercurrent, as if something were building up to a climax. Though when? He had much bigger fish to catch than a few stolen cases, even though some of their contents were lethal.

But he must hide his worries. He mustn't spoil Rowena's happiness, whether it included Miles Gilbert or not.

"I hope you have a pretty costume to wear. Who are you coming as?"

"Ah! That's a secret. You'll find out tomorrow." He had changed the subject so abruptly, she hesitated. He obviously didn't want to talk about the island and its hidden contents. She wondered why he had clammed up. Didn't he trust her? She pulled away slightly, hurt by his withdrawal, but he seemed not to notice.

"I'll look forward to then." He moved to the stairs. "You'd better get your beauty sleep; see you in the morning." She watched him go, a small ache in her heart.

CHAPTER FOURTEEN

The early morning, bright and clear, gave promise of a lovely summer day. Rowena was up at the crack of dawn supervising the last minute polishing and cleaning. She and Jason cut great bunches of flowers from the gardens while the dew was still on them. The various vases were already filled with water awaiting her arrangements.

She worked eagerly all morning, darting from one area to another, trying not to fall over the caterers, or the workmen who were organising extra tables and chairs to place around the Great Hall and on the terrace where the guests were to sit for dinner.

Earlier in the week, she had decided that everyone should see Queen Elizabeth's portrait, so the library, also, was opened for guests. Her decision had not been without a tinge of fear. She hated the thought that this might be the last time she would see Her Majesty in her true setting, with Gulls Walk in festive mood. But this morning she refused to think of that as she placed a bowl of yellow roses beneath the portrait. *ET QUAM SALUTAMUS CUM OBSEQUIO* . . .

She chuckled over the words, and with suitable humility, she curtseyed to the stately lady. "I hope you enjoy the ball, too." The rough translation, 'OF SHE WHOM WE DO HOMAGE PAY WITH OBEISANCE . . .' seemed so apt.

Rowena even opened the box in which the chain with its bronze medallion lay. She put the contents on display in the glass case beside Morgan Pentraegon's diary, his other papers, and the history pamphlet. Usually the case was kept locked, but everything that was part of Gulls Walk deserved an airing that day. She lingered over the diary, opening it and reading one of her favourite passages: it seemed so appropriate

The House must be kepet Cleansed, and oft Perfumed, Sweet Scents being a thing most agreeable to Us. To this ende,

Lavender, Rosemary, Apple Mint and Sweetbrier Rose shall be Planted with other Herbs, the names of which I wot not.

Dear old Morgan, she thought. She could just imagine his bluff manner as he gave his orders. And there was another passage;

We shall not be Pent up in narrow ill-favoured Roomes. The men must bee Carefulle to doe Things curiously and thorowly well from the first, For Our most plentifull and certain Gaine after with Long Continuance.

There was nothing narrow or ill-favoured about all the efforts that had been made to make Gulls Walk look beautiful that day. She sighed. If only the 'long continuance' were possible.

But determined to make the manor live up to the original Morgan Pentraegon's expectations, she urged her staff on. And the outside was not forgotten as a group of men, under Bartlett's directions, strung pretty lanterns among the trees, and placed spot lights at strategic points so that the house would glow like a jewel when darkness fell.

Even Rob came from his wing to help. He good-humouredly fetched and carried tables, chairs, vases of flowers, whatever was needed. Just before lunch, Rowena noticed him working near her, so she asked again if there was any news. His answer was abrupt, and his eyes darted around the terrace where they were standing.

"No. Not now, Rowena." The Spaniard moved away just as Miles came out of the library.

Feeling snubbed, she greeted her neighbour with a warmer smile that usual. He grinned delightedly at her.

"Good morning, Precious. I've come to see if there is anything you need." He put an arm around Rowena's shoulder and nodded to Olivares, who turned back to placing chairs in casual groups.

"Oh, thank you, Miles. I think we are pretty well organised at the moment, but Megan is in the kitchen helping Jeannie. There's sure to be something there that needs doing." Her smile faded as he cheerfully went in through the terrace door. She hesitated, wondering if she dare ask Rob again about the smugglers. But not wanting another rebuff, she placed the last candle under its chimney and followed Miles, leaving the terrace to her tenant.

She didn't see his grim expression as he watched her enter the house.

Later in the afternoon, a few hours before the first guests were to arrive, Rowena stood in the Great Hall checking that everything was ready. The various servants were in the kitchen having a quick meal and a rest before they were needed on duty. Miles had left, and Megan and Rob had gone to their respective quarters. And so must she if she were not to be exhausted before the ball began.

She wandered from room to room. The whole house looked so beautiful. She was pleased how all her efforts had come together. She felt the wonderful warmth of anticipation. It was going to be such a lovely party.

Head on one side, she examined the hearth where she had placed an enormous urn full of velvety pink hollyhocks, blue delphiniums, the tallest of the Shasta daisies, and long fronds of fern and ivy, with clouds of Queen Anne's lace to soften the outline. It was a delightful arrangement, but it seemed to lack something, dwarfed by the size of the huge fireplace. She frowned as she cast her mind over the various tall plants in the garden, trying to decide what would help.

Then she had a brain wave; some branches of those same sweetbrier roses the diary had mentioned. They had been planted in abundance all round Gulls Walk, and replaced over the centuries; their sweet-scented leaves and pink flowers were an integral part of every summer. And bulrushes; Miles had plenty of them growing round the pond by his main barn.

She changed into a pair of Wellington boots, grabbed a pair of secateurs, and hurried out of the house up the path to Home Farm. She skirted the cobbled courtyard as quietly as she could, not wanting to disturb Miles' elderly guests in case they were resting before the evening's activity.

The bulrushes, with their long golden-green fronds and deep brown heads, were beautifully tall; the recent rains combined with the warm weather had not exactly stunted their growth. They were perfect. She visualised in her mind how well they, with the sweetbrier, would fill up the soot-darkened gap behind the urn.

She waded into the middle of the clump and was just about to start cutting when she heard voices coming from the barn through a window set high in its stone walls. She ignored them at first, for it was nearing milking time, and Heron's men must have been at their usual evening chores. It was all pretty meaningless, anyway. Then she heard a voice raised in exasperation.

"Hell, you're taking no chances. It's not your neck!"

The snuffling and champing of the cows munching on their evening feed made it difficult to hear the reply. There must have been some sort of negative answer, for a laugh followed, then another, deeper voice. "But it has to be tonight . . . London wants the goods . . . Other boats . . . guests . . . ."

Rowena frowned. What did they want delivering? Cows? Miles' pedigree herd was valuable, she knew. Yet they were never transported by boats.

The speech was cultured; certainly not one of the cowhands. More whispers and a jumble of voices. She couldn't make out the words. Then another laugh and the first voice again.

"Couldn't be better . . . need to see inside . . . plans will help . . . . When we take over . . . ."

Inside: take over: inside what? thought Rowena. Someone was plotting something. As silently as she could, she waded closer to the wall. Thank goodness she was behind the barn, so no one in the farmhouse could see her.

Next a harsh laugh. ". . . large cellars . . ." Another agitated whisper.

"That's settled then." were the next words that Rowena could make out. There was a shuffle of feet across the barn floor.

Then came a jumble of agitated whispers, none of which she was able to understand. Again the cultured voice. ". . . so what if it take hours?"

Again the whispers.

The first voice replied.

". . . no moon . . . lights on the house . . . shadows deeper."

More jumbled sounds and another harsh laugh.

"It can't be more than thirty miles."

Thirty miles. That was about the distance to the island. Suddenly it all began to make sense. Rowena had almost forgotten the smugglers, so wrapped up had she been in the ball. Dear God, what would they do if they knew she were listening? She crouched down, oblivious to the cold, dank water.

She missed the next few sentences; then louder words.

". . . get a good idea of the house . . . storage . . ." A pleased, hearty laugh this time. "It couldn't be better timing . . . No one will stop us . . . ."

Yet again an agitated whisper sounded some sort of protest.

Back came the first voice. ". . . can't wait for that damned Spaniard to leave . . ."

A jangle of argument. Then: "Hell, what are you afraid of? You're earning your money for almost nothing." The deep voice was louder, angrier.

The barn door creaked drowning the rest of the sentence; someone was pushing it open.

Rowena sank lower, hoping they would go straight to the farmhouse. She tried to piece together some sort of meaning to the jumble of words.

It was the deep voice again, loud and clear, the tone, now almost jovial, that spoke last. "Certainly these cattle are of excellent quality."

She heard steps moving away from the barn so, carefully, she peeped around the corner of the wall. There were two men, one much taller than the other who was thicker set and seemed older. She didn't recognise either of them; though, obviously, they must be Miles' guests. She watched as they, without looking back, turned the corner of the farmhouse.

Beginning to shiver in spite of the warmth of the day, she remained crouched among the rushes, not daring to move. If one of them saw her and realised that she might have overheard their conversation, she dreaded to think what they might do. And there been a third voice, though only a whisper. Heron, one of his labourers, even Miles. Whoever it was, she could still hear the rustle of movements in the barn. Now what should she do?

The slimy water was running into her Wellington boots, but she was too frightened to notice or care. Bending on hands and knees, she began to crawl further away from the building, deeper into the pond but keeping in the bulrushes. Gradually, she worked her way across to the shadows of some willow trees that dripped their fronds into the waters. Straggling weeds clung to her clothes, even her hair, as she eased herself onto the bank. She grimaced at the mess she was in, but she didn't stop.

Out of sight of the farm and the barn, she scurried up the slope and climbed over the stone wall to the road beyond. Crouching low, keeping to the grassy verge, she made for the stable yard rather than the manor house. Relieved that no one had seen her, she entered the tack room hoping to clean off the worst of the mud.

"By gosh, Miss Rowena. Where've 'ee been? 'Ee sure be proper dirty. Did 'ee fall in yon pond?" The burley figure of Jason appeared from one of the horse stalls. He couldn't help laughing as he saw the mess she was in.

"No, Jason, I didn't fall in!" She was too frightened to be concerned by her stable hand's grin. And there wasn't time to explain. "Look, we've got a problem. I can't tell you more now. Go fetch Senor Olivares. Please, Jason. Hurry. Don't speak to anyone else." Startled at the urgency of her voice and the fear in her face, he turned and ran.

She dragged one of the horse blankets around her shoulders as she leaned against the door of Goemor's box. He nudged her gently and she turned and buried her face in the smooth, silky comfort of his coat. Oh, Gramps, she thought, why did you have to leave me?

The sound of running feet brought her back to the present. Rob, with Jason behind him, hurried into the stable.

"Mother of heaven, Rowena; what on earth have you been up to?" His lips quirked into a smile. "I hope you're not going to the ball like that!" Seeing her shiver, he pulled her into his arms totally unconcerned by the mess she was in. For a moment, she worried about transferring the slime and damp to him, but it was such a relief to lay her head against his broad shoulders. Yet she mustn't crumble. Now was not the time. She drew back.

"Of course I'm not. Oh, Rob; listen. There isn't much time." She hesitated, shattered by what she had heard, and Miles' possible involvement in something she didn't understand. Bewildered, she still wasn't certain whom she could trust. "Er, Jason." She looked desperately at him.

"Oim 'ere, Miss Rowena. If 'ee be in trouble, oi'll 'elp 'ee. Your grandfather, 'e told un oi mun all'us look ar'ter 'ee." Stubbornly he crossed his arms and glowered at the Spaniard. Obviously nothing short of dynamite was going to shift Jason from his duty.

Hesitating no longer, Rowena told them both most of what she had heard. Until today she had kept her word to the Spaniard and spoken to no one about the cave, but Jason had to know. She had never questioned the loyalty of her staff before, and now was not the time to begin.

"Oh, Rob, it must have been Heron, or Miles, the other person, the whisperer, the one I didn't see."

"Now we can't be sure." The Spaniard hesitated, seeing the hurt in her eyes. Damn the man, he thought grimly. No wonder she was distraught.

"What luck that you overheard them; I'll take it from here. You've been quite marvellous. We've been waiting for a break like this. And just think, when these so-called guests of Miles come to the ball, they won't know that we are on to them, thanks to you." He tried to soothe away her fear, for he couldn't bear to see the frightened look on her face.

With a smile of assurance, he continued, "I'll get on to my contacts who'll handle everything. It seems as if those men intend to sail to the island this evening; we can catch them red-handed. Don't worry about them, they'll be dealt with." She needn't know that his own involvement now was going to be far deeper. And there was more at stake than those bottles of wine. He watched a tentative smile appear. "And we have no reason to believe that Miles is involved."

"I b'ain't never been too fond on 'im," muttered Jason, looking hard at Senor Olivares who had shown no surprise at Rowena's revelations. The stable lad was beginning to realise that the Spaniard was not what he seemed. But if

Miss Rowena trusted him, then so would he. "That blasted Master Gilbert! I seen 'im tease Miss Rowena too many times."

He clenched his fists in exasperation as he watched the Spaniard draw Rowena back into his arms. Jason grunted in some satisfaction, though. It seemed right that she should be there, particularly since he had long feared that she might marry Miles Gilbert.

"Come, my love, we've got work to do." Rob grinned down at Rowena. "I somehow don't think you want our guests to see you looking like a decidedly damp water nymph." Warm chestnuts, she thought for a moment. Then, in startled remembrance of the time and her filthy state, she pulled herself together. There were less than a couple of hours before the ball was due to begin.

"Oh, my hair," she groaned.

Inwardly breathing a sigh of relief, Rob laughed. She would be all right now. Feminine vanity was a wonderful thing.

"Ee! Thee do be that dirty." Jason joined in the laughter.

Rowena, with the Spaniard, ran across the yard and through the side door. Jason watched them go, the amusement fading. Then he, too, hurried after them. His face hardened with resolve. Come hell or high water, he was going to be at the ball where he could watch over his mistress, not working behind the scenes as had been his original instructions. Nothing was going to happen to her if he could help it. The Senor's men could look after parking the guests' cars and overseeing the mooring of the boats of those guests who would be coming by sea.

But first he had better find himself some suitable clothing so he could be presentable. Maybe the Spaniard's servant Bartlett could lend him a waiter's jacket.

Meanwhile, Rob had work to do. He helped Rowena remove the waterlogged Wellingtons, then watched her creep up the back stairs to her bedroom, avoiding the kitchen where the servants were beginning the final preparations. Next, he drew out his cell phone, making sure no one was near, and dialled a number. There was no time to waste. He spoke softly for some minutes, then ended, "I hardly think much before at least eleven because of the tide. My men will be watching. And I'll need that equipment."

He put away the phone with a satisfied sigh. He had hated the waiting. He bounded up the stairs two at a time. Now they could make progress. And his instinct had been right, Rowena was not involved. He felt as if a great load had been lifted from his shoulders. Thank God his analytical mind had been wrong.

But he couldn't shake the other concern; she cared for that damned Gilbert, and he for her; his repeatedly calling her 'Precious' proved that, and she had accepted the endearment. It must have been shattering to discover that the friend she had known all her life was possibly involved in something illegal. He shook away the thought. He still had much to do before he could go to the ball.

Rowena scrubbed her hair until she thought her scalp would peel. Repeated showering gradually removed the dreadful stench and, after drenching herself lavishly in perfume, she blew-dry her hair, twisting it into ringlets, for she had no time to style it any other way. Its flyaway tangle, she hoped, might be considered appropriate for a sixteenth century maid, if not for a twentieth. The merest touch of make-up and she was ready to dress.

She slipped on her costume, fastened her grandmother's necklace, and pinning the lace handkerchief in place so the drop earring glistened on her forehead.

There! She looked at herself in the mirror. Her face was flushed. The vivid green, embellished with the sparkle of seed pearls, was a perfect foil for the rich red of her hair. She wondered if that first Rowena had been similarly dressed. In almost a daze, forgetting the present, her mind wandered back those hundreds of years. Perhaps she understood a little how her ancestor must have felt. How miserable and lonely she must have been, waiting and hoping. Rowena shivered with a queer sense of depression, almost déjà vu.

There was a quiet knock at the door.

"Come in." she called, thinking it was Megan.

"Captain Roberto Igado Guilio Alberoni Olivares at your service, Ma'am." Looking incredibly handsome, in the rich costume of a Spanish grandee, flourishing a wide-brimmed, feathered hat, her tenant bowed low.

Rowena felt a strange frisson of excitement ripple through her body. She swallowed, trying to control the sudden, rapid beating of her heart.

"Captain Olivares," she curtseyed. "The first Miss Rowena Pentraegon bids you welcome." She kept her head low, trying to hide her wild blushes.

"Does she, little Porcupine?" His voice was deep and soft. He moved into the room and took her hand, helping her to rise. "You look lovely. I might have guessed that you would come as your ancestor."

His eyes drank in the tiny waist, the creamy skin, and the vivid, dramatic costume. A far cry from the sodden, bedraggled pixie he had held in his arms in the stable. He found himself wanting to bury his face in her glorious mane of titian hair; a Botticelli painting personified. He moved closer. Shyly, she lifted her head.

Suddenly Rowena gasped. She pushed on the hard chest and stumbled away. He saw astonishment, then horror, drain her face of colour. She backed across the room, her hand to her mouth, fearful eyes on the chain around his neck.

"No," she moaned. "No, it can't be. Oh, it'll happen again. Dear God, no!"

Turning from the Spaniard, she flew to the door, running as fast as her legs would carry her. She hardly knew how she got down the stairs.

When she reached the library door, she paused, trying to control her tumultuous heart beat. Was there a simple solution?

But of course. He must have been there first. He'd seen the medallion in the case and had borrowed it; it had to be that one.

What on earth had she been thinking? The shock, on top of the jumble of incoherent thoughts that she had been dreaming, imagining herself to be that long dead Rowena, had almost unhinged her. One minute, she had been gazing at a black velvet doublet shot with gold embroidery, conscious of her heart beating faster as the Spanish sea-captain drew nearer. Then her eyes had rested on dull, bronze links from which was suspended the large, round disc, just like the one the first Morgan Pentraegon had valued so much.

Thrusting open the door, she rushed over to lift the glass lid under which she had placed the open box.

But it still contained the original! How could that be?

She felt the tears on her cheeks, cutting away the centuries like cold slivers of ice. The diary had said that the first Rowena's sea captain had left long before Gulls Walk had been built, and had taken his medallion, the replica of this one, with him. So had she imagined the chain, with its ancient coin, around her tenant's neck? Was it a dream?

Now came the harsher realisation, which her subconscious mind had known for weeks. She would be utterly devastated if Rob were to leave. She had tempted fate. Would this evening's ball mark the end of her secret yearning? She sank over the display case, overwhelmed by her own realisation.

The door crashed open behind her, and she was dragged to her feet.

"What is it, Rowena?" The Spaniard pulled her close, iron arms refusing to release her in spite of her struggles. "No, keep still; tell me what's the matter."

"This medallion," Hardly daring to believe it was real, Rowena touched it. "Where did you get it?"

"It's been in my family for centuries. Why?"

He followed her finger as she pointed to the glass case.

"Good Lord! It's the same." The crude Spanish galleon glinted in the long rays of the evening sun. He remembered that he had put on his own medallion with the same face in view. "But why did you run away? What frightened you? There must have been many of these made. Mine is a relic of the time of the Armada."

"So is mine. And there were only these two." His attempt at a rational explanation only served to agitate Rowena more. "Look, read the pamphlet." She took it from its place next to her own medallion. "You don't understand. It's all in the diary. He left, and he didn't come back."

"Who left and didn't come back?"

"The captain, the Spanish captain; oh, read the book. It explains it all." Her thoughts flew raggedly round her mind. She couldn't seem to grasp the present, so bewildered was she by the past.

Rob took the pamphlet from her and drew her to sit beside him on the window seat. She watched him as he read.

"So this is the story of Gulls Walk. But why the tears, Rowena? The coincidence is remarkable, but surely not frightening."

He was right. She must pull herself together. One last sob escaped her.

"He left, and didn't come back," she repeated.

Then she got to her feet quickly; she shouldn't have said that. Suddenly, the library seemed to swirl around her as the combined shocks of the day took their toll. She couldn't seem to find the glass case to return the pamphlet. The shadows darkened and she began to fall.

When Rowena came to her senses, she was stretched out on the window seat. Gradually she remembered what had happened and tried to struggle to her feet. She could hear the sounds of the orchestra tuning up. Guests would be arriving soon.

"Don't move," a voice admonished her. The Spaniard rose from where he was kneeling beside her. She became aware of amber lights, chestnuts, and warm fires. She couldn't seem to concentrate. A whimsical expression lifted the corners of Rob's mouth softening his look of concern. "Here, drink this." He held a glass to her lips. "It will make you feel better."

She spluttered as the fiery brandy burned her throat, but it did the trick. Colour began to return to her cheeks.

"So you think that history is about to repeat itself, do you?"

Rowena lowered her eyes. She had already said too much. Ignoring the question, she mumbled an apology. "I'm sorry I fainted. It must have been that wretched duck pond." She gave a shaky laugh. "I got rather cold. And seeing that medallion threw me. But I'm fine now."

"No more secrets, little porcupine." There was a new light in his eyes and his voice had deepened. "History won't repeat itself, I promise you." He put an arm around her shoulder, then hesitated. Perhaps now was not the time. There was still the enigmatic Miles to deal with. First things first. He touched the medallion on his chest.

"The original owner was certainly a captain of a ship of the Armada, one of my family's ancestors. Perhaps he was that same captain who loved Rowena in your story. I don't know. But in any case, he could not have returned to England, however much he wanted. He died in prison."

For a moment, she was too startled to take it in. So the first Rowena had not been forgotten.

"But why? What happened? Who imprisoned him?"

"When he returned to Spain, without his ship, of course, a less than grateful nation stripped him of most of his possessions and condemned him. This medallion was one of the few things his family was allowed to keep, for it was considered worthless, though he set much store by it. Sadly, he only lived a short time. King Philip had little understanding of failure. So you see, he couldn't come back to Cornwall." He watched the light return to Rowena's eyes.

"How sad," she murmured softly; "but I'm so glad he didn't just forget his Rowena."

And neither will I, thought the Spaniard.

There was little time for further explanations, for voices could be heard in the Great Hall. Rob touched Rowena's cheek.

"Does that make you feel better? And this Spanish captain certainly has no intention of leaving Gulls Walk just yet, if you don't want him to?" He made it a query as he got to his feet.

Not want him to? Dear God! she thought. But was he just being kind?

Rowena put down the remains of her brandy and tried to reply. She sensed pity, and that was the last thing she wanted. Perhaps she should explain just why she had fainted; how her jumbled thoughts had seemed so real; how the ghost of her ancestor had walked over her grave. Though surely that first Rowena need never haunt Gulls Walk again.

Gulls Walk! Her heart had lifted; now it plummeted once more. The millstone of her problems was not about to go away just because one mystery had been solved. The threat of the probate office still hung over her head.

And there was the more immediate problem. A feeling of foreboding touched her with its chill. Miles and his guests. But she tried to pull herself together, to catch again the pleasure and anticipation of the morning.

She smiled as brightly as she could. "Yes, I feel so much better. Though it's such a sad story, I'm sure my ancestor is at peace now. I think I'll wear the other medallion to celebrate." Rowena ignored her tenant's query. She would think about that later. She got to her feet, walked over to the glass case, and lifted the chain from its box. She held it out for Rob to compare.

"You're right. They are the same. At least, on the front." He turned them both over rubbing his fingers over the uneven backs. "Curious." he said; then carefully, lifting her hair, he hung the original around Rowena's neck. His fingers rested for a moment against her soft skin. Unnerved at the tingle of his caress, she pulled away.

"Our guests. What must they think of us? We must go."

He was quicker than she and caught her arm as she tried to reach the door. "Is that all?" he whispered. There was something false about the brightness of her smile. For a few moments the barriers had been forgotten, but now they were back again. She crumbled against his broad chest. "One of these days you are going to have to stop running, you know, little porcupine." He lowered his head, his eyes flaming. This time the gentleness was gone; just a hungry need remained. His mouth covered hers and his arms wrapped her close. "Promise me you'll be happy this evening," he muttered against her lips.

If only life were that simple. Tomorrow she would try to explain, she told herself. What right had she to be happy? Would he understand how bound she was to Gulls Walk's desperate need? But, dear God, she could not resist his kiss.

Neither of them heard the opening of the door, nor the startled gasp before it was closed again.

CHAPTER FIFTEEN

Surely it was only a moment, but it seemed like an eternity. The sounds of laughter and voices outside the library door brought them both to their senses. Breathing deeply, the Spaniard released her.

A woman's voice could be heard, "And have you seen Gulls Walk's treasures? There is a portrait of Queen Elizabeth in the library." Not waiting to hear more, he hurried Rowena through the door onto the terrace beyond. He paused for a moment, not ready to greet their guests. Where could he take her? There were lights everywhere. He grinned down at her, his eyes brilliant with laughter, a younger, almost carefree Rob.

"Quick, my apartment. I'm not about to share you yet."

At last a bubble of happiness rose in Rowena's throat. Perhaps this was more than sympathy, which had been all she had dared to read.

Though what was the use? For she was still a girl with a millstone of debt around her neck. She tried to draw away. "No, Rob. We must go back. Our guests will be wondering where we are."

A faint frown touched the Spaniard's face. Again a mercurial change. He sighed; would he ever really get through to her? There was still something holding her back; and yet when he had kissed her he had been so sure.

Suddenly he made a decision. He must trust her; show her his trust; be totally honest with her. Then, perhaps, she would trust him.

Quickly, he reached for her hand again and hurried her across the terrace to his own wing. He pushed open the door and drew her inside.

A very different Bartlett was pouring over some maps when they entered. He seemed taller, more assured. Hurriedly, he attempted to shield the table from Rowena's view.

"Don't worry, Tom. It's about time our landlady knows the set-up. Rowena, my love, meet Sergeant Tom Bartlett of the Special Branch. He's not exactly a valet or butler, but at least his wife is an excellent cook."

Startled, Rowena's eyes darted from one to the other. If he were a policeman, then what was Rob?

"I'm sorry that we had to deceive you, Miss Pentraegon, but someone had to look after the Senor and his problems, not only his stomach." Both men grinned at her. But there was no answering sparkle in Rowena's eyes.

"You mean your being at Gulls Walk was all planned?" She frowned at Rob. A cold, hard stone seemed to sink where her heart had been. "You're not here because any place in this part of Cornwall would do? You're not here for a holiday, for a rest?" She shivered. She had been manipulated. "What if I hadn't wanted a tenant?"

"Oh, that was a Godsend. It couldn't have been more opportune; though we would have found somewhere near if not." The Spaniard frowned. There was a coldness to her questions.

"But why? Did you already know about the smugglers? That there were illegal activities going on here? You obviously must have thought that I, as well as Miles, was involved."

"Well, not exactly." How could he tell her that suspicions had been of her grandfather at first, long before any plans had been made to stay at Gulls Walk? After all, the bill of lading, which had been found in the truck way back in early spring, had the address of Pentraegon Cove. The police had assumed complicity between Gulls Walk and Home Farm since they were the only properties in the small valley. But months of observation and careful inquiries had turned up nothing. Perhaps the commandeering of the truck had forced those involved to lie low.

But he could tell her that Pentraegon Cove seemed to be the source of contraband, and the police had decided to make closer contact; hence, the planting of himself right on the spot.

"I volunteered to help since quantities of my own shipments of wine had been stolen," he finished his shortened explanation.

Rowena's expression hardened. She was no fool.

"So that was why you were so angry at the beginning." She wrapped her arms around herself to stave off the sudden chill. "Even before you had found out who I was, you had decided that someone in this house was guilty. No wonder you showed no interest in leaving. That wouldn't have suited you at all. Perhaps you had already marked me as the criminal; you certainly stalked me like a cat stalking a mouse."

Vividly, she remembered his behaviour in the library that afternoon weeks ago when he had discovered who she was. And his attempt to mend his fences that same evening.

"It seems that you are a remarkably good actor, Senor Olivares."

"Not always, little porcupine." His words were soft. "Look, I can understand your anger, but you have to trust me now. There isn't time for long explanations. What I did was necessary. You must realise it was essential. There is much more at stake than a few hurt, personal feelings." He reached to take her in his arms again. "Look, my sweet, all that is past. I'm trusting you completely now. Of course I know that you're totally innocent. Don't you want to see these criminals caught?"

He sighed as she shrank back angrily. The light and warmth had died from her face. "Please, Rowena, we still have a great deal to do, and a trap to set. And I need your help. We mustn't let Miles, or anyone, suspect we are watching." Perhaps action would jolt her back to the urgency of the moment. Damn Miles Gilbert, he thought.

Her help? Rowena was startled. She tried to pull herself together. Of course. Why had she not realised? It had all been a ploy. He wanted her on his side, not Miles'.

But her anger subsided as she realised she was not being fair. She dug deep into the little strength she had left after the many shocks of the day. She had grown up considerably in the last few weeks. Her indignation faded. What right did she have to be angry? She had no right, even, to query the Spaniard's presence at Gulls Walk. He came, he paid his rent, and he was a well-behaved, congenial tenant. She, on the other hand, had been the porcupine he chose to call her.

And her worries over Gulls Walk suddenly seemed almost out of proportion. She wouldn't be the first one to have to sell her home; life would go on. It was amazing how numb she felt. During the past weeks, she had lived for nothing but this intense desire to retain her birthright. Oh, granted, she had been absorbed in her efforts for the ball, and her growing awareness of Rob. But through it all had been this single-minded purpose.

Now that same purpose was as chaff blowing in the wind. She couldn't seem able to hold on to it. She suddenly realised that she had been trying to resurrect the history, the past security, to retain and relive the family life she had lost. Bricks and mortar could not do that, and she knew all those things would remain in her heart, whether she retained Gulls Walk or not. No wonder the sight of the Spanish medallion had so unnerved her. She had deliberately shut herself into a time warp, and yet she had functioned in the rational of today.

She lifted her hands to her eyes as if to wipe away the last of the mist. No more looking back, she thought.

What was it Rob had said? Oh, yes; he had asked for her help. The smugglers; she must concentrate, for she remembered the underlying, grave concern she had seen on Rob's face in the cave.

It had left a curious thought, which she had not really faced until now. Those cases had contained something other than wine; otherwise, why had Rob shaken the bottles? And wine, valuable as it was, would hardly have caused the involvement not only of the police, but the Special Branch and Interpol as well.

"Yes, I'll help." Rowena took a deep breath. She would bury her jumbled feelings. She had been a fool to imagine a future. Her Spanish tenant was here to do a job, and she was nothing more than a pleasant piece of flotsam washed up on the shore of his life, a piece that would be washed away with the tide when he left.

She lifted her chin. "Of course I'll help. But first, I must know something."

The Spaniard studied her face warily.

"Is this drug related?"

Both men looked grim. She was such a young slip of a girl. Trust was one thing, but Rob had hoped to spare her the knowledge of their suspicions about a new pipeline through which a cartel of drug dealers intended to flood the country. A smuggling group, she could handle, but it might destroy her to know that Miles Gilbert could be involving in selling death.

"Oh, Rowena, I had wanted to spare you this." Again he reached to hold her. Again she stepped away.

"It's all right. I hate drugs just as much as you do." She had seen students at college who had played Russian roulette their own lives. Her personal worries seemed far less important. "What can I do?"

This was a new Rowena. Mingled with concern was a glint of admiration in her tenant's eyes. It gave her strength. "First, I expect we had better show our party faces to our guests." Rowena answered her own question, allowing herself a small, grim smile. The world might suddenly be an evil place, but she was not a Cornish lass for nothing.

"You're right, of course." Her tenant paused. "Tom? Will you handle everything? I'll be back as soon as I can." Rob took the girl's arm and steered her across the room to the door. "You're sure, Rowena? Are you feeling well enough?"

"Of course. This is my house, and my country, remember. Do you really think that I would let a little thing like a faint stop me from doing my duty?" She swallowed. She would manage somehow. "And I am just as capable of acting as the next person." The small dig gave her another ounce of adrenaline.

With that, she swept out of the room as proudly as any previous mistress of Gulls Walk.

Many of the guests had arrived, and the orchestra was playing lively music to which some were already dancing. Slowly, Rowena and Rob mingled, greeting old friends and introducing those whom each had not met. All, without exception, congratulated Rowena on the beauty of the house; and many amused compliments were banded back and forth at the attempts of each guest to authenticate a true Elizabethan character.

The fireplace by now was hidden by a group of guests, all much too busy to notice any lack in floral decoration. Rowena grimaced to herself. It had seemed so important just those few short hours ago.

Down the stairs from Rob's quarters came a Spanish Grandee and his lady. Rowena, who knew neither of them, walked forward, forcing a welcoming smile.

"Good evening, my lord, my lady; I'm Rowena Pentraegon. Welcome to Gulls Walk." She made a deep curtsey to both of them.

"Miss Pentraegon, we are so pleased to meet you. Rob has told us such delightful things about you." The lady exclaimed as she and her husband greeted Rowena. "And this house; it is so beautiful. No wonder my dear brother has fallen in love with it." Below the exquisite black mantilla, laughing, amber eyes sparkled with great kindness.

Chestnuts, brightly glowing fires, Rowena could not fail to recognise the same warmth. "Oh, you must be Margarita. I'm so glad you could come." She remembered the photo in the yacht's cabin.

Both her hands were taken and held between long, slender fingers. Then the smiling face looked beyond Rowena. "And speaking of the devil."

"Ah, so you're finally ready, dear sister. Let me introduce you to Miss Rowena Pentraegon, my charming landlady." Rob grinned as he placed a firm hold on Rowena's shoulder. "Margarita and her husband Dr. Carlos Mendoza arrived while you were dressing. They're here for a few days."

"Yes. And glad to be here, Miss Pentraegon. I managed to re-arrange my surgery schedule and steal some time off. I wouldn't have missed seeing . . ." A nudge from his wife changed what Carlos was about to say. "Gulls Walk." he concluded with a grin.

"So you approve of this treasure I've found?" Rob questioned his sister.

There was a twinkle in Margarita's eyes as she answered. "Oh, the house is just wonderful. All it needs is a crowd of children. Your nephew would love it." She gave a far from lady-like wink to her brother as a surprised Rowena turned her head to look up at her tenant. "I always knew you had impeccable taste," his sister finished.

"And you, my dear brat, need a spanking." He smiled as Carlos gently kissed Rowena on the cheek.

"Your servant, Senorita. You mustn't mind these two." His expression was kind. "Thank you for including us, and for allowing us to see your remarkable home. I work much of my time at Great Ormond Street in London, the children's hospital from where we often send our recuperating patients to places like this. Ideal. Privacy, fresh air, freedom to romp and play in safety. I must talk to you sometime about the possibility."

"Now, Darling, please get off your hobbyhorse for one night at least." Margarita had noticed Rowena almost flinch, and lower her eyes. "It's party time!"

For a moment, the future, which she had tried so hard to put on one side, came flooding back. She felt Rob's fingers tighten as he, too, was aware of her withdrawal. She shook away her morbid thoughts and determinedly she smiled. After all, it really was party time.

The next to arrive was a group of her grandfather's elderly friends amongst whom was James Whitford, the family lawyer. He, appropriately, had dressed himself as an Elizabethan man of law. With his own black court robes, a white, legal cravat at his neck, and a scull cap on his almost bald head, he looked every inch an Elizabethan prosecutor. In spite of his twinkling eyes, his costume reminded Rowena of what happened to smugglers who were brought to justice. And those who couldn't pay their probate taxes. She faltered, then pulled herself together.

"Mr. Whitford, I'm so glad you could come. The old girl looks a bit happier than when you last saw her, don't you think?"

"My dear Miss Pentraegon, it is good to be here. You are to be congratulated. Gulls Walk certainly is as beautiful as I have ever seen her, and I am glad that Senor Olivares is able to make such good use of all her amenities." Rowena had made quite sure that Rob's name had been on the invitations. She wanted no misunderstanding about who was the host; therefore, who was paying the bill.

"Yes. I'm so happy he wanted to have his party here." With a slight dryness in her tone, she shook the old man's hand, for Megan had been the instigator.

"So am I." James Whitford looked around with nostalgic pleasure. "I remember the wonderful times we had when your grandmother was alive."

He reminisced for a few minutes. Rowena hardly heard as she smiled and nodded in the right places, for her mind was on Miles. She had deliberately suppressed the thought that he might be a criminal. Now, vivid pictures of him standing in the dock, in front of a public prosecutor, filled her mind.

Pleading the arrival of other guests, she excused herself. She needed a moment to pull herself together. Her eyes searched the Great Hall for Rob, desperately needing reassurance. He was chatting and laughing with a group as if he had not a care in the world.

Feeling a hand on her arm, she turned to find Jason looking rather uncomfortable in a jacket a size too small.

"Miss Rowena," he whispered; "They be here." She glanced beyond him. Her neighbour, and two strangers, were standing in the entranceway.

Miles was dressed in the elaborate costume of an Elizabethan courtier. His doublet was of rich, purple brocade with silver embroidery. A link chain lay under the wide ruff at his neck, and a jewelled sword hung at his side. She could not help noticing that his legs, encased in hose of the same purple shade, were not exactly well muscled. He was sporting a goatee beard and a flourishing moustache, which, with his black hair and pale skin, gave him a dark, satanic look. Grimly appropriate, Rowena thought.

"Sir Humphrey Gilbert at your service, Mistress Pentraegon." He swept off a velvet cloak that hung from one shoulder. "Perhaps I should lay this down for my princess to walk on, as my ancestor's step-brother, Sir Walter Raleigh, was purported to have done for his queen." He grinned at her, rather ridiculously twirling his moustache. "How are you, Precious?" He kissed her on the cheek.

Rowena was not inclined to be amused; truth to tell, she had a hard time even keeping a polite smile on her face as Miles turned to introduce his guests. Before he could do so, in a cultured voice, the shorter, older of the two interrupted him.

"Thank you so much for your kind invitation, Miss Pentraegon. I'm afraid that these costumes were the best we could do at short notice. I do hope that we are in keeping. Pirate Redbeard, at your service, and this is my friend, the Queen's executioner." He laughed, making no mention of their real names.

Rowena braced herself to greet the strangers. Her eyes widened. No one could possible recognise them again. Their costumes totally disguised their faces.

The pirate was sporting an enormous, false, red beard and a broad moustache. Above one eye was a bushy, equally false, red eyebrow, and over the other, a large black patch. A bandanna completely covered his head, and under it, wisps of false, red hair protruded. Even his clothes, a loose shirt and baggy trousers, obviously stuffed to increase his corpulence, were sufficiently nondescript to conceal his real shape. No wonder he had no qualms about being seen.

And the other's costume was even more bizarre.

The executioner was taller, younger, hard-bodied, and yet equally impossible to recognise. He wore loose breeches and a leather jerkin over his powerful chest; conventional enough for a sixteenth century peasant. But there the conventionality ceased. Over his head and shoulders sat a black, silk hood. All that was visible of the face underneath was the gleam of eyes through two narrow slits. He carried over his shoulder an axe, obviously a stage prop, but looking lethal enough to shine coldly in the bright light.

Rowena shivered. She wondered if he were truly capable of chopping off heads. He certainly looked as if he might. He stood with his arms crossed, appearing quite deliciously evil according to the group of admiring girls who 'ooed and aahed' at him as they passed.

Pulling herself together, Rowena welcomed him, managing to cover the slight tremor in her voice with a small laugh. "I hope we have no particular traitors you intend to drag to the tower." The man merely bowed, silently keeping in character. She indicated the direction to the bar and watched all three move away.

So much for Rob's hope that Miles' guests would be recognisable.

There seemed to be no more new arrivals just then, so Rowena drifted casually among her guests with some vague idea of keeping a distant watch over the three; though what she expected to accomplish, she had no idea. She felt helpless, not knowing what plans were being set.

Miles, she noticed, quickly became immersed in conversation with Mr. Whitford, while the other two leaned on the bar, apparently content to watch the swirling crowd. Deciding that for a few minutes at least she could carry out her duties as hostess, she went to the dining room to see that everything was set out properly in readiness for supper, which would be served later. From there she wandered onto the terrace where small groups were enjoying the evening air and dancing candlelight.

Her spirits lifted a little. The scene was enchanting. Dear Gulls Walk, she thought. I hope tonight will make up for some of the years of neglect. But her worries soon sent her back to the Great Hall.

Meanwhile, Miles was doing some research of his own.

"It's a shame that she will have to sell, Mr. Whitford. I've offered her a loan, but she won't take it. You and I will have to put our heads together to at least keep Gulls Walk in the family, so to speak."

Shrewdly, the lawyer looked at the moustached and bearded face. Miss Pentraegon's business was private, and he was not to be drawn. "I expect it will all work out," he said noncommittally.

Unaware of the snub, Miles continued.

"I told Rowena that I'm willing to buy that land if she decides to sell. I'll give her the best price, for the land, or the house, or both." He could afford to be magnanimous. When they married, whatever money he paid, after the death duties were sorted out, would be his anyway. But he had no intention of allowing anyone to say he was marrying her for her property. He smiled to himself. He could almost taste the pleasure. After four centuries, the Gilbert family would no longer be in the shadow of the Pentraegons.

"Oh, that may not be necessary." The lawyer had never liked Miles. And yet, business was business. "I'll let you know if we have to sell, though." He allowed a cool smile to touch his lips. After all, the owner of Home Farm might be prepared to pay more than a less interested buyer. Personal feelings must never close the door to a good sale.

Well satisfied that he had laid the groundwork for first chance to purchase Gulls Walk, Miles wandered in search of Rowena. His guests would be fine for a while. He found her with Megan and a group of old school friends. He put an arm around her shoulder and drew her onto the dance floor.

"Hello again, Precious. You really have excelled yourself. It's a wonderful ball. We should do this every year."

"And where do you think the money is coming from?" She felt annoyed at his presumption, and tried to pull away from his too-tight hold. Then, remembering the Spaniard's warning, she swallowed any further retort and attempted a laugh. "We'll have to dig up a pot of gold at the end of the rainbow, won't we? Or Morgan's treasure."

"Or do a little smuggling, perhaps. All self-respecting Cornish men have to do a little gulling once in a while. Who knows? I just might try my hand for you."

Rowena flinched, startled at his boldness. How dare he be so blatant? "Oh, Miles. How could you?"

"What do you mean, how could I? Of course I could. Your family has not been exactly innocent. Where do you think that wonderful old silk came from for those curtains you've made?" He laughed somewhat cynically.

Startled, she had not thought. So recent generations of Pentraegons had their secrets to hide, too. And she had profited from their illegal trade. She looked down at her own costume in some distress.

"Oh, don't worry, Precious; I'll never tell." Complacently, he pulled her closer. Another point to his advantage.

Numbly, she allowed her head to rest on his shoulder. How many more shattering revelations could she take? Perhaps even her grandfather had been involved. She shied away from the implication. And yet, here was Miles, practically admitting a similar guilt. What was she supposed to do now? Did he expect that she would be party to some sort of co-conspiracy?

They danced in silence until the music ended.

Keeping his arm around her shoulder, he guided her to a quiet corner away from the bar where most of the guests were happily quenching their thirst.

"Marry me, Precious." He still held her close. For a moment, she was startled by his sudden words. "Marry me and I'll take care of your problems. I'm becoming quite a rich man, so I'll buy Gulls Walk; then you can use the money to pay the probate taxes. I'll give the house back to you as a wedding present." Confidently, he smiled down at her.

Suddenly, she came to her senses. Hastily, she pulled away as a shudder, almost of revulsion, swept over her. No more could she endure his touch, not after he had practically admitted smuggling complicity. And yet she dare not be rude. She had told her Spanish tenant that she was as capable of acting as he, so now she must prove it.

"Oh, Miles. That's so sweet of you." She almost gagged on the words. "But no, I must sort out my problems myself. I know you are just being kind."

She tried to sound light hearted, to act normally. In spite of the conversation in the barn, and what he had seemingly revealed, she still could not believe that he was all bad. How could she? Old loyalties die hard. She tried a light laugh. "But thanks for caring. And you may take me into supper later." It would be as good a way as any to keep an eye on him as Rob had asked her, particularly as she had no idea who else was watching Miles or his guests, or who among the Spaniard's people were police.

She searched for an excuse to leave. "Meanwhile, I'd better see to my hostess duties."

With a quick smile and an airy wave of her hand, she slid from his arms. Barely noticing where she was going, she twisted her way through the couples beginning to assembly for the next dance. Miles watched her go, a little annoyed, but he had no intention of giving up so easily. He moved to the bar; he needed a drink.

The evening was warm, even for July, with a hint of thunder in the air, and Rowena was about to seek the cooler breezes on the terrace and avoid another request to dance when she saw her tenant watching her, a grim expression on his face. She found her heart beating a little faster and turned away, moving into the shadows of the staircase. She needed to calm down, to pull herself together. Perhaps she wasn't as accomplished an actress as she pretended. But before she reached the wall, she was halted by a hand on her arm.

"Hiding, little porcupine? Don't you think the host should dance with his hostess?"

At that moment, the lights dimmed, and the soft strains of a romantic ballad filled the air. The small sound of denial caught in her throat as the Spaniard drew her close.

"Come. Forget your responsibilities. Let's enjoy the moment. You look quite remarkably lovely." His eyes had darkened, but there was none of the velvet warmth. A flare of angry passion matched the grim lines beside his mouth. "Your friend Gilbert has had his turn. Surely I deserve the same treatment?" His arm tightened as he deliberately dragged her closer making her aware of solid bone and muscle. "You show a remarkable partiality to someone who could be as guilty as hell." Damn it, he thought, just what was the relationship between Miles and Rowena?

She shivered, whether from reaction to his bitter words, or the strange frissons of emotion tingling through her body, she didn't know. "But you told me to keep a watch on him." Worriedly, her eyes searched his. "I didn't want to dance with him, but it would have looked strange if I had refused."

What could he say? That she had been dancing too close, that she had hidden her face against his shoulder? God! He sounded like a love-sick Shakespearean swain. Damn you to hell, Miles Gilbert, he thought.

He tried to relax. Perhaps he had read more into the dance than had been intended. His grasp softened as they swayed to the music, but he still kept her close. "Well, you were certainly having a long conversation." He tried to focus his mind on the smuggling. "I hope you didn't say anything about my reasons for being here."

"Oh, no. Nothing about you, or today, or what I heard." She had to remove his expression of disbelief. "Actually, he proposed."

She felt his body become rigid.

"And?" His voice was cold.

"I said no, of course. Really, it's more of joke than anything." She couldn't quite keep the quaver out of her voice. She hadn't been so sure this time. "I think he just feels it's his duty, Gramps being gone." She stumbled through something about brotherly love. She was still shaken by the blatant comments on smuggling that Miles had made; but the shame of her own family's involvement in past years stayed her tongue.

Yet it seemed as if Rob were condemning him, too? Though a man was supposed to be innocent until proven guilty, wasn't he?

The Spaniard looked down at her lowered head. He sensed her withdrawal, and an element of fear. She knew something; and whatever it was, it had brought back that same cloak behind which she had hidden so many times. But instead of anger, he felt a deep desire to protect her. Dear God. If only he knew from what.

Perhaps he could lighten the moment. "Let's forget him and enjoy the music." He rested his face against her hair and chuckled. "You certainly smell sweeter than you did in the stable." Rowena pulled away remembering the conversations from the barn. How could he laugh?

He sensed her indignation. That was better. He smiled down at her. "It's all right, Rowena. Everything has been taken care of. The police are prepared. Trust me, my little porcupine." The warm glow was back in his eyes. He drew her close again, and they danced slowly around the hall until the music ended. Perhaps she could forget and just enjoy the moment. What could she say? What could she do? With a small sigh, she relaxed.

Finally, Rob returned her to a group of friends and excused himself. "Thank you, Mistress Pentraegon, I must go to see how my sister is enduring her husband's heavy feet." He grinned as he left her, but not before whispering again, "Trust me."

At last, when the long summer twilight faded, it was time for supper. The candles on the terrace were flaming brightly, and the guests meandered through the dining room, filling their plates.

Miles came to join Rowena as she listened to the compliments from the hungry people. Jason, who had been hovering around most of the evening, served them from the buffet, which groaned under the magnificent spread.

Sea food and salmon; garden and jellied salads; a huge roast of beef; slices of the large pig which had been the nearest thing to a boar the caterer could find; pheasant and duck; delicious tiny hors d'oeuvres, concocted in shapes reminiscent of Elizabethan times; dainty Cornish pasties; fresh fruits and cream; comfits and sweet tartlets. Rowena looked at her plate when they had seated themselves at a vacant table, and wondered how she was going to eat any of it. But Miles dived in with obvious relish, and no apparent concern except for the food in front of him. Oh, how can he? Rowena thought.

Megan came onto the terrace. She had a local farmer in tow, and they were looking for a table. With relief, Rowena called to them. Conversation would be easier if there were four.

They both had had a fair quota to drink, and Megan's eyes seemed to have a feverish brightness as she flirted with her bemused partner. Rowena was puzzled. This was so unlike her friend. Come to think of it, there was something different about Megan. Conversation was stilted as the men concentrated on their plates, though Megan, too, seemed not to be hungry. Finally, the meal was over.

"Well, Rowe, who're you going to marry?" Laughing somewhat shrilly, Megan drew herself away from the arm of her rather red-faced farmer who was beginning to nod off.

"To marry?" Rowena had been buried in her own thoughts and had not followed the casual chatter.

"Yes, who's to be the lucky man? Lots of money, that's what you need. After this ball, I suppose you think that Senor Roberto Olivares wins hands down. You're hogging all the men. That's not fair."

Rowena was startled. What on earth was Megan getting at?

"I've no intention of marrying anyone." Rowena knew she could and would not change her decision. 'Millstone, millstone.' The jingle went round and round her head. The responsibility was hers alone. Marriage was out of the question when she owed God knows how much money in taxes. Megan was so wrong. Yet the delicious memory of Rob's caresses still lingered, in spite of her realisation that it had been little more than manipulation.

"Oh?" Disbelief was patently obvious in Megan's voice. "You didn't look exactly negative when I saw you kissing in the library."

Aghast, Rowena frowned. This was no light-hearted banter.

Miles, too, was looking hard at her. His eyes had narrowed.

"Sorry, Miles; am I telling tales out of school? Did you think you were her only suitor?" Again the trilling laugh. The word seemed incongruously apt as they sat there in Elizabethan finery.

Rowena looked at him, not knowing what to say. How could Megan be so cruel? They had all been friends for so long. She hesitated, then turned back to protest.

But the brittle laughter had died, and there was such a look of misery on Megan's face. With it, a blazing realisation came to Rowena. Megan may have been half drunk—she would hardly have spoken like this if she had been sober—but the truth was there to see. How blind Rowena had been. While Miles had paid his seemingly well intentioned, though half-humorous court to herself, Megan had hidden her own yearning for him. No wonder she had turned her attentions to Rob.

Suddenly, Megan began to cry. She had forgotten the young farmer who, by now, was snoring peacefully. She had even forgotten the ball and the other guests.

"Miles asked you to marry him again, I heard him, back there in the hall, before supper. I knew he would. It's been 'Precious' this and 'Precious' that. I expect you're going to keep him dangling on a string." She was ignoring the subject of the conversation; all her enmity was directed at Rowena. "He didn't see what I saw, though. Why don't you tell him that he hasn't got a chance? Or do you intend to be a dog-in-the-manger? Why can't you make up your mind? You have everything."

The revelation had not only been Rowena's. Visibly shaken, Miles reached a hand to touch Megan.

"She's had too much to drink. We'd better get her out of here before she makes more of a scene."

But with an angry flounce, Megan jumped to her feet. "Damn you, Miles Gilbert! You never had any hope with her. Don't you know that!" Holding up her skirt, she ran from the terrace.

"Oh, Miles, I'm so sorry." Rowena's words seemed hopelessly inadequate. Forgotten were the police; the words in the barn; the crates hidden on the island. She had been so absorbed in her own life. How self-centred she had been. Her poor, dear Megan. Ruefully, she touched Miles' arm, but she didn't know how to bridge the awkward silence, nor to expunge the feeling of guilt.

Miles looked stunned. Megan had sounded so positive. Were his plans all for naught? He had been so sure.

"I think I'd better go." He had forgotten his own guests who had left earlier. They would serve as an excuse. Uncomfortably, he got to his feet. Murmuring some sort of conventional thanks, he left the terrace.

He felt hollow. For the first time he wondered if his desires for Gulls Walk were as important as he had imagined. He had always been so determined to live there—as had his father, and his father before him. He had been so sure that he would win, that he would marry the heir to the house, that his family name would supersede that of the Pentraegons.

But just what had Megan seen in the library? Rowena always seemed to want to keep out of Olivares' way, and certainly had shown little interest in her tenant whenever he, Miles, was around.

His head was bowed as he slipped out of the back entrance and crossed the courtyard. He had no wish to mingle with the other guests who were still in a festive mood. The party was over for him.

Rowena watched him go. What could she say? What could she do? She had been so absorbed in her own problems that she had not seen what was in front of her nose. Fond though she had been of Miles all down through the years, her affection had been based on propinquity, not desire, and she had assumed the same had been Megan's.

Feeling thoroughly ashamed of herself, she was in no mood to go back to the ball. She knew that she should be there to bid good-bye to those who would soon be leaving, but she couldn't face them.

What a travesty the evening had become. She watched the candle under its glass shade flicker and die, and a sad wisp of smoke drift up into the dark sky and disappear on the evening breeze. She sat for a few minutes longer, feeling as if all her hopes were as ephemeral as the candle flame; then she, too, slipped through to the kitchen and out of the side door.

She wandered across the lawn at the front of the house where all was quiet except for the wistful strains of some old love song, muted on the soft night air. Slowly, keeping to the grass and the shadows of the trees, she finally reached a stone seat set against the wall that divided the manor from the farm. Behind it was the track down to the beach. She sat in the darkness, looking back at the twinkling lights. Bartlett had certainly done an excellent job, she thought, as she watched Gulls Walk gleam complacently in their glow.

Yet curiously, the face of the house was blank. This side had a flat elevation, and none of the upper windows was lit. The small buttresses dividing the lower casements looked like gaps between smiling teeth. Large, greedy teeth. Rowena shivered.

For the first time, she looked at Gulls Walk dispassionately. It had been the focal point of so many lives, almost obsessively so. She, too, had become obsessed, unaware of the emotions of others. Poor Megan; somehow she must make it up to her.

There was a faint rattling of stones the other side of the wall. Someone must be coming down the path. Whoever it was stopped, and Rowena heard the low murmur of voices. She remained quiet, for she was in no mood for questions, or long-drawn-out good nights.

"We'll wait here. No one from the house can see us."

Startled, Rowena turned her head.

"Heron'd better hurry, we must be back from the island before anyone wakes up."

"You worry too much. If anyone sees us when we return and asks, we've just been for a casual fishing trip. There's no reason for anyone to suspect anything else."

Dear God. She recognised the voices. These were Miles' guests, the men in the barn, the pirate and the executioner. She froze, hardly daring to breathe.

The men stood in silence until more stealthy footsteps could be heard coming down the pathway.

Shaking off her fear, Rowena knelt on the seat and carefully peeped over the wall. Now she would find out who else was involved in the clandestine activities on the island, for surely this group must be part of the smuggling organisation her tenant was trying to uncover.

The narrow passageway was so dark she could barely make out a third man, wearing heavy rain gear as were the others, as he moved onto the soft turf carrying part of a bundle over his shoulder. Behind it, his face was hidden. He had his arm around another man who staggered under the other half of the load that looked like a fishing net. Rowena could just make out a dark cloth around his mouth, like a gag, as he stumbled and fell to the ground. His partner looked down at him in disgust.

"Get up, you damn fool." He turned to the waiting men. "Sorry I'm late," he whispered, barely loud enough for Rowena to hear; "you gave him a hell of a beating and he can hardly walk. I've had to half carry him." He shifted the load on his shoulder. "Here, help me with this. It's heavy."

"What the hell? I thought we'd decided to leave him behind." One of the waiting men stepped forward.

"I couldn't risk it, leaving him trussed up like a chicken in his state. The last thing we need is a body. He has his uses."

Rowena leaned farther, hoping to hear more of the whispered words and catch a glimpse of the various faces, unaware that her head might be silhouetted against the lights.

One of the waiting men spoke again, "You damn fool. I've spent months setting this up."

And that was the last she heard. Involuntarily, Rowena gasped. It was her undoing.

The blow caught her high on the temple, and suddenly the fairy lights around the house seemed to dance and blaze in a kaleidoscope of colour, then die into thick, deep, silent blackness.

CHAPTER SIXTEEN

Most of the evening, Jason had busied himself collecting empty glasses as he kept an eye on the chattering guests. Just before supper, he was standing in an alcove by the stairs watching Miss Rowena and Miles Gilbert dancing when he saw the two guests from Home Farm quietly sidling out through the front door. They made no attempt to look for their hostess to give normal, polite thanks. Feeling curious, Jason put down his tray and followed them. No one else seemed to be noticing their departure in spite of Senor Olivares' promise to have them followed. He wished he knew more what was going on. And where was the Spaniard, anyway?

He watched the two men cross the drive to the side path leading to the farm buildings. They were keeping to the soft grass and the shadows. Strange that they had not waited for Gilbert. Jason silently followed them and stood among the trees for a few minutes until he saw them enter the main building of Home Farm. Then he turned back wondering if he should alert someone, but Senor Olivares had said that everything was under control. He wished he could be sure.

As he re-entered the house, people were leaving the dance floor and moving into the dining room for supper. He made his way through the crowd searching for Miss Rowena, finally finding her with her neighbour. Hurrying over, he offered to serve them from the buffet. That gave him an excuse to hover close, for the Spaniard had told him to keep an eye on Master Miles as well as his guests.

After Megan and her partner joined the group, and he had served them, Jason returned to the Great Hall to look for Senor Olivares or, at least, Bartlett. He could find neither, so he went back to the front of the house hoping to find one of the Spaniard's men on watch.

Eventually, as he stood in the courtyard, he saw Miles Gilbert leave through the kitchen door and take the same side path to the farm house. He followed him part of the way to be sure.

Knowing now where all three men were, Jason definitely had to find the Senor who would decide what to do. Hardly had he returned to the entrance to Gulls Walk when the side door reopened. This time it was his mistress. Now what was Miss Rowena doing? Surely she, too, wasn't going to the farm?

Standing in the shadows, Jason watched her walk up the lawn until she was lost beyond the glow of lights. Loathe to let her out of his sight, he stealthily followed her, keeping to the darkness of the trees. She seated herself on a stone seat by the wall surrounding the property. Jason waited, uncertain what to do.

Ten minutes: fifteen: but still she sat. She looked so sad.

Yet this wouldn't do. He must find Senor Olivares who would know what the next move should be. There was no sign or sound of any activity at the farm, so surely his mistress was safe. Jason hesitated, then turned back, creeping quietly so she didn't see him. She wouldn't like it if she thought he were watching her. He would find the Spaniard, then return.

The faint crunch of footsteps on gravel made him pause. He caught a glimpse of the shadow of someone else, probably one of the Senor's watchers. Feeling happier, he continued his silent way. He had almost reached the last shrubbery by the front entrance when he heard a faint cry. Probably only a night owl, he thought. He carried on to the kitchen door, then paused. The beat of the music throbbed, cutting out any further sound. Perhaps he had imagined it, but surely there had been a human element to that cry.

He stood for a minute, then he shook his head. Perhaps he was worrying unnecessarily.

He turned back to the front entrance and looked into the ball room, but he couldn't see the Senor, or Bartlett; so just in case, he carefully and quietly retraced his steps. Once beyond the limit of the spotlights, he cursed the darkness as he stumbled on. It would have to be a night when there was no moon.

He neared the wall and looked round for his mistress. There was no sign of her. The seat where she had been sitting was empty. Now, even more worried, he crept on through the trees towards the farm. Reaching the road, he paused, listening for any sounds. Nothing. Only silence. Even the music from the orchestra was little more than a pulse on the night air. Yet surely she must have gone to the farm, or to the stable. She certainly hadn't returned to the house; he would have seen her.

Realising that circumspection was needed, Jason moved as cautiously as he could. No sense in annoying his mistress by appearing to snoop.

All the farm buildings were in darkness. Though Jason peered through the windows, he could see no sign of anyone. No sound. Nothing. Not even any of the Spaniard's men. Carefully, he tried both front and rear doors, even that of the guest quarters; all were locked. Next he tried the barn, but that, too, was in darkness. In the stable, both horses were dozing placidly. The whole group of farm buildings seemed wrapped in the silence of sleep.

Jason ran back to the sheltered wall where he had last seen Miss Rowena. Perhaps she had merely moved to another place, and he had missed her as he had crept through the trees. He looked around where she had been seated.

A crumpled piece of something white caught his attention. There, lying crushed under a fallen log, was the delicate lace handkerchief she had worn as a head-dress. The clip, which had held it in place, was still fastened to the material, and a long, auburn lock of hair was snagged under it. She must have felt it catch, and surely she would not have left it there of her own accord.

Now he was really frightened. He hurried back to the house and cast his eyes wildly round the Great Hall. Where was the Spaniard? The laughing, chattering crowd was still dancing and drinking, everyone thoroughly enjoying themselves, but there was no sign of Senor Olivares. Whom should he tell? Who else knew what was going on?

Bartlett. Yes, the butler would have to do. He had certainly understood Jason's concern when lending the jacket. There wasn't time to go searching for the Spaniard, and Bartlett had returned to the bar where he was supervising some of the staff.

Drawing him to one side, Jason told him what had happened and showed the handkerchief. The bright light over the bar illuminated a deep red stain, which, in the darkness, Jason had not seen when he removed the cloth from the broken branch.

"See, it's blood. Oi just know sommat bad's happened to Miss Rowena. Thee must be quick and find the Senor." He grasped Bartlett's arm in frantic concern. "He said as 'ow there be people keeping watch, but Oi b'ain't seen but one out there."

"Come." With the firm voice of authority, Bartlett signalled to a couple of the bartenders. The four of them hurried back to the east wing to the Spaniard's living room. Most of the guests were too tipsy to miss them. There, Jason was amazed to see that on the dining table was an extremely efficient-looking, computerised tele-communication system. In front of it sat the Spaniard with a pleased smile on his face.

"Ah, Jason. All is under control. The police are out there in force but carefully hidden. It's going to be a simple matter to catch the smugglers red-handed. We've seen them leave the harbour, and our men are under cover on the island just waiting for them to attempt to remove the contraband. We've nothing more to worry about."

"But Senor, 'ee don't know what's happened. They got Miss Rowena."

In shocked horror, the Spaniard got to his feet. Grimly, he listened to Jason's story.

"But there were only four men who boarded the fishing boat. Are you sure? My people would certainly know if one had been a woman." He turned back to the panel and switched through to his various watchers who had all converged on his yacht.

After a few moments, he had the answer. The bundled fishing net, which the watcher at the farm house had seen carried over two men's shoulders, seemed larger and heavier as it sagged suspended between its carriers when they boarded the waiting fishing boat, particularly since one of them staggered under the weight. Their faces were hidden behind the heavy mesh, and their rain gear completed their disguise. But satisfied that these were the same men who had left the farm house, it had not occurred to either watcher to check the size of the net.

"Mother of God, if they have harmed her . . . ."

Rob's voice hardened as he began to issue orders. "Bartlett, call the police. Tell them what's happened. On no account are they to attack until I get Miss Pentraegon off that trawler. Come with me, Jason, and you two." He included the pseudo-bartenders. "I'll keep in contact. I'll patch into one of the police boats. But meanwhile, double check the grounds in case. Don't worry any of the guests. This still has to be a secret operation." He led the way through the door onto the far side from the terrace.

As quietly as they could, keeping to the shadows, the four men skirted the spot lights, which were shining on the guests who were still enjoying the warm evening listening to the music that swirled through the windows and across the lawn.

Jason looked back with a sense of unreality. Gulls Walk glowed unconcernedly in the twinkle of fairy lights. He hastened his steps to catch up with the Spaniard.

In an agony of fear, Olivares cursed himself. He had come to Gulls Walk willing to believe that all the occupants of Pentraegon Cove were guilty, and now his blundering had brought danger to the most innocent of them all. He should have kept her by his side this evening, as had been his original intention.

He increased his pace. As they clambered onto his yacht, the ropes mooring it to the dock were untied, and the engine spluttered into life. Rob took the helm and coaxed every last ounce of speed. Would they be able to catch up with the trawler, which his men had watched creep quietly into the cove, pick up its passengers, then equally quietly, nose out to sea? That must have been over half-an-hour ago.

Once on course, Rob contacted Bartlett. "Did you get through?"

"Yes. The coast guards have the trawler on their radar. It'll be a while before it reaches the island. They don't seem to be in any hurry. I passed on your message, and the police are prepared to hold off until they have more instructions from you. But they can't wait too long. They can't afford to risk the whole operation." Bartlett hesitated. "I'm sorry as hell, Rob."

Grimly, the Spaniard hung up the phone. He eased back the throttle. His first intent had been to keep open wide his yacht's powerful engine and tear across the water to storm the trawler. But then the element of surprise would be lost, and what might happen to Rowena in the fighting? Though surely Gilbert, if he were one of the men, would not let any further harm come to her.

Aware that the trawler almost certainly had radar, too, he veered north of his original course. The smugglers must have no suspicion that they were being followed. He set a course to bring the yacht in a big loop round to the West Side of the island. There were many fishing boats in the area, and his would not be noticed, if, indeed, anyone on the trawler were watching the screen.

He eased the throttle forward a little. He had to reach the island before the smugglers and be in place to board while they were ashore. Surely they would do her no further harm until they had examined the contraband. He gritted his teeth. The knowledge that police manned some of those fishing boats trawling their nets near to the island was little consolation.

Groaning, Rowena was aware of a sledgehammer beating her head. She touched it gently and winced. There was a bump the size of an egg, and it was sticky; hastily, she drew her hand away, appalled at the amount of blood. Barely conscious, she tried to remember what had happened. Where was she, and why? There was a single overhead light that seemed to swing from side to side as she tried to concentrate.

Aware of the creaks of timber and the pulse of an engine, she struggled to sit up. What was she doing on a boat? And whose was it? Sitting on the stone seat at the top of the driveway was the last thing she remembered. Then bits of the conversation filtered through her misty memory. The two men. They'd been talking about the island. She suddenly remembered that, too.

The smell of fish assailed her nostrils. Somehow or other, she must have been caught and now was on one of Miles' trawlers. That accounted for the bump. But who had hit her? She winced again.

She looked around what was little more than a sail locker. She was lying on a cramped bunk with a rough blanket thrown over her. Well, at least someone didn't intend that she should die just yet, she thought as she tried to ease her fears. She lowered her feet to the floor of the cabin and gingerly moved across to the porthole. All was black. Of course, no moon, she remembered.

The throbbing pain in her head grew worse and, feeling dizzy, she dragged herself back to the bunk, pulling the blanket over herself. She was hardly aware of the rattle of the door as it opened, or of the face which bent over her. She kept her eyes shut, too sick to make any effort to protest as a hand roughly shook her.

"She's still out. Good. Let's hope she stays that way." The door closed and Rowena vaguely heard the key turn in the lock as she drifted back into unconsciousness.

The increased turbulence of the sea eventually woke her. Feeling a little better, she got to her feet and looked through the porthole. Realising that the cabin light was preventing her from seeing out, she reached over to the switch by the door and turned it off. When her eyes had adjusted, the reflected phosphorescence of the waves at least gave her an horizon. In the distance she could make out the riding lights of a boat. Probably another trawler. If only she could attract its attention. Somewhat hopelessly, she looked round the cabin.

The light!

She wracked her brain. S.O.S. That was the old international distress signal. She reached for the switch. Dot dot dot, dash dash dash, dot dot dot. She tried it again, and again, then went back to the porthole. There was no answering flash.

Dejectedly, she left on the light, then sank back onto the bunk. What was the point? Probably those fishermen were much too occupied with their nets. A lethargy of inevitability crept over her and she closed her eyes. For a while, she slept. She was hardly aware of the decrease in speed, nor of the dropping of the anchor.

The grating of the key in the lock jarred her back to consciousness, and she struggled to sit up as the door was opened. She pushed her hair away from her face, determined to hide her fears. Acceptance was not the way. Cornish women were supposed to be strong. Pentraegon pride. Yes, that's what she needed.

"Good morning, my dear Miss Rowena." The portly figure of pirate Redbeard entered the cabin. His disguise was still in place. Even the black patch remained. The one eye she could see was as cold as the fish she could smell, belying the softness of his tone. "I hope you have slept well. I am desolate that my hospitality is not as, shall we say, generous as yours. But if you will stick your pretty little nose in what is none of your concern, then I'm afraid you must suffer the consequences."

"Who are you? What am I doing here? Where are we?" She managed to keep her voice steady. Her head throbbed, but she wasn't about to let her fears show.

"Now, now, my dear. You don't really expect me to answer, do you? All in good time. Meanwhile, I have a visitor for you. We need some co-operation from him, and he doesn't seem willing to comply. Perhaps you can persuade him."

The door was pushed wider and a dishevelled Miles Gilbert was thrust into the cabin. He stumbled and fell to the floor. Gone was the trim goatee and moustache; his clothes were dirty and torn. There was an ugly bruise over one eye where the skin was cut, and his lip was swollen and bleeding. He looked so different from his usual elegant self. His poise and most of his control were gone.

"Oh, Miles, what have they done to you?"

Rowena clambered down from her bunk and knelt beside him. She attempted to cradle his head. With a groan, he managed to sit up and tried to smile.

"I'm all right. Just a little difference of opinion." He touched the corner of his mouth. "It appears that Heron's guests have nothing to do with farming. They are damned thieves."

"Strong words, my dear Mr. Gilbert. But you'd better co-operate." With a grunt, the pirate leered at Rowena. "It would be a shame to harm such a pretty face." He looked down at Miles, once more. "Remember that." The gleam in his visible eye grew cold and malevolent as he left the room closing the door behind him. The key grated in the lock.

Tearing a piece of her underskirt to wipe away the blood, Rowena attempted to clean Miles' wounds. "I don't understand. Why have they hurt you?" Bewildered, she clutched his shoulder.

"Hell, I've been a blasted fool. I've made such a mess of things, Rowena. I thought . . . ." His voice trailed away.

"What is it? Please, Miles, tell me."

"That pirate and his friend, they're no more cattle buyers than the man in the moon. They're smugglers!"

Rowena looked at him uncertainly. She knew that; but they had all been so sure that Miles was involved.

"Smugglers?" She managed to sound startled. Yet if he were not one of them, then who had been the third person in the barn? "But they are your friends. Surely you must have known." Later she would tell him what she knew, but not now. She took a deep breath, trying to keep her head clear.

"No, I damn well didn't. I may have been somewhat devious in my time, but I certainly am no thief on their scale!" His tone was so adamant that she had to believe him. "But what were you doing at the wall, Rowena? What did you hear?"

"Oh, I'd just gone there to have some peace and quiet." She ignored the second question. It seemed a lame reply, but she needed more answers to her own questions before she divulged any information. If only her head didn't hurt so much. She tried to concentrate. "Tell me first, why are you on this boat? Why have they beaten you up? You say you knew nothing."

"I walked in on a conversation that obviously I was not meant to hear." Miles frowned, touching his injuries gingerly. "I was quiet when I returned to the farm. I didn't want to wake my guests. But they were still up, in the living room, talking to that damned Heron. The window was open, though the lights were off." He cursed himself for being such a bumbling idiot. He had barged in when he had heard himself called a fool who saw nothing, even if it were under his very nose—Megan's revelation about his blindness over Roberto Olivares as a potential suitor for Rowena still smarted. "They talked about being ready to expand their smuggling operations. That's when I got the first of these bruises. When they discovered me listening."

Miles flinched as Rowena's hand pressed too hard on a bleeding cut. But the sharpness of the pain was nothing compared to his anger at his own stupidity. How had he been so blind?

"Apparently, this has been going on for the last couple of years. Maybe I suspected something, but I've paid very little attention to the working of Home Farm and the fisheries. When my father died and I hired Heron, he seemed to do such a good job, with plenty of money rolling in for me—hush money, now I realise—that I left it to him; I'd interests elsewhere, which required much of my time. Even when I came home, it was mainly to see you or your grandfather, to keep in touch."

His voice trailed away; he was not about to admit that his obsession to make enough money to own Gulls Walk had so totally consumed him. "You were away at college most of the time, anyway."

A couple of years? Rowena cast her mind back. Miles had explained that the continual supply of food from the farm, in exchange for the use of Gulls Walk's pastures, had started about then. It must have been Heron's suggestion, and of course Miles had insisted on carrying on with the deliveries after Gramps had died. No wonder Heron meticulously followed Miles' instructions, she thought. The less contact Gulls Walk had with the outside world the better. They all had been gullible fools. How Heron and his friends must have laughed.

Then she remembered the leer on Redbeard's face. And his demands.

"This co-operation. He said he needed co-operation. What does he want?" she asked.

"I'm afraid you won't like it, Precious." He touched his bruised jaw. Uncertainly, he continued. "It's a long story, but I suspect we don't have much time." Miles glanced at the door. "They want, insist that . . . Look, they've just beaten me again, trying to persuade me because at first I refused to co-operate when I discovered that I have been used as their pawn. But then they told me you're included."

Rowena drew back. What sort of co-operation could they possibly want with her? Her head was beginning to spin again. "Why me?"

"It's Gulls Walk. They want the house under their control. And they will have it if you and I . . ." He swallowed his words. "I told them that you wouldn't sell, even though you needed money. They laughed at me and said that they would have both the house and the farm."

The old arrogance returned.

"It's my . . . our valley, Rowena. Ours. Our families have lived here for hundreds of years."

"Yes, I know all that, Miles. But why do they want Gulls Walk? We haven't even known these men existed until now."

Miles took a deep breath.

"They want the whole valley under their control, so there will be no risk of anyone finding out about their activities; activities they intend to expand. Very few people come here. Only the servants, and they can be changed. And Whitford; he's old enough to be pensioned off, any way. Another lawyer of their choosing can be put in charge of Gulls Walk affairs. Even Olivares is only temporary; another few weeks and he will be gone.

"It's access to the sea they want; total, uninterrupted access. And no change in the status quo; no new people; no different activities. And for that, you and I need to be married if we are to continue to live in the valley. Wives don't give evidence against husbands."

He winced as her curiosity changed to disgust.

"Look, Rowena, I care for you. I've always wanted to marry you, long before these men appeared on the scene . . . and live at Gulls Walk." He had the grace to look ashamed. "After your grandfather died, I thought I could persuade you because you had no one else to turn to."

"But why is that important to them?" Rowena was angry, but bewildered, too.

"Two birds with one stone." Now came the worst part. "They want total control of all the buildings in the valley." He attempted to sweeten the bitter pill. "But in return for our co-operation, they'll pay off the death duties; the house will be ours and my income will continue. There'll be no more need for tenants. The whole valley will, ostensibly, be under my control. You'll have no money worries, and we can live happily ever after. We won't even be aware of their activities. It'll be just like before."

"But why should I agree? I've told you that I don't intend to marry you, Miles. There's no way I'll co-operate with them, with smugglers." Gulls Walk was hers alone. The hammer-like beats in her head were making it so difficult for her to understand.

Miles pushed on with his persuasion.

"But think what will happen if you don't. In any case, whom can we accuse if they do let us go? Only Heron. I didn't meet Redbeard and his partner until they were wearing their disguises. And I expect the names they gave were false, anyway. We don't have any evidence; we don't even know what they are smuggling, or from where."

He hesitated. He hadn't wanted to tell her his worst fears.

"They've got me caught in their damned web, Rowena. If they do let us return, and we don't keep their secret so their activities are discovered, they'll make sure the police think that I am responsible for the smuggling.

"My signature is on everything. They have used my transport, both ships and trucks, all under my name. I won't have a leg to stand on. They'll make sure that my bank account will make me look as guilty as hell. I'll be destroyed. You've got to help me, Precious."

Rowena shivered. She was beginning to hate that name. She had thought that Miles really cared for her, as well as the house. But he had shown little concern for her, so absorbed was he in his own troubles. Thank God she had not told him about the island, and the whereabouts or contents of the contraband.

She moved away from him and returned to the bunk. Wrapping her arms around herself, she tried to think. She realised she should not be surprised at Miles' attitude. She remembered the smile on his face the morning after the funeral when she had told him of her straitened circumstances. Deep down she had known it was the house he really wanted. Oh, Gulls Walk, what have you done to us? she thought. She roused herself to continue her questions.

"But if we don't do as they say, they're hardly likely to let us go free." Drug smugglers, she was sure, would have no qualms about snuffing out a couple of lives. It would not be too difficult to manufacture an accident. She and Miles might have gone for a sail to celebrate the ball; the trawler could sink, and they, apparently, would be drowned at sea. Their bodies would wash ashore.

She shuddered at the vivid picture her mind was creating.

The fisherman, of course, who had brought the boat to Pentraegon Cove, would never be found. He could easily resurface elsewhere with a new identity. Even Heron would not be involved. There would be nothing to point to his presence on the trawler.

Rowena felt so cold. What hope had they? She laid her head on the pillow in sheer exhaustion. She couldn't seem to think any more.

Miles dragged himself from the floor and covered her with the grubby blanket, then tried to offer her some sort of solace.

"You have to understand, Rowena. With co-operation, Pentraegon Cove will be totally safe for us as well. What's a bit of smuggling, anyway?"

Rowena was startled. She had forgotten that Miles knew nothing of the contents of those apparently innocuous bottles.

"And we will be wealthy, too." Desperately, he pleaded with her. If this were the only way he could take what his family had coveted for centuries, then why not accept the inevitable?

But his words seemed to have little effect. He tried another tack. "I'm afraid there's something else." This should clinch it, he thought. "If necessary, they can incriminate your grandfather."

No! Not her beloved Gramps.

"How . . . ?"

"Don't you remember? The sea chests with those bolts of cloth; the covers and curtains are all there for anyone to see. They were surely smuggled goods. These men can easily trump up something. And your grandfather is not here to defend himself." It all seemed so logical to Miles Gilbert; no matter that the material had been stored long before Gramps had been born.

Terror turned her body to ice. She lay there, frozen in fear. An awful helplessness shrouded her mind.

But the nightmare continued. The final blow came as if from a great distance.

"And if we still won't co-operate, they'll burn Gulls Walk!"

Aghast, Rowena shivered. She had known Miles all her life—or thought she had. Suddenly, she felt very small, unimportant, a piece of flotsam floating on a tide of greed. Dear God. Gulls Walk seemed to have become more important than any of them.

A millstone.

It felt worse than that. As if a great weight were pulling her down and down.

CHAPTER SEVENTEEN

Rob was glad of the darkness as he dropped anchor off the south-western corner of the island. The yacht had made good time in spite of the wide arc; better than the much slower trawler, he hoped. He had changed his Spanish sea-captain costume, and Jason and the others had pulled on navy sweaters to cover their white shirts, and balaclavas to cover their faces.

The wind shifted and brought with it a spattering of rain. The sea mist curled in, blocking out the stars. Good, thought Rob, the darker the better.

With the minimum of noise, the dinghy was lowered. Now they were ready to go. Before leaving, he switched on his cell phone and contacted the police whom he knew were in an innocent-looking trawler fishing well to the south of the island.

"They've just arrived and taken a boat ashore," was the answer; "and someone on board isn't happy." The dimly blinking lights of the S.O.S. had been seen long before the sudden squall blacked out the horizon.

"Thank God." Rob heaved a sigh of relief. "That has to be Rowena. I had feared she might be hurt." Or worse, he thought. How better to dispose of a body than at sea. Quickly, he gave instructions.

"Don't make any move until you hear from me. I'm going to get closer to find out what they're doing. You've got all your surveillance equipment in place, so whether you capture the smugglers in the cave or on the mainland won't matter, particularly if they remove some of the boxes to the boat. Indeed, in case something goes wrong, it will be just as well that they aren't aware how much we know about the island. I'll signal if I can't get through, but keep this line clear, anyway."

He didn't expand on how he intended, while the crew was in the cave, to board the trawler and rescue Rowena. He knew the police would try to stop him, for they wanted to catch the smugglers red handed; but who knew what would happen to Rowena in the melee? Only after that, would he allow them to mop up the whole operation.

Grimly, he packed the phone, with a torch and his gun, into a waterproof case and dropped into the waiting dinghy. Leaving one man behind on the yacht to relay any messages, he and the rest of the men, quickly and silently, rowed toward the jagged cliffs. He doubted if the motor would have been heard, but he was taking no chances.

The sea was no longer the summer calm it had been, and the waves were beginning to roughen. The white spume gleamed in the darkness as the heaving rollers from the Atlantic battered the high, granite walls. Steering well clear, for the last thing they wanted was to crash on the rocks, the dinghy rounded the headland into the calmer waters of the tiny cove where they could just make out the lights of the trawler through the increasingly heavy rain.

The men's faces were grim as they neared the squat hulk. They had no means of knowing if any smugglers were still on board.

The flare of a match for a cigarette illuminated the face of one man sheltering on the bridge. Damn, thought the Spaniard, but he seemed to be alone; perhaps the others were all ashore.

Hauling in their oars, Rob and his crew drifted on the tide. They dared not let any sound disturb the watcher, though the pouring rain would block out most of the noise. Surprise must be the key.

Suddenly, there was a flash of light from the beach illuminating a small boat drawn up on the sand. Men clambered aboard and its engine pulsed into life. With its greater speed, there was no doubt that it would reach the trawler before the Spaniard's dingy, so the possibility of overwhelming a skeleton crew was now gone, and with it, the opportunity to reach Rowena before her captors did.

"There's one chance. I'm going to try to get aboard secretly. Perhaps two of us can make it." Rob quickly contacted the police boat telling them what he was going to do, ignoring their demands to wait. Then he wrapped the phone back in the waterproof case and tucked it away under his sweater.

Kicking off his shoes, he issued final orders. "The rest of you get back to the yacht. Return to Gulls Walk, but for heaven sake, not in a direct line. We don't want the smugglers to have any suspicions. Inform the police; they'll follow, but tell them to keep to the south, apparently just a fishing boat returning to Penzance. That shouldn't arouse any suspicions. I'll contact you later. But if you don't hear from me, the police can board the trawler before it docks. Jason, can you swim?"

There was no need for an answer. With a broad grin, the stable boy dived into the black water after the Spaniard.

The sound of the trawler's engine springing into life jangled across the cove as the smugglers reached its side and clambered aboard. In the dim deck lights, the cases they were carrying were barely visible. They wedged their burdens adjacent to the bridge, then went below.

The rain beating down smoothed the surface of the water, and the two swimmers desperately increased their speed until they were in the shadow of the hull and were able to grab a couple of the fenders hanging over the side. They heard the anchor clank as it was hauled up, and they hung on grimly as the trawler turned and began to move slowly out to sea.

Heaving himself up to the rail, Rob peered through the gloom. Only one man was in the comparative shelter of the bridge; the others seemed to have gone below out of the driving rain.

Signalling to Jason to follow him, he climbed onto the deck and hid behind a pile of fishing equipment. Cupping the light in his hands, he flashed a quick beam from his torch in the direction of the now-invisible dinghy to let his crew know he was safe.

So far, so good. But how were he and the stable boy to get below to search for Rowena?

Impatiently, they waited, their eyes searching the gloom. They could just make out that the cases the men had brought on board were, in fact, flat containers in which fish, smothered in ice, was usually packed for immediate customer delivery. Obviously no chances were being taken with telltale wine cases, and the transfer had been made on the island.

There was a clatter of feet and a group of men, heavily garbed in rain gear, climbed up to the bridge carrying cups of coffee. The aroma drifted on the wind and the hidden watchers shivered. The temperature had dropped, and their sodden clothes clung to their cold bodies. They needed to get to shelter quickly; otherwise, they would be too numb for any sort of action.

Pointing silently to the closed hatchway through which the smugglers had come, Rob moved from their protective screen. Dear God, he thought, let's hope no one is still down there and that none of those on the bridge looks back.

Keeping to the shadows, they slithered across the deck and gently eased open the hatch cover. There was no sound from below, so taking a deep breath, they crept inside. The sudden change from the biting cold was a relief, but neither man dared relax. The powerful odour of fish assailed their nostrils, and Jason pinched his nose. "No wonder I b'ain't a fisherman." He chuckled in the Spaniard's ear.

"Shhh." But Rob couldn't help grinning at the ever-ebullient stable boy. The lad was actually enjoying himself. Carefully, they moved down into the main cabin. It was empty. A thin line of light showed beneath a door at the end; could that be where Rachel was being kept?

There was one light in the galley that enabled them to make out a pile of nets lying on the table, probably the ones in which Rowena had been carried aboard. Along the wall were hooks from which were hanging more of the heavy oilskins that his watchers had seen the smugglers wearing.

Skirting the table, which took up most of the space, they ventured toward the end cabin. The key was in the lock. Carefully, Rob turned it, gun in hand.

Telling Jason to keep watch in the main cabin, Rob eased open the door. A couple of bunks heaped with dirty blankets, and on the floor, piles of boxes and equipment, were all that were visible. The Spaniard's face was grim. He had been so sure that here he would find Rowena; otherwise, why was the door locked? He moved further into the tiny cabin The blankets could be covering something. He lifted a corner then gasped as he saw the bright auburn tresses, dimmed and darkened with matted blood.

"My God, Rowena, what have they done to you?" he whispered. His face tautened as he drew back the blankets.

Hardly daring to hope, he gently eased away the hair, feeling for a pulse. It was faint but sure, beating in time to the dull throb of the engine. Yet Rowena did not stir. A sense of desolation swept over him.

"My sweet love," he whispered as he bent to kiss the white face. Whoever had knocked her out had been thorough. He felt the bile of bitter anger rise in his throat. Yet the S.O.S? She must have come to her senses for a little while at least to send it. "Rowena, little porcupine, wake up." He shook her gently. But she slept on. He bowed his head to rest on her still body, his hands clenching the rough blankets. He had brought her to this. She was innocent, and he had not protected her. Anger flared, but he pulled himself together; there was little point in recriminations.

A sudden noise startled him. Rob whipped round as a bleary-eyed Miles Gilbert stagger through another door at the rear of the cabin; it led to a small washroom, the ship's head. He was wiping his bruised and swollen face, hardly able to see out of his almost closed eyes. "What the hell? Who is that? Are you one of them?" he questioned in a frightened voice, not recognising the balaclava-covered face.

Signalling to Jason to keep out of sight, the Spaniard's eyes narrowed. The dishevelled appearance of Gilbert was not what he would have expected. And why was he locked in with Rowena?

"No, I'm not! Just the opposite, in fact," whispered Rob, his voice muffled; but he had his own questions. "Why are you locked up here? Who did this to her?" He gently examined Rowena's wound.

"They did. Those bastards." Miles jerked his head in the direction of the bridge. "If you're not one of them, who are you? How did you get here? We're all in danger." Miles' face was grey with fear. He must be suffering some sort of reaction, he thought. He was having difficulty making out the figure in front of him. Was he police? The whole cabin seemed to sway in and out of darkness as he tried to concentrate, to hold on to his carefully built plan to own Gulls Walk. It was disintegrating in front of his eyes.

"I'm well aware of the danger." Rob had no intention of explaining their presence, but he needed answers, too. "Just what is your part in all this? We saw you and your friends carry her aboard in the fishing net. Kidnapping is breaking the law." That would do for now.

"No. I wasn't part of that." Miles protested his innocence. "We've both been kidnapped. These men are smugglers." His mind was almost too shattered to concentrate as he tried to tell the bare bones of his own capture.

"They hurt Rowena when they caught her listening as well. She's been barely conscious. When I told her what they had done to me, since I had overheard them talking about smuggling, she passed out again." He tried to focus his eyes on the still girl. "Look, I swear I didn't know anything about them being smugglers. If I hadn't heard what they were saying in the farmhouse, they wouldn't have beaten me up and dragged me aboard."

He had no intention of explaining more than necessary. He doubted if he could, anyway. His head was swimming so much that he began to black out again. Then through the haze, he was aware that he might not be believed. "They'll be back soon. They want us to co-operate." He stumbled on; "If we don't, who knows what they'll do." There was anguish in his voice.

Was he dreaming? Was he imagining someone had come to help? He staggered as waves of pain increased the nausea he had been trying to control. He tried to look through the dark mist but could no longer make out the figure in black, then with a groan, he sank unconscious to the floor.

Rob clenched his fist. Any cooperation will be over my dead body, he thought.

"Senor, you be wasting time." The matter-of-fact voice of Jason interrupted them. "We got to have a plan of action." Nothing more was going to happen to Miss Rowena if he could help it.

"Jason, I don't know what I would do without you." Rob's mouth lifted in a grim smile.

The stable boy continued.

"We better find a place to hide for when these blasted smugglers come back. There b'ain't owt we can do for Miss Rowena right now." The prosaic logic was obvious.

Rob looked round the small space for inspiration, to the other door that led into the tiny washroom. Perhaps there would be some sort of first aid kit, and maybe enough room for one of them to be concealed.

"Gilbert?" He shook Miles' shoulder. There was no response from the unconscious man. "If he wakes up, let's hope he has the sense to say nothing about us." Rob frowned.

He turned back to Jason. "Those men hadn't better find us. At least Miss Pentraegon is sleeping through all this." He looked at her with deep concern, though with some relief remembering that she had returned to consciousness earlier to send the S.O.S., even if it had been only for short periods of time.

Then it struck him. The key. The door had been locked. It must be locked again; otherwise, anyone who came to check on Rowena and Gilbert might be suspicious. He took Jason's arm.

"I'll be in the head. But you must be outside to turn the key." They looked back into the main cabin. There was only one possible place. "Can you squeeze past that table and under the seat? Those draped nets should cover you." What their next move would be, Rob had no idea.

Suddenly the sound of footsteps on the deck above sent them hurrying to hide, but not before Jason locked the door.

The hatch opened and the short, burly figure of Redbeard descended the steps. Rob quickly hid as the pirate crossed the main cabin and turned the key.

Rob held his breath. His hand closed over his gun. If Gilbert gave him away, neither man would go unscathed.

"So. Have you made up your minds yet?" The sagging flesh visible above the red beard looked greasy in the weak, yellow light. At the sound of the pirate's voice, Rowena stirred. She had been dreaming. A lovely dream; Rob had kissed her, but she hadn't been able to reach out to touch him. Now the dream was gone and the nightmare was back.

Redbeard's voice jolted Miles to some vague consciousness. "It's all right, Precious." He tried to drag himself onto the bunk, but he was too weak and collapsed to the floor again. Surely someone else had been there. But it must have been a dream. The pirate's eyes gleamed as he heard the term of endearment.

Rowena was groggy and waves of nausea prevented her from answering; the blow on her head must have caused some sort of concussion. She seemed to be wandering in and out of darkness, too.

"We're working it out." Miles' voice was little more than a whisper. Rowena tried to protest, remembering something about co-operation, but his groan silenced her. "Go home . . . Rowena?" It was the best he could do. He hoped her answer would be innocuous enough to placate the pirate.

"Oh, yes. Please can we go home?" She felt so disoriented and her head hurt so much that the events of the past hours were swirling mists. She reached to clasp Miles' hand for comfort. "Gulls Walk." she muttered.

Rob, behind the door, waited for the reaction of Redbeard.

"Good. I'm glad you decided to be sensible. I really didn't want to set the . . . er, home fires burning, Miss Pentraegon." He gave a harsh laugh.

"But I've had second thoughts about your fiancé. I've a better idea. We'll take Mr. Gilbert to London with us for a little while. He won't be missed. He's always travelling somewhere. That should definitely ensure your co-operation."

He grinned without humour.

"And remember; if you change your mind and go to the police, no one will believe you. You have no idea who we are, so whom can you accuse? And if you try, an anonymous citizen will present a list of extraordinarily damning evidence against your boy friend. Then Gulls Walk surely will go up in flames. It will be a nuisance as far as I am concerned, but just that; a nuisance. There are many more areas we can use for our business. You are not that important to us."

Miles cringed. The dark shadows still wavered through his mind. Where were they going to take him? And what would they do to him if there were no rescue? Just a barely conscious girl; and himself, little better; there seemed to be no chance of getting away. Had he imagined the policeman? Even if he were indeed real, it would be a miracle if they escaped from the trawler. It seemed none of them could prevent whatever Redbeard intended.

And to cover up what? Miles didn't even know what was being smuggled, or from where. Co-operation was to have solved so many problems. He felt

Gulls Walk slipping through his fingers. But just in case, he'd better hedge his bets. He roused and dragged himself to the bunk.

". . . won't go to the police. Will you, Precious?" He made his final comment to the pirate as assured as he could before collapsing against her.

With a grunt of satisfaction, Redbeard smiled complacently. "I'll be back just before we reach the dock, in an hour or so. We'll come to fetch you both then. Meanwhile, sweet dreams." He reached down, dragged Miles from the bed, then crashed his head against the bulkhead. "That should quieten you for a while."

He laughed as he locked the door behind him. He had been sure that Gilbert's easy life style was too comfortable to give up, and fear of incrimination would keep him toeing the line, especially after a little incarceration. Also, Heron had assured him that Miss Pentraegon, who was practically engaged to Gilbert, loved Gulls Walk too much to risk anything happening to the house. A valley peopled with those whom he could control was ideal.

What, potentially, had seemed a disaster when Gilbert had overheard their conversation, was turning out to be perfect. The whole situation couldn't be better. The other solution would have been messy. There could have been all sorts of uncomfortable inquiries, and a waste of considerable time if a 'lost at sea, believed drowned' was arranged.

He whistled cheerfully to himself as he negotiated his way back on deck.

As soon as Redbeard left, Jason crept up to the hatch; he eased it open an inch. Peering through the heavy rain he was just able to make out the men huddled in the shelter of the bridge. He counted carefully, then hurried back to the locked door and turned the key.

"It b'ain't too bad. There be only four of them out there." Life was simple to the stable boy. He and the Senor, with the element of surprise, should be enough to handle old Redbeard and his cohorts. Then all would be right with the world again. He looked eagerly at the Spaniard, who was standing in the shadow of the washroom door.

But Rob's attention was centred on Miles Gilbert, who lay as if dead to the world. His eyes were closed.

"What's going on?" Jason looked in turn at each man. Only Rob had heard the conversation with Redbeard.

"It seems that our friend has wedding plans." Dryly, the Spaniard replied.

Miles was too lost in the wavering mists caused by his pounding headache to answer, but he reached a hand toward Rowena, who had sunk into a shattered silence. She stirred. The sound of Rob's voice penetrated the dark tunnel of her mind, and she struggled to the surface. Dimly she became aware of the new sounds, the new faces. Perhaps it was all a nightmare and she would wake up to find herself in her own bed.

"Is that true, Gilbert?" The Spaniard's words were harsh.

Ah! But one must never under-estimate the simple country mind. Miles Gilbert ignored his nemesis.

Jason sprang across the small cabin and dragged him from the bunk. "Like hell!" One short, sharp blow, with all the power of broad shoulders behind it and Miles returned to cold darkness. It was the last straw to his already-battered body.

Smoothing his knuckles with an unconcerned shrug, the stable boy grinned at Rowena. He didn't believe in all this talk. Action was much better.

"Oi know that be not true, Miss Rowena. 'Ee got too much sense to marry 'im." Calmly, he pulled off his balaclava as he stepped back to the wall, waiting for whatever instructions his mistress or the Spaniard might care to give. Life was black or white in his book. There were good and bad people, and he had long made up his mind in which category lay Miles Gilbert. Miss Pentraegon would never want to marry the likes of him!

Senses slowly returning, Rowena gazed at her stable boy. Where had he come from? "Oh, Jason." she murmured. A small bubble of hope began its difficult way up from her heart. The pure beauty and trust of Jason's mind was a revelation. He was right. Of course she would never marry Miles. Come what may, she would live up to that trust.

Suddenly, she was aware of the brooding figure standing in the doorway. The Spaniard removed his disguise, too.

"Rob!" She pushed herself off the bunk and staggered across the cabin. "You came." All her fears and worries dissolved. Nothing mattered any more. She was safe. She held out her arms, wanting to bury her head in his shoulder to hide the tears. Redbeard's threats, and Miles' attempts to persuade her, all jumbled around her mind; there was so much she had to explain. But that could wait. The moment was all that mattered.

Yet Rob held her away, and she winced as his clasp tightened on her wrists.

"Really, Porcupine, you do seem to get yourself into some pickles." The words were cool, with no amusement in the Spaniard's voice. His face was hard granite.

Rowena flinched, bewildered. He seemed a stranger. She drew back. Where were the warm chestnuts, the cosy fires?

"But I gather you are quite prepared to co-operate, according to Gilbert." His words were in icy contrast to the blazing jealousy that burned through him.

He glanced down at the supine Miles, then turned to the stable boy. "Jason, I'll deal with you later. You can keep your opinions to yourself. Meanwhile, see if you can find something for Miss Pentraegon's head. She and Gilbert can make their wedding plans later, if we ever get out of this." He ignored her protest. His eyes were cold, hard agates. This on-again-off-again marriage. Cynically, he remembered he'd believed her twice before.

He twisted her round. "Let me look at your head. It's not still bleeding, thank goodness." Then his voice gentled as he touched the broken skin. "Does it hurt too much?"

Numbly, Rowena allowed him to examine her. What had Miles said? She barely remembered any of the conversation. And Redbeard? Her mind was still spinning and she couldn't seem to concentrate. For a few moments, her heart had filled with such a wonderful feeling of relief. Rob had come to rescue her, and all misunderstandings were no longer important. She remembered how he had kissed her in the library. Oh, why hadn't she trusted him?

"No, it's not so bad." she murmured. Pentraegon pride. That was what she needed. "Thank you for coming." It seemed such a banal statement, but she didn't know what else to say. All the light had gone from her face. How could he believe that she would marry Miles? She had told him again and again that she would not. And knowing what she did about the contents of those cases, it was even less possible. His lack of trust hurt.

Rob swore to himself as he watched her face close up. Bitterly, he wished that Miles Gilbert were at the bottom of the sea. Jealousy was hell. Why couldn't he just hold her close, as all his instincts demanded? It was so hard to accept that Gulls Walk was everything to her. He felt as if the very bottom had dropped out of his world.

Jason was aware that he had missed something. He didn't understand why Miss Pentraegon was not in the Spaniard's arms. It was where she should be. He wouldn't put up with that sort of nonsense with his Jeannie. And standing here all polite like b'ain't doing no good, he thought.

"How be we getting off this boat, Senor? We'm better have a good plan." Action was what they all needed. He fetched a damp towel and gave it to the Spaniard, and then he rummaged through the washroom's tiny cabinet to collect medical supplies.

Careful not to open the wound again, almost mechanically Rob wiped away the worst of the blood and covered it with anti-biotic salve. It was the best he could do. Rowena didn't flinch. Truth to tell, she was too numb with emotional turmoil to notice any change in the dull ache.

When he had finished, he took out his phone and switched on to try to make contact with his yacht. He still had a job to do. Jason was right. Now was the time for action. But the heavy static from the storm caused so much interference that the interchange of information was virtually impossible. Maybe nearer the shore he would be able to reach Bartlett.

Meanwhile, another signal, perhaps, could be seen. He reached for the switch in the washroom. The porthole there was on the starboard side, so he hoped the light would be visible to the distant police launch masquerading as a trawler. Someone on board must be using night glasses to penetrate the darkness even though the storm was still raging.

When he returned, Rowena was standing waiting for him. Icy control kept her hands by her side. The hurt had gone deep, yet she had to try to penetrate the granite.

"I don't know what Miles has told you, but I think my word is more trustworthy than his is. I am not going to marry him."

Jason's reaction had given her strength. It suddenly seemed so important that her tenant should believe her.

"I know I prevaricated when we first met, yet I have never actively lied to you, Rob. That pirate demanded our co-operation, but I haven't agreed. I certainly wanted to get back to save Gulls Walk. But Jason is right. I cannot marry Miles, and I won't co-operate, even to save my home. Not even that is worth the potential evil of those drugs coming into the country. Do you think so little of me that you could believe I would put my house, or my life, before that?"

Exhausted with the effort, she lay back on the bunk.

Her quiet dignity shattered his selfish bitterness. Dear God. What had he done? Damn his analytical mind. Rob reached his arms to her.

But he was too late.

She ignored him and turned to the stable boy, conjuring up a smile. "You're right, Jason. We do need a plan of action."

In some bewilderment, Jason looked helplessly at the Spaniard, at the bleakness in his eyes, and the hurt in Miss Rowan's. He sighed. But standing there was going to do no good. "Can't we just get rid of them smugglers? They won't be missed?"

Rob dragged his gaze from Rowena as a sudden gleam of an idea began to crystallise.

He understood her withdrawal. He blamed himself. If only he had not been so damned jealous; but explanations would have to come later. Obviously nothing he could say or do just now would close the chasm that had formed between them. Next time he would react only with trust, not with jealous condemnation. He was a fool.

"Get rid of them? That's the best idea you've had all night, Jason. And I think I know how it can be done." He eyed the stable boy for a moment. Yes, it just might work.

His mind stretched beyond the immediate present to the long term. What he had in mind could ensure the safety of the valley far into the future, for to remove old Redbeard and his partner was not enough; there were others involved. He needed to know who had hit Rowena, for instance. And who was waiting back in some big city ready to distribute the death those bottles contained?

Yes, he would concentrate on that. But his eyes lingered on the proud figure of Rowena, crushed though she was in all her Elizabethan finery.

CHAPTER EIGHTEEN

Closing the door carefully behind them, Rob and Jason moved into the main cabin. It was better that Rowena did not know their plans just yet. They had settled her down, hoping she would sleep for a while. She had swayed as she had tried to keep control, for the blow to her head was still bothering her. Miles was showing no signs of stirring, so giving Rowena strict instructions to tell him nothing should he do so, Rob persuaded her to try to rest.

First, they searched through the jumbles in the various corners of the main cabin. Next, they worked out the details of their plan. There would be very little time to put it into action, so they needed to co-ordinate their movements. Success depended on who came to fetch Miles and Rowena. Grimly, Rob dared not consider failure.

"It's time I went back. You're sure you can handle it?" Rob watched the stable boy's eager reaction.

"It be my pleasure." Jason chuckled. "Oi'll do 'bout anything to help Miss Rowena." He pulled the item they had gathered into the shadows. "You got no need to worry, Senor, you do your part and I'll do mine." The stable boy followed the Spaniard to the small cabin and locked the door behind him as he entered; then Jason returned and crawled back into the darkness under the table.

Rowena, wide awake, was lying watching the door as Rob entered. "How are you feeling?" he asked.

"I'm fine," she answered, her white face belying her words.

"Rowena, I . . ." He reached to touch her. He could not bare the misery of her expression.

"I'm sure we don't have time for personal discussion," she interrupted him, sitting up and pulling away from his hands; "what is this plan? Can I help?" While she had been lying there, she decided to close away any romantic notions. She would look at them another day: if there were other days.

Pentraegon pride. Perhaps it is better this way, thought the Spaniard. Perhaps it would give her the strength she needed, strength necessary if she were to act her part.

"It's quite simple really. We're going to change places."

Rowena's eyes widened. "Change places? Who's going to change places?" Rob proceeded to tell her.

Eventually, there was the clatter of footsteps and the pirate returned.

When the key grated in the lock, Rowena was kneeling trying to revive Miles who was showing little signs of waking. He must have taken quite a beating before Jason's fist knocked him unconscious.

"Oh, help me," she exclaimed, turning to Redbeard as he entered; "he has passed out. You hurt him badly, I can't revive him."

Leaving the door open behind him, the pirate moved closer and bent down to look at the still figure. He never heard the faint sound of a swish through air, nor felt the crunch of the heavy iron bar as he collapsed at the feet of the grinning Jason who had crept into the cabin after him.

"One down and three to go." The stable boy chortled. He and the Spaniard between them hauled the unconscious pirate into a sitting position and dragged off his disguise. Rob was silent as he looked at the face, searing each feature into his memory.

Sending Rowena into the main cabin to keep watch, the two men removed Redbeard's clothing and boots, and the cushion strapped to his waist. Finally, they bundled him behind the door of the head.

Quickly, Jason removed his own damp jersey and pants and donned the discarded garments, making himself appear as fat as the pirate had seemed. The boots pinched, but he managed to squeeze into them. The beard had been held around Redbeard's ears with wire pieces, and it was only a moment's work to fasten it in place on his own face. After placing the patch over one eye, he pressed down the still-sticky false brow over the other. Then he wrapped the bandanna, with its ring of hair, around his head. Rowena gasped when she returned to the cabin. The transformation was incredible.

Winking broadly with his one eye, Jason made his way through the cabin to the hatch. He pushed it open and gesticulated to Redbeard's partner. He knew his voice would be almost lost on the wind, so he had no fear of it being recognised. "Ahoy," he yelled, then returned to the waiting Rowena. Meanwhile, Rob hid himself behind the half-open door of the cabin.

"What's the matter?" With hood in place, the executioner came clattering down the steps to where an apparent Redbeard was kneeling over Miles.

"You'll have to help us." Rowena was entering into the spirit of things, and her own white face and dishevelled appearance certainly helped. "He's sick and too heavy to lift. He might die!" She looked up pleadingly at the tall man. Showing his irritation, he bent over to look. He, too, heard nothing as the heavy bar crunched bone, and he collapsed beside the still-unconscious Miles.

Jason grinned delightedly as Rob threw the bar into a corner. "I enjoyed that." He certainly showed no compunction.

Again Rowena kept watch in the outer cabin as clothes and disguise were stripped, and again the Spaniard looked long and hard as he uncovered the face of Redbeard's partner.

But time was short. Rob donned the clothes and boots, then the hood, causing Rowena to shiver, and Jason to laugh as he commented, "We look a right evil pair, don't we?" It was extraordinary how similar they looked to the real smugglers.

The stable boy returned to the main cabin to search for the ropes.

"Oh, I can help you there." Eagerly, Rowena lifted her skirts and unlaced the farthingale she had created out of curtain cord. "Rope's too thick; this will be much more secure. There's enough here to tie up an army." She began to unwind the cord and handed an end to the Spaniard.

For a moment, their hands touched. She looked up and saw that the warm chestnuts were back. Suddenly, she felt ridiculously happy. It must be the concussion, she decided. How could she so quickly forget his mistrust? She lowered her head as she tried to shake away some of the remaining cobwebs.

When the two smugglers were trussed up like turkeys, and strips of material from Rowena's underskirts used as gags, they were both bundled into the tiny floor space in the head and wedged so they couldn't use their feet to bang on the walls.

The same key to the cabin fitted that lock, and Rob, with considerable satisfaction, turned it, then put it in the pocket of his jeans and bundled them, with their discarded clothes, under the bunk where the police could find them later.

"So far, so good. It b'ain't likely them men on the bridge 'll get in there in a hurry." The stable boy chuckled. "They'll think old Redbeard took the key by mistake. The police'll enjoy our little presents."

"Oh, Jason, what a treasure you are." Rowena reached up to stroke his beard. "But I do prefer you clean shaven." She laughed. It was hard to believe that such a short time ago she had been so desperately afraid.

Rob watched the interchange and ruefully touched his own cheek. He would have given anything for the same caress and smile.

There was a change to the sound of the engine, and he realised they must be near the shore. Now he could make contact with Bartlett, but he would have to be quick. He took out his phone.

". . . don't interfere. Remember, we're the ones disguised as the smugglers now. Above all, keep your men hidden, unless I shoot. And watch for Rowena as we near the house; I'll send her in through the library and up the back stairs. Don't disturb the servants, or Megan. Have Carlos check the wound, but speak to no one else. Who knows who may be watching."

If only they could get away with the next stage of his plan. They must somehow avoid arousing the suspicions of the two men on deck. And there was still the walk to the farm house.

A voice called down to the cabin. "We're almost there; bring 'em up. Wrap up the girl again if she's a nuisance. If not, I'll get the net. You can carry a couple of the containers. They won't be much heavier a load than the first one." There was a snigger. "The rest, I'll take to the warehouse. Better done now than later. It will be dawn soon, but the rain'll hide you."

For a moment, the three looked at each other, they recognised the voice. So Heron was involved. And he intended going back to Penzance before returning to the valley. Good, the Spaniard thought. He had been concerned about the farm manager.

But now was the main test. Each man donned the smuggler's rain gear; a couple more such coats were taken from the cabin wall, one to cover Miles, and another for Rowena. Rob hoisted Miles over his shoulder, first concealing his gun at his belt where the body would cover it. He was taking no chances. He knew the dangers, even though Jason seemed to think that the whole escapade was a joke.

And Rowena. So much now depended on her. He hoped she could carry out her part. She should be under a doctor's care, not acting out a dangerous subterfuge. Grimly, he signaled for her to precede him.

"What the hell . . . ?" Heron looked at the girl, and the body of Gilbert.

"Oh, careful. He's so hurt. Don't bang his head again. Watch the hatch." With an almost hysterical commentary, Rowena backed up the gangway ahead of Rob. A surprised Heron stood watching. "Move away, can't you. Oh, if you've killed him, what'll I do?" She turned to Jason who was guiding Miles' legs through the narrow space. "Gently, gently. Don't drop him. Oh, here's the dock." A rope was thrown over a bollard. "You get down there first and help

him." Rowena pointed to Jason as she dithered like a flustered hen, not giving
Heron the opportunity to look closely at the two apparent smugglers.

"Hell! You've certainly got your hands full there." The farm manager
whispered, then turned to Rowena. "Keep your voice down, woman." He
peered through the darkness at the Spaniard's yacht moored further along
the dock. A twisted smile touched Heron's usually dour face. No more would
he have to kow-tow to the lady of the manor. He moved over to the hatch as
Rob, with his burden, negotiated the transfer to the walkway.

"Forget the nets." Heron kicked the pile out of the way. "You'd better take
just one box. You can't take more. I'll put it ashore; you'll have to manage
it between you. The others I'll hide in the warehouse with the fish I've got
to deliver to make the trip look authentic." There were half-a-dozen other
containers stored farther down the deck. He removed one from where it had
been wedged near the bridge.

Rowena carried on fussing. Deliberately falling over her skirt, which was
now, conveniently, too long without the farthingale, she insisted on a helping
hand from Heron to step onto the dock. Intermittent murmurs from Rob
and Jason were all that were necessary.

As the farm manager let go of Rowena, he leered down at her. "Don't you
forget. One word out of you to the police and your boyfriend will die."

"Oh no. I promise. I won't tell the police. I'll cooperate. Don't hurt him.
Please don't hurt him." She contrived an anguished look.

"Good." He gave a satisfied grunt. "Get her back into the house."

With a wave from Heron as he returned to the deck, the trawler slipped
away into the gloom.

Delightedly, Rowena opened her mouth to proclaim their freedom.

"Not yet," cautioned the Spaniard; "we still don't know who hit you.
Whoever it was may still be watching. We don't know if Heron contacted
anyone while we were returning to harbour. We're not out of the woods
yet."

There was a groan from Miles. The night air was reviving him. Indicating
the necessity for speed, Rob hurried up the slope toward the house. The last
thing he wanted was a conscious Gilbert who could give them away.

Jason easily hefted the container of supposed fish to his shoulder and gave
a helping hand to Rowena who was struggling with her cumbersome skirts.

Next time I go to a fancy dress ball, I'll go as a smuggler, too, she thought,
as she watched the easy, purposeful stride of the Spaniard in front of her. A
small giggle broke from her. She couldn't help it. She must still be light-headed,
she decided. It was difficult to concentrate. She swayed a little.

"Easy, Miss Rowena." Jason kept his voice low. It sounded eerie through the rain and the mists that were swirling in from the Atlantic.

The spot lights and fairy lights around the house had been switched off. A dim glimmer from one light left on in the Great Hall, barely outlined some of the windows. Halting at the bridge, well away from any possible listening ears, the Spaniard gave his instructions.

"Rowena, can you manage? Carlos will be there to check that wound." He wished he could accompany her into the house. "Go straight to bed. If you meet anyone else, don't say anything. Go to sleep." He reached to touch her cheek, then changed his mind. "Don't worry. We'll sort everything out in the morning." Tomorrow would be time enough for explanations.

He hoisted Gilbert higher on his shoulder and led the way through the darkness to the library door where Bartlett and the doctor were waiting just inside. Rowena removed her rain gear and gave it to Jason; then, with considerable relief, she hurried into the warmth. Watching her enter the house alone was one of the hardest things Rob had ever done. But the charade had to be played out to the end if they all were to be safe.

"Come on, Jason. We've still got work to do." He shifted his burden and they pressed on to the farm guest quarters. Jason took out the key that Redbeard had kept in the pants pocket of his disguise.

As they reached the door, Miles coughed and began to struggle. Once inside, Rob eased the barely conscious body onto a couch and signalled for Jason to draw the curtains. Then the Spaniard switched on a low light and looked down at his dishevelled burden.

A disoriented Gilbert opened bleary eyes.

"What the . . . where . . . how the hell did I get here?" Anger and fear mingled in equal quantities as he looked at the mask of the executioner. Rob remained silent. Jason's appearance at the door as Redbeard was the final straw. Gilbert's jaw dropped.

The startled expression was almost ludicrous, but the Spaniard had no time or inclination to laugh. With a groan, Miles turned his face to the wall.

"I'll co-operate," were his last words as the supposed smugglers left the room. It had all been too much and he sank back, out to the world. Cynically, Rob reflected that there was no likelihood of Gilbert doing otherwise. A little more suffering he well deserved, and the police would be happy to keep him locked up.

But there was no time to waste. The first grey glimmerings of dawn were beginning to filter into the room.

Jason and Rob packed the cases of the smugglers; then they went into the main farmhouse for Miles' clothes. His wallet was tucked into the back pocket of the jeans he had discarded before dressing for the ball, and with other clothes, all were packed in his overnight bag. Taking the car keys from where they had been carelessly thrown on the guest bedroom dresser, everything, including the apparent fish container, was bundled in the car parked at the back of the farm. Next, they tied Miles' hands and blindfolded him. They were taking no chances of him recognising who they were or where they were going. Then, leaving the cumbersome rain gear behind, they bundled him onto the back seat and quietly drove away, their disguises still in place. They wanted no hidden watcher to have any doubts as to who was in the car.

Once well beyond Gulls Walk and the farm, Rob pulled into a side road, took out his phone and got out of the car. He was taking no chances of Gilbert overhearing him.

"You've certainly taken your time! I've contacted the police and they're screaming for action." Bartlett's voice sounded desperate. "Carlos has tended to Miss Pentraegon's wound. She's now in bed. She'll be fine, he says."

"So everything's under control." Rob allowed himself a deep sigh of relief. They had been lucky. He explained in detail what had happened on the boat, but now the next stage of his plan had to be handled. "Here's what I want you to do."

As Bartlett listened, he began to feel more hopeful. "Do you really think it will work?"

"I don't see why not, providing everyone does their part. Get the police to come to pick up this car quickly. It has to be well hidden, and Gilbert locked away as soon as possible. Tell them to hurry, for we need to have enough time to get back before people start moving about at Gulls Walk. Nobody has followed us. Thank God for the rain and fog." Giving instruction as to their whereabouts, Rob and Jason settled down to wait.

The nearest unmarked car was only minutes away, and the exchange was quickly made. They borrowed coats from the police men and removed most of their disguises, and Jason now became the driver, apparently returning to the house having driven some servants home, or possibly guests who were probably too drunk to drive themselves.

He parked the car in the courtyard, making no attempt at concealment, and whistled cheerfully as he scrunched noisily over the gravel to the stables and bed. He didn't see the silent watcher crouched by the farm entrance who paid little attention, discounting the stable boy as unimportant.

Meanwhile, Rob had slipped from the car at the corner of the last turning and silently made his way behind the high walls until he reached the rear of Gulls Walk. A much thicker fog was rolling in from the sea, following the diminishing rain, shrouding him as he crept to the side door of the east wing.

Bartlett quickly let him into the darkened room and hastily checked the heavy curtains before switching on the light. Rob stood tensely waiting. He desperately wanted to check on Rowena. "Are you sure Miss Pentraegon is all right?"

"She has a mild concussion, very mild. She needs a couple of day's rest, that's all, then she will be as right as rain, Carlos told me. He's gone back to bed now. They were as quiet as mice, and no one else was around. All the servants had either gone to bed or home. She's going to be fine, Rob."

"Thank God for that." Rob breathed a sigh of relief as he sank, exhausted, into a chair.

Bartlett smiled to himself. Their pretty lady-of-the-manor didn't know how single-minded his Spanish friend could be, or how he usually got what he wanted. She'd not been pleased with Olivares at the beginning of the ball, but he'd lay odds that wouldn't last. He smothered his rueful chuckle as Rob hauled himself to his feet and began to pace back and forth.

"What's the latest information, Tom?"

"The police are all ready; we should be hearing soon. Two of them are now dressed as dock hands and will follow Heron and the other fisherman when they bring the containers ashore."

The erstwhile butler grinned as he continued. "They'll probably not return to the trawler, for Heron will be in a hurry to get back here to seem as if he has never left. Then it will be easy for our men to board the boat. There is one hell of a fog, so anyone wandering around will be much too busy trying to cope with their own business. Removing the live cargo should be easy."

"And Heron will be no wiser." At last, Rob relaxed. "I just hope he makes no attempt to go to the cabin before he leaves the boat. We trussed up Redbeard and his partner sufficiently well that they won't be able to make enough noise to be heard. And Heron doesn't know where we hid the key."

But having no idea who else was involved in the kidnapping, who had hit Rowena, or where any further danger was likely to come from, were still Rob's major concerns.

A short time later, the light on the communication system flickered and the Spaniard switched on. It was the chief inspector.

"All taken care of. I had no idea what a brilliant tactician I had engaged when I decided to use you, Senor Olivares. Heron locked the containers in the Pentraegon Cove warehouse, and he and his skipper have driven a van in the direction of Gulls Walk. He's left no one watching the boat now, so I'll let you know when the er . . . live cargo are secure. My men have been told where the key is, so they'll collect your clothes, and then remove our smuggling friends, all covered up in rain gear, in a matter of minutes."

"Thanks, Chief Inspector. Now everything depends on Heron having no inkling that he has been set up. If that happens, we'll have no control over any others in the drug ring. There's more to our plan than just catching 'Pirate Redbeard'" Rob switched off. "All set!" He grinned at Bartlett in relief.

Now for a different kind of action. First, he wanted a shower. The smell of fish on his person was the last thing he needed. But he had to hurry, for the first glimmers of sunlight were beginning to filter through the fog, and surely the servants would soon be moving around clearing up the debris from last night's ball even though they had all been told to take their time this morning.

"You wait for the call, Tom. I've got to show my face. Maybe I can catch a guilty look. Who knows?"

CHAPTER NINETEEN

Quickly and quietly, the Spaniard crossed the Great Hall to the staircase, meeting no one on the way. After he had showered, he went down to the kitchen where Jeannie was tackling the load of dishes in the sink.

"Nobody to help you yet?" he questioned.

"Oh, no, Sir, it be too early. But it be all right, I want to get these out of the way before we do the clean-up. It be some mess out there." She started to giggle. "The Old Lady, she surely had a fair goings over last night."

"You're right, Jeannie, but it was a good party, wasn't it?"

"Too good for some folks, I see." She laughed, giving the Spaniard a coy look. "You'm got a bit of a hangover, I'm thinking, Senor."

Rob looked sufficiently chastened. He had been very much aware of dark circles under his eyes when he had shaved. "Perhaps." he agreed. "Any sign of Miss Rowena yet?" He wouldn't put it past her to drag herself down stairs in spite of Carlo's instructions.

"No, Sir, but I be thinking of taking her a cup a' tea. I know she'll want to be up soon. I don't know what time she went to bed; I didn't see her when the last folks left, and that must'a been in the wee hours." Her brow creased in momentary concern. "She worked that hard, she did. She must be real wore out."

"I'm sure you're right. So let her sleep a little longer. I'll take her tea up later if I may, and I'll insist that she remain in bed. I'd like to thank her for all her efforts. Perhaps she'll have breakfast upstairs. She deserves to be cosseted a little and allowed a lie-in." He wanted Carlos to check her first, too, before any of the servants saw her.

He couldn't help feeling guilty that he was not taking Jeannie into his confidence, but he wanted no one to talk to Rowena until they had time to work out their story. Of course, the maid could not possibly have anything to do with the kidnapping, but she was quite a chatter-box, and he had to suspect each and every member of the household, as well as the farm hands, until he discovered who had knocked Rowena unconscious.

Though he had told Jason to tell none of the staff or guests, he hadn't mentioned Jeannie by name, but he knew that the stable lad was well aware that secrecy was essential, and her very innocence would be a perfect buffer to anyone asking questions

First things first. He needed to talk to the police. He returned to the east wing to make the call.

"As soon as possible, start removing all the contraband from the island. We don't know whether Heron might take it into his head to go back there."

That was the first part of his plan taken care of.

Later, when the reports told of no glitches, that Redbeard and his partner had been removed safely and were being taken off to prison, he returned to the kitchen. Carlos had already peeped into Rowena's bedroom and found her sleeping peacefully, so now Rob could check on her himself. Carrying her tray carefully, he made his way up the stairs.

His first knock elicited no answer. He knocked again.

"Rowena, it's me, your Spanish sea captain," he called softly. He paused for a moment. "I've brought you your breakfast."

There was a rattle of the latch, and Rowena opened the door. She was fastening her dressing gown. She pushed her hair away from her face as she managed a wan smile. "Good morning." Her voice was husky with sleep. "Come in," she looked at the daintily-spread meal. "Thank you, you shouldn't have, I was coming down just now." She led the way across her bed-room to the window seat where Rob placed the tray on a table beside it.

He hesitated as he watched her pour herself a cup of tea. "How are you feeling?"

She showed little eagerness at his presence. She remembered his lack of trust. Her voice was cool. "Oh, a little better, I managed to sleep. Did you?"

"Actually, no. But then I haven't been bashed over the head. How is it? May I look?" Frowning, he moved to sit beside her. There seemed to have been no further bleeding, and the professionally dressed wound appeared to be healthy enough, but the egg-like bump looked so tender. She stiffened her spine, a haughty expression on her face.

His frown softened, but he could not hide the deep concern in his eyes. She obviously still intended to keep her distance. But if she only knew how jealous he had been of Miles Gilbert.

Suddenly, the fear of what might have been was overwhelming. To hell with misunderstandings. He reached for her and drew her close, his strength overcoming her resistance.

"Dear God," he muttered. "I went through purgatory wondering what was happening on that damned trawler when we were following it. And then when Miles seemed to stake his claim, I could have . . . . If I had lost you . . . ."

He cupped her chin, his eyes searching her face.

"Oh, Rowena," he whispered. "I could not have borne it." Gently, he touched her lips with his fingers. "Mistress Pentraegon, this sea captain is not going to let you wander off by yourself again." The harsh emotion changed to a wry smile. She was like a delicate piece of porcelain, too fragile to crush in his arms as every nerve in his body demanded. Her eyes had widened: pools of uncertainty.

For a moment, she tried to draw away from his touch. The memories of the previous night were a jumble of contradictions. He had spurned her arms when she had reached for him, showing that he didn't trust her. Now she so needed the trust that she herself had spurned in turn. She felt the barriers crumble. Then, as his lips trailed across her cheek, everything seem to dissolve in a vivid flame of desire.

"Oh, Rob," she moaned. Her arms reached up, her hands burying themselves in the crisp curls. There was only the moment. The night was a dream; a nightmare, yes; but still, just something in the past. She felt as if the cocoon of darkness had opened, and she now was floating on a cloud of glorious, blissful happiness. The morning was a great blaze of warmth and light. She turned her head, reaching for his mouth.

The Spaniard felt the softness of her curves through the thin material of her robe, the slender length of her limbs pressed close to his. He felt as a man in the desert, longing to slake his thirst. His whole body shuddered with a torment of need. Raining kisses over her eager lips, across her face, her eyes, her cheeks, down the long, slender column of her throat, he could not taste enough of her.

She no longer had any resistance. A startling shaft of ecstasy set fire to her, sending deep ripples of passion to the very core of her being. It was as if nothing else in the world existed; just the moment, and the magic.

"Damn Miles Gilbert." Rob muttered against her tender softness.

Rowena gasped. She came back to earth. The harsh world of reality broke the spell. This was not the time, maybe there never would be a right time. She must not forget the threats of the smugglers on her childhood friend, the house, her grandfather. Others could come, even though Rob and Jason had captured Redbeard and his partner.

She pushed away the Spaniard's eager hands and dragged together the folds of her robe.

His eyes narrowed as he looked at her flushed face. Why the withdrawal? "What's the matter, little porcupine?"

"I'm sorry. You must think I'm a weak-and-wan, Elizabethan damsel in distress, or something. I'm fine, you don't need to comfort me." She lifted her chin. The last thing she wanted was pity.

"It's certainly not mere comfort." He drew back. Why was she doing this? She had pulled down the shutters again. "Rowena, one of these days you are going to stop running." His voice was gentle. "You won't escape me then."

She shied away from his words. It could not be. Her enormous load of responsibility was almost too much to bear. The smugglers, Gulls Walk with its millstone of debt, her ancestors, they all seemed to be closing in on her.

And Miles! What was going to happen to Miles? Perhaps it was the aftermath of the concussion, but it was all too much to resolve. Yet inevitably she needed answers.

"What news have you heard? Did the police take the smugglers? Does Heron know what we did? And Miles? What have you done with him?" She determined to concentrate on today. She couldn't endure thoughts of the morrow. She tried to make her voice business-like.

"Slow down!" Rob smiled. If that was the way she wanted to play it, then he would go along. "I can't answer so many questions at once." He settled his back against the windowsill. "First, yes, the police have the smugglers. They are in prison by now. Second, no, Heron doesn't know. When he left his boat to come back to the farm, he was smiling, according to the police. And third, your friend Miles is . . . in good hands." Rowena winced at the touch of sarcasm. "He thinks he is being held by the smugglers."

"But can't you tell him? He must be scared out of his mind." Privately, the Spaniard thought that wouldn't do him any harm!

"No. If we are to succeed, he must know nothing more about the smugglers. Just trust me, Rowena." In any case, he was not ready to divulge all the details of his plan yet. He raised her fingers to his lips. She trembled a little.

"So what's going to happen next? Heron might carry out the threat to burn Gulls Walk when Redbeard and his partner don't show up." She bravely tried to hide her fear.

"Now why on earth would he do that? He certainly can have nothing to gain. He has no reason to believe that since Gilbert, as far as he knows, is out of the way, you have any intentions of reneging on his promise to co-operate. If you meet Heron, just show how scared you are. That'll keep him happy!"

It all sounded so easy. She twisted the napkin in her lap round and round. "Then what do we do?"

"We wait. Heron will be worried when he hears nothing. His line is tapped and the police will soon find out who are the leaders of the smugglers. One thing more. The police are removing the contraband from the island, so if Heron goes to check, he'll find nothing. He'll think that he and his organisation have been duped, that old Redbeard has scarpered with the lot. Then we'll see them all chasing their tails . . . right into our net.

"And you know what is wonderful? They have no idea of our involvement."

He injected as much confidence into his voice as he could; he so wanted to drive away the fear that still lurked in her eyes, for there was no point in worrying her about the unknown quantities: one in particular. Who was last night's unknown assailant? He must find out soon. His burning need to protect Rowena was paramount.

A sharp knock on the door startled them both.

"Rowena? Are you awake? It's me, Meg." The voice was loud. "I hope you don't have a hangover like mine. I'm going to make a hair-of-the-dog-that-bit-me. Want one?" The knock sounded again.

Quickly, Rob got to his feet. The flames of fire in his eyes softened leaving the warm glow of chestnuts. Dropping one final touch on her shoulder, he went to open the door. Rowena buried her face in her cup of tea to hide conflicting emotions. She so wanted to believe her tenant.

"Oh." Megan looked disconcerted.

"Thank you, that's sweet of you, Megan." Rowena called. Her voice was husky. She cleared her throat. "But Rob brought me a cup of tea, which is serving the purpose." She took another sip.

Ruefully, she remembered Megan's bitterness last night. But her friend seemed to have forgotten it. Perhaps it had only been the drink talking. If Megan didn't remember how she had parted from Miles and herself in anger, then Rowena, thankfully, was not going to bring it up. She looked at the Spaniard who gave an almost imperceptible shake of his head as he put an arm on Megan's shoulder.

"I've got a pretty good remedy, Megan. Come, I'll make you one while we leave Rowena to her breakfast. She's feeling a little fragile this morning.

Somehow, she fell last night and cut her head. She thinks she must have been unconscious for a while. But my brother-in-law has treated her and says she will be all right." He turned back to Rowena. "You stay up here, at least until lunch time. I'll come to see you again then." His tone was matter-of-fact, even business-like. Rowena felt uncertain again, until he smiled and winked at her unbeknownst to Megan as he firmly lead the girl through the door. He closed it quietly behind them.

Rowena leaned back against the cushions, looking out at the glistering of sunlight on the fast-fading morning fog swirling like thin gossamer over the freshly washed earth. The rain and accompanying heavy clouds were gone, leaving shimmering, sparkling crystals of dew on the flowers beneath her window. Mingling with their scent was the sweet smell of summer grasses and the sharp, clean tang of the sea. She listened to the trill of song birds blending with the gentle buzz of lazy bumble bees; and above all, the ever-present call of the gulls searching for their next meal.

Since time immemorial, the morning sounds had been the same. Yet today, they were different. The sharp etchings of fear, mingled with hope, made the world seem infinitely precious.

Rowena stretched her arms above her head, her aches forgotten. She knew she should worry about Miles, the smugglers, Gulls Walk, probate, what was going to happen next; but for the moment she allowed herself to hold on to the Spaniard's confidence, and the memory of his kiss.

In a little while, she would go downstairs. She was suddenly hungry. After breakfast, she would shower. There was no hurry, though she must look a dreadful mess. But it had not seemed to matter to Rob. Small, pearly teeth crunched on a slice of toast. It was weeks since Trevy's home-made marmalade had tasted so good.

"Well, did you enjoy the party?" Rob barely listened to Megan's burbles of delight, which needed no extra encouragement from him. His thoughts dwelled on the moments with Rowena. He hoped he had managed to convince her.

They reached the kitchen where Jason and some of the servants had just come in.

"Morning' Senor, Miss Megan." The stable boy hesitated, knowing nothing of events at the harbour in Penzance and wondered how he could ask. "How be you, Sir?"

"Absolutely fine, Jason. A little hangover, perhaps. But it's a lovely morning."

The stable boy mentally heaved a sigh of relief. Obviously the Spaniard's plans had gone well. "Good, Sir. I'll be getting to my chores then." He longed to find out if Miss Rowena was all right, but he wasn't about to ask any questions in front of the others in the kitchen. The Senor had told him to keep mum.

"Thank you, Jason. I've just taken Miss Pentraegon her breakfast, and she says you were all towers of strength last night." His eyes swept the assembled group as he patted the boy on the shoulder, then turned back to Megan. "Now, about that hair-of-the-dog-that-bit-you . . . ."

Jason heaved a sigh of relief.

It was midday before Rob heard again from the police. Everything had gone according to plan. The two smugglers were being allowed no contact with the outside world. Proof of their involvement with drugs saw to that. And apparently the blows on their heads from the iron bar had been sufficiently effective to keep them in a groggy state for a few hours yet. What words they had managed to exchange with each other as they were driven away were of murderous anger at a double-cross, for who else but Heron and his fisherman partner could have been responsible?

The eaves-dropping police couldn't have been more delighted! And the contraband removal was underway.

With a pleased smile and a sigh of relief, Rob now looked for an excuse to find out what was happening over at Home Farm. Jeannie had run out of milk for the lunch-time coffee, so he offered to fetch it.

"Good morning, Heron." He met the farm manager in the yard. "We've run out of milk. We all need plenty of coffee to wake us after last night. Everyone is busy clearing up, so I've been given my orders." He grinned as if he had not a care in the world.

"Oh, right, Sir." The man looked bleary-eyed. He led the way to the dairy.

"And how're Mr. Gilbert and your guests today? I hope they all enjoyed themselves." Rob asked.

"I'm sure they did, Sir. They left first thing this morning. Mr. Gilbert, too. They had to get back to London. It was kind of you to include them." The dour expression almost became a smile.

"Oh, no problem; they were welcome." Perhaps he was wrong, but Rob was sure he saw malice in Heron's eyes. "I'm surprised that Mr. Gilbert left so early. I thought he would have had too much of a hangover."

"I think he did, but business called." Quickly, the farm manager changed the subject. "And did every one at the manor have a good time at the ball?"

Interesting, thought Rob.

"I hope so. The last guests stayed well past three o'clock." He had checked with Carlos, who had valiantly stayed up until the last reveller had left.

"Thank you, oh, do we need our coffee!" He turned away with the jug of milk in his hand. His own eyes twinkled as he imagined the smug thoughts going through Heron's mind.

Now for the next step.

"Tom," Rob closed the door to his apartment behind him. "I want you to contact the police again. When Heron hears nothing from his friends, he'll begin to worry. I expect he'll call someone in the organisation who will worry, too, since no one will know where Redbeard and his partner are. When Heron eventually checks the island, he'll believe he has been set up. So will his friends! Then the fat will be in the fire.

"But I want no more involvement from us, if possible. Miss Pentraegon has endured enough."

"Yet if you're right, we'll have more visitors." Bartlett frowned.

"I expect so. But the police can take over from there. Since Heron's phone is tapped, we can quietly and innocently fade from the picture." He wondered if that were wishful thinking.

He continued. "Heron will want to show his friends those containers holding the bottles he took from the island; they're in his warehouse. After all, they are the only proof of his loyalty. And that's when arrests can be made. The police will, apparently, follow those visitors from London."

Not to Gulls Walk, he hoped.

"As far as Heron knows, we innocent residents of Pentraegon Cove have no idea about the island, or the type of contraband, so can have nothing to do with the disappearance of the smuggled drugs. The rest of Redbeard's group will be chasing their tails."

"But there is one thing you have forgotten." Bartlett looked toward the closed door. "Who hit Miss Pentraegon?"

"No. I haven't forgotten, but whoever it is will surface. He'll have to contact Heron to find out what happened on the trawler. Remember, every phone call will be monitored. After all, the smugglers have no idea that we are aware of what is going on." He thought for a moment.

"I'm pretty sure that Redbeard will hardly have spread the word from the boat that Gilbert is a prisoner, or that Rowena, supposedly scared stiff, is intending to co-operate. Remember, we couldn't get through on our radio phone until we were near to shore, and that was just before we knocked out the pirate and his friend."

Surely the storm had been sufficiently bad for it to be too difficult for the smugglers to make contact with land any earlier. And he was pretty sure that Redbeard had not sent any information about the captured two at the beginning of the trip to the island. He would want to consider his options before telling of the foul-up.

The Spaniard sent up a silent prayer.

"Only Heron knows," Rob continued; "and he is not likely to volunteer information about Redbeard's decision. He's probably little more than a go-between in the set-up, anyway. Indeed, he's caught between two stools. He doesn't know where Redbeard is or what's happened, so he's sure to keep his mouth shut.

"He's the only one, apart from the boat's skipper, who knows that Miles and Rowena were on the trawler; and it must have been his information that persuaded Redbeard to use pressure to make them co-operate. He's not about to admit anything that suggests that Pentraegon Cove is no longer safe for further smuggling. He's been making a good living from his activities, and I'm sure he wants it to continue."

But they'd have to make sure. There was one last thing he required of Rowena. He wished he didn't need her help. At least, they had a little time; but she was the key.

It was afternoon when Rob tapped on Rowena's door. She had just finished dressing and bade him enter. The sunlight pouring through the windows lit a vivid halo around her glorious auburn hair. He longed to take her into his arms. His eyes darkened. She deserved so much more than the brief explanations he had given her just before the ball. No wonder she had found it hard to trust him. Yet she had acted the role he had asked her to play on the fishing boat uncomplainingly, magnificently.

"You look so much better. Not at all like a girl who endured what you did last night. We couldn't have escaped without your wonderful efforts. And I forgot to thank you." He grinned and swept her a truly Elizabethan bow. "My humble appreciation."

"You're welcome, Rob." Her eyes brightened. "It was rather fun, actually. And I haven't thanked you either." She managed to enter into the spirit of things. Somehow, her worries seemed less when he was near. She reached up to touch his face. "But I like you better without that awful executioner's mask."

With a wry smile, he took her hand and kissed it.

But there was still much to do, and he needed her help again. First he must fill her in on some, though not all, of the details. He drew her to the roomy window seat. Rowena listened in dawning understanding. When he had finished, she sat in silence, then lifted her head.

"So Miles only knows what he heard from the smugglers, and nothing about our escape? But surely he knows that Jason and you were in the cabin? Won't he wonder how you got off the boat?" Rowena clasped her hands together. "Is he to know nothing more?"

"I think not. After all, the balaclavas disguised our faces, too. And at the moment, he is still suffering from his beating and wanders in and out of consciousness; so he doesn't remember very much, and there is no one to jog his memory. He hasn't said anything about us being on board, so perhaps he really doesn't remember. He must be worrying himself sick wondering what has happened. It must be like a nightmare. After all, he still thinks he is in the hands of Redbeard's friends, and the police are quite skilful at picking the brains of an unsuspecting witness." Rob frowned as he continued.

"He may not be part of the smuggling ring, but he must have had some inkling of what has been going on. Even he cannot totally believe that his income came only from cattle, flowers and vegetables!"

Suddenly, he was not so sanguine. "I'd give anything to keep you out of this, to send you away to safety. For if anything goes wrong, I'll never forgive myself." His eyes darkened.

"But nothing will." She touched his cheek again. He trusted her, and he needed her! A feeling of elation swamped any fear she might have had. "Remember, I'm just as much involved as you. I have a duty to help. Gulls Walk is mine, and she's as responsible as anyone else. I'll be fine, Rob. Really I will. Now just tell me what you want me to do."

The light of battle shone in Rowena's eyes. The sheer relief of total trust was wonderful. Nothing could take that away now.

But the Spaniard's face was grave as he looked at her innocent smile.

"Actually, I need you to look fearful and grim, not glow like Joan of Arc!" He tried to smile. "You really are an extraordinary young woman, my porcupine?" He still remembered her feisty behaviour the first time he met her. "At least we probably have a day's grace." Then he explained what he wanted her to do.

CHAPTER TWENTY

The morning's activity saw Gulls Walk restored to her usual self, and the warm, sunny afternoon settled drowsily over the house now that the extra servants had left. Jeannie went to her room for a well-earned rest, first insisting that her mistress should rest, too. Jason hung around the stable, half-heartedly cleaning tackle. He, too, needed more sleep after the night's exertions, but he could not bring himself to relax entirely. Bartlett sat at his communication centre, wondering when the police would call. The farm phone had not rung at all. The waiting was hard, but he was determined that Rob should catch at least a few hours sleep.

By evening, there had been no calls, no visitors, nothing. When the Spaniard got up to take Bartlett's place, all was silent and still. He dozed off and on through the night stretched out on the long sofa with a blanket covering his legs. He, too, found the waiting hard, but he spent the time going over and over his plan. Nothing must go wrong if Rowena and Gulls Walk were to be safe.

When the first glimmerings of dawn touched the horizon, and Bartlett came to relieve him, he returned to his bed, weary with going over every contingency.

That morning, the household lay low.

Jeannie, who had received the usual supplies from the farm, innocently chattered to Heron about Rowena's fall.

"She fell and hurt herself after the ball. She looked that pale when she got up yesterday afternoon. That Doctor Carlos was a bit worried about her at first, thinking as how she might be a bit concussed or something. Oh well. It's over now, so she can rest as much as she likes. She surely deserves to, I know that."

"How did she hurt herself?" Heron had questioned, and when Jeannie said she didn't know, he told her to give Miss Rowena his best wishes for a speedy recovery. He smiled as he walked away.

Rob heaved a sigh of relief when a gleeful Jason passed on the message. Apparently the farm manager had no suspicions and must be gloating that his friends had obviously secured her silence when they returned her to Gulls Walk. Now they had more breathing space.

The household settled down to wait. Rowena pleaded her sore head and stayed in her room under Carlo's orders of rest and quiet. Megan went back home—since no one was around to talk to, she told Jeannie. And Rob disappeared, ostensibly on business, taking with him his sister and her husband. The hot summer day continued, and the manor house basked in apparent peace.

Bartlett constantly checked back and forth with the local police, the Special Branch and Interpol, but there was no news. The only one who seemed totally calm was Heron, who went about his normal business, sometimes with a half smile on his face.

Jason decided to work on some much needed repair to the stone walls on either side of the lane between Gulls Walk and Home Farm. He nodded at the farm manager and a couple of the farm workers as they guided the cows into the barn for milking. He even discussed the ubiquitous weather, for he was determined to keep a watchful eye on any fresh comings and goings.

In the evening, Rob returned to find Bartlett champing at the bit. Heron had just received a phone call. The eaves-dropping policeman had quickly passed it on through the usual channels.

The voice had been angry. A harsh, grating voice with a heavy accent.

"Where are they, and the goods? They were supposed to be here yesterday at the latest."

"Haven't they arrived? Hell, I don't know what's happened. They left here the morning after the ball. All went according to plan. They should have been with you by now."

"Well, they aren't here. You said it would all be easy. I want answers! Now! Get back to me."

The phone was slammed down. What Heron's reactions were, the listening policeman could only guess. But there would certainly be action.

And there was.

A few minutes later, Heron made a phone call to Penzance.

"Have you heard anything? They haven't reached London. They left here at the crack of dawn after the ball, according to our watcher. That's much too long."

"I've heard nothing. You don't suppose . . . ?"

"Don't even think it. There'll be hell to pay if they've double-crossed us. But just in case, I think we'd better go fishing. Get here fast."

Again the policeman heard the slamming of the phone.

Now it was time for Rowena to play her part. Rob needed to make sure there was no doubt in Heron's mind of Rowena's and Miles' innocence. Grimly, the Spaniard, hidden behind a curtain, watched her walk across the courtyard to the farm house just as Heron was leaving.

"Oh, I'm sorry; you're in a rush." She made her voice as apologetic as she could. She knew she looked flustered. That was easy to do. "I just wondered. I haven't heard about Miles since . . . you know. Is he all right? I've been so worried." Her eyes were large, innocent pools, with the nice touch of a couple of tears. Dear heavens, she thought. I should be up for an Oscar.

"Your boyfriend? Ha! He's being well taken care of. He'll get over a few bumps and bruises." An ugly leer crossed Heron's face. Then a sudden thought struck him. The girl needed to be kept dangling. "You'd better keep you mouth shut, or you won't see him again. Meanwhile, just take yourself home to Gulls Walk, and look at what you'll lose if you disobey me."

He grabbed her arm and steered her back toward the manor house. He stood for a few moments watching her disconsolate figure trail down the gravel driveway, and half smiled, enjoying the power; then his face set into its usual grim and dour expression. What the hell had happened to his cohorts? He hurried down to the dock to await the trawler.

"Yuck!" Rowena shivered as she entered the Great Hall where Rob was standing waiting. "The man is horrible! He actually gloated over poor Miles' injuries."

"Now, don't worry, the police say that he is improving. All he is suffering from now are a few bruises and a headache." And a healthy fear, which would do him no harm, Rob thought, feeling little sympathy for him.

"How can you be so callous? He hasn't really done anything wrong. Oh, I wish the police would tell him that they know everything, then he needn't worry. I don't see why they have to keep him in the dark, letting him think he's still in the hands of the smugglers. After all, we know that he has nothing to do with them." Rowena found it hard to understand Rob's cynicism.

He did not remind her that the financial status of her life-long friend was far too suspect for any element of trust to be given to him. The less Miles Gilbert knew about the present situation, the better.

"Maybe. We'll cross that bridge when we come to it." Rob longed to take her in his arms. Truth to tell, he was far more concerned for her than he wanted to admit. "Anyway, it seems we can be sure that Heron has no doubts about you, and no inkling of my involvement." Whatever happened

over the next few days, no suspicion must fall on her. These drug cartels
had long arms.

By the time the last, deep shadows of twilight were fading, Rowena
couldn't keep her eyes open. She had curled up on the sofa in the Spaniard's
apartment while he and Bartlett kept contact with the police. The trawler
had picked up Heron, and radar was keeping track of their direction, but it
would be at least another hour before they returned.

Rob gently woke her.

"You should be in bed, Porcupine. Carlos told me to make sure you had
plenty of rest and sleep." She shook her head, not wanting to leave. "Look,
even if you do stay up, there will be little to report. The surveillance equipment
is still in place on the island, and it will pick up Heron's comments when he
finds the cave empty. It's all in the hands of the police now. They won't need
us any more." Rob helped her out of her comfortable seat. Longing to kiss
away her worried frown, he cast about in his mind for something to take her
mind off the smugglers.

"Oh, by the way, I had an idea about our medallions. I have mine here."
He drew it out of his pocket. "I've been meaning to take another look at
yours."

Curiously, she examined it. Anything was better than this awful waiting.
Yes, it did seem different, Rowena had handled hers so many times that she
could pick out the pattern blindfolded. Leading the way to the library, she
opened the glass case to where she had returned it yesterday.

Rob held it up to the light.

"Yes, look. These shapes on the back could make letters, backward letters.
Now if we had an ink pad . . . ."

"There's one in Gramp's desk, I think." Thoughts of sleep vanished.
Eagerly, she searched through the drawers. "Yes, I knew he had one. Oh,
Rob, perhaps it's a clue."

Taking a sheet of paper, he carefully inked first one, then the other
medallion. Lining each galleon side by side, he pressed down. He twisted
and turned the pieces of paper, but the lines and curves made no sense
at first. Then he had a brain wave; he re-inked one of the medallions and
printed it over the marks of the other. After a few tries, he managed to print
them in alignment. Apparently, they were letters, though they were rough,
and not very clear. **OBSEQUIO**, he managed to decipher. What on earth was
that? His Latin was decidedly rusty; something Uriah Heepish, he thought,
remembering a character from Dicken's David Copperfield. Humble rubbing
of greasy palms.

"Well, so much for my thinking it might be a clue to buried treasure. I think the old man must have been having the last laugh, telling the Spanish captain to bow to a superior Englishman. Oh, well. It was worth a shot."

"No, wait a minute, it must mean something. Come look at Queen Elizabeth's portrait. There. Below her hands. Old Morgan had those words written long after the picture was painted. We always wondered why.

EI QUAM SALUTAMUS CUM OBSEQUIO ET HUMILI TRIBUTO TENEMUS
IN MEMORIA ILLIUS DIEI ET EIUS REGALIS OMNIPOTENTIAE

"'Of she whom we do homage pay with obeisance and humble pence we keep in memory of that day and of her omnipotence.'" She translated. "It seems such an odd word. I realise now there has to be a reason other than to make the captain squirm. I never could imagine old Morgan using it; all his writings speak of his pride. To give homage was enough. He might bow to his queen, but not in a servile manner. And obeisance could be translated as obsequious behaviour. It does seems to be the same in English as in Latin."

Rowena lifted her hand and traced the words with her fingers.

"I think you have a good point." Rob was thoughtful, thankful he had found something to distract her.

To submit, to fawn, to be dutifully obedience, servile. Where in heaven's name does one bow down? he wondered. There's no church on the property, so it can't mean an altar. Where the servants worked? Is that a possibility? But the Spanish sea captain, who was a carefully treated prisoner, wouldn't know much about the servant's quarters.

"Rowena, we've got to think how that first Morgan would have thought. He was master in his own house. Look how he wouldn't let poor Rowena marry the Spaniard, though he allowed the man to live. But maybe he had some distorted sense of honour with regard to ownership of whatever he removed from the galleon. And you say there have been rumours of buried treasure down the centuries."

"You're right, Rob. Morgan was little more than a pirate at that time, and he must have been awed by his distinguished captive, even though he saw no immediate future there for his daughter."

"So if there is treasure, it's got to be somewhere in the living area. Bow down, serve, kneel. Ah, a throne? Has there been a particular place where Morgan sat dispensing justice?"

"Good heavens, no! He gave orders to his family, obviously, but he was no feudal Lord-of-the-Manor. He was a pretty jovial character by all accounts."

"But why in Latin? I know it was still the educated language of the church, but the Spaniard must have spoken English, otherwise he would not have been captain of an invading galleon. And why are the words painted on the portrait?" Rob got to his feet and examined Queen Elizabeth closer. "Yes, probably the words were added at the same time as the painting of the house, or maybe later. Can there be some connection that we are not seeing?"

His fingers traced the letters, **OBSEQUIO.** They were exactly under the front entrance to the house.

Hmmm. He tried to imagine back four hundred years. He supposed one did bow when one came to call at that time in history. "Let's go out and look at your front door." He led the way, quickly followed by a now wide-awake Rowena. He lifted the heavy latch and walked out to the gravelled driveway. Then he turned and made a bow to Rowena as she stood under the arch.

"Does that suggest anything to you?"

Rowena giggled. "No, except I think it's a shame bowing went out of style."

"Just ask and I'll bow to you any time, my sweet." Rob laughed. "I'll even go down on bended knee. Will that be obsequious enough for you?" Then his eyes darkened, the laughter suddenly gone from his face. Rowena lowered her head as a shy blush touched her cheeks.

"I think . . ." She hesitated. "Do you have any more bright ideas . . . about buried treasure?"

Oh, yes, he had many more ideas. About treasures, too. She was all too tempting. His expression softened and he began to smile as he watched the blush spread. But it was late. Time for sleep. At least she now had something else to think about other than smugglers and drugs. He closed the front door and helped her up the stairs. Tomorrow was another day.

Early the next morning, Rowena and Rob took out the horses for what they intended to be a gentle amble. They had both missed the daily exercise, and so had Goemor and Firefly. But once away from the house, they gave the animals their heads and allowed the breeze to whirl away their problems. The crisp air lifted the last of Rowena's headache and they both returned to the house refreshed and optimistic.

But when Rob entered his apartment, leaving Rowena to go upstairs to shower and change, his optimism plummeted at the sight of Bartlett's grim expression.

"Do the police have news of Heron?"

"Oh, yes. He's as mad as a rattler. According to the conversation he and his fisherman friend had in the cave yesterday evening, they think old Redbeard has pulled a fast one on them. It's just as you expected. It hasn't occurred to them that anyone else might be involved. I would love to have seen their faces when they found the crates all gone." Bartlett allowed himself a small smile, then his face grew grave again. He hated to be the bearer of his next piece of news. "Early this morning, there was another phone call. We now know who knocked out Miss Pentraegon."

CHAPTER TWENTY-ONE

As she dressed after her shower, Rowena mentally went over every room in the house, trying to imagine any connection with the word on the medallion.

There were letters and documents written by other ancestors who had been equally curious, but they had found nothing. They, too, had searched possible places mentioned in old Morgan's diary: the too expensive sundial, under which an empty chamber had been found, and the mounting block that had been placed over a brick-lined hole.

At the sundial, one bowed to 'time's fell hand'—she remembered her Shakespeare—and at the mounting block, one bent one's knee to mount one's horse. *OBSEQUIO'* could apply to both. And the number of holes dug around the mulberry tree over the years certainly also required much bending of the knee. Had treasure been buried in any of those places once? Earlier ancestors had certainly searched there. If so, it was now long gone from those locations.

But old pirate Morgan had been insistent that a share of what he salvaged from the galleon should go to the Spanish captain, if he returned. Rowena remembered the words in the pirates diary.

Of such Treasures as J hath, He shalle share when He returne, but not Tille then, that of Mye Beloved Rowena

And none of her ancestors had admitted to finding any of the treasure.

Rowena sighed. They were no nearer solving the mystery, and she had been so hopeful when Rob had worked out the message on the bronze discs.

Ah, well; she had better things to do than waste time on a dream. Visions of returning part of the treasure to the Olivares family, or handing over a large cheque to a nebulous probate officer, faded from her mind. She wandered onto the terrace with ideas of picking some roses to freshen the flower bowls, but the sun was so tempting she settled into a comfortable chair and, still tired from broken nights, soon was fast asleep.

Meanwhile, after seeing Carlos and Margarita off to Penzance for the day, Rob questioned Bartlett for more details about Rowena's assailant.

"The inspector played the tape back to me. They had a real old slanging match, each angry with the other over the events of that evening. Heron particularly was furious that Miles Gilbert and Rowena had come poking their noses into what was none of their business; if only they had remained at the ball . . . . Without their interference and necessary capture, the whole operation would have been straight forward.

"But we noticed Heron didn't say anything about Redbeard's coercion of the two into the co-operation he was determined to have. Heron seems to be keeping that to himself; and nobody has any idea what's happened to the smugglers, or Gilbert, whom they presume is with Redbeard and the executioner. The conversation gave no more details, but certainly showed how both Heron and his friend are desperately concerned."

Bartlett rubbed his chin thoughtfully. "One good thing we discovered. They have no intention of telling their bosses about events leading up to and on the trawler; accusations will fly if they do. For them, it's bad enough not knowing what's happened to the bottles on the island without incriminating themselves." He paused for a moment. "But Heron thinks that with Gilbert's disappearance he has Rowena in the palm of his hand, scared to death, and no one else need know that. He seems determined to persuade the head of the smuggling ring that Pentraegon Cove will be as peaceful as ever, so maybe he can arrange a new set-up, and the money will keep rolling in."

"And what about the drugs? Was any mention made of them?"

"Curiously, no. I got the impression that they both still think the contraband is just wine."

"I suppose we should feel relieved about that." But Rob's expression remained grim.

"There was one other thing. About Miles Gilbert. They both are positive that he knew nothing about the island cache, or that he could be party to its removal. Heron has never told him that his lucrative income is not from cattle. If Miles had not got in the way, he would still be free. Not that Heron expressed anywhere near as much concern for the man as he did for the wine. It's the other one who is worried about what has happened to Gilbert."

With some relief, Rob wandered over to the window and looked out. He saw Rowena there, peacefully sleeping. One piece of the news he had to tell her was good. At least they could corroborate that her friend Gilbert would be exonerated in part. But the other information, the name of her assailant; he wondered how long he could keep it from her.

The phone rang again. Rob reached to answer it.

"There's been another call from London." It was the Chief Inspector. "You were right, Senor, the same voice as before; we've traced the call and know who he is. We have long suspected his involvement but haven't been able to prove anything until now. He's coming down to see the cases Heron has stored. He's mad as a rattler that the contraband on the island has been removed. I don't fancy being in Heron's shoes. I'm not sure he's convinced the farm manager isn't connected with its disappearance."

"How's he coming? By car?"

"Yes, so it will be quite feasible for him to think we have followed him from London when we catch him. I'll have secret surveillance equipment in place so we can find out as much information as possible before we pounce. He doesn't expect to be here until evening, and Heron has to be at the warehouse early, waiting for him."

"And no plans to come to the farm?"

"No. Just the warehouse. The island and the contents of the containers are what interest him. And we have no intentions of allowing him to extend that interest." The inspector chuckled. "I've been waiting for this day for a long time. Thank you, Senor Olivares."

"My pleasure, believe me. But what about Miss Pentraegon's assailant?"

"Oh, after we have dealt with our London friends, having found the goods in their hands, the mopping up operation will be easy."

When he rang off, the Spaniard looked at his watch. The rest of the day had to be got through. He could hardly deliberately avoid telling Rowena the news. But not yet. At least, he could distract her enough so she wouldn't ask for too many details.

"Wake up, sleepy head." Carrying a couple of cups of coffee, Rob walked onto the terrace. "Well, where shall we look first?"

"Look?" Rowena blinked and sat up.

"Yes. Buried treasure. Surely you have all sorts of ideas."

"Well, no, actually. All the obvious places have been searched over the years." Rowena reminded him of the entries in old Morgan's diary. "There seems little point in wasting the time."

"Wasting time? But what else do we have to do?"

"The smugglers, and the cases on the island . . ." Her voice trailed away.

"Oh, everything is under control. The police are all set to catch them. No more worries there, so let's fill in the time until we hear from them. It's a lovely day, and I feel like a treasure hunt."

They wandered around the house, Rob suggesting all sorts of ridiculous and humorous places until he had Rowena in fits of giggles. He laughed with her, but often he turned away as sombre thoughts brought a worried frown to his face.

Finally, they ended in the library to read again the words under Queen Elizabeth's portrait.

"You know, the one thing I don't understand is that the medallions were made before the house was built. How could the old pirate know where he was going to bury the treasure?" Rowena turned over the disc she had removed from its case.

"That's not too difficult to work out." Rob took the chain from her fingers. "He probably had various places in mind, and prepared them as the building grew, intending to decide later. Indeed, maybe he needed several places, for the treasure must have been considerable. There were many soldiers, as well as sailors, on the galleon, who required their pay; and food and lodging were to be needed. Remember, the intention of King Philip was to take over the country and return it to the Catholic religion, not rape it."

That made sense, thought Rowena; but why was none of the treasure found in those obvious places, places to which Morgan had pointed not too subtly in his diary?

Each sat slumped in their chairs. The effort to keep up the laughter had tired them both. The Spaniard glared up at good Queen Bess. "You know something, old woman. What's your secret?" He got to his feet and peered closely at the one-word clue. "OBSEQUIO, why would the old pirate place that word exactly below the middle of the house? There has to be a connection."

Rowena shook her head. "I'm sure he had his reasons, but I have no idea." The hopes that had been raised now plummeted. What was the use?

Rob was not willing to give up so easily. And he desperately needed something good to happen before he told her his bad news. He peered again at the picture.

"Have you a torch, Rowena? I want to look closer." The superimposed house was something of a blur, and the brush strokes were far from perfect.

Taking one from her grandfather's desk drawer, Rowena handed it to him.

"I don't suppose you have a magnifying glass as well?" Rowena found that, too.

"Can we move this display case so I can get closer?" He was positive that the word must have a connection. Gingerly, for the woodwork was no longer very stable, they drew it away from the wall.

Inch by inch Rob examined each letter, but none seemed different from the next. He looked higher and examined the roughly-stroked overlay of the house. Window and door details were more of a suggestion than clearly painted in, but something was not quite right. Of course, not all later extensions were included, and that was to be expected. But still, there was something else . . . .

Suddenly, he turned to Rowena and pulled her to her feet.

"Come; I want to take another look at the front." Giving her no time for explanations, he dragged her across the Great Hall and through the entrance way. Still holding her hand he crossed the drive way to the grass verge of the lawn.

"Look." he said. "There's something missing, and I don't know what."

Rowena's eyes moved back and forth over the elevation. She had no idea what the Spaniard meant, but dutifully she tried to find something different; she had walked through the front door so often, of course, that she had ceased to be aware of it.

Dragging her back inside, Rob peered again at the picture. The number of windows was the same; the decorative embellishments, though proportionally somewhat larger than those that had been carved into the stone all those centuries ago, seemed the same, too.

Once again, he returned to the drive way, Rowena, by now, just as intrigued as he.

"That's it. That's what is missing." He pointed to the blank area above the ornamentation.

Rowena shook her head. "I don't understand. I can't see what you mean."

With a huge grin on his face Rob put his arm around her shoulder, "You will, my little porcupine. Come back inside and look for yourself."

When they entered the library, he pointed to the crudely marked decoration above the door of the painted manor.

"What do you see at the top?"

"Just squiggly marks, some sort of shape, but it's so rough."

"Look closer. What do you think they represent?" He handed her the magnifying glass.

Rowena still looked bewildered. Then suddenly her eyes widened. "Oh, perhaps a ship? Yes, the galleon. But the one above our entrance must have worn away with time."

"No, Rowena. Go look again. There is plenty of ornamentation, but nothing like a Spanish galleon!" Back they went to re-examine the facade.

"Oh, Rob, you're right. But how does that help us?"

"I'm not sure yet, but I'm damned well going to find out. What's up there, behind the wall? There are no rooms at that level, apparently." He glanced along the brick facing below the castellations of the parapet looking for windows.

"No, but there are some rather small, dirty attics. Only junk is stored up there. Certainly no treasure trove!"

"I expect you're right, but it's worth a look." Rob was glad that Rowena's intrigued interest seemed to have pushed out of her mind thoughts of smugglers and drugs. A few cobwebs were little to endure if they meant total absorption in today: not yesterday, or tomorrow.

Taking the torch with them, they clambered up the rickety back stairs to the top floor. There was a long corridor, which was lighted by a couple of weak bulbs, and various doors that led to mostly empty attics. Judging the centre of the building, Rob pushed open a door to a room over the front entrance. This was where the old sea chests were kept, now mostly empty, because Rowena had used nearly all the old silks and satins.

"See. I told you there was no treasure here. At least, not now." Rowena smiled as she told her Spanish tenant how they all had worked so hard beautifying his quarters.

"Hmm. I wonder." He listened to her story but seemed preoccupied as he paced back and forth. Leaving that room, he repeated his pacing in the next.

Finally, he returned to where Rowena was standing.

"Well, my sweet," He reached for her hands and pulled her close. "We just might have found the secret of your umpteenth ancestor." He kissed her quickly, then hurried her back down the stairs. "Let's find Jason. I'm going to need his help, and he deserves to be in on this."

"But what have you found?" Rowena's excitement bubbled over in eager laughter.

"You'll just have to wait." With a wide grin, Rob led her back down to the Great Hall. "I'll only be a moment." He hugged her briefly and hurried through to the kitchen. Jeannie would know where Jason was.

As Rowena paced up and down in eager anticipation, she heard the crunch of tires on gravel, and then the door bell. Megan had returned.

"Oh, Meg, I'm so glad to see you. Come in, come in. You'll never guess what's happened." Giving her friend no time to reply, Rowena took her by the hand. "Follow me, I'm not sure what Rob has found, but I think it is old Morgan's treasure. Isn't it wonderful?"

New visions of sharing filled Rowena's heart with gladness. She had felt so bad about her own selfish introversion, her unawareness of Megan's unhappiness over Miles; now she could alleviate at least some of that sadness.

She pulled Meg behind her up to the top floor and along to the open door of the central attic. Out of breath, she stopped and, with a beaming smile, looked back.

There was no answering smile.

Instead, a strange, taut grimace; and eyes that glittered.

"So now you have it all. The house, Rob, the treasure, and you never even wanted Miles, did you?" There was an ugliness in her expression as Megan moved forward. "What happened on the boat? Why did they let only you come back? Where is Miles now? He was innocent. He knew nothing."

Rowena gasped. "The boat? How do you know?" Suddenly her eyes widened in dawning understanding. "It was you who hit me."

"Of course. You don't think I was going to let you spoil our scheme. Damn you Rowena. I wish I'd hit you harder."

"But why, Megan? I didn't know you needed money."

"You stupid woman. It wasn't for me. Don't you understand? It was for Miles. He wanted Gulls Walk more than anything in the world, and only pretended to want you. If I had money and could help him buy this house, then he would marry me. Me! Do you hear? For two years I've taken my share of the smuggling proceeds; that's because I told Heron about the cave. And this was to have been the big payoff. Just the right time since you don't have the money to settle the death duties! You've never loved him. I've loved him ever since I can remember."

Rowena shrank back, appalled at Megan's bitter anger. The distraught girl continued.

"Why did they let you go free but not Miles? Is he to be the hostage to keep you quiet? I've just been to ask Heron, but he's gone. I came here because you must know. You must tell me. I have to know." She reached a claw-like hand to Rowena's face. "Where is Miles now? Where have they taken him? I saw the smugglers carry him back to the farm, and then put him in the car and drive off. He seemed to be hurt, to be unconscious. I waited until dawn for Heron to come back, but he said he didn't know and would tell me nothing. How badly hurt is Miles?"

Her voice became a high, piercing shriek. Her eyes, almost opaque, were glazed as she lunged. Rowena stumbled backward. One of the chests was behind her and it probably saved her.

As she toppled over it, Megan dived after her, her strength almost doubled in the wildness of her grief. "It's your fault, Rowena Pentraegon. All your fault!"

Rowena twisted and rolled away as Megan crashed into the wall beyond them. There was a splintering and rending of wood. Then there was silence.

Rowena shivered as she dragged herself to her feet. She looked in horror at the crumpled figure. Megan lay across broken pieces of timber with other slats leaning drunkenly into a dark hole beyond. Most of the wall, obviously become fragile through the passage of years, had collapsed under the weight of her diving body. A beam lay across her shoulders; it was that which had knocked her unconscious.

Sinking to her knees, Rowena fearfully felt for a pulse. "Oh, Megan. I would gladly have given Gulls Walk to you both rather than have this tragedy. Please don't die." she moaned.

Dear God! What obsessions this house has created, she thought. Gulls Walk, you truly are a millstone!

Her fingers trembled as they found the faintest of beats. She dragged great gulps of air into her lungs, for she, too, had almost passed out with shock.

Just then she heard the clatter of feet on the stairs.

"Rowena, Rowena, are you all right? What was that noise?" Rob tore along the corridor, Jason just behind him. He became aware of particles of dust, still rising from the broken timbers, drifting slowly over the two girls. Rowena tiredly lifted her head and the Spaniard saw the trickle of tears.

He reached for her and drew her close before bending down to touch the crumpled figure of Megan. "What happened?"

Rowena started to explain. Quickly, he silenced her. Even in her apparently unconscious state, Megan might still be able to hear.

He and Jason carefully removed the fallen beam from Megan's body and checked her for broken bones. There seemed to be none, but they dared not move her until she had been examined more thoroughly. After sending the stable lad for Carlos who, with Margarita, had returned from Penzance, he drew Rowena out of the room and down to the end of the corridor. Megan must not hear their conversation.

With anguish in her voice, Rowena explained what had happened. Furious with himself for having allowed Rowena to be in such danger, he held her close. If only he had repeated to her the inspector's call that morning, had told her that Megan was involved with the smuggling ring, she would never have brought the girl upstairs, or told her of old Morgan's treasure.

"Oh, Rob, what has Gulls Walk done to us? It must have been a temporary madness. I never understood. We should have told her that Miles was all right."

"Now you know we couldn't do that." He kept his voice low. "It is essential that we keep that secret. There must be no possibility of any of the cartel finding out about our involvement, and those people have their methods of infiltrating the prison system. Imagine what would happen if Heron discovered what we had done. Your life would be in jeopardy. And I am sure Gulls Walk would have gone up in flames." Rob paused. He hated to spell out the very real danger, but she had to understand.

"Part of the success of drug cartels, the Mafia, indeed, any crime organization, is due to the swiftness of their retaliation, or more simply, perhaps, plain revenge on those who defy them. This continues to create fear, dissuading all those who wish to fight their power. They cannot afford to lose; hence, swift elimination of all opposition as a warning to others. So you see, we must absolutely avoid any possibility of our involvement being discovered. And who knows with whom Megan may still have contact. Even if she eventually goes to prison, she can still talk."

Rowena shuddered. She had not realised just how great was their danger. It had all seemed simple. The police were about to capture the drug dealers; Redbeard and his partner were already in prison; Miles was safe, though he didn't know it; so she had thought surely that was it.

And they now knew about Megan.

But the Spaniard tried to soothe her horror. "Now we cannot blame ourselves for Megan's unstable reaction but must count our blessings that we discovered her part in the criminal activities in time. Thank goodness we didn't tell her what happened on the boat."

Rob held her close. "I'll just have to watch you like a hawk if I'm to keep you safe." He forced a grin to his face; Rowena looked so desolate. "She's going to be all right, I expect she is just stunned. Tit for tat, I'd say. She clobbered you, and now old Morgan has returned the favour!" He managed a chuckle. Even Rowena raised a small smile.

Carlos came hurrying up the stairs and Rob filled him in with a quick explanation. "Remember, you know nothing. Just that she fell against a wall and a beam crashed down on her. That's all Rowena has said to you." He led the doctor to the attic where Megan lay, still unconscious.

Rowena remained in the corridor, for she could not bare to face her erstwhile friend. Carlos checked Megan thoroughly. When he had finished and was satisfied that she could be moved, Jason carried the girl to her bedroom and went to fetch Jeannie to help clean her up.

Rob led Rowena back to the Great Hall, his arm around her shoulders, where they waited for the doctor's diagnosis

Eventually, Carlos came down with a wry smile on his face and joined them as they returned to Rob's apartment.

"When she woke sufficiently to talk, I asked her what she had done, 'Rowena told me you knocked down a wall.' I said. 'Now if you had an irate husband, I'd certainly understand.' I laughed rather pompously at my own joke, and all she did was glower at me! She's going to be fine, but I gave her a knock-out dose to make sure she sleeps." A good sleep was not only what she needed, but it would keep her secure until the police had dealt with the smugglers. "I've left Jeannie cleaning her up. Rowena, thank goodness your maid knows nothing of what is going on. Wise move there, Rob. Fill me in on the details when you have a moment."

They heard Jeannie's steps on the stairs, and her angry mutters. Rob went to meet her.

"That there Miss Megan! She was so rude. I told her off, I did. She mumbled something about it being Miss Rowena's fault; what for, I don't know; but she didn't look too happy, and I don't believe Miss Rowena would 'a done anything to her. I be not too keen on looking a'ter her. Your doctor Senor, ye can tell him that."

The maid stomped off to the kitchen, carrying a bowl and the first aid materials.

Rowena, who had been listening with considerable concern, found herself wanting to giggle in spite of her distress. Never had she seen Jeannie so irate.

Her tenant couldn't help smiling as well, for he, too, doubted the sleeping tablets would help Megan to a better mood; though under the circumstances, keeping her sedated was important.

But he was not smiling when he explained to Carlos the full story of what had happened in the attic.

"I must get onto the police to tell them that we have Megan, and that we'll keep her here until they come for her."

"Don't worry. I'll make sure she stays in bed. Even if she feels well enough to get up in the morning, I'll think of some medical mumbo jumbo to keep her there. After all, I officially know nothing; just that she fell. She won't escape, I assure you." He went off to find Margarita who was enjoying the peace of the terrace.

Relieved, Rob took Rowena's hand as he phoned the Chief Inspector.

"I'm so sorry Miss Pentraegon was attacked. Is she all right?" the policeman asked. Rowena assured him she was fine and that she had a lucky escape. But remembering the crash and the shattering of timbers, her mind visualised the scene, and Megan's bitter anger. That hurt far more than a few bruises.

When Rob finished his call, having established that all was ready in the warehouse and Heron was there, he turned back to Rowena.

"Everything is set. There's nothing more for us to do except wait. So how about finishing our treasure hunt." His eyes twinkled as he looked down at the worried frown on Rowena's face. "I'll put in a good word for Megan." he finished, gently.

That went against the grain, for as far as he was concerned, she deserved punishing. But he was beginning to understand his landlady's sense of loyalty. A lifetime's friendship could not lightly be thrown away. And he supposed he would have to do the same for Miles Gilbert. His own jealousy and general lack of trust gave him no right to be judge and juror.

Rowena smiled tentatively, perhaps the end was in sight. "Thank you Rob. I feel so guilty. I never knew how unhappy she was. If only Miles had been satisfied with the farm. Gulls Walk is responsible for so much."

Frankly, the Spaniard thought human greed was more responsible, but now was not the time to argue. Much better to think of other things, things such as soft lips and eyes to drown in. He took her into his arms, not wanting to let her go.

But before he could forget the world, Rowena pulled away. The problems of the manor house, and now her friends, still remained. If there were treasure, perhaps it could solve some of them.

"Rob, we didn't look behind the broken wall. It was so dark, and we were concerned about Megan."

Personally, Rob wanted to consign Miss Megan Haversham to the devil and ride away with his porcupine to a place where smugglers and buried treasure did not exist. He sighed as he released Rowena. Damn. The house was taking over again.

"You're right, and we have time now. Let's go." He placed a hand on her shoulder, needing to keep physical contact. So many times, like a will-o'-the-wisp, she had drifted away from him.

They re-climbed the stairs and entered the dark attic. Rob switched on the torch. The dust had settled, and he quickly moved aside the broken wood and the beam, clearing a path to the gaping hole beyond. He shone the light to make sure the area was safe, then he stepped back. Rowena deserved the right to go first.

It was difficult to see, so, taking the torch from the Spaniard, she bent down and squeezed through the hole.

She didn't know what to expect; perhaps sea chests like the ones that had held the bolts of material. But there were none of those. No boxes, no sacks, only a pile of metal in the corner, dulled by years of dust and neglect. Disappointed, Rowena shone the torch higher. She had been so sure that here she would find old pirate Morgan's treasure.

There was a shelf above her head, and an ancient desk at the side with a stool pushed under. The whole space was barely three feet deep. No wonder previous searchers had been unaware that the wall had concealed the tiny room.

Disappointed, she crawled back through the hole.

"If it held any treasure before, it doesn't seem to have much now."

"Let me see." Rob took her place.

He lifted one of the pieces of metal and brought it out to the light. It was curved and engraved with some sort of pattern. He rubbed it with his sleeve.

"Well, I'll be damned! It's a soldier's breast plate. I do believe we must have found your sea captain's armour." He crawled back and brought out more pieces. There was a typical, sixteenth century, Spanish, broad-brimmed helmet; the paldrons that protected the shoulders; and vambrace to cover the arms. "This is a wonderful find. I know quite a few museums that will love to have this. Sets of such sea-faring armour are rare."

Rowena tried to look pleased. At least someone would benefit from their search. "Oh, well. The secret of the galleon's treasure is a secret no longer.

But it has been fun looking for it," It had helped to put aside her memory of Megan's attack.

"Now, let's not be hasty. I saw what looks like a box on the shelf." Rob crawled back through the hole and brought out a leather case covered in cobwebs. He, too, was now coated in the dust and debris of centuries. Rowena couldn't help smiling, remembering how her tenant had rubbed away the soil on her nose the evening before the ball.

"I'm afraid my hanky is not as large as yours." She pulled it from her pocket and brushed the filmy coating from his face. He grinned at her.

"But much more effective." He wasn't referring to his cleaner state.

In some confusion, she wiped the top of the case and the small lock on the side. "Open it, Rob, please. Maybe there is treasure after all."

The catch was brittle and easily gave way, but the lid was tight and it took him a few moments to force it open. A heavy velvet cloth covered the contents. Lifting it gently, they both gasped as the dim light from the bulbs in the corridor was reflected off an untarnished metal. This was not the steel of the armour. Twinkling among intricate, gold scroll-work was the rich glow of precious stones.

"What is it?" Rowena queried. She removed the velvet and reached into the box. In awe, she brought out first one, then two more exquisite chalices.

"Of course." breathed the Spaniard. "These must have been the ones your sea captain used for Mass on the ship. They probably were family treasures, which he brought to ensure that God was on his side, he hoped. And Morgan, though no Catholic, apparently respected them and kept them safe for the captain when he returned."

Rowena sat down abruptly on one of the sea chests, her mind in a sudden turmoil as she pictured the religious fervour the sea captain must have felt for his mission; how he had saved and cherished such important symbols from the sinking galleon. She found herself looking at old Morgan's secret hiding place with a new perspective. What right did she have to mercenary gain? She had been thinking of this treasure as hers, but it was not; the house was only its temporary sanctuary.

"Then we must keep them safe, too, until we can return them. They shall go back to your family," she said, quickly; "we have no right to them, even though they have been here for four hundred years."

"I could kiss you for the thought, my sweet, but we'll discuss that later." Rob put a hand to her face and gently caressed the soft skin. He would never consider allowing that. They truly were hers after so many centuries; they

were too valuable and could be sold for an enormous sum. Then he turned
back to the dark hole.

There seemed to be nothing else, but why?

The desk had a drawer, and he wondered if in there he might find a clue.
It was not easy to open, having been sealed by the dust of centuries.

Rowena searched among the jumbles of old, discarded objects in one of
the other attics and found a broken knife. Easing along the rim of the drawer,
Rob finally managed to jar it from the desk frame. A piece of cloth wrapped
around something, was wedged, preventing the drawer from opening; so inch
by inch, as carefully as he could, he gradually worked the material loose.

Suddenly the whole drawer gave way. Gingerly holding on to the sagging
wood, he removed the tightly wrapped bundle. He carried it into the lighted
corridor and placed it on an old table, which Rowena had dragged from a
corner.

"You open it, Rowena. This must be of value since it is wrapped so
carefully." Strangely, he felt a deep sense of disappointment. He should have
been happy for her. He was aware how concerned she seemed to be about
money. But he wanted to be the one to give her treasures. Not some long-gone
ancestor, a pirate, who had acquired his riches by dubious means—little
different from the smugglers using Pentraegon Cove today.

He stood back as she carefully unwrapped the cloth. He almost didn't
want to look.

"Oh. It's a book. It's a diary, I think. It looks like the one in the case in
the library. Old Morgan's diary."

The Spaniard looked sharply at Rowena. Her voice did not express
disappointment. But surely she was hoping for other valuables, ones that
could be changed for good, hard cash.

"This probably will tell us much more than does the diary in the case in
the library. Oh, Rob, isn't it exciting. At last we may know the whole story.
Let's take it downstairs to where we can examine it in a brighter light."

Her eyes danced; and Rob felt the harsh tightness of disappointment
melt away. The value of the chalices was inestimable, but no thought of that
seemed to have entered her head. Bless you, my love, he thought. Casually,
she gave to Rob the case containing those golden cups, but held on tightly to
the re-wrapped diary as if it were the most precious possession of all.

Carlos and Margarita had left the terrace and were standing in the Great
Hall when they reached the bottom of the stairs.

"Come into the library and see what we have found." Eagerly, Rowena reached a hand to Rob's sister. She danced ahead of the two men who quickly assured each other that all was under control. Megan was fast asleep, and the police were ready and waiting in the warehouse.

When they reached the library, Rowena pulled back the curtains to catch the full light from the evening sun. She placed the precious diary on a small table next to the window seat and indicated to the men to pull up chairs.

They were just about to open the book when there was a banging on the door. "Come quickly. It's all systems go. Heron's friends must have made better time driving down from London than they expected." The excited voice of Bartlett brought them to their feet.

Hesitating, Rob looked at Rowena.

"It's all right," she said. "Old Morgan's not going anywhere. In any case, we will all enjoy uncovering Gulls Walk's beginnings so much better if we know that our smugglers have been taken care of." She was the first to leave the room and hurry in the direction of the Spaniard's apartment.

When they entered, the sergeant told of a quick phone call from the Chief Inspector that had explained how concealed microphones were ready to pick up all conversation, and Rob's equipment had been patched in.

"Heron's boss has gone into the warehouse. In fact, four other men are with him. We think they are important men in their organisation, so we should make an even better haul than we dared to expect." Bartlett turned to the receiver. "The police are waiting until Heron and they open the bottles."

A clatter of doors opening and closing, and the scuffle of feet interrupted him as he turned up the volume. A deep, guttural voice, immensely angry, came clearly over the speaker.

"You'd better have some answers for me. Have you heard from my people?"

"No, not a single phone call. But I went to the island after they left, since I has heard nothing, and the rest of the boxes were gone. They must have taken the bottles. I know nothing about it, I swear."

"Why the hell should I believe you? Those men have been part of my organisation for years. I'll kill you for this. No one double crosses me. You told me this was a sweet set-up, as easy as . . . ."

"I'm not the double crosser." Heron's frightened voice was almost a scream. "It's your men, the men you sent. It has to be. They said they were going back to London, but obviously they didn't. Nobody else knew anything." The rustle of packing material could be heard as Heron continued. "Look.

Would I be here? Would I show you these if I had stolen the rest of the wine from the island?" There was a clink of bottles.

A whispered conversation followed, obviously not intended for Heron's ears.

"Have you opened any of them?"

Heron's reply sounded bewildered. "No, of course not. What good would be an opened bottle of wine?"

Again a mutter too low to hear.

Then Heron continued. "Look, we can find other places to hide the crates. Ones your so-called partners don't know about. Entry to our cove is a cinch. A marvellous place for bringing in contraband. The loss of a shipment of wine is not the end of the earth." The fear was still there in Heron's voice, but now he tried to sound conciliatory. He obviously was loathe to lose his profitable operation.

There was a harsh, contemptuous laugh. "Do you really think I would come down here to investigate a petty operation involving just smuggled wine? You are a fool, Heron." There was the noise of a struggle and the sound of broken glass.

Blazing anger this time. "See. There was over a million pounds in raw heroin in some of those bottles in the cave. Just the beginning of a supply that would have brought profit beyond your wildest dreams."

"But . . . you told me it was wine. Damn you. I never said I would smuggle drugs. Is that what I have been smuggling over the last couple of years?"

"Certainly not. Only a few of the bottles contained drugs. Most of them held wine. We needed to make sure the pipe line was fool-proof. And now we are ready, the whole shipment has gone. I trusted you, Heron. And you know what happens to people who cross me."

"I haven't broken your trust. Hell! I'd no need to. It was a sweet set-up. Like I told you. There was no need to send anyone to check, so why did your partners come? No wonder they wanted to go to the island. I thought it was for security. But it wasn't, was it. They set you up."

Suddenly Heron's voice pitched higher, almost hysterical. "You thought you could trust them. How they must have laughed at us all. And I led them there." His voice broke. "So you're blaming me. Damn you to hell, the lot of you." Anger, bravado, fury all were there. He must have known that his life was worth nothing. Suddenly there was a shot.

A cacophony of sound: running feet, further shots, screams of rage, and the heavy voices of authority. In minutes it was all over.

"So that's it." The Spaniard's voice was curiously quiet as Bartlett switched off the receiver. Each person in the room sat in silence. The noises from the warehouse had told the story as vividly as any picture.

At last, Rowena spoke. "Thank heavens Heron didn't mention Megan, or Miles." She sighed in relief. "Does that mean it's finished?"

"Oh, Miles is unimportant. Since he knew nothing of the operation, the smugglers are hardly likely to bother about him. Anyway his and Megan's involvement were most probably only with Heron; and I doubt she actually knew who Redbeard and the executioner really were."

He had a feeling the police would call her later as an accessory, though. But that worry he would keep from Rowena a little longer.

But she wanted to know more.

"Who was shot? Dear heavens. Do you think Heron was killed?" Rowena's sudden realization was hard to watch. Rob reached for her hand. "Oh, Gulls Walk. Are you cursed?" she anguished.

"Now we don't know who's been hurt, but we'll hear soon enough. It's all out of our hands. Think of what we have prevented by shutting down this operation. Think of the potential lives we have saved." He needed to mitigate some of the horror Rowena was feeling. She relaxed a little. Rob was right.

"There will be some mopping up operations, and questions will have to be answered, but as far as you are concerned, this is the end. Gulls Walk and Pentraegon Cove are safe."

But was he being too hopeful? The sense of deflation was hard to shake. Would Rowena ever feel the same about her home? He must help her pick up the pieces.

CHAPTER TWENTY-THREE

Margarita was the one to break the spell. All of them seemed glued to their chairs, for the ending had been so sudden.

"Well, that's that, then." She tried to lighten the gloom as she got to her feet. "I think it's about time we solved another mystery. Come on, Rowena. Let's get back to that wonderful book. To think it hasn't been opened for four hundred years."

They all stirred. Bartlett promised to stay by the phone and shooed them away. He, too, was aware that Rowena had suffered more shocks over the last few days than she could be expected to endure. She needed to have her mind taken off the near disaster. And certainly she did not need to dwell on the shots they all had heard.

"Wonderful idea!" Rob grinned gratefully at his sister. The servants deserved to be in on this, he thought, but he could hardly include both of them. He remembered the night on the trawler, and later, his guilt at not allowing Jason to tell Jeannie of their discoveries. Mentally, he shuddered to think how little, initially, he had trusted any of the members of the household.

Pulling herself together, Rowena remembered that she was, after all, the hostess, and she hurried to the kitchen to make some sandwiches. Jeannie had gone off duty until dinner time, so she raided the fridge alone. The activity gave her time to come to terms with the horror of the events in the warehouse. Surely now she could expunge some of the heavy sense of guilt and responsibility that she had carried on her shoulders. She just hoped that Megan was going to be all right.

Her mind was a swirl of jangled emotions, for somehow she seemed to have had so little control of her life over the past few days. Let the tumblers fall where they may, she finally thought; though perhaps there really was a light at the end of the tunnel. A small smile lifted the corners of her mouth. She had created so many metaphors in the last weeks, but at least she no longer felt like flotsam on the sea shore, to be swept away by unfeeling waves.

She returned to the library carrying a tray. Her guests were seated around the table, eagerly waiting for her to open the dusty book. Carlos had been up to check on Megan, who was now sleeping soundly, with Jason on duty outside her door. Rob brought in ice and drinks from his apartment, and they all helped themselves as Rowena smoothed away the grime of centuries.

Gently, she opened the cover and turned the first leaf. The pages were dry and stiff, partially stuck together, so she had to be careful not to tear them.

The writing was remarkably legible.

This Thirteenth day of October in the Yeare of our Lord, 1591
Mine Good Enemy, thou hast not Come. I have kept Thine
Share well hid. I shall Showe thee how Mine hath been spent.

Rowena read the words, her curiosity peeked. "It seems that the old pirate intended to be quite scrupulous. He's made a list of expenditures."

She turned the book so that the others could see. New clothes were mixed up among building materials and the purchasing of farm animals. A penny here, a sixpence there, even the enormous sum of two guineas for a mare for Morgan's daughter. The list covered half-a-dozen leaves, then there was a blank sheet. Rowena turned to the next page.

This Twentyeth day of December in the Yeare of Our Lord, 1592
This shall be a sad Christmas, my Good Enemy.
Why doest thou not Come? Our beloved Rowena doeth pyne for
thee and has taken the Sickness. Thou muste come soon.
Here followeth my expenditure.
My House is well done but I fear too costly.

"How sad." Margarita said. "It seems his joy in building his manor was less than it had been. I wonder if his Rowena got better."

Rowena skimmed through the list of purchases and turned further pages until she reached the next date. Rob sat quietly, watching her absorption. The constant introspection at last seemed to be gone.

This fourteenth day of March in the Yeare of Our Lord 1593
Today we laid to Reste mye Beloved Rowena.
There is little need for Thy return Mye Good Enemy.
But I shalle keep mye Accounts lest thou doest.

Rowena looked up, tears in her eyes. "His list is quite short. I suppose he didn't have much interest in building while his daughter was dying." She turned back to the book. There seemed to be only a few more pages on which there was any writing:

This laste day of June in the yeare of Our Lord 1595
I hath builte Apace and have not time to keep my Records
Mye Moneys are well Spente. Mye Manor is wondrous Good.
I shalle Showe Thee Alle, Mye Good Enemy, if thou doest Come.

A few items were mentioned, but as lump sums, for roofing, gardens, and tree planting. One final comment on that page was intriguing.

Tis fitting that Thy moneys are Placed under Time,
since Thou doest not be Aware of it.
And Should Thee come, climb upon thy Horse with Care.

The men laughed. "The old man was pretty fed up, I think. A touch of sarcasm there." Rob pointed out to Carlos, through the window, the sundial under which the sea captain's share must have been placed for a while. "But he certainly left plenty of clues. That accounts for the hole under the mounting block that you told me about, my sweet."

Rowena read on. The next pages were much of the same, except inferences were made to the removal of the treasure to other hiding places. Finally, an entry startled them all.

Tis not Easy, Mye Good Enemy. I hathe need of some husbandry,
I muste Borrow from thee. I hath spente Thy Monys well. Stables
for Mye Horses, a cow byre for mye cattle Which hath Increased

many fold, More land, and I must house mye Grown Sons, hence mye newly added rooms, and my Farm. It is All good.

The list that followed was much longer. "It seems the old pirate got tired of waiting. No wonder there was little treasure," said Rob; "he obviously went on a spending spree. He must have tried to forget his dead daughter." For a moment, his own agony at the possible harm to which Rowena might have come gave him some insight to old Morgan Pentraegon's mind. He shook away the thought and concentrated on her eager face.

Rowena turned more pages that showed the gradual expansion of the Gulls Walk property. Finally, she came to the last entry. It was dated, as had been most of the other.

This Twentyeth Day of October in the Year of Our Lord, 1599.
I had wished that thou hadst Come, Myne Good Enemy. Tis near the end of this Century. I have none to telle of thy last Treasure but shalle Hide it Here. Mye Sons hath no Love of Popery. If thou boweth to Mye Queen, mayhap Thou wilt see thy Galleon as I told Thee to search. Mayhap Thou shalle find it then. I do wish that Thou wilt read mye Record Mye Good Lord, for Mye Maker Cannot frown on mye care of Thine Mass Chalices.
Sadly, I leave thy sea chests Empty. The rest of Thy Treasure be in mye Propertys. Indeed, the Halfe of what I leave, mye Home and Lands, is thyne.
Mye Sons shalle not know of this unless thou Cometh.

Rowena's look of relief surprised Rob.

"So the old man spent it all. But he hid the sea captain's special possessions behind the galleon emblem as you guessed, and just as old Morgan wrote. I suppose if he had used one of the other hiding places, he would have marked that with a galleon." She decided she must be light headed. Why wasn't she worried? Somehow the millstone seemed so much less. "So half of this house belongs to your family, not mine, to the Olivares."

"Oh, no, my sweet. We have no claim. Indeed, the connection is so tenuous no court of law will agree." Rob reached to take her hand as she closed the old pirate's diary. "But I'm sorry there is not more treasure for you, though the chalices are immensely valuable."

"No." Rowena was adamant. "I told you, I'll have no part of them. They must go back to Spain. To a church, or to a museum with the suit of armour—whatever your family feels is right. Obviously Morgan wanted them to be returned, and I shall follow his wishes. I can't possibly benefit from them. Actually, the whole discovery is a great load off my mind. For years, Pentraegons have worried over the lost treasure. Now I can forget it."

"But you have been so concerned about money, about probate." He hated to mention it, but Rowena needed to be more realistic and less altruistic.

Rowena was startled. "Probate? You knew?"

"Of course. Mr. Whitford warned me that my lease may not stretch as far as I intended. You don't think he would make a legal contract without giving me a full picture."

Rowena was stunned. To think she had worried so much and had carried the load on her shoulders for so long. She had been so concerned that her tenant not find out. She began to laugh.

"How stupid I've been. I've worried and worried about how I can take care of everything, and now it is all over. I'll sell Gulls Walk to someone who will love it just as much as I have, and half the proceeds shall be yours, in spite of what you say." Rob vehemently shook his head, but Rowena ignored the gesture. "And no longer will I be responsible for her. You have no idea what a relief it feels." Truth to tell, the avaricious desires of Miles and Megan had so badly hurt her feelings for the old house that she wondered if she would ever feel the same.

"But why sell, Rowena?" Carlos chimed in.

"Oh, I'll have to. I don't have the money for probate, and I can't afford its upkeep. She costs an arm and a leg." She managed a chuckle. "But they're not going to be mine!"

Carlos glanced quickly at Rob who was frowning. "Let's not make hasty decisions. Tomorrow is another day." The two men got to their feet and helped clear the plates and glasses. Each was deep in thought.

A quick check with Bartlett assured them that all the drug dealers were in prison, though two were badly hurt. Heron, who had received the first bullet, was barely holding his own in hospital, and two burly policemen at his bedside ensured no visitors. The whole situation was under control; only the interrogation of Megan was needed to clear up any last questions.

Jeannie, when she came to clear away the dishes, was delighted to hear of the discovered treasure, and of old Morgan's diary; and she was glad to see her Miss Rowena so happy. Determined that the happiness should continue, she put aside her own concerns for Jason's and her future when she heard of Miss Rowena's intention to sell. "I be glad 'ee no longer be so worried, Miss Rowena."

She bravely smiled at her mistress then returned to the kitchen where she raided the deep freeze for the last of Trevy's meals and made dinner for the guests.

Rob brought a couple of bottles of his Spanish wines to the dining table, and as they ate, he, Margarita and Carlos told hilarious stories of their childhood to keep away thoughts of tomorrow. It was a happy evening.

When Rowena climbed into bed, she was so exhausted that she fell asleep almost instantly. Yes, tomorrow was another day.

Morning came.

Jeannie, feeling guilty because she had not been very polite to Miss Megan, got up early to check the patient. It was almost twelve hours since the doctor had given the sleeping tablets. She found her groggily sitting up in bed.

"How be you this morning, Miss Megan? I brought 'ee a cup'o tea." Bruises around the eyes and on the side of her face caused Jeannie to feel some sympathy. "My, how did 'ee do all that?" The swelling was more obvious than it had been the night before.

"I fell, I told you. But I have to get up and go home. I'm well enough."

Jeannie was not too sure, but she had no right to argue and began to leave the room.

"One moment. Have you seen Mr. Gilbert?"

"Why no, Miss Megan. He went off to his London business right a'ter the ball. Mr. Heron, he told me. He ain't been back."

"Are you sure?"

"Well, I ain't seed him; 'e comes here for his morning coffee if 'e be at the farm." Her eyes widened in some bewilderment. People didn't usually ask her about the comings and goings of their neighbour.

"Do you know how Miss Pentraegon hurt her head after the ball?"

The interrogation was not over.

"No, Miss Megan, that I don't rightly know." She frowned. "It do be strange that she fall and bang her head and knock herself out. But she be better now. Except that she be tired, and she don't talk much."

It was obvious that the girl had no further knowledge of that night. And any more questions might raise suspicions, so Megan dismissed Jeannie and staggered out of bed to get dressed. Apparently, Rowena had told no one, thank goodness, and was keeping quiet to save Miles, wherever he was.

Perhaps she herself should disappear for a while. There was no telling what Heron might say to the head of the smuggling group, even though her own involvement had been his and her secret alone, until she had met Heron's two smuggler guests. Before, it had been nice to sit back and receive money and sink it into a secret bank account; but now . . . ."

She shivered as she remembered the cynical laugh of those two, who had insisted on seeing her in the barn on the afternoon of the ball. When she made the map of Gulls Walk for them, she had not known their intentions and had protested their entry to the house. Though her attempts to dissuade them had failed, she had managed to avoid showing them around the place once they were inside. It was much too dangerous and she wanted no part of that. Something that had not exactly endeared her to them, she supposed.

It was from that point that everything seemed to fall apart. But their demand to meet her in the barn before the ball began had been backed up with a nice cash inducement, too tempting to resist

It was her need for money that had started it all. She'd only been protecting it when she crept up to where Rowena was sitting by the wall. She had to hit her. This would have been the biggest haul yet; her share, much larger than before.

Though she had heard none of the smuggler's conversation, she had seen Miles there; but not wanting him to see her and realise how involved she was, she had run from the scene, only stopping to watch the two smugglers drag Rowena away.

What a fool she had been. And Heron would not be above somehow shifting the blame to her for the disappearance of the contraband to save his own neck.

Had he done that when he met with the London group at the warehouse?

Would there now be two groups of smugglers who knew of her involvement? Heron had assured her that only he and his two guests had known. But now . . . . Dear God! She was in over her head.

The only good thing was that Rowena seemed to have told none of her staff about the boat trip, obviously because of equal worry about Miles. And Rob and his family? Carlos seemed to know nothing, so Rowena had kept her secret from them, too. If only she herself had not been so crazed with misery and anger last night, Rowena need never have known of her involvement, either. For one short moment, she thought bitterly of Old Morgan's treasure and wondered what it was. Rowena would never sell the house now. She quietly opened the door and began to creep along the corridor. She had to get away.

Rob was crossing the Great Hall when Megan reached the bottom of the stairs. Since midnight, he and Jason had taken turns to watch her bedroom door lest she wake early and try to creep away. They could not lock her up in case they raised her suspicions, and they both disappeared when Jeannie took up the cup of tea.

For the last few minutes, Rob had been in the kitchen listening to the maid's puzzled comments on Miss Megan's questions. Again he was glad she knew nothing, so Megan must still think her secret was safe. Showing apparent concern, he hastened over to her.

"Hello, Megan." he greeted her. "Are you sure you should be up? My brother-in-law is coming to check you out in a few minutes."

"I'm fine. It's time I went home." Her voice was abrupt. She was fearful of what Rowena had told her tenant.

"Not yet, I think. You look decidedly pale." He was all warmth and sympathy. "Rowena was deeply sorry that the wood was so rotten and that you hurt yourself so badly. She's still in bed, but I'm sure she'll be down soon to see how you are. Come, let Carlos examine you. I don't know how you fell into that wall in the attic, but you certainly gave yourself one hell of a bump. Rowena said you were just chatting and you slipped." He solicitously took her arm and led her to his apartment. All the surveillance equipment had been removed from the table and was stored away. Margarita and her husband were having breakfast.

"Carlos, can you check Megan? She seems to think she can go home." He gave his brother-in-law a meaningful look.

"Why of course." Taking a tiny torch from his pocket, the doctor shone the light into Megan's eyes. He frowned as he put it away. "I'm afraid you'll be doing no driving today, my dear. I don't like the look of you. Flat on your back is where you should be. A fall such as yours can damage the retina or an ocular nerve. Of course, it may be nothing, but we need to have you examined more thoroughly. We'll take you to hospital where they can do the proper tests, won't we, Rob?" He led her to the couch and insisted she lie down.

Margarita came over to offer her felicitations, and they all showed sympathy and natural concern for her.

Silently, Megan searched their faces for any anger at the previous night's disaster. She breathed a sigh of relief, for it seemed Rowena had told them nothing other than that she had fallen. Obviously Rowena's concern over Miles was still keeping her mouth shut.

Now all she had to worry about was how she was going to disappear, and whether there really was something wrong with her eyes. There had been moments of shadowy blackness causing her to sway as she dressed.

Suddenly, the door banged open and in rushed Jeannie. "I just been up to the farm for the morning milk since nobody brung it. You never saw such a kafuffle. There be a whole lot of police. It be that Heron; he's been shot, they say. They come asking questions of the farm hands. My! What a noise there be. All them cows is waiting to be milked, and nobody ain't doing nothing."

There was a startled gasp from Megan. Rob pretended not to notice. He jumped to his feet. "Good Lord! Who shot him? Did they give you any information, Jeannie?"

"Oh no, Sir. They b'ain't tell me no more. Said it be none of my business and to go home."

Rob interrupted. "He must have had a row with someone, he always was rather morose. Maybe one of the farm hands. How is he? Did they say?" The Spaniard continued to ignore Megan who was as white as a sheet.

"No. The policeman wouldn't tell me nothing." She held up the can in her hand. "And I b'ain't got the milk, neither." Typical Jeannie, practical to the end.

Sending her back to the kitchen, Rob turned to Carlos. "I think I'd better go see what it's all about. When Rowena comes down, keep an eye on her. She's been somewhat depressed lately, though she seemed happy enough when we found the treasure." He looked across at Megan as if he had just remembered she was there. "Stay here until we've sorted this out, then either Carlos or I will drive you to the hospital."

As he hurried out of the room, he wondered just what was going through the girl's mind; she had looked so strange.

Frankly, it was terror.

She had to get away. Something must have gone dreadfully wrong. Both she and Heron had known that the bosses were angry at the loss of the wine, but neither had expected guns. First, Miles was gone, who knew where; and now Heron was shot. He could be dead.

Would she be next? Another victim of the smugglers? Her world was falling apart.

A blankness began to overtake her. She seemed to be in a tunnel. A long tunnel.

She was falling. Falling.

And at the end, there was Rowena. Rowena! Everything returned to Rowena. She was the cause, the problem, the fatal flaw who had destroyed all Megan's hopes.

The tunnel narrowed, then wavered. A light seemed to be guiding her. Yes. There had to be an end. It was up to her to find it.

Carefully, Megan managed to get to her feet. Now, everything was suddenly so very clear. The light brightened. It was beckoning her.

Then it wavered and shrank to only a pin-point. Weaving a little, now aware only of a misty glimmer, she struggled to the door.

"I think I'll go back to bed. I feel . . . . Please excuse me." Carlos and Margarita jumped to their feet to catch her, and they fussed with apparent concern as they helped her to her bed. "I'm all right. Just tired. I can find my own way." she mumbled.

She meant to the light.

But the Spanish couple seemed not to understand as they covered her.

Yet they mustn't stay with her.

She must send them away. She must get up. The light was bright. Then it was dim. But the tunnel beckoned her on.

Then it was dark. Dark. Sleep. She would pretend to be asleep. Then they would leave her. Go. They must go.

Carlos' eyes narrowed. At first, he had assumed that there was not much wrong with her, other than a guilty conscience, and shock at Jeannie's information. Now he wasn't so sure. His torch was not sufficient for a proper assessment. They needed to get her to hospital to have that examination, and soon. He now was worried about her mental state. Meanwhile, bed was certainly the best place for her.

Yet he found he had little sympathy, hardly a good doctor's attitude, though she deserved to be in prison. Well, they knew where she was if the police came.

The girl closed her eyes, seemingly ready for sleep. The best thing for her under the circumstances. He waited until her breathing settled, then hurried down to the telephone to call the hospital and make arrangements for admittance, and for an ambulance to collect her. But not before finding Jason and establishing him with a polishing cloth, ostensibly rubbing the furniture in the Great Hall. Carlos was taking no chances.

Megan was not asleep, though.

A light seemed to quiver, bringing her out of the mist. She sat up and dragged herself off the bed. There was something she must do.

Now. It had to be now.

One step, and another. Then one more. Out of the room. Now to the right. What next?

She stood silent and still for a moment, trying to decide where she must go.

No. It was not here she had to be. She must go farther.

. . . Here at last. This was the door she had to go through. The light from the tunnel was shining on it. She must enter.

She held out her hand. The light shone brighter. Yes. This was where she must go.

She knocked.

Rowena had locked the door, as Rob had insisted the night before when she had gone to bed. It must be he coming to see her, she thought. She had just finished dressing and was making her bed. Eagerly she hurried to open the door.

Aghast, she tried to close it when she saw the strange glitter in the eyes of her visitor, but she was no match for the uncanny strength of the girl. The door fell back and she shrank against the wall as her friend entered.

"Oh, good morning, Megan." Apprehensively, she wondered what else to say. Glazed eyes held her mesmerised. Then came a monotonous moan.

"You . . . . It's your fault. You're in the way. It's always been you. Sorry, so sorry. They're coming for me. I'll be next." The tall figure moved forward. "You shouldn't have . . ." A frown appeared and the distraught girl bent her head sideways as if trying to remember something. "You shouldn't have . . . have . . . Miles is gone."

Rowena took a step back. What was the matter with Megan? She seemed, almost, to be sleep-walking. The door banged shut.

With a lunge, Megan reached for Rowena, twisting her arm behind her. "Sorry. Sorry . . . you should be sorry. You took him. Where is he? Where is Miles?" Her voice had risen.

Suddenly, the bright rays of the morning sun glinted on the staring eyes. Rowena screamed. But the walls were thick. And nobody heard.

CHAPTER TWENTY-FOUR

Eagerly, Rob returned to Gulls Walk from the farm.

A quick, private conversation with the inspector, and an exchange of information was all he needed. Then, in front of the other farm hands, an abrupt, more public refusal by the policeman to give details of the shooting of Heron, established his ignorance. He intended to miss no opportunity to ensure the innocence of those at the manor house. Who knew what stranger might later come asking questions?

Satisfied, he entered his apartment where Carlos and Margarita were waiting.

"Oh. Where's Megan?" he asked as he looked around the room.

"I put her in bed. I think she is rather more hurt than we thought. I shall feel much better when we get her to hospital. I'm not too happy about her mental state." Worriedly, Carlos was feeling a little guilty at his own lack of sympathy. "The ambulance should be here in another half hour."

"Good. Perhaps we had better get her ready. Hasn't Rowena come down yet?"

"No, she hasn't. I'll get my bag. It's in our bedroom. You go on. I'll be with you in a minute."

Eagerly, Rob followed Carlos across the Great Hall, stopping only to speak to Jason who was industrially polishing away and keeping an eye on the stairs. With some satisfaction they agreed that Megan in hospital would simplify her interrogation by the police. And there need be no hurry for that since Carlos could order the length of her stay. Yes. All the loose ends were being tied up nicely.

But why did he have this strange sense of foreboding? He quickened his pace, taking the stairs two at a time.

He hesitated outside Megan's door, which was closed. A few more minutes wouldn't matter. She must be asleep. He hurried back to Rowena's room. That door, too, was closed. He knocked sharply.

"Rowena? Are you awake? May I come in?"

There was silence.

He called again, with greater urgency. "Rowena, my sweet, open the door, please." He reached for the handle and turned it. Damn. It was locked. But then she must still be inside, otherwise Jason would have seen her come down stairs. Why didn't she answer?

With a sharp exclamation, he returned to Megan's door and pushed it open. The room was empty. Where had she gone? What was it Carlos had said about her mental state? Dear God! He rushed back to Rowena's locked door. He was about to rap hard on it again, then he hesitated. Bending his head, he put his ear to the keyhole.

Aware of harsh breathing, his worst fears almost overwhelmed him. It had to be Megan. The sound was not normal. Faintly, he also heard a tiny whimper.

A jangle of thoughts rushed through his mind. Uppermost was the awful dread that Megan had hurt Rowena. A great, murderous anger almost took charge as he raised his fist to beat on the door again. But that could only do more harm. Whatever else he did, he must not startle Megan. He heard steps along the corridor and he hesitated. It was Carlos.

Raising a finger to his lips, Rob stopped the doctor from speaking. He swallowed his fury and reached for calm. Megan must not be pushed further out of control. He forced a normal tone. "Come down when you are ready, Rowena. Jeannie's made breakfast for you." With steady footsteps, he walked back to Carlos and down the staircase. Keeping his voice low, he started to explain.

Reading the fear and anger, Carlos interrupted him. "She's in there with Rowena, isn't she," he whispered. It was a statement, not a question. The anxiety, which had been at the back of his mind, became a deeper concern. "That blow; it must have had a greater effect than I had thought. Damn. I could kick myself. I'm so sorry, Rob. When I looked at her eyes this morning, I was aware that there were all the signs of concussion, but I didn't think it could cause any mental problems. Not that we know for sure it has, but we must get into that room and find out." Apprehensively, he touched Rob's arm. "Perhaps we need Jason again."

"Ah, yes. Jason. What we would do without our steadfast Jason?" Rob led the way across the hall to the stable lad. Quickly, he explained what had happened.

"We dare not attempt to break down the door." said Carlos. "Who knows what sort of reaction Megan might have." He was aware that blows to the head could be unpredictable.

"Then how the hell are we going to get in there?" Rob's voice was desperate.

As Jason spoke, even his usual calm was ruffled. "We'm just have to play hide-and-seek. There b'ain't nowt about this house I don't know. My father, 'ee worked 'ere all his life and knew every nook and cranny. And there be plenty o' ways into rooms with locks." He sized up the two men. "There be a way into that room. It'll take a bit o' crawling, mark you. There b'ain't much space. You'm too big, Senor. I ain't been there since I was a nipper, but I'll try."

Carlos interrupted him, for he was the slightest of the three, and eagerly volunteered. Jason nodded.

"Maybe that be best. I can use a ladder to get up to her room; there be one by the garden wall that we used for the lighting at the ball. Miss Rowena, she al'us likes her windows open, so I can get in that way. But Miss Megan, she better not see me or the doctor." He looked speculatively at the Senor.

"That's where I can help." The prospect of action cleared Rob's mind. He was back in charge again. "I'll talk to her through the door. Hold her attention. Keep her there."

The shooting of Heron had obviously been the final straw. Megan's white face when Jeannie had brought the news of Heron had been a mirror of fear. He'd reassure her, concoct some story, string it out, keep her at least listening. "All right, Jason. How does Carlos get in?"

Quickly and quietly, the stable lad led the two men back upstairs and along the corridor. Between the east wing and the central wing was a gap that held a tall window; beneath it was a wide, deep window seat. Jason lifted the lid. Inside were the heating pipes and electrical wiring that extended into the various bedrooms.

Carlos looked with some distaste at the accumulated dust of years, and at the narrow space through which he was going to have to crawl.

"It be not so bad." Jason whispered as he glanced dubiously at the pristine clothing of the doctor. "It goes to the little bedroom where Miss Rowena used to sleep when she was a child. It's next to the bathroom and the big bedroom. There be a seat just like this one. You've only got to push up the lid. It's mostly a store room now, so that there Megan won't be paying it any attention. And it ain't locked."

He got to his feet and looked out of the corridor window, pointing out where he intended to place his ladder, then he hurried back down the stairs.

Carlos reached into his medical bag before gingerly climbing into the open window seat. "I feel like a damned mole," he muttered.

Now it was Rob's turn. He listened at Rowena's door and heard a faint mumble of sound, the same voice repeating the same jumble of words. He could make out the name Miles, but much of the rest was lost. He took a deep breath and knocked.

"Hello, Megan. I've got some more news about Heron. Do you want to hear it?" Dead silence. Then a faint shuffle as if someone had moved nearer to the door. "I spoke to the police." Rob waited. "They've taken him to hospital. He's in a coma."

Again the shuffle. This time, there came the same faint whimper he had heard before.

Thank God. Rowena must be all right still. "I have some details of what happened. Do you want to know?"

He glanced back, but he could no longer see Carlos.

"I didn't hear your answer, Megan." He took a hasty look out of the corridor window to the bedroom casement where Jason intended to place his ladder. There was no sign of him yet.

"I thought you and I could go into Penzance for the day, just like we did before. We had a good time didn't we? We can go to see Heron."

There was a strangled cry from the bedroom. Rob clenched his teeth. He so desperately wanted to break down the door. "Megan, I'll send for Miles." Could that name be the key? "He'll come back to take care of his farm."

Suddenly the silence was broken by a great, keening cry. "Miles. Where is he? He's gone. He's gone."

"No, Megan. He'll come back. I promise you, he'll return." He spread his hands wide on the locked door, longing to reach through. He felt it shudder as if someone were pressing on the other side.

The tragic voice again.

"No. He can't. They've taken him. He'll never come back to me. Miles, Miles." Again the deep moan. Then the voice changed. "It's your fault, Rowena. It's all your fault. You never wanted him. You only cared about the house. That's all you ever thought of. He wanted it, too. And you were the key. I loved him . . . ."

The Spaniard called to her again.

"No, Megan. Listen to me. Miles is fine. He'll be coming back soon. Megan, I promise you. Megan." He beat on the door in frustration. Oh, hurry Carlos and Jason, he whispered to himself.

A crash; a shriek of terror; a jangled cacophony of angry voices. Then silence.

Rob froze. Dear God! He felt all the frustration of despair.

The sound of the key in the lock brought him to action.

"We be a'having a rare lot of bashing on people's heads, but I b'ain't done it this time." The prosaic calm of Jason's voice was music to his ears, but pausing only to squeeze the stable lad's arm in thanks, Rob rushed past him into the bedroom.

An incredibly dirty Carlos was holding Rowena, and both were looking down at the limp body of Megan sprawled at their feet.

"It's all right, Rob. It's all over." The doctor paused and took a deep breath. "She must have heard Jason as he climbed through the side window. She knocked Rowena to the ground and was about to climb out of the window opposite. I'm sure she was going to throw herself out. There was every indication that she was suicidal. Jason charged across the room and grabbed her, giving me time to stick my hypodermic into her arm. She whirled around and I managed to grab her hand, nails and all, before she could do much harm."

He looked in surprise at the trickle of blood on his wrist. She had been much stronger than either of them had expected. Thank God she had dropped like a stone as the anaesthetic took effect. Abruptly, he sat on the bed as Rob pulled Rowena into his own arms. He was more shaken than he cared to admit.

"Oh, Rob. If Jason and Carlos hadn't come . . . . Megan had one hand over my mouth. I couldn't call out. She was going to . . . to jump out of the window, I think. Her eyes. They were so wild. She couldn't have known what she was doing. My poor Megan." Rowena buried her face in Rob's shoulder.

Poor Megan, be damned, he thought as he held her close. His own eyes were dark with a mingling of anger and relief. "It's all over now, my love." He tightened his hold. "You two. Thank you both. Jason, I owe you." His words were heartfelt. "If we had been any longer . . . ."

But now was not the time for that. "Come, Carlos. We'll get your bag and clean you up. Jason, perhaps you'll watch Miss Megan while we see if the ambulance is here." The sooner the unconscious girl was in hospital the better. She would be secure there.

Rowena looked back as she was led out of the room. "But why, Rob? What caused her to go berserk? Carlos, could just a blow to the head make her so . . . so dangerous?"

"I expect so. Such injuries can be unpredictable. But I wish I had read the signs better. I feel responsible. I'm so sorry, my dear. But treatment and quiet will help her, I'm sure. Now don't you worry any more. I'll see that she has the best of care." Carlos longed to take away the deep hurt in Rowena's eyes. Her concern seemed to be so much more for Megan than for herself.

But a grim Roberto Olivares felt none of that sympathy. He held Rowena close as they returned to his apartment. Thank God that one more loose end was now tied up; but it had so nearly been a tragic ending.

When the ambulance left, Carlos accompanying it, Rob called the police inspector and told him of Megan's breakdown. "We can only assume that her connection with the smugglers, and the fear of retribution, was at the root of her behaviour: that, and the blow from the wooden beam. Carlos seems to think that it will be some little time before you can question her, but it's one hell of a relief to know that everyone involved has been accounted for."

It was a most satisfactory talk with the inspector. The mopping up operation was going according to plan. Charges of murder would be laid against the prisoners since Heron had not recovered. In a few days, Miles was to be 'allowed' to leave and need never know that the police had been his warders. If he came back to Gulls Walk, surely it would not be for long. He would be too fearful of being caught again by the smuggling ring.

Yes. It was all most satisfactory. Neither Heron, Miles or Megan had any idea of the widespread net that had been set to catch them. But Rob still had one major concern. Did Miles remember the presence of himself and Jason on the boat? Had he worked out who they were? Or did he really think they were police? Or might he think it had been a dream, or nightmare? He had not told his interrogators anything about them. And certainly his physical state had been poor enough for his memory to be hazy.

But still there was a nagging doubt. The Spaniard could only wait.

It was three days later. Carlos had insisted that Rowena rest in bed and had given her sedatives to make her sleep that first day. He was aware of how worn out she must be. But the following morning, she insisted on going to see Megan and crept into her hospital room while the doctor waited at the door. She looked down at the still figure with a great sadness.

But now, almost recovered, she and Jeannie spent the afternoon polishing the chalices until they shone. They finally placed them under the picture of Queen Elizabeth as much as to say to her, 'Just look at what secret you have held all these years.'

Later that afternoon, Carlos again visited Megan. She still was in a coma and looked to be so for some time to come.

Immediately after she was put into hospital, Rob had gone to London to wind up the last pieces of the investigation, and both he and Carlos were due back that evening, with Margarita. She had taken the opportunity to do some shopping since Bartlett and his wife had returned to London now that their presence was no longer needed. Rowena had hugged them both before they left, knowing she would never forget the policeman's solid strength.

Determined to give her tenant and his family a celebratory dinner, Rowena stood looking with some concern at the almost empty deep freeze.

There was a knock at the door and in walked Mrs. Trevain.

"Darling Trevy." Rowena rushed over to greet her. She knew the house keeper was soon to return, but she had not expected her that day. "How wonderful to see you. Are you all right?"

"Of course I am. And about time, too. I be going crazy with nothing to do. And how be you, Miss Rowena?" The twinkling, black-button eyes took in the slenderness of her mistress. "Now, what you been doing? You'm lost some weight, I see."

"A little, but it's fashionable." Rowena laughed. It was so good to see the old lady.

"Well, now I'm back, we'll put a bit of flesh on those bones. Fashionable indeed!" she snorted indignantly. "I'll just put my things away and then I'll see about dinner. And I'll see how that Jeannie has looked after my pots and pans."

She bustled into her room and soon was back fastening an apron round her plump waist. She, too, examined the deep freeze in satisfaction.

"Almost empty, I see. I remember a certain young lady telling me I don't be needing to cook so much. I think I'd better get started filling it up again." With a pleased smile, she allowed Rowena to hug her. "I heard how that Mr. Heron got himself killed, so I expect them farm deliveries be at sixes and sevens." The light of anticipation glowed in her eyes as if she were going to battle. "It be just as well I be prepared!"

She reached for the shopping bags she had brought with her. And on that satisfactory note, she shooed Rowena out of the kitchen.

Collapsing with laughter, Rowena sank into her grandfather's chair in the library. Trevy was back, and all was right with the world. Remembering how down through the years she had relied on her beloved housekeeper, a deep sense of contentment spread through her. Somehow, whatever news the men brought back, she would be able to handle it. Maybe for the rest of the summer she and her staff could remain at Gulls Walk, then sell the manor, buy a small house, and Trevy could carry on being the only mother she remembered.

She hardly dared allow another dream to surface.

The phone rang and, reluctantly, Rowena went to answer it. She didn't really want to be dragged back to the cares of her world just yet. Putting her dream aside, she spoke into the mouth piece.

"Gulls Walk."

"Precious, thank God you're there. I didn't know if you would be. It's me, Miles. They told me they'd released you from the boat and sent you home. You haven't said anything to the police, have you? My imprisonment was their security that you wouldn't talk."

"No, of course not. Where are you? What happened? Are you all right?"

"I'm fine, a little groggy still. But last night, I managed to escape. They must have thought I was still too hurt to try anything. They had packed some clothes for me when they brought me here, and thank God I had left my wallet in my jeans pocket. I managed to force the lock with a credit card. I was kept in some isolated house on top of the moors, and I've been walking most of the night, but this morning I reached a village and found a phone."

"What are you going to do? Are you coming home?" She was back to earth with a thump.

"Not likely. Do you think I'm a fool? They told me that our cove was no good to them any more, but I'm taking no chances. They threatened me, but there wasn't much I could tell them. I had never known what they were smuggling, wine probably, or who they were. They wore disguises, like Redbeard and his partner; I remember them dragging me from the farm, but those two didn't come to see me again. Cattle buyers indeed!"

His voice sounded puzzled. "The whole ghastly experience on that damned boat was like a dream. I still have a bump on the back of my head like a golf ball, as well as more bruises than I care to count.

"I can't seem to get a clear picture from the time I left the ball, though. I vaguely remember being on the boat and telling you we had to co-operate, but little more. I kept getting the strangest flashbacks. I even thought the police were there. I didn't tell the smugglers that, though, and they didn't mention them. If only they had come to rescue us. No. Wishful thinking on my part, I expect. Now I don't want to know. I just want to forget it all."

Rowena gave an involuntary gasp. "But . . . But I saw no police." That was the truth.

"I know. It was my muddled imagination." Miles paused. "Whatever you do, Rowena, keep silent about everything. I expect the smugglers thought I was no danger to them since I knew so little, but I was so sure they were going to kill me. They told me Heron has been shot, so there'll be no more smuggling from the cove. But now I've escaped, I don't intend to stay around in case they change their minds."

"Not stay around? What do you mean?"

"I'm going to sell up. Too many bad memories. In any case, I may have to pay a hefty fine as accessory to the smugglers, even though I knew so little about them. And without Heron, who will look after the place?" She heard him sigh.

"I'm going to call Whitford. Maybe he can find a buyer for the farm. I've had time to think over the last few days, Rowena. I feel so damned ashamed of myself. Since I was a child I have been brought up with this obsession about owning Gulls Walk. For generations, the Gilberts have worked to that end. So much so that nothing else seemed to matter. Except money, of course. The more we made, the more land we could buy from the Pentraegons. And when Megan was so angry after the ball . . . ."

"Oh, Miles. She has been so hurt. I didn't know how much she cared." Rowena stopped. She had almost blurted out that Megan had been involved with the smuggler, too. But Rob had said to tell no one what had happened.

Miles interrupted her. "I know that now. These last few days have given me plenty of time to realise what a fool I have been. She was always special. But the house was so important. Tell her; oh, hell. I've nothing to offer her. But tell her I care."

"Will you be back? Will I see you?" Whatever he had done, Miles was still her life-long friend.

"No, Precious. Maybe sometime down the line, but not now. I'll hide out for a while. But I'll call you one of these days. Give my love to my farm, and to Gulls Walk." His voice broke. "And to Megan." There was shame as well as sorrow as he said good bye; then the phone went dead.

How deep must be his fear for him to give up his heritage, Rowena thought. Yet perhaps it was just punishment for his greed, for he had been quite prepared to take hers. Sadly, she stood looking at the instrument. There had not even been an opportunity to tell of the coma Megan was in. She supposed that was just as well, for Rob had been so determined that Miles should be unaware of Rowena's deeper involvement.

But she could not help feeling some relief, particularly as Miles seemed so uncertain about any unknown presence on the boat.

So finally, the police had fulfilled their promise and allowed Miles to escape. And now there would be no more 'Precious'. Oh, how she had come to hate him calling her that. Yet there was also a deep sense of sadness. This was the end of an era. She returned to her chair in the library to wait for the return of her tenant.

CHAPTER TWENTY-FIVE

The sound of laughter in the Great Hall brought Rowena back to her feet. The voices were those of the returning Spaniards, each of them chuckling over their many parcels. She heard Trevy bustling from the kitchen. "And who might you gentlemen be?"

Rowena grinned wryly as she opened her door and saw her housekeeper puffed up like a pouter pigeon. Dear, dear Trevy. She would protect her chick to her last breath.

"Ah! You must be the inestimable Mrs. Trevain." Rob looked at the apron, now liberally sprinkled with flour. "I must thank you for that wonderful food you left in the deep freeze. I'm Roberto Olivares, by the way, Miss Rowena's Spanish tenant; and this is my sister Margarita, and her husband, Dr. Carlos Mendoza." He held out his hand.

Rowena watched. Did her darling Trevy actually simper? The turning on of Rob's charm was making a new convert. Join the club, she sighed to herself as she went to meet them.

"Good afternoon, all of you. Have you had a good day?"

"Certainly, my love." Her tenant answered for them as they moved toward her. Then Rob smiled at the housekeeper. "Let us just take these bags of food to the kitchen. We thought the cupboard might be bare by now. I wonder, dear Trevy, could we have coffee in the library?" With a nod and a smile, the old lady bustled away.

Good Lord, thought Rowena. Already she's willing to take orders from him; just like the rest of us. The men followed the old lady into the kitchen with the groceries while Margarita, with a smile and a wave of her hand, went up to her bedroom to put away her personal shopping.

When the men entered the library, bringing the coffee with them, Rowena told of the phone call. Rob smiled his relief when she explained Miles' decision to sell, and his jumbled memory of the supposed police. Even though so many of the cartel were in prison, the faintest of suspicions could bring vengeance upon Gulls Walk. Rob was not so naive to think that someone in the future might not attempt to ask Miles questions. But the longer he remained away, the less likely that became. He changed the subject.

"You're sure he's not coming back to Home Farm?"

"And he's decided to sell, lock, stock and barrel, has he?" Carlos looked pleased.

"Yes, since he knows Heron won't be here to look after the farm. I didn't tell him anything that has happened. Nothing about Megan. He didn't give me a chance. Come to think of it, he never even asked what happened to me."

He might have shown just a little bit of concern she thought. But now she was looking at her ex-neighbour in a new perspective. Most of her childhood had been spent in pleasing him, so why should he think of her now? Pushing the thought away, she remembered his message to Megan and was glad he had shown concern for her. That was more important.

"Good. That's one thing settled." Rob was pleased to see her slight irritation. He had been so worried lest her feelings for Miles still might colour a sense of responsibility.

He got to his feet and began to pace the floor. "The police have more or less finished all their moping up. A farm labourer and two of the fishermen have been taken into custody, but they seem to know very little; another seems to have disappeared, probably the one who skippered the boat. But the police are quite sure they will eventually capture him. A couple of men from the village are replacing the labourer and Heron.

"Redbeard and the executioner, also their bosses, will be incarcerated for a long, long time: in different facilities of course. If they ever do manage to contact each other, think how they'll be sure that the others are lying!"

He watched Rowena's face lighten. With a grim smile, he continued. "But I've one more piece of news. It concerns Megan." He came to sit on the window seat beside her. "Do you want to press charges against her?"

"Oh, of course not." How could she?

"I thought not. Well, since there will be no complaint against her from you, the charge will be less, particularly as we want as few people as possible to know what has been going on."

"Then does that mean she goes free?" Rowena looked eagerly at her tenant. She knew she had no right to expect that, but Megan was her friend.

"Not completely. She will, eventually, have to answer some serious questions, but the case will be kept very quiet. Of course, there will be a fine. She cannot be allowed to keep the illegal moneys she acquired from the smugglers; but any imprisonment may be reduced to probation since she took no active part in the smuggling activities, though she was an accessory. But it will be a long time before she is well. That fall did more damage than we had thought."

Frankly, he thought Megan was getting off much too easily; he would have loved to see the wretched girl locked away for a good long time. He watched Rowena try to accept the inevitable. With a sigh, finally she smiled.

"Well, at least Pentraegon Cove can settle back into its usual peace."

How glad he was of that. But he had been straightening out one last detail. Perhaps the change of subject would help.

"We have been to see Whitford. The probate officers have made their decision. It was less than he thought. Apparently when the inspector came, the house looked in such a poor state that it was estimated to have a lower value." He hesitated. "In any case, I've taken care of it. I've paid them off."

Rowena rose to her feet in protest. Megan faded from her mind. The porcupine prickles were back. "No Rob, absolutely not. That's my problem. I told you I am going to sell the house. It has bitter memories now. As soon as I do, I'll pay you back."

She didn't know who would buy the property, but she could accept nothing from him. She couldn't bear to have his pity. Pentraegon pride raised its head. "Thank you for helping me, Rob, but I cannot allow that."

"Now just a minute, Rowena. There's more. A substantial reward for the capture of the smugglers will be yours, eventually. With that, you will have no need to sell Gulls Walk; and I, too, absolutely insist that I pay my dues to this wonderful old manor. It was to have been the unwilling centre of the cartel's activities and deserves compensation."

Rob grinned to himself, thinking of the feisty old lady who had glittered and glowed for their summer ball. "Now, instead of selling, Carlos has an idea that might appeal to you. Listen to him, Rowena. Wait until you hear his suggestion." He reached for her hand and drew her back to the window seat. The doctor came to sit on the other side her.

"My dear Rowena, in spite of what you have said, I'm sure you don't really want to sell the house. In fact, I hope I can rent part of it from you. Rob is very generous in supporting the various rehabilitation homes we have for our recuperating children, both here and in Spain; and he has long promised to help fund a new one. What better place than Pentraegon Cove? That probate money you can count as part of a rental agreement if you wish."

He watched her indignant protest change to bewilderment. "Now you've told us about the farm being for sale, I'm even more excited about the project. We will buy the buildings. Imagine; fresh, home-grown food right on our doorstep, and extra accommodation for staff. I have talked to the local hospital people, who are equally enthusiastic about Gulls Walk. National health finances, good as they are, cannot stretch to all the extras sick children need. And there are, indeed, so many needy children."

Rowena looked in amazement from one to the other. Could this be a solution to her problems? The phrase, needy children, struck a chord. She, too, surely had been needy. And her present tenant had come to her rescue.

She remembered the generous rent he had paid, resulting in the face lift she was able to give Gulls Walk—the ball, with the evening's glamorisation of the old lady—the daring rescue he and Jason had made, both of her and Miles—the brilliance of his scheme to free Gulls Walk from the retribution of the smugglers—his discovery of old Morgan Pentraegon's treasure—his help, with that of Carlos and Jason, in her escape from Megan—even his mitigation of whatever intentions of prosecution the police might have had of her erstwhile friend. She was pretty sure that he had been the persuading factor there.

He had indeed responded to her need.

An enormous, overwhelming relief brought tears to her eyes, "Oh, Rob, I am so grateful to you, because I have been needy, too. I have so much to thank you for." She turned to Carlos. "And you, as well, dear Doctor. Of course you may rent the house if you want. And if there is a reward, let me use it to help you fund your project. I'm sure there will be many alterations and improvements you will require. You can have it all. I don't want any part of a reward. I would always think of it as tainted money."

Her eyes clouded as she thought of the broken lives of her two best friends. "And Rob, you will take back the chalices, in gratitude." It was a statement, not a request. She was so glad she had something to offer him. Indeed, half of all she had was his anyway.

With a sudden, sharp expression of anger, her tenant got to his feet. "Damn it. It's not your gratitude I want. And certainly not the chalices. We can give them to a church if you wish." He had no intention of being paid; he could well afford much more than the probate bill.

Just then there was a knock on the door. It was the housekeeper.

"I'll take then dirty coffee things now. How many for dinner, Miss Rowena?"

"Thank you Trevy, four, I think. We have some plans to make." She looked uncertainly at her tenant.

"We will be delighted, dear Trevy; I would not want to dine anywhere else." He swallowed his anger. He was well aware how much the old lady meant to Rowena. When they had taken their groceries to the kitchen, he had asked her to stay on as housekeeper if Rowena agreed to the proposed project.

"Dr. Carlos, and his Mrs. will be the other two, I suppose?" Rob nodded. "I be right pleased. Miss Rowena, they told me what you all be hoping to do here, and I be right pleased about that, too. This old place has been so lonely and has become quite sad over the last years. I bet it's glad to give up old Morgan's treasure. They told me about that, also. And children will bring the old lady to life again. Lots of them. But you keep that east wing for yourselves and your own children when you come for a holiday!"

With a meaningful look at them, and a satisfied chuckle, Mrs. Trevain picked up her tray and began to leave the room. Rob had obviously told her more than what they hoped was going to happen to the house.

He broke into laughter, "I can see you have my measure already, dear Trevy. Which reminds me. If Jason is there, will you send him in." As she left, his voice softened. "I have a feeling she already is planning much more than the future of Gulls Walk, don't you?" He smiled ruefully at Carlos' splutter of amusement.

Before Rowena could think of an answer, the stable lad hurried in.

"You wanted me, Sir."

"Ah, yes, Jason. I don't think we have really thanked you properly for all you have done. We would never have solved Gulls Walk's problems without you."

"Oh, it be nothing. Actually I b'ain't had so much fun in a long time." He grinned from ear to ear. "Anything for Miss Rowena." He blushed as his mistress added her thanks.

She and Rob then told him of Miles' intentions.

"Perhaps when you and Jeannie marry you will like to live in the farm house." Carlos concluded. "I expect Trevy has already told you about our plans for Gulls Walk, and since Gilbert wants to sell Home Farm, and we, to buy it, it will need a new manager." The simple delight of the stable lad was a joy to see.

"That there Master Gilbert? He be not coming back?" He grinned from ear to ear. "Good! Yes. It be about time I wed my Jeannie. She be wondering where I keep going off to with 'ee, Senor." He chuckled. "It be my turn to thank 'ee. Sir, Miss Rowena, and you, Doctor." He reached to shake the extended hands. "But if 'ee have any more adventures, 'ee let me know."

He left to tell his Jeannie the good news. He had to admit he had been worried just what their future might be. Now all was right with his world.

Rob watched the stable lad go. He would be for ever grateful to him. Now to his own unfinished business.

"Carlos, go and tell your wife about the farm. If I know that sister of mine, she'll be organising us all even before we have the project off the ground." He smiled at his brother-in-law. "And don't come back for a while."

Grinning delightedly, Carlos left the room.

"Now, I've some questions to ask you, my girl." He turned to Rowena. "And let's get one thing out of the way first, one that has been burning my gut ever since I first saw you with that damned Gilbert. Why did you allow him to call you Precious if you weren't going to marry him?"

"It's just a nickname, Rob." She laughed in surprise. She was so used to it that it had never occurred to her what interpretation someone else might put upon it. Did it really matter to the Spaniard so much? A tiny glimmering of hope began its difficult way through the barriers she had created in her mind.

"A nick name?" Rob's laugh was a mixture of chagrin and enormous relief. "Mother of God. You have no idea how many sleepless nights I have spent." He listened as she told him the story of the long-ago frog in the old woman's basket. Damn Miles Gilbert, he thought.

But he had another question he needed to ask; her feelings of gratitude over his help, though sweet, were not only what he was hoping for. He got to his feet and moved to the glass case where Rowena had placed the second diary beside old Morgan's original one.

"May I?" He found the key as Rowena nodded and unlocked the lid. He carefully lifted out the two books. Turning the pages, he re-read some of the entries.

"The old man was pretty emphatic about his intentions, wasn't he?" Rob examined the words of his will.

Hereafter I do bequeathe my house, Gulls Walk, and mye lands to mye Firstborne Son and to his son after him, on and on, in Perpetuity Maye no Man or woman, be they King, Queen or Commoner, yntrude upon the House of the Pentraegons.

He turned the brittle pages until he found another entry.

Of such Treasures as I hath, He shalle share when He return, but not tille then, that of Mye Beloved Rowena!

"I think the old man would have liked the sea captain to have come back to Gulls Walk. Perhaps he regretted sending him away, though the political climate must have been the stumbling block." He opened the second diary. "Morgan repeatedly questioned why he did not return. Do you get the impression that he would have allowed the Spaniard to marry his daughter?"

Rowena looked confused.

"Yes, perhaps." Surely that was all in the past now.

"But one thing we are certain about; he was determined that Pentraegons would always inherit his Gulls Walk."

Rowena agreed again.

"I'm glad you have changed your mind about selling. Old Morgan would have turned in his grave if you did. Now his descendants can still inherit. Their second name can be Pentraegon even though their last name will be that of your husband." Replacing the diaries, he returned to the window seat. "Do you think that would satisfy the old man?"

"I . . . I think so." The harsh angles of his face were bewildering her even more. A few moments ago he had been all smiles as he sent Carlos away.

"And would that be agreeable to you?"

Until the last week, she had been so wrapped up in her determination to save her inheritance, and to fulfil her responsibilities to her ancestors, that she had thought of little else.

"Your children will carry on the line and learn to love the old place as your ancestors have." He wanted to say 'our children' but was determined to put no pressure on her. Gratitude might be all she felt for him, and he was well aware of her strong sense of obligation.

"Oh, of course it would. But only if it were agreeable to my . . . my husband. He would . . . will help choose names and decide where we live." Why were his words so curiously impersonal. Her heart sank.

"So you would be willing to live elsewhere? Come back, perhaps, for holidays only?"

"Yes." Her answer was heartfelt. To have the joy of visiting, with none of the heavy load of the millstone of the past months, seemed like heaven.

With a sigh, Rob reached for her hand and lifted it to his lips.

"And that leads me to my next question." The Spaniard paused.

"I have a house. Actually, it's a castle, even older than Gulls Walk. It is quite beautiful, but it needs . . . it needs you. As I do. Quite desperately, my beloved Rowena." Old Morgan's description of his daughter seemed so right. "I have loved you since that first day when Goemor threw you, almost at my feet, and I pulled off your riding hat. Then I saw your glorious hair. But I fought my feelings; you looked so young. I was so angry because I could not shake away the attraction. And since then, I've . . . . Marry me, my darling."

Tentatively, Rowena lifted her hand and touched the harsh grooves around his mouth. They softened as he turned his face to kiss her fingers "Is that yes?" he asked as he pulled her close. She nodded, her own heart too full to speak.

With an enormous feeling of relief, he tightened his arms. "So you will put me out of my misery?" She snuggled close. "I can't bear to let you out of my sight, my sweet, I'll happily take all your stabs any time. Marry me soon, my love."

As she raised her face for his kiss, she remembered her original reaction to her Spaniard. His eyes had been like the amber gleam of chestnuts glowing in a winter fire. So they were now, but no longer did they hold the aloof anger of that first meeting.

When Rob finally lifted his head, he was aware of the golden rays of the evening sun forming a halo around her head. My Botticelli angel, he thought to himself.

But as he looked down at her, with a tender smile, he whispered, "My precious porcupine."